I0729898

The Hallow

The Tether

Elizabeth Chappelle

HUMMINGBIRD PUBLISHING LTD

Contents

Prologue

The screams carried through the woods like something torn out of a nightmare, raw, desperate, rising and falling in waves that echoed against the trees until they dissolved into the night. The forest was vast, a stretch of ancient timber that seemed to go on forever, swallowing the moonlight and shrouding everything in thick shadows. Branches arched overhead like bony arms. Somewhere deep within, startled birds took flight, their wings beating furiously as they burst through the canopy, their cries joining the chaos for a fleeting moment before the silence swallowed them again.

Detective Lora Matthews eased her car to a stop at the forest entrance. The flashing blue lights of patrol cars and ambulances painted the darkness in stuttering bursts, throwing long, jagged shadows across the tree line. The buzz of radios, the murmur of voices, and the low growl of idling engines tangled together into a symphony of unease. Reporters lingered at the tape line, their cameras flashing, their hushed commentary feeding the storm. Forensics teams moved like ghosts in the chaos, their white suits glowing eerily under the strobing lights. The coroner's van was already there, parked with grim finality.

Lora pulled the handbrake, her gaze fixed on the forest as though it were daring her to step inside. She muttered to herself, barely above a whisper, "Oh boy... here we go again." The words hung in the stale air of the car, a mixture of dread and resignation. She exhaled slowly, squared her shoulders, and stepped out into the night.

The sound of boots crunching on gravel approached. Detective Chief Sam Matthews, her boss, her ex-husband, and the one man she thought she'd never have to work beside again stopped just a few feet away.

His voice was steady, clipped with professionalism, but she knew him well enough to catch the tension underneath. "Detective Matthews," he said by way of greeting, his tone measured.

She nodded once, her own voice tight. "Chief."

They stood for a beat, the space between them weighted with years of unfinished sentences and unspoken regrets. His eyes, though calm, flickered with something she couldn't name worry, maybe, or the same exhaustion she carried. He thought she looked tired, drawn, but still sharper than anyone else he had on his team. Reliable. Relentless. Dangerous to his peace of mind.

You shouldn't even be here, he thought. And yet... I'm glad you are.

They turned toward the forest. As they ducked under the tape, the chatter of the scene behind them dimmed, swallowed by the looming darkness ahead. Together they walked a few feet into the trees, their footsteps muffled by the damp earth and fallen leaves. The forest seemed to lean in around them, each tree standing tall and silent like a sentinel.

Lora slowed to a stop, her eyes flicking upward toward the treetops. She raised a hand sharply, silencing Sam. "Shhh. Do you hear that?" she whispered.

He frowned, scanning the darkness. "No. Hear what?"

She lowered her voice further, almost reverent, as though speaking too loudly might shatter something fragile, "The stillness. It's an eerie silence."

Sam shifted uneasily, his instincts prickling. He tried to play it off, but his voice betrayed him. "Yeah... I don't like it."

"Me neither," Lora murmured, her eyes never leaving the shadows above.

The silence pressed against them, heavy and unnatural, as though the forest itself were holding its breath. Both detectives felt it the weight of something unseen, waiting.

Sam's thoughts turned bitter. Another body, another night, another horror I'll be cleaning up after. And with her by my side... damn it, it's going to cut deeper this time.

Lora's stomach tightened. This place feels wrong. Like it knows what's waiting for us. Like it's watching.

They stood in the hush of the forest's grip, two fractured souls, bound together again by duty and darkness, on the edge of something neither of them wanted to face.

Chapter One

The screams had ended, but the echo of them still lingered in Detective Lora Matthews' ears as she stepped deeper into the forest. Every footfall sank into damp soil, muffled by layers of fallen leaves and moss. The deeper she went, the more the chaos of flashing lights and murmuring voices behind her faded until all that was left was the hush, the kind of silence that clung to the skin, that whispered of things unseen.

Sam walked just a step behind her, the beam of his flashlight slicing through the dark. His jaw was set, his posture rigid, but she knew him too well. His silence wasn't composure it was unease.

He feels it too, she thought. He just won't admit it.

"Scene about fifty yards in," Sam said, keeping his voice steady, as though facts could shield them from whatever waited ahead. "Patrol found a trail. Lots of blood. They think." He stopped short, the words catching.

Lora glanced over her shoulder. For a heartbeat, she almost saw the man she once knew the husband, not the chief. His eyes were shadowed, the mask of authority slipping. Then he straightened, clearing his throat, the moment gone.

"Let's just see for ourselves," he said flatly.

They pushed deeper. Branches cracked underfoot. The trees seemed to close in, taller, darker, whispering overhead. Lora tilted her head, listening. That stillness hadn't broken. No crickets, no rustling, no calls of night birds. Just the sound of their breathing and the faint hiss of distant radios.

She shivered, pulling her coat tighter around her. This forest isn't just silent. It's listening.

Up ahead, the glow of lanterns broke through the dark. Uniformed officers stood in a loose circle, their faces pale and grim in the artificial light. The forensic team was already at work, their cameras flashing, their gloves slick with dew.

And at the centre of it all.

The body lay crumpled at the base of an old oak, its bark scarred by deep, fresh gouges. The victim was a woman, young, her pale skin stark against the earth. Her mouth was open in a frozen scream.

Lora stopped cold. For a moment, her pulse faltered, her breath caught. Something about the angle of the body, the way her arms were stretched as if clawing at the ground, hit too close. God, she looks like she was running for her life.

Sam's voice cut low beside her. "She didn't make it far. Just inside the tree line." His tone was detached, but his hand flexed at his side, curling into a fist.

"Someone wanted her found," Lora whispered.

He looked at her sharply. "What makes you say that?"

She gestured at the scene. "If she ran from deep in the woods, she'd have been further in. This feels... staged. Placed just close enough to be discovered."

Sam's gaze followed hers, and unease flickered across his face before he shoved it down again. She always sees too much. Always.

A uniform approached, hat in hand. "Detectives. No ID yet. But uh you should see this." He motioned toward the tree.

Carved into the bark, just above the victim, were words scrawled in jagged letters, as though gouged in desperation or fury:

CRIES INTO THE NIGHT

Lora's breath caught. Her eyes traced the letters, each one uneven and raw, cut deep into living wood.

Her voice was barely audible. "It's a message."

Sam muttered under his breath, almost to himself, "Or a warning."

They stood side by side, the weight of the forest pressing in around them, the silence deeper than before. The air smelled faintly of iron and damp earth. Somewhere beyond the lantern glow, the darkness seemed to shift, waiting.

Lora's thoughts spiraled. This isn't just another murder. It's the start of something worse. And if the past has taught me anything... it's that nothing good ever comes crawling out of these woods.

Sam looked at her, his expression unreadable. Here we go again. And God help me, I don't know if I can protect her this time.

Lora stepped closer, the crunch of her boots sounding unnaturally loud in the hush. The lantern light flickered across the victim's face, illuminating wide eyes glazed over in terror, her lips parted as if her final scream had been ripped from her throat.

Lora crouched down slowly, careful not to disturb the soil. The damp earth smelled of iron and moss, and beneath it, something else, something faint, acrid, like burned wood.

Her gloved fingers hovered near the victim's wrist, not to check for a pulse, she already knew there wasn't one but as though some part of her needed to bridge the chasm between the living and the dead.

How many times have I done this? How many times have I knelt in the dirt, staring at someone else's nightmare, pretending I don't carry it home with me?

Behind her, Sam shifted, his boots grinding against the leaves. She didn't need to look to know his arms were crossed, his jaw tight. That was his armour, stand tall, stay cold, don't let it in.

But she could feel him watching her. Always watching her.

"She was terrified," Lora murmured, more to herself than anyone else. "Look at the hands, fingers clawed, nails broken. She ran."

"Ran from what?" Sam asked quietly.

Lora lifted her eyes to the gouged words carved into the bark. Cries Into the Night. The letters almost seemed to pulse under the lantern light, the grooves raw and fresh.

"From whoever left that," she whispered.

Sam followed her gaze. His stomach twisted, though he refused to let it show. A message. A taunt. Or something worse. And of course, it had to happen here. In these woods. On my watch.

The uniformed officer cleared his throat nervously, shifting his weight. "Detectives... there's something else."

He pointed toward the base of the tree. Lora leaned closer. The victim's shoes mud-caked sneakers were worn, almost threadbare. But it wasn't the shoes that caught her attention. It was the soil beneath them.

A trail. Barely visible in the lantern light. Scuffed earth, pressed leaves, a path leading deeper into the forest.

Lora's pulse quickened. She glanced at Sam. "She wasn't alone."

Sam's eyes narrowed. His instinct screamed at him to call it, to wait for backup, to seal off the trail and let the forensics team crawl through every inch. But he knew that look in Lora's eyes the one that said she was already two steps ahead, already walking that path in her mind.

He ground his teeth. Damn it, Lora. You're going to get yourself killed one of these days. And I'll be the one left holding the pieces.

"We don't know that." he said flatly, trying to anchor her with logic. "Could've been animal tracks. Could've been."

"It wasn't," she cut in, her voice firm, unshaken. She rose to her feet, dust clinging to her knees. "This wasn't random, Sam. Someone brought her here. Someone led her here. And if there's a trail…" Her eyes shifted into the dark, where the lantern glow didn't reach. "…then maybe they're still out there."

For the first time all night, Sam felt the hair rise on the back of his neck. He forced his voice to remain steady. "Don't go jumping ahead. We'll follow protocol."

But the silence pressed harder now, thicker, more suffocating, as if the forest itself resented the intrusion.

Lora folded her arms, her voice barely above a breath. "Protocol won't save us from what's in these woods."

Sam stared at her, searching her face for the woman he used to know the partner who trusted logic, who leaned on evidence. But what he saw in her eyes now was something different. A knowing. A quiet dread that mirrored the feeling coiling in his gut.

He turned away before she could read his expression. "We'll call in another unit to sweep deeper," he muttered.

But the trail was already pulling at Lora like a thread unravelling, tugging her into the dark. And no amount of tape, protocol, or caution would be enough to keep her from following it.

The circle of lantern light flickered like a fragile island against the dark. Beyond it, the forest loomed, silent and endless. Each tree stood like a watchman, their bark damp with dew, their branches clawing against the night sky.

Lora let her gaze linger on the carved words again. CRIES INTO THE NIGHT.

The grooves were jagged, uneven, dug with desperation. Sap bled from the cuts, running like veins down the trunk. She stepped closer, reaching up with a gloved hand. Her fingertips hovered above the rough letters, almost as if touching them would whisper the truth of who had made them.

But she didn't touch. She couldn't.

It's fresh. Hours old at most. Whoever did this was here. Watching. Waiting.

She swallowed hard, the taste of copper on her tongue, though she hadn't bitten anything.

Behind her, Sam's voice carried, low and gruff. "Why here? Why write that?"

Lora didn't answer right away. She traced the words with her eyes again, letting the silence stretch. Finally, she said, "It isn't just a message. It's a name."

Sam frowned. "A name?"

She nodded slowly. "Cries Into the Night. That's what they want this to be called. It's a story they're writing, Sam. And she..." Lora tilted her chin toward the body..." she's their first chapter."

The words hung heavy between them.

Sam hated how much sense it made. He hated the way her instincts always pierced straight through the noise. And he hated most of all, the way his gut agreed with her.

The forensics van finally arrived, headlights sweeping the scene before snapping off. The silence fractured with the shuffle of boots and the rustle of tarps as the team moved into place. Their cameras flashed, cutting the dark with staccato bursts. The soft whirr of evidence bags, the clipped voices of technicians marking samples it all felt clinical, too clean against the raw horror that lay in front of them.

One of the techs knelt near the body, murmuring to an assistant, but Lora tuned them out. Her eyes never left the victim's face.

The woman's hair was tangled with leaves, her jaw slack, her skin ashen under the lantern light. A faint line of blood had dried along her temple, but it wasn't enough to explain the terror etched in her expression.

You saw something, Lora thought. Something so awful that it froze you in that last scream.

She felt a twist in her chest. Not pity. Not yet. Something colder. Fear.

A twig snapped behind her, sharp as a gunshot in the silence. Lora spun, her hand instinctively brushing her hip where her weapon rested.

It was only an officer, young, wide-eyed, holding up an evidence bag. Inside lay a torn scrap of fabric, stained dark.

"Found it about fifteen feet along that trail," he said, pointing into the woods. His voice cracked on the last word.

Sam's gaze followed the line of the officer's finger. The trail again. The scuffed earth, the bent undergrowth, the path that waited.

Forensics murmured approval, marking it down, but the discovery only deepened the quiet dread in Lora's chest.

She wasn't running alone. She was being chased.

The thought pulsed inside her, steady as a heartbeat.

Sam stepped closer, speaking low so only she could hear. "We don't go deeper without backup."

Lora's jaw tightened. She wanted to argue, to step into that trail and let the woods answer for themselves. But the forest seemed to press tighter around them, listening, waiting.

Then, one by one, more officers joined. Flashlights clicked on, beams cutting into the shadows. Radios crackled. Orders were given. The crime scene held, but the deeper trail beckoned.

Sam looked at Lora. She knew that look reluctant, wary, but resolved. He wasn't going to let her walk into the dark without him, "Alright," he said, voice firm. "We go together. Careful. Slow."

Lora gave a single nod, her stomach tightening as if the forest had already swallowed them.

The two of them, flanked by a pair of uniformed officers, ducked past the tree and into the trail. The glow of lanterns faded behind them, swallowed by the dark. The deeper they walked, the heavier the air grew. Damp, dense, and cold.

Sam swept his light left to right, catching glimpses of twisted roots and pale fungi clinging to trunks. Every sound seemed amplified the crunch of boots, the faint hiss of breath, the rustle of leaves disturbed.

And yet beneath it all there was still that awful silence.

Lora whispered, almost to herself, "It feels wrong in here."

Sam's reply came rough, quiet. "Feels like we're not alone."

Neither of them disagreed.

The forest breathed in long, cold intervals, as if the night itself were holding its lungs in check. Lantern light behind them pulsed faintly through the branches, a heartbeat they were leaving behind.

Lora stood under the carved words and let the hush settle on her shoulders. CRIES INTO THE NIGHT. The letters bled sap, a tacky sheen that caught her beam and turned it wet. She didn't need to touch to feel the roughness; her fingertips twitched as if the story had grain and could catch a nail.

Granddad used to say trees memorize the weather and the sins. Rings for the rain. Scars for the rest.

Sam lingered at her periphery, posture squared, a silhouette of control. The little tells still leaked: a jaw that clicked once, an exhale he kept shallow so his breath wouldn't show.

"You see the depth?" Lora murmured. "Not a pocketknife. Something heavier. Chisel, maybe. Or a screwdriver pounded in." She angled the light. The cuts were not elegant; they were obsessive. Some strokes overlapped, dug again as if the words weren't real until the tree flinched.

Sam's gaze tracked the grooves. Someone took time. Stayed long enough for their hands to ache. He swallowed the thought. "Forensics will cast it," he said, as if procedure were a spell strong enough to clear the air.

Beyond the tape line, cameras popped and clipped voices carried in sterile fragments. Close by, the victim lay with her hair webbed in damp leaves, one shoe half off, the aglet bright as a fish scale. Lora crouched, the earth cool through her knees. She did not look directly at the face this time. She looked at the small things: a scrape across the knuckles, dirt under three nails but not the fourth, a faint ash smudge along the sleeve seam.

Burned wood. I wasn't imagining it. The smell threaded through the loam, acrid and thin. Not campfire. Not leaves. Plastic? Wax?

An officer Riley, young, jittery shifted too fast and his radio hissed at his hip. The sound broke like glass. Lora's hand went to her holster before she could stop it. Riley flinched, mouth already opening to apologize.

"It's fine," she said without looking up. It wasn't fine, but saying so would feed the wrong thing.

Patel, older and quiet, stood a little behind Sam, his beam low, careful with where it went. He focused on what most people missed:

the edges. The places where a story tries to seam itself to the world and fails.

"Forensics," a tech called, "needs five minutes uninterrupted on the bark. No touching. No shadows across the upper lettering."

Sam nodded, hands clasped behind him, the picture of a chief who could wait. Inside, a clock he didn't wind ticked harder. Every minute out here is another minute the trail goes cold. And still no birds. No frogs. Not even a fox bark. What scared this place quiet?

Lora stood. "She ran," she said again, softer. Saying it twice took the certainty from cold to warm. "She ran and he...." She bit the word down. Don't gender the monster yet. Don't give it a silhouette before you have to.

Patel angled his beam beyond the oak. "The track continues," he said. "Light. Pace increases there longer scuffs."

Sam looked to Lora. They didn't nod. They didn't need to. Agreement thinned the air between them for a second, like two magnets finding their alignment.

A pinecone plummeted through the branches and thudded near Riley's boot. He yelped and then laughed at himself, too loud. The laugh died immediately, as if the trees absorbed it out of embarrassment for him.

"Keep your lights between knee and shoulder," Sam said, voice even. "No strobing. If you spook something, it spooks you back."

He always was good at sounding like the adult in the room, Lora thought, and immediately hated that the thought felt like comfort. She turned that discomfort into movement. The acrid thread of scent tugged her forward.

Behind them, the forensic tech finished shooting the words and began framing the bark with a measuring ruler, his assistant marking logs. The camera whirred, indifferent to dread.

"Alright," Sam said to the circle of lanterns. "Scene is yours. We'll be on the trail. Two officers with us." His eyes flicked to Patel and Riley. "You're up."

Blue tape lifted and fell behind them. The lights blurred out like buoys vanishing in fog.

They moved single file. Lora at point, Sam on her right shoulder, Patel steady behind, Riley bringing up the rear with a beam he couldn't stop from shaking. The path narrowed and then forgot it had ever been a path. Brambles reached. A thorn hooked Lora's sleeve and held; she paused, freed it with slow fingers. The thorn bit the glove anyway. Tiny pain. Real. Grounding.

They went another ten yards. Twenty. The ground fell away then rose, slick with leaf rot. The forest had gradients the eye couldn't measure until the calves began to protest.

False movement churned in the edge of Lora's vision dark on darker, a shade less black than the rest. She stilled, lifted a hand without turning. The group froze behind her in that ripple you only get from people who've trained together.

Something burst from the undergrowth to the left, a blur of muscle and panic. A deer, small and gaunt, tore past and vanished, its pale tail flashing once before the dark swallowed it whole. Lora let out a breath she hadn't known she'd been holding. Riley's involuntary "Jesus" sounded much too human in the hush.

When the deer's hoofbeats faded, the silence returned, deeper, as if the forest had been waiting to reset.

Animals are brave until they aren't, Sam thought. And that one... He didn't finish the sentence. He didn't like where it went.

They found the first certainty as quiet as a whisper: a thread of fabric snagged on a blackthorn, high, shoulder-level. Lora pinched it between gloved fingers. Synthetic. Pink once, now dirt dulled. The same tone as the torn scrap in the bag Riley had shown them. She breathed through her mouth, fighting the useless thought that if she could inhale the fabrics past it would tell her everything.

"Direction holds," Patel said softly. "See the bracken? Pressed inward like something came through at speed." His beam skimmed without lingering, respectful.

They went on. The acrid smell strengthened in increments, faint, then faint-plus, then a thread you could follow with your eyes closed.

A twig snapped to their right, soft, deliberate weight, not wind. All four lights swung, cutting lattice into the trunks. The beams shook. Nothing there but trees. And still, Lora felt watched in the way teeth feel watched by a dentist's tray before the instruments come out.

Stop it, she told herself. The forest isn't a person. But the forest disagreed.

A shape interrupted her light at ankle height she halted inches from it. A length of twine spanned the path, tied low between two saplings. Sam's hand shot out, catching her elbow. They both stared.

Riley breathed, "Trapline?" too loudly.

Patel crouched, steady. "If it is, it's crude." He traced along the twine carefully. It ended at a tin can half buried in leaves, a cluster of small stones inside. Not a bomb. A rattle. A noisemaker, simple as childhood, meant to announce the crossing to anyone listening in the dark.

Lora straightened. "Someone wanted to hear us coming."

"Or hear her," Sam said. The word hung there, reassigning the line to a different hour. He swept his beam ahead. "Step over. One at a time."

They did, careful as surgeons. The twine twitched once and the stones in the can clicked against metal with a sound like tiny teeth.

Everyone went still. The air listened with them. Nothing answered. The quiet resumed.

The smell was stronger now. Lora tasted it at the back of her tongue. Plastic and something sweet gone wrong. A low-grade chemical note that didn't belong to trees. The canopy thinned ahead, and a lighter patch of night suggested a clearing.

"Lights low," Sam said. "Patel, hold left. Riley, right with me. Lora...."

"Centre," she finished, already moving.

They broke into the clearing like divers breaching the surface of a black lake. It was small, an oval scraped raw. The ground here had been bullied: leaves pushed aside, soil churned, a shallow bowl of ash and melted something at the center. Around it, stones had been placed not tossed, placed in a loose ring. Candle stubs pooled into puddles of wax had slumped and fossilized along the rocks. Blackened wicks stuck up like tiny antennae.

Lora's light found a shape jutting from the ash: the warped skeleton of a cheap lighter, its metal spine gleaming. The acrid note spiked. Ash dust climbed her nostrils. He burned something here. Or tried to. She thought of the smear on the victim's sleeve. Here.

"Don't step in," Sam warned, but his voice dropped, thinned. Fire. He wanted light here? Or wanted to erase traces? The ring felt ceremonial, and he hated the word for it. Rituals belong to religions and families and griefs. He didn't want a killer borrowing it.

Riley circled too close to the right; Lora shot out a palm without looking. He stopped, boot hanging over the edge of the churned soil. He swallowed. "Sorry." In the beam, his wrists shook.

"Look," Patel said.

On the far side of the clearing, not obvious at first glance, a crude ladder had been cut into the face of an old beech: cross-pieces nailed into the trunk at uneven intervals, the wood of each step a different age. Some fresh, sap bright at the cut. Some old and grey. Above, a platform sat wedged in the crook of branches small, makeshift, almost invisible from below. A hunter's stand, but wrong. Angled toward the clearing. Angled toward the ring of candles.

Sam's gut went cold. "Blind," he said. The word felt too benign. He watched. He sits and watches and waits.

"Stay," he added to Riley, who already looked ready to volunteer. "Patel, with me. Lora"

But Lora was already moving to the base, head tipped back, reading the story in the geometry of wood. He didn't build that at midnight. This is older. He's used it. He's had time. The beam picked out fresh scrapes along the trunk where hands had climbed recently, where boots had ground bark away.

"Careful," Sam said. For the first time that night, the word was not procedure. It was personal.

She climbed. The wood gave a little and held. Each step bit into the soles with a creak that sounded too loud, every foot of height stretching the silence tighter. At the platform she paused, drew a breath, then hauled herself over the lip and into a square of shadow that smelled of old rope and cheap smoke.

She crouched, pivoted slowly, every motion measured. Her light found a nest of ball of tape, a flattened cushion, a bottle of water capped and half full, condensation beading even in the chill. Not abandoned. Used. Recently. A Styrofoam coffee cup lay on its side, lip stained with a crescent someone had bitten while drinking.

And there, tacked to the inner post, was a scrap of glossy paper pinned with a small nail. Lora's beam caught a slice of pale face, blurred, and a smear of handwritten ink beneath.

She leaned in. The photo was a Polaroid, the kind that develops into truth whether you want it or not. The subject was the clearing below from this very angle, candles mid-flame, empty of bodies, the ring complete. The ink scrawl under it wasn't a note. It was a number 2.

Lora's mouth went dry. First chapter back at the tree. She did not, would not, finish the counting aloud.

"Lora?" Sam called up, voice low but carrying. "What have you got?"

She didn't answer right away. The forest pressed close to the little platform, close like it wanted to hear her say it. She tamped down the urge to tear the photo free with her teeth. She took a breath, made her voice a steady instrument.

"Blind's active," she said. "Supplies. Fresh. And a Polaroid view of the clearing. Numbered."

Below, Sam's jaw ticked once. He's composing this. Out loud, he said, "Anything else?"

Lora's light eased along the post. Another nail hole under the first. Another above it. An empty bracket where something had been and was now gone. A faint rectangle of clean wood in a field of grime, as if a device had lived there and been removed. She pictured a small black box with a glass eye.

"Trail cam mount," she said. "Missing now."

Patel breathed a sound like the first hint of weather. "He watched her. And us."

Riley, from the path edge, shifted and set off the tin can rattle far behind them. The stones clicked, small and precise. Lora's head snapped to the sound, then back to the clearing. The forest didn't move. That was the worst part. The forest didn't have to.

Lora slid the Polaroid into an evidence sleeve she kept in her inner pocket, the plastic whispering. You don't belong to him anymore. She took one last look at the platform, the cushion, the cup with the moon of teeth, the faint chemical sweet that clung to wood like a touch someone hadn't asked permission to give.

She climbed down, slow, each step translating her pulse back into earth. Sam's face tilted up to meet her. They were eye to eye when her boots hit soil.

He said nothing. He didn't need to.

She nodded once. "He was right here," she said. "Close enough to count our breaths. And if this is two…"

Sam finished it, because she wouldn't. "Then one was the tree."

And the woods, finally, let a single sound in an owl, sudden, one note that cut clean through the cold. It sounded like a question it already knew the answer to.

"Mark the clearing," Sam ordered, voice returning to its hard edges. "Call it in. Full team. And we keep moving. Carefully."

The ring of stones glimmered under their beams. The path out of the clearing narrowed like a throat. Lora looked into it and felt the shape of the mystery sharpen not a fog anymore, but a blade.

"Alright," she whispered, to herself or the trees she didn't know. "Show me chapter three."

Chapter Two

The woods did not give them answers. Only silence and the faint pull of a trail that seemed to go on forever. Every step deeper felt like a dare, and every snapped twig underfoot felt too loud, like breaking glass in a cathedral.

They lingered in the clearing longer than they should have, circling its edges, cataloguing every stone, every wax-dripped stub, every bent blade of grass. And still nothing. Nothing but the ash pit and the memory of heat.

By the time they began retracing their steps, the air had shifted. A pale wash of light threaded through the branches overhead, dim at first, then brightening. Sunrise had started to push against the horizon, turning the black sky to bruised grey.

The transition felt wrong. Wrong because the forest should have welcomed the dawn with noise—with chirping sparrows, with the rustle of squirrels, with the low hum of waking life. Instead, the silence remained, dense and stifling. The light made the shadows longer, harsher, as if the trees resented the intrusion.

Lora caught herself squinting at the bark of every trunk, searching for more words carved into the wood. She half expected to see new messages scrawled just out of reach, waiting for her alone to find them.

Her chest ached with exhaustion, though she fought to ignore it. Her mind still hummed with the Polaroid, with the number scrawled beneath it. 2.

If there's a two, there's always a one before it. Always a three after. A sequence. A plan.

She hated walking away from a story unfinished. Hated the idea of leaving pieces scattered in the dirt while the killer moved them like chess pieces.

Sam broke the silence first. His voice was steady, low, but it carried the weight of command.

"We're pulling back."

Lora stopped dead in her tracks, the words striking her harder than she expected. "What?"

"It's dawn. Forensics needs clean light to work the site. Patrol will hold perimeter, mark where we left. We'll regroup, get the lab's input, then resume."

Her heart thudded in protest. "We're already here, Sam. You saw the ladder. The stand. The photo. He was right there." She gestured into the thick woods, her hand trembling despite her control. "He could still be."

"Gone," Sam cut in. "If he was close, we'd never have reached the blind in the first place." He stepped closer, eyes locked on hers. "You know that."

Lora clenched her jaw, anger prickling hot under her skin. He's retreating. Again. Always the cautious one. Always the one who knows when to quit. And me—I'm the one who keeps dragging us forward, even when it burns.

"Every second we waste," she snapped, "is a second, he's setting up the next scene. You want to wait until it's three? Until we're chasing him from behind?"

Sam's gaze hardened, but behind it was something else a flicker of fear. Not for the case. For her.

She doesn't stop. She never did. And one day, that's what will kill her.

His voice softened just enough for her to hear it wasn't just an order. "We call it here. That's final."

The two officers glanced between them but said nothing. Riley's shoulders sagged with relief. Patel only shifted his flashlight lower, quiet and unreadable.

Lora's breath hissed between her teeth. She wanted to argue, wanted to scream, but she knew him too well. Once Sam planted his feet, there was no moving him. Not in the field. Not in life.

She turned away, her throat tight. "Fine." The word was sharper than she intended.

Sam gave the order aloud, for everyone's benefit. "Mark the path. GPS the last point. We resume at nineteen hundred hours, no earlier."

Patel unclipped a can of orange tape from his belt, tying a strip around a branch at eye level, the fabric flapping faintly in the early morning breeze. Riley placed another marker a few feet down. Together they worked in silence, leaving breadcrumbs in the forest's teeth.

The walk back felt longer. The dawn light spread thinly, touching the moss, painting the trunks in weak gold. It should have been beautiful. Instead, it looked raw, as though the forest had been skinned open.

When they finally broke back into the perimeter, the crime scene buzzed with renewed life. Reporters leaned harder into the tape, cameras eager to catch glimpses of tired detectives. Forensics fanned out in the better light, combing every inch of the oak with the carved words. The body had already been covered, readied for transport, but the shape beneath the sheet was still a scream in the soil.

Lora paused at the edge of it all, the morning breeze cold on her face. She breathed in deep, hoping for clarity. All she caught was the lingering tang of ash.

Sam stepped up beside her, his shadow long in the early light. His voice was low, meant for her alone, "We'll get him."

She didn't answer. Her eyes stayed on the treeline, on the place where the trail disappeared into the green.

You don't stop a story halfway through, she thought. Not when someone else is writing the ending for you.

And though the sun had risen, the forest still felt like night.

The precinct was awake before the city was.

Reporters had followed them back like vultures, their voices echoing down the station steps in waves of shouted questions: "Detective Matthews, was it ritual?" "Chief, is this connected to the disappearances last year?" "Do you have a suspect?" The cameras flashed, popping white light against the glass doors as though trying to burn their way in.

Sam ignored them, shouldering past with the practiced calm of a man who had been chased by microphones for decades. Lora trailed behind, jaw tight, the flashbulbs stinging her eyes. She wanted to stop, to snap back at the vultures, but she didn't. Not yet. Her silence would be twisted no matter what she said.

Inside, the air was no less stifling. The bullpen buzzed with phones, keyboards, and voices too loud, too fast. A dozen detectives leaned over files and screens, their faces lit by the glow of monitors and coffee steam. Conversations clipped and cut off the moment Sam and Lora walked in. The weight of the night had already travelled ahead of them.

In the glass-walled investigation room, the first pieces of evidence were already being laid out. Photographs of the victim on the forest floor. Close-ups of the gouged bark. The carved words CRIES INTO THE NIGHT printed on glossy sheets, larger than life.

Pinned beside them was the Polaroid. Number two scrawled beneath it.

Lora stared at it too long, her chest tightening with something she refused to call fear. It looks worse in here. Under fluorescent light, it feels like it doesn't belong to the woods anymore. It belongs to him. To me. To everyone who stares long enough for it to breathe.

A younger detective, Hayes, leaned back in his chair with a smirk that grated on her nerves. "So, what's the verdict? Some nutjob with a wood chisel and a flair for the dramatic?"

Lora shot him a look sharp enough to cut. "That 'nutjob' staged a scene, laid a trail, built a blind, and left us a numbered Polaroid. You think that's amateur hour?"

Hayes faltered, the smirk fading under her glare. The room stilled. Sam's eyes flicked between them, his silence sharp with warning.

Patel, ever steady, broke the tension with his low voice. "This isn't his first time."

Heads turned.

Sam nodded once. "Agreed. And it won't be his last. Which means we move carefully. We move smart."

But Lora's gaze hadn't left the Polaroid. Two. The number whispered at her like a taunt, like a countdown she hadn't agreed to. She imagined the killer tacking it to the wood with a steady hand, smiling to himself in the dark.

Her knuckles went white around the chairback. What's one? What's three? How many more chapters until we're written into the story ourselves?

The day stretched long. Statements taken. Evidence logged. Press briefings drafted. And through it all, Lora stayed in motion until Sam finally put a hand on her shoulder and said firmly, "Go home, Lora. That's an order."

Her apartment was dark when she entered, a silence that was almost merciful after the chaos of the precinct. She didn't bother turning on the lights. She kicked off her shoes, let her coat fall across a chair, and sank onto the couch.

She closed her eyes but sleep never came. Instead, the forest replayed itself behind her eyelids: the victim's frozen scream, the carved words bleeding sap, the ash pit ringed with stones, above all, the Polaroid, the number two.

It pulsed in her thoughts like a heartbeat.

If there's a two, then there's already a one. Did we miss it? Did we walk right past it? Or is one still out there, waiting for us to find it?

The sound of her phone buzzing broke the loop. She glanced at the screen. Sam.

For a moment she considered ignoring it. But she didn't.

"Matthews," she answered, her voice hoarse with exhaustion.

"Lora." His tone was softer than it had been all night. Not the Chief. Just Sam. "How are you holding up?"

She hesitated, "Tired." A pause. "But I can't stop thinking about it."

"I know." His sigh crackled through the line. "That's why I called. I need to know... did you have any more of your...." He faltered, careful, "Visions?"

Lora pressed a hand against her eyes. *Visions. He still calls them that. Like they're ghosts and not instincts I can't explain.*

"No," she whispered. "Not yet. Just... a feeling."

Silence stretched. Then his voice, low: "You're extraordinary, you know that? The way you see things. The way you cut through the noise. I've never met anyone like you."

Her throat tightened, and she hated how much she needed to hear it.

"But," he continued firmly, "you need to rest. You push yourself too hard. Always have." His voice softened, the crack of old care leaking through. "Get some sleep. I'll see you later."

The line clicked dead.

Lora lowered the phone slowly, her reflection faint in the black glass of the screen. *Extraordinary. Or cursed.*

She lay back on the couch, eyes open in the dark, as dawn spilled pale light through the blinds. The number two burned behind her eyes.

And still, sleep would not come. Lora tried to obey.

Chapter Three

She woke late, though it wasn't real sleep just a thin layer of exhaustion that covered her eyes like film. The second she sat up, the weight of it all pressed back down: the body, the message, the photograph.

She showered, dressed, forced coffee down. She opened her blinds, then shut them again. The morning light felt wrong, like an intruder instead of relief.

Her apartment was quiet, but her thoughts weren't.

Don't chase it, Lora. Sam told you to rest. Just breathe. Just stop.

But she couldn't. Every corner of her mind bent back to the Polaroid. That 2. It was louder than the city outside, louder than her own heartbeat.

She paced her living room, bare feet slapping against the floorboards. She pulled open old boxes stacked in her closet files from cold cases, unsolved killings, the kind she never let go of. She flipped through them, scanning photos, details, names.

Looking for patterns. Looking for number one.

Her fingers shook as she traced photographs from years before victims left in parks, alleyways, the edge of rivers. No carvings. No Polaroids. But something lingered. Something that felt familiar in the angles, in the way the scenes had been staged.

She pressed her palms to her eyes, breath coming too fast. Am I forcing it? Seeing ghosts where there aren't any? Or is he out there, weaving all of this together, laughing while I claw at scraps?

By noon she had spread case files across her floor like puzzle pieces, but none of them fit. None gave her the one thing she craved: certainty.

The compulsion gnawed at her, sharper with every hour. And beneath it fear. Not of the killer. But of what he might mean for her. Of what this case was already starting to do to her insides.

When dusk finally touched the windows, she realized she'd been holding her breath all day. Waiting for the hour when she could return.

Rest was never an option. Not for me.

The squad room pulsed with energy by the time Lora arrived. The sun had dropped low, leaving only bruised light outside the windows. Fluorescents buzzed overhead.

Clusters of detectives leaned in over coffee cups, whispering theories. Words like ritual and black magic hung in the air, spreading from mouth to mouth like infection.

"It was staged. Had to be," one voice said.

"Pentagrams, fire pits… it's a damn ritual," another muttered.

"You don't carve something like that for fun."

"Witchcraft. Satanic stuff."

Lora stood at the edge of the room, listening. Not correcting. Not yet.

She hated gossip it always felt like noise distracting from the truth but tonight, she couldn't deny the weight of it. There had been ritual in that clearing. The stones. The ash. The blind. It wasn't random.

Sam appeared from his office, coat slung over his shoulders, eyes sweeping the room until they landed on her.

For a heartbeat, they just looked at each other.

She read him like she always did steady, grounded, the centre of the storm. But beneath that composure she saw the same unease in his eyes that she carried in her chest.

He feels it too. Even if he won't say it.

He crossed to her, his voice pitched just above the buzz of the room. "Ready?"

She almost smiled, but it didn't reach her lips. "I've been ready all day."

His gaze lingered a moment longer than it should have. A flicker of something softer, something familiar. Then he nodded, brisk and professional, and turned toward the waiting officers.

Within minutes, the team was assembled. Maps were rolled up, gear checked, weapons holstered. The chatter died down into clipped orders.

As they filed out into the night, Lora's chest tightened with anticipation. Fear, yes but also hunger.

This is it. The forest has more to tell us. And tonight, I'll listen.

And beside her, Sam walked in silence, his thoughts heavier than his footsteps. God help us if she listens too closely.

The convoy rolled out at nineteen hundred sharp. Engines hummed low, headlights slicing across the tree line as the vehicles pulled up in staggered rows at the forest's entrance.

Blue tape still stretched across the posts, sagging slightly in the cool night air. Flashlights cut through the gloom as officers checked equipment, their voices low, subdued, as though speaking too loudly might wake something better left asleep.

Lora stepped out of her car and tilted her face upward. The forest loomed taller tonight. Shadows clung to its edges, thickening with every breath of dusk. The first stars blinked faintly above, drowned by the forest canopy the deeper she looked.

She felt it before she heard it: the hush. The woods seemed to lean in, waiting.

Her skin prickled. It feels different tonight. Heavier. Watching me.

Sam came up beside her, his presence as solid as the ground under her boots. "You good?"

She nodded, though her throat was dry. "Yeah. Just... it feels thicker than last night."

He scanned the treeline with narrowed eyes. "That's because we know what's in there now. Or at least, part of it."

No, she thought, but didn't say. It's because something else is waiting.

The officers pushed aside the blue tape, letting it flutter as the group crossed the threshold. The forest swallowed them slowly, one step at a time.

Flashlights darted ahead in beams, catching glimpses of bark, roots, and leaves that looked too much like reaching hands. The crunch of boots on soil was the only steady rhythm. Occasionally, a snapped twig or the flutter of a bird startled someone into jerking their light skyward only to find nothing but branches and silence.

Lora stayed close to Sam, though she hated needing the comfort. Her pulse matched the swing of her light across the undergrowth. Every shadow seemed to bend toward her, every hollow seemed to breathe.

Her inner voice gnawed at her: This is where he lives. Not in houses, not in alleys. Here. In silence. He wants us lost in it. He wants us to hear him without sound.

"Stop." Lora's voice came sharp, surprising even herself.

The line of officers stilled, lights swinging back.

Sam turned to her. "What is it?"

She listened.

The forest was dead quiet. Too quiet. Even the crickets that had carried through the dusk were gone.

She whispered, almost to herself: "Do you feel it? The stillness?"

Sam's jaw tightened. "Yeah." He nodded to the group. "Stay sharp."

They pressed on, and the forest grew darker, as though the night itself had roots. The beams of light seemed weaker here, swallowed by the trees. A mist had begun to gather low along the ground, curling between trunks like pale fingers.

One officer cursed under his breath when a branch cracked behind him. They all turned, beams slicing the dark, only to find emptiness.

False scare.

Lora didn't laugh it off. She couldn't. Her instincts pressed harder, whispering warnings in a language only she understood. *He wants us nervous. He wants us scattered. Don't give him what he wants.*

Sam's voice, low beside her: "Keep moving."

Then, the trail bent sharply. And there it was.

Another marker.

A tree, its bark stripped bare in a square panel. Nailed into it clean, deliberate was another Polaroid.

The light from their flashlights struck it at once, the glossy surface reflecting back like an unblinking eye.

This time, the number beneath it read: three.

For a moment, no one spoke. Only the mist moved.

Lora's chest tightened as though a fist had closed around her lungs. *Not one. Not two. Three. He's building something. A sequence. A story. And we're only just turning the pages.*

Sam's hand hovered at his belt, his jaw rigid. He's pulling us in, step by step. Damn him, he knows exactly how we'll move.

The officers muttered, theories slipping out in fragments, "Another photo, it's numbered..." The officer paused for a bit and shivered as he spoke the words, "Ritual, has to be."

But Lora didn't hear them. She was staring at the photo, unable to look away. The way it was placed. The way it waited for her.

Her whisper cut through the dark, trembling despite her steel: "He's leading us deeper."

Sam met her eyes, the unspoken weight heavy between them.

And deeper, they would go.

The officers closed in around the tree, their beams cutting across the nailed photograph.

Sam stepped closer first, pulling on gloves, his movements slow, deliberate. He plucked the Polaroid free from the bark and held it up for the lights.

Gasps stirred through the group.

The image was of a body another woman laid out across the forest floor. The frame was tight, her face turned away, but her arms were spread wide, palms upward, as if in offering. Twigs and leaves had been carefully arranged around her head like a crude halo.

The shot was fresh. Too fresh. Whoever had taken it had done so within the last twenty-four hours.

"Christ," one officer muttered, looking away.

But Lora didn't look away. Couldn't.

Her eyes had already drifted past the body to something else in the photo. The way the halo had been shaped. Not random, not careless deliberate lines, a pattern.

Her breath caught.

Not just a halo. A symbol.

The branches formed into a rough spiral, broken twice, curling inward like a maze. It struck her with the familiarity of a dream she couldn't place.

A tremor passed through her chest. She knew she had seen that spiral before. Somewhere deep in the recess of her past cases or maybe further back. Childhood stories, chalk symbols scrawled in alleyways, scrawled notes she once dismissed.

No. It's more than that. This... is for me.

Her stomach turned. The thought felt like truth, though she had no proof.

Sam's eyes flicked to hers. He saw the shift in her expression instantly. "What is it?"

She swallowed hard, voice low. "That symbol. He's not just numbering them. He's... speaking. To me."

Sam's jaw flexed, but he didn't argue. Not here, not in front of the others. He only tucked the photo carefully into an evidence sleeve and gave the order to spread out, comb the surrounding trees for signs of the body's location.

As the team moved, tension bled into the air. Every snapping twig now sounded like a scream waiting to happen.

And for Lora, the image of the spiral clung to her mind, burrowing deep. He's ahead of us. Always ahead. He knows I'll follow the trail. He knows I can't not follow.

The forest seemed to breathe heavier as they moved deeper. The breadcrumb had been placed, and they had taken it.

The game was shifting.

The forest had swallowed the sound of their voices.

Every step forward felt heavier now, the weight of the Polaroid pressing against the evidence sleeve in Sam's pocket like a live wire.

They moved as a tight column, flashlights slicing narrow corridors of light through the dark. Their boots crunched on damp leaves, each footfall punctuated by the distant drip of water deeper within.

The number on the photo burned in Lora's mind. three. Not just a number. A message. A taunt. A countdown she couldn't quite decipher.

Her eyes scanned every tree, every patch of earth, the symbol replaying in her head. The spiral. The breaks. She could feel it under her skin now familiar, invasive, like a memory she didn't want but couldn't shake.

Sam glanced at her, his voice low. "You're somewhere else, Matthews. Talk to me."

She shook her head, not looking at him. "It's... nothing. Just focus."

But it wasn't nothing. It was everything.

A sharp bark cracked through the quiet.

Heads turned as two K9 units emerged from the path behind, the handlers straining to keep the dog's steady.

"Got 'em from the city," one of the handlers said, breathless. "Fresh scent pulled from the clearing earlier today. Thought we'd sweep the deeper grid."

The dogs hit the ground running the moment they were loosed, noses to the soil, tails stiff with alert tension.

Lora froze. Her gut twisted as if it already knew where this would lead.

"Matthews," Sam called, but she was already moving, boots pounding the dirt, chasing the sound of claws scraping bark and leaves scattering under frantic paws.

Branches whipped across her arms and face, but she didn't slow. Every breath tore through her lungs like ice.

The forest grew denser, closing around her in suffocating silence until the dogs stopped as one. Their bodies stiffened, then dropped low to the ground, paws clawing at the earth.

They dug in synchronized desperation, dirt flying in ragged arcs, sharp whimpers cutting through the stillness like knives.

Lora dropped to her knees beside them, shoving branches and soil aside with frantic hands. "Come on," she muttered. "Come on, don't...."

And then a flash of fabric. Blue.

Not random. Not discarded. A sleeve. A badge half-buried in the dirt.

"No," Lora whispered, the word strangled. Her nails clawed deeper, adrenaline surging until her fingers bled against the roots and stones.

The earth gave way in clumps, revealing pale skin, a familiar jawline streaked with mud, hair matted and dark.

Her chest seized.

It was Detective Rachel Meyers.

Her partner. Her friend. Someone who had sat across from her in a dozen late-night stakeouts, trading terrible coffee and darker jokes. Someone who had been there when Lora's marriage imploded, when the job almost broke her.

Rachel's eyes were closed. Dirt clung to her lashes. The spiral the same spiral from the Polaroid had been carved, shallow and precise, along her left forearm.

Lora's scream was raw, ripped from somewhere deep as she fell back, breath gone, the world tilting violently around her.

The dogs threw their heads back and howled, the sound so sharp and mournful it seemed to pierce the night itself.

Sam crashed through the trees behind her, froze at the sight, then forced himself forward, jaw clenched so tight it hurt.

"No," he whispered. Then louder, to the team, his voice shaking but firm: "Call it in. Now. Lock this entire area down."

He knelt beside Lora, his hand hovering above her shoulder but never quite touching, as though unsure what she'd do if he did.

Her hands trembled in her lap, streaked with blood and soil. She couldn't take her eyes off Rachel's face.

She was mine to protect.

The spiral burned behind her eyelids when she blinked, etched into her thoughts like a brand.

And in the stillness of that clearing, the forest felt alive again. Watching. Listening. Waiting for the next move.

Voices barked orders through the cold night air. Radios crackled with overlapping static, calls for backup, for the coroner, for more lights, for more people as though numbers could contain the horror that had rooted itself here.

But none of it touched Lora.

She knelt in the soil, her knees damp, her gloves caked in dirt and blood, her eyes fixed on the hollow stillness of Rachel's face. Every detail burned into her memory the pale skin, the strands of hair tangled with earth, the spiral carved into her arm with surgical precision.

Not Rachel, her mind whispered, frantic and broken. Not her. She wasn't supposed to be here. She wasn't.

Her chest constricted, breath coming in ragged, shallow pulls that tasted of dirt and iron.

"Matthews."

Sam's voice. Low, rough. Close enough to reach her but careful not to.

She blinked once, slow, as though dragging herself up from water, but she didn't look at him. Couldn't. Her body felt cold, hollowed out.

"She was supposed to be off tonight," she murmured. The words sounded alien in her own voice, barely audible. "She said she'd... she said she was visiting her sister in Boston."

Sam crouched beside her, boots sinking slightly in the damp earth, eyes burning with quiet fury not at her, but at the thing that had done this.

"She must've followed a lead," he said, voice tight but steady. "Or... maybe..." His words faltered, the unspoken possibilities curling in the air between them like smoke.

"No." Lora finally looked at him then, sharp and wild, eyes glinting wet in the beams of the flashlights. "No. She wouldn't do that without telling me. Not Rachel."

Sam didn't argue. He knew better.

Around them, the forest felt smaller, pressing in closer as the evidence techs moved with clinical precision, cameras flashing, tape unspooling, markers set carefully in the dirt.

The spiral carved into Rachel's arm seemed to stare back at them all.

The dogs were restless now, pacing in tight circles near the tree line, low whines threading through the air. One barked sharply toward the darkness beyond the clearing, but the handler pulled it back, muttering something about scents fading too fast.

Lora barely heard him.

Her mind spun in jagged fragments: Rachel laughing over stale donuts. Rachel teasing her about Sam. Rachel's voice on the phone just days ago, telling her to get some sleep, promising she'd cover her shift next weekend.

Now, silence.

And the spiral. Always the spiral.

This is what he wants. To make it personal. To make me bleed before this is over.

"Lora," Sam said softly, as though her name alone could tether her. "Look at me."

Her eyes lifted, glassy and sharp all at once.

"You're no good to her like this," he said, voice thick with something she didn't want to name. "We need to work this. We need to find him. But right now, you've gotta breathe. For me. For her."

For a moment, she wanted to scream at him, to shove him, to let the grief explode into the violence building in her chest. But instead, she drew a sharp, trembling breath that burned her lungs raw and forced herself upright.

Sam stood with her, steady and solid, the way he'd always been even when she hated him for it.

The coroner arrived, and the clearing filled with the sterile glow of portable floodlights. White tarps unfurled. Gloved hands moved with clinical reverence as Rachel's body was prepared for transport.

Lora stood just outside the tape now, numb, arms folded tight across her chest as though to keep herself from shattering. She couldn't look away.

When they lifted Rachel, the spiral carved in her arm caught the light one last time.

Lora's breath hitched.

She turned her face away, the trees spinning around her, the weight of the night pressing down like a physical thing.

He's escalating, her thoughts hissed. And now it's war.

Sam's hand brushed her shoulder, firm but wordless. A brief touch steady, grounding before he stepped away to bark orders into the radio, his voice low but commanding.

The forest held still around them, as if even the night itself understood what had been taken.

Somewhere, far off, an owl called once. Then silence.

The kind of silence that promised nothing good.

The clearing had transformed into a command post.

Portable floodlights hummed, their harsh glow painting the trees in sterile white and sharp shadow. Officers moved like clockwork snapping photos, tagging evidence, stringing more tape to keep the scene intact but there was no escaping the undercurrent of dread that clung to every motion.

Sam's voice cut through the night, sharp and steady.

"I want a five-hundred-yard perimeter. Nobody in or out without my clearance. K9s stay on standby. And for Christ's sake, lock this down tight I don't want a single goddamn thing disturbed."

His words carried authority, but even in the clipped commands there was an edge, a crack of fury and disbelief barely restrained.

Lora stood a few feet from the epicentre, the soles of her boots caked with damp soil, her breath shallow and uneven. The clearing buzzed around her, but none of it truly registered.

Her eyes kept drifting back to the patch of disturbed earth where Rachel had been, as though some part of her refused to accept the emptiness left behind.

She replayed it all in jagged flashes. Rachel's laugh. Rachel's voice in her ear on late nights.

Rachel's promise that she'd always have Lora's back.

And now gone. Stolen, and staged like a grotesque message.

Why her? The question burned hot and bitter, but the answer sat just out of reach, taunting.

"Matthews."

Sam again.

She blinked, dragged back to the present, to the sight of him moving toward her with that same calm exterior he'd perfected over years, but his eyes betrayed him. They were sharp, tired, and raw all at once.

"You need to sit," he said quietly, almost an order but not quite.

"I'm fine," she muttered, though the tremor in her voice betrayed the lie.

"You're not."

The silence stretched. Somewhere beyond the tape, a camera shutter snapped three times in rapid succession. A radio crackled. The forest was too loud and too quiet all at once.

Sam exhaled slowly, rubbing the bridge of his nose. "Listen... I know what she meant to you. But I need your head in this. Not just for the case for you."

Her jaw tightened. Her hands curled into fists at her sides.

"You think I don't know that?" Her voice cracked like glass. She turned away sharply, eyes locking on the path deeper into the woods, the trail swallowed in darkness. "I will find him, Sam. You hear me? I don't care what it takes."

He didn't argue. Not now. He just nodded once, quietly, the muscle in his jaw flexing.

As the team continued to process the scene, the forest seemed to grow colder, heavier, as if mourning along with them. Every rustle of leaves in the distance set nerves on edge; every snapped twig had officers whipping their flashlights toward the shadows, fingers hovering near triggers.

The spiral.

Lora kept seeing it in the dirt, in the bark, even in the shape of the breeze through the treetops. It followed her, etched into her mind, into her bones.

And beneath the weight of grief, something darker began to bloom a resolve sharpened to a dangerous edge.

This wasn't just a case anymore. This was personal.

The coroner's team finally lifted Rachel's body into the van. The clearing dimmed in their absence, the floodlights feeling colder, harsher, as though their glow no longer reached far enough.

Sam started issuing final orders, his voice hoarse but unwavering: "Grid the area. Catalogue everything. We regroup at dawn. No mistakes."

When the last evidence bag was sealed, when the last perimeter check confirmed nothing more to be found for now Sam approached her again, his expression unreadable in the fractured light.

"We're done here for tonight," he said.

Lora didn't move. Didn't blink. Her eyes stayed fixed on the tree line, on the darkness that had swallowed Rachel and spat her back out like a warning.

Finally, slowly, she turned to him. "Then we hit it harder tomorrow."

His silence was an agreement, heavy and unspoken.

Chapter Four

The precinct was alive with static and noise.

Phones rang off the hook. Radios barked updates. Officers moved briskly through the narrow halls, some wide-eyed, others tight jawed, the weight of the night settling like lead across every face.

The bullpen felt like a storm-controlled chaos, but chaos, nonetheless.

Reporters crowded the lobby downstairs, their voices sharp with questions, hungry for answers. Demanding to know how another victim and not just any victim, but a decorated detective could have been taken under their noses.

Sam barked for the blinds to stay closed, for the noise to be contained, for the press to stay where they belonged outside.

Inside the war room, walls were lined with pinned evidence: photographs, maps of the forest, snapshots of carved symbols now circled in red marker. Victims. Timelines. A board that grew more grotesque by the hour.

Lora stood apart from the chaos, arms folded, her gaze locked on the photos.

Rachel's face stared back from one corner.

Her throat tightened, but she forced herself to look, to see. She wouldn't turn away now.

You wanted me to rest, she thought bitterly, remembering Rachel's voice. Guess you didn't know you'd be the one keeping me awake.

Sam appeared at her side, his presence quiet but grounding.

"You're running on fumes," he said, voice low so only she could hear.

"Then I'll run until the tank's dry," she shot back without looking at him.

He studied her for a moment, weighing his words carefully. "Lora... you're an extraordinary detective. But you're not indestructible. You burn too hard, you burn out. And if you burn out now...."

"I won't," she said sharply. Then, softer, almost a whisper: "I can't."

There was no arguing with her when she sounded like that. Sam knew it.

Still, his voice softened, almost reluctant. "Then at least go home for a couple hours. Clear your head. Call me when you're ready to come back."

Hours later, her apartment was dark and silent.

Lora sat on the edge of her bed, still in her clothes, the city beyond her windows blurring into meaningless streaks of light.

Sleep wouldn't come. Every time she closed her eyes, the spiral burned bright, and Rachel's face surfaced, pale and still in the dirt.

The vibration of her phone startled her. Sam.

She answered without a word.

"You, okay?" he asked softly.

"No," she said. She didn't bother lying.

There was silence on the line, the kind that only years of history could carry. Then his voice again, quiet but steady:

"You're an extraordinary detective, Lora. But you need to rest. We'll hit it hard in the morning. I'll see you later."

She closed her eyes, her throat tight. "...Yeah. Later."

But when the line went dead, the silence roared louder than ever.

Chapter Five

The forest was different in daylight, but no less suffocating.

The morning haze clung to the air like wet gauze, soft light spilling through the canopy in fractured beams. The crime scene tape still fluttered at the entrance, a thin line of blue against a thousand shades of green, but no one was there to stop her.

Lora ducked under the tape without hesitation, boots crunching over damp earth.

She retraced the steps they'd taken the night before; each twist of the trail burned into her mind. Her body knew the way now her heart remembered every tree, every stone, every breath of dread that had followed her through the dark.

When she stepped into the clearing, it hit her.

The stillness.

The quiet.

The absence.

Rachel had been here. Rachel had died here.

Now, the space was hollow, stripped bare except for the churned earth and faint outlines of the grid marks left by forensics.

Lora stopped where Rachel's body had lain and froze.

Her throat tightened.

And then it came unbidden, sharp, too real.

She was running.

Breath ragged, lungs burning. Branches snapping underfoot, tearing at her arms as she stumbled through the dark.

Her own voice a hoarse, desperate whisper in the back of her mind. Keep moving. Don't look back.

But she did. She always did.

A flash of something behind her movement, a shadow, a figure just out of focus.

She tripped, hitting the ground hard, pain lancing through her knees. Panic swallowed her whole, but she scrambled up, forcing her legs to move again.

Then nothing. Just trees and darkness, and the echo of her own heartbeat.

The vision snapped like a rubber band, and Lora staggered, bracing herself against the nearest tree.

Her chest heaved, breath ragged.

What the hell was that?

Was it a memory? A hallucination? A piece of Rachel's final moments bleeding into her mind?

Or something worse?

Questions tore through her skull like claws:

Why was Rachel here alone?

Who was chasing her?

Why couldn't she see their face?

Where the hell was victim one?

The spiral lingered behind her eyes like an afterimage, twisting tighter the longer she stood there.

She forced her eyes shut, took a long, deliberate breath, and let the silence settle around her.

The forest didn't answer. It never did.

By evening, the forest was no longer empty.

Blue lights flashed faintly at the treeline as the team returned, their voices low, their steps heavy.

The mood had shifted no longer just the grim determination of an active case, but something darker. Grief sharpened into rage.

Rachel's absence was a wound, raw and gaping, and everyone felt it.

Officers moved in pairs, their radios muted, every crack of a branch sending nerves flaring.

Sam stood near the entrance, briefing the team in clipped sentences. His tone was steady, but his eyes betrayed the strain, the exhaustion pressed deep into his bones.

"We sweep the grid again," he said. "Two teams, staggered intervals. K9s are on standby. We're looking for any sign any breadcrumb. And I don't care if it's a cigarette butt or a single hair, you bag it and tag it. Understood?"

A unified murmur of assent rippled through the group.

Lora joined the line silently, her presence a weight the others could feel but didn't acknowledge.

She could sense their whispers, the sideways glances.

The legend of Detective Lora Matthews the woman with the instincts that bordered on psychic had been whispered through these halls for years. Now those whispers had changed. She wasn't just brilliant anymore. She was haunted.

And maybe they were right.

Sam's eyes found hers briefly as the teams prepared to move. There was something unspoken in that look a mixture of warning and worry, the same message he'd been trying to press into her since Rachel's death: don't lose yourself in this.

But Lora said nothing. She just adjusted the strap of her flashlight and stepped forward into the darkening woods.

Night came quicker this time, swallowing the last blush of dusk as they pressed deeper into the forest.

The air grew heavy, damp, as though the woods themselves were holding their breath. Every rustle of leaves sent adrenaline spiking; every bird taking flight sounded like the sharp crack of a branch under someone's foot.

Somewhere behind her, one of the rookies muttered under his breath something about black magic, about curses and rituals.

The words slithered through the line like smoke.

Lora didn't turn, but her jaw tightened.

She didn't believe in curses. But she knew evil when she felt it. And whatever was out here... it wasn't finished.

The search crept forward, flashlights sweeping, boots crunching.

Every step felt like a question waiting for an answer.

How many victims are there?

How many messages has he left?

How many spirals until this end?

And beneath it all, a whisper she couldn't shake:

You're not hunting him, Lora. He's leading you.

The deeper they moved into the forest, the more it felt like stepping out of time.

The world narrowed to the rhythm of boots on soft earth, to the shallow beams of flashlights cutting through the dark, to the laboured breathing of the team around her.

But Lora... Lora drifted somewhere between the moment and the pull of something unseen.

Every step forward felt directed, guided not by instinct, but by something colder.

Halfway through the grid, the temperature seemed to shift.

A cool wind threaded through the branches, sharp enough to raise goosebumps along her arms.

She froze.

"Stop," she whispered, though she didn't remember deciding to speak.

The team halted, puzzled glances darting toward her. Sam was the first to step forward, his brows drawn tight.

"Lora," he said carefully, low enough that only she could hear, "what is it?"

She didn't answer. Couldn't.

Because in the darkness, in that unnatural stillness, she heard it.

A sound soft, almost delicate.

A whisper.

Her name.

Not out loud, not in the physical sense, but inside her head, as clear as the memory of Rachel laughing.

Lora...

She stiffened, breath locked in her chest, her flashlight trembling in her grip.

Run.

The word skittered across her mindlike nails on glass.

She spun, flashlight beam slashing through the trees, but there was nothing there nothing but shadows and the wide, unblinking eyes of her team.

"Matthews?" Sam's voice sharpened now, a commander's voice. "Talk to me."

But her pulse thundered too loud to answer.

Was it real? Or was it just you losing control?

Then the dogs barked sharp, frantic.

Handlers yelled as the K9s pulled hard against their leashes, noses low to the ground, tracing an erratic path off the grid.

"Go!" Sam barked. "Stay close to the dogs!"

The team surged forward, lights swinging wildly as they plunged deeper into the dark, the ground sloping unevenly beneath their boots.

Branches clawed at Lora's sleeves as she ran, her breath coming faster, sharper, the earlier whisper still clinging to her ears.

The dogs stopped almost in unison, a keening whimper cutting through the heavy night.

They pawed at the base of a massive oak, nails clawing at the damp soil.

Then they started digging.

And whimpering.

That sound that broken, almost mournful sound twisted in Lora's gut.

"No," she breathed, sprinting the last few steps, dropping to her knees beside them. "No, no, no…"

She dug with her gloved hands, frantic, dirt and mud filling the spaces between her fingers.

And then a glimpse of fabric. Dark, mottled with soil and blood.

"Sam!" she screamed. "Here! I've got something!"

The world tilted as they unearthed the rest.

A body.

Face-down, stiff, cold.

The spiral carved into the bark above the shallow grave, clean and deliberate.

When they rolled the body over, the breath went out of her lungs in one brutal rush.

She knew that face.

The world narrowed to a single, suffocating point.

"Jesus Christ..." Sam's voice was ragged now, breaking through the chaos like static.

Because this wasn't just another victim.

This was Detective Marcus Hall, her first partner, the man who'd taught her half of what she knew, the man who'd called her kid until the day she'd outpaced him on a case.

Now he lay at her knees, his throat bruised, his skin pale, his lifeless eyes open to the canopy above.

The forest erupted around her, commands, shouts, radios spitting coordinates but all of it sounded muffled, as if she were underwater.

Her fingers trembled as she reached out, brushing dirt from his sleeve.

Why Marcus?

Why now?

Sam's hand closed over her shoulder, steady but firm, grounding her as she trembled under the weight of it.

He didn't speak. Didn't need to.

Because in that moment, with the spiral watching them from the tree above and Marcus Hall lying cold in the soil, they both understood the same truth.

This wasn't random.

This was personal.

And they were running out of time.

The woods had gone silent again.

No rustle of leaves, no hum of insects, no whisper of wind through the canopy.

Just stillness.

Heavy. Oppressive.

And Marcus Hall, lying in the dirt as though the forest had claimed him.

Lora knelt there, frozen, unable or unwilling to move.

The light from her flashlight trembled where it lay discarded beside her, casting warped, uneven shadows over Marcus's face.

Her brain refused to catch up. It wouldn't connect the image in front of her the lifeless body, the spiral above them carved clean and precise with the man she'd known. The one who used to hum Sinatra under his breath during stakeouts. Who'd once told her she'd make detective of the year by thirty if she didn't burn herself out first.

"Why..." Her voice cracked in the stillness. She swallowed hard, tried again. "Why was he here?"

Sam crouched beside her, his expression carved from stone but his eyes raw, dark with something close to rage.

"I don't know," he said quietly. He glanced at the spiral, then back to Marcus. "He didn't tell me he was looking into anything. Not... not lately."

Lora's mind spun, racing through memories conversations, texts, brief passing mentions of old cases. Nothing stood out. Nothing that screamed he was onto something.

Unless he hadn't wanted anyone to know.

Unless he'd been working something off the books.

Her hands curled into fists, dirt grinding into her gloves. Marcus. Damn it, Marcus, what the hell were you doing out here?

Behind them, the dogs whined, restless, handlers murmuring low as they pulled them back from the grave site. Officers kept their distance now, their voices hushed, their movements deliberate as they began marking the perimeter.

Every so often, one of them would glance their way at her, at Sam and quickly look away.

Lora felt the weight of those glances but didn't care. She couldn't.

"This wasn't random," she said finally, her voice a raw whisper.

Sam exhaled slowly, the sound tight and sharp, and sat back on his heels. "No," he said. "No, it wasn't."

His gaze swept the clearing the torn earth, the spiral, the careful placement of Marcus's body.

"This," he muttered, almost to himself, "is a message. And we need to figure out what the hell it means."

Lora stared down at Marcus, her throat aching with something sharp and ugly.

She wanted to scream. To demand answers from the forest, from the killer, from Marcus himself. But the words stuck like barbed wire in her chest.

Instead, she whispered his name. Just once. Quiet enough that only the trees heard her.

The radio crackled sharp, jarring. A call from the perimeter. Forensics was en route. The coroner's team would follow.

Sam stood first, his hand brushing her shoulder as he rose.

"Lora." His voice was softer now, but steady. "You need to step back. Let them do their job."

She looked up at him, her eyes glassy but defiant.

"I'm not leaving him," she said.

A pause. Then a nod.

"Then you stay," Sam said. "But stay behind the line. Let's do this right. For him."

She stayed and watched as the forest filled with more light, more voices, more movement the sterile precision of forensics setting up grids, cameras flashing like lightning in the darkness.

Every click of a shutter. Every measured voice. Every ripple of the blue tape.

It all felt unreal because Marcus Hall mentor, friend, steady anchor in the chaos was now just another number.

Victim number four.

Lora stood there until the last evidence marker was placed, until the coroner zipped the black bag closed and loaded it carefully onto the gurney.

Only when they wheeled him out through the trees did she finally let herself close her eyes, sucking in a breath sharp enough to sting.

The drive back was swallowed in silence.

The forest was a dark blur in the rearview, receding with every mile, but Lora could still feel it the damp earth under her knees, Marcus's lifeless eyes, the spiral carved into the bark above him like a brand.

The steady hum of the engine did nothing to quiet her thoughts.

Sam's knuckles were white around the steering wheel, jaw tight, the blue lights reflecting off his profile as they cut through the back roads toward town.

Finally, his voice cracked the silence.

"I'm taking you off the case, Lora."

She blinked, slow and disbelieving, before turning her head toward him.

"You can't do that," she said, her voice steady but low, threaded with steel. "You need me, Sam. You know you do. No one else sees what I see I can pick up the clues no one else even thinks to look for."

His grip on the wheel tightened, his knuckles pale.

"I'm not disputing that," Sam snapped, his voice sharp, edged with something raw. His eyes flicked to her for a fraction of a second, then back to the road. "But I need to keep you safe. That's my priority right now."

Silence filled the car again, thick, suffocating.

Neither of them spoke.

The only sound was the hum of the tires on the asphalt, the occasional crackle of static from the police radio, and the quiet ache of things they couldn't say.

Then, softer, rougher:

"Goddamn it, Lora..." Sam's voice trembled, the mask slipping just enough for the truth to bleed through. "I still love you. And I still care for you. You know that don't you?"

She stared out the window, the trees blurring past in streaks of shadow and moonlight. Her throat tightened, too full to form words.

A tear slipped free, tracing a cold, wet line down her cheek.

Sam noticed.

His hand left the wheel, hesitated for a heartbeat, then found hers, warm and firm and trembling just slightly.

She didn't pull away. She couldn't.

Chapter Six

The precinct was a storm when they arrived.

Reporters were already swarming the front steps, their cameras flashing like lightning as Sam pulled the car into the underground garage.

Inside, chaos reigned.

Phones rang off the hook. Uniformed officers darted through the halls, barking updates and evidence requests.

In the bullpen, the investigation room had been transformed into a war zone case boards covered in photographs, maps marked with bright pins, evidence bags stacked in neat, sterile rows.

The spiral symbol was everywhere; a haunting reminder taped to every surface.

Lora stepped in, every eye flicking toward her. Conversations dipped into hushed tones, but she could still hear the words.

"Fourth victim... a second detective ..."

"Hall and Meyers were one of ours. Jesus Christ."

"Whoever's doing this... they're escalating."

Her jaw tightened, but she kept walking, ignoring the stares, ignoring the whispered questions.

She headed straight for the board, her gaze locking on the photographs the Polaroids, the spirals, the faces. Marcus's photo stared back at her now, pinned at the centre like a cruel centrepiece.

Sam trailed behind her, already barking orders to the task force.

"Expand the grid. Every inch of that forest gets mapped; I don't care how long it takes. Pull Marcus's case files all of them. I want to know what he was working on, what he touched, who he talked to in the last six months and Meyers."

"Yes, Chief," someone answered, already moving.

Lora sank into a chair at the corner of the room, hands folded tight in her lap, eyes distant but sharp.

She could feel the grief simmering beneath the surface hers, the team's, all of it boiling into something jagged and restless.

Marcus and Meyers weren't just another body.

They were family.

And now he was a clue in a puzzle she didn't understand.

Her phone buzzed in her pocket, dragging her back into the moment.

A message. A blocked number.

She opened it with trembling hands.

No words.

Just a photograph.

The spiral.

Carved into another tree.

Somewhere... deeper.

The second message came through before Lora could even lower her phone.

A single sentence.

You're supposed to be dead.

Her body locked. Breath stalled in her throat, her pulse roaring like static in her ears.

Across the room, Sam caught the look on her face pale, frozen, unreadable and was at her side in seconds.

"What is it?" His voice was low, clipped. Urgent.

Wordlessly, Lora turned the phone toward him. The first photo of the spiral still burned on the screen, and now the second message sat beneath it.

Sam's expression shifted instantly confusion flashing first, then something colder, heavier. Fear.

"Jesus Christ," he muttered. He stepped back just slightly, as if distance could dull the weight of what he was holding. His eyes darted to hers, searching, as though he needed to confirm she was still real, still here.

Lora, meanwhile, stared past him past the walls, past the precinct, back into the woods. Her voice was flat when it came, quiet but sharp enough to cut glass.

"I think that's the killer," she said.

Sam exhaled hard, his hands tightening on the phone before he passed it to Detective Alvarez.

"Trace this number. Now. I don't care if it's blocked, ghosted, whatever. Run it through every system we've got."

"Yes, Chief," Alvarez replied, already moving toward the tech desk.

Sam turned back to her; his face etched with something between frustration and desperation.

"That's it, Lora. I'm enforcing this you're off the case."

Her head snapped toward him, a storm in her eyes, fury flaring like a live wire.

"No," she said, sharp and unwavering. She stood, her chair scraping hard against the floor. "You don't get to do that. Not now. Not when we're this close."

"You don't understand."

"I understand perfectly," she shot back, stepping toward him, voice low but shaking with the force of her anger. "This is my case, Sam. Mine. He's talking to me. Sending messages to me. You take me off; you lose your best chance at stopping him."

The bullpen had gone silent; all eyes now fixed on the two of them.

Sam's jaw clenched, muscle twitching, but before he could reply, the room erupted again voices overlapping, evidence boards snapping as new files and images went up.

The task force had shifted to full-blown crisis mode.

"Two patterns," someone barked. "He's escalating faster, tighter timelines between kills."

"He's taunting us now," another voice added. "This is a game. He wants us chasing shadows while he lines up his next victim."

"Or he's telling us, "A third said grimly, "That his next victim is already chosen."

Lora's phone was handed back to her and it buzzed again in her hand, vibrating like a live thing, but when she glanced down this time, there was nothing. Just an empty screen.

She looked up, locking eyes with Sam.

A silent understanding passed between them.

She wasn't waiting for permission.

Without another word, she turned on her heel, the room's noise dimming behind her as she strode toward the exit.

"Lora!" Sam's voice thundered after her, but she didn't stop.

The cold night air hit her like a slap as she stepped out of the precinct, her mind already spinning, retracing steps, piecing together patterns only she seemed to see.

If the killer wanted to taunt her, to draw her in, then fine.

She would follow.

But this time, she swore to herself, it wouldn't be to another body.

Not if she could stop it.

"Goddamn it, Lora!" Sam's voice cracked through the bullpen, but the echo of her footsteps was already fading down the hall.

For a moment, no one moved. The precinct buzzed around them phones ringing, papers rustling but here, in this corner of chaos, there was only stillness.

Then Sam snapped out of it.

"Alvarez! Peterson!" His voice was sharp, cutting through the room like a blade. "Get a unit on her now. She's headed to the woods. I want eyes on her, but you keep your distance. No engagement until I get there."

"Yes, Chief!" Alvarez barked, already reaching for his radio.

Sam grabbed his coat, slinging it over his shoulder as he stormed toward the door. Every step was fuelled by anger, by fear, fear that this was exactly what the bastard wanted.

"Goddamn stubborn woman," he muttered under his breath, keys biting into his palm as he hit the garage.

The forest greeted her like an old, waiting predator.

By the time Lora arrived, the sun was nothing but a ghost behind the clouds, shadows stretching like fingers across the ground.

She parked at the trail entrance, the hum of her engine the only sound for a long moment before she killed it, plunging herself into silence.

The woods loomed, ancient and unmoving, as if holding their breath.

She walked in slowly, each step sinking into the damp earth.

Her thoughts spiralled, a cyclone of questions she couldn't quiet.

Marcus. Rachel. The spiral carved into bark, into her dreams.

The messages. You're supposed to be dead.

Her pulse thrummed in her ears as she reached the clearing the place where Rachel had lain.

She stopped.

She could feel them, eyes she couldn't see, pressing in from between the trees.

A twig snapped somewhere behind her.

Her breath hitched, her body stiffening, but she didn't turn.

Instead, her voice rang out, sharp and ragged, slicing through the stillness.

"What do you want from me?!"

The forest swallowed her words. For a moment, nothing. Not even the rustle of leaves.

Then it came.

A voice wrong, distorted, crawling through the trees like a cold draft.

"Lora..."

She froze, every muscle taut, her hand instinctively hovering near her holstered weapon.

"You know what I want..."

Her chest rose and fell in sharp, shallow breaths, eyes darting through the shifting dark.

"No..." Her voice cracked, the word trembling. "No, I don't. Remember what?"

The voice came again, closer now, slithering over the damp air.

"Come... come, Lora... remember..."

Her heart pounded so hard she thought it might burst from her chest.

"What the hell are you!"

A sudden rustle, the crunch of boots on damp leaves, snapped her around.

"Lora!"

Sam's voice rough, real ripped through the clearing, shattering the moment like glass.

He emerged from the tree line, flashlight beam cutting through the dark, Alvarez and Peterson just steps behind him, weapons drawn, scanning the woods.

"Jesus Christ," Sam muttered, his face tight with fear and fury as he closed the distance. "You don't ever come out here alone like this again. You hear me?"

But Lora wasn't looking at him.

She was still staring into the black, her breath uneven, her eyes wide and glassy as though she'd seen something no one else had.

Sam stepped closer, his hand brushing her arm firm, grounding.

"What did you hear?" he asked, low but urgent.

Lora swallowed hard, her voice barely above a whisper.

"It... it knew my name, Sam." Her gaze flicked to his, desperate, trembling. "It... it told me to remember."

The forest had gone utterly still.

Not even the whisper of wind through the leaves. Not a bird. Not the distant hum of night insects.

Just the silence thick, suffocating, as if the trees themselves were holding their breath.

Sam's hand was still on her arm, warm and steady, but Lora felt miles away from him.

Her pulse thrummed in her ears, loud enough to drown out reason. The words clung to her skin like frost.

Come, Lora. Remember.

She blinked, dragging her gaze away from the tree line to find Sam's eyes on her sharp, searching, afraid in a way she had never seen before.

"Talk to me," he said softly, though there was an edge in his voice. "What did you hear, exactly?"

Lora licked her lips, throat dry as ash.

"It... it wasn't human, Sam," she said finally, voice trembling but quiet, almost reverent. "It knew my name. It... it wants me to remember something but..." Her gaze darted back into the endless rows of dark, ancient trees. "...I don't know what."

Behind them, Alvarez and Peterson exchanged uneasy glances. Even seasoned, battle-hardened cops weren't immune to the oppressive weight pressing in on them now.

Every shadow looked sharper. Every branch that groaned in the wind sounded like footsteps just out of sight.

Sam tightened his grip on her arm, grounding her, his jaw clenched like stone.

"Listen to me," he said, voice low and steady, though his eyes flickered nervously toward the black tree line. "It's trying to mess with you. That's what this is. Mind games. Don't let it in."

But Lora barely heard him.

Her gaze traced over the clearing, the faint scarring of the earth where Rachel's body had been lifted, where Marcus had stood beside her just nights ago.

A chill prickled down her spine, threading through her bones like ice water.

Mind games, Sam had said.

Then why did it feel so real?

From deeper in the forest, a sound broke the stillness faint but distinct.

A whisper of movement.

Low. Distant. Then gone.

Every flashlight beam snapped toward the direction of the sound, white cones of light cutting through the darkness.

"Chief," Alvarez said tightly, scanning the perimeter. "Something's moving out there."

Sam didn't release Lora's arm, his voice sharp now, commanding.

"Fan out. Keep your spacing. Quiet and slow. If he's watching us, I want him flushed out."

The team moved like shadows, boots barely whispering over the forest floor, radios muted, breaths sharp and controlled.

Sam stayed close to Lora, his presence protective and suffocating all at once.

"You shouldn't be here," he muttered under his breath, the words for her alone.

She didn't answer. Her focus was locked ahead, on the trail that wound deeper, coiling like a dark vein into the forest's heart.

Something was waiting for them out there.

Something that wanted to be found.

As they pressed deeper, dusk finally surrendered to night.

The air grew colder, damper, the forest closing in tighter around them until the canopy above swallowed even the glow of the moon.

Lora's fingers twitched near the butt of her holstered sidearm, every nerve lit, every step deliberate.

The deeper they went, the heavier it felt the silence, the darkness, the sense that the forest was bending, subtly, inexorably, toward them.

Then, suddenly, a soft, sharp sound snap cracked through the trees ahead.

Not loud. Not close. But enough to send a ripple through the team.

Sam froze, hand instinctively brushing the grip of his weapon.

"Positions," he murmured.

The trail ahead yawned like an open throat.

And somewhere beyond, the forest waited, breathing slow, patient.

The forest swallowed their footsteps as they advanced.

Every beam of light trembled over roots and undergrowth, slicing through the shadows but never quite banishing them.

Sam moved closer to Lora, his free hand brushing hers. For a heartbeat, he hesitated then laced his fingers with hers.

Her hand was ice-cold and trembling.

"You good?" he whispered, eyes never leaving the dark ahead.

No answer. Just a small, tight squeeze of his hand.

The sound had come from ahead deeper, toward the forest's unseen core and every instinct screamed that they shouldn't be going this way.

But they moved anyway.

Step by step.

Breaths shallow.

Weapons ready.

The air grew heavier the deeper they went, the smell of damp earth thickening until it tasted metallic, like old blood at the back of the throat.

Then, just as Sam raised his hand to halt the group, Lora stopped dead.

"Sam..." Her voice was soft, fragile.

His eyes snapped to her, then forward following her gaze.

There, nailed into the trunk of a massive oak, was a wooden plaque.

It was weathered, stained. The letters carved into it rough, frantic.

A crude spirals the same one carved into the bark near Rachel.

And beneath it, in jagged, uneven letters:

"To find the fourth, follow the path where silence screams."

The words bled dread into every corner of the clearing.

No one spoke. Even the radios, muted and silent, seemed to hum with a strange vibration.

Lora stepped closer, her light trembling across the carved spiral.

Her stomach turned. She could feel Sam behind her steady, solid but it didn't help. Not here. Not with this.

"This... this isn't just a clue," she breathed. "It's... a warning."

Sam's jaw flexed. His eyes swept the tree line, instinctively searching for movement for him.

"Or an invitation," he said, voice low, tight.

The forest seemed to lean closer, its shadows bending toward them as though listening.

Lora's breathing quickened, the edges of her vision darkening as that strange, crawling sense the same one from the clearing wound around her again.

Her mind whispered that something was ahead. Waiting.

"No," she said suddenly, sharp and urgent. She turned, her flashlight shaking in her grip. "Sam... no. We need to turn back."

Sam froze, eyes narrowing, "Are you sure?"

Lora nodded quickly, too quickly, her chest rising and falling in shallow bursts, "I don't... I don't know why," she admitted, her voice breaking. "But if we keep going... someone else won't come out."

For a long, tense beat, Sam just stared at her, reading the raw fear etched across her face.

Then, reluctantly, he squeezed her trembling hand again and gave a tight nod.

"Alright," he murmured. "We do this your way. For now."

The woods didn't protest.

But as they slowly began to backtrack, every step felt heavier like the forest was trying to hold them in place.

And somewhere beyond the veil of trees, unseen but listening, something chuckled.

The hum of the SUV's engine was the only sound.

No radio chatter. No nervous small talk. No bravado.

Just silence.

Lora sat rigid in the passenger seat, her eyes fixed on the blur of trees beyond the window, their dark spines retreating as the forest loosened its hold on them.

But she didn't feel free.

Not even close.

Her fingers still tingled where Sam had held her hand.

She flexed them slowly in her lap, trying to ground herself, to breathe.

But the words carved into the wood looped endlessly in her mind:

To find the fourth, follow the path where silence screams.

A path.

A fourth victim.

A promise.

"You're shaking," Sam said quietly, breaking the stillness.

His voice was soft too soft. Like he was speaking to glass he didn't want to break.

"I'm fine," she said, her voice hoarse.

But she wasn't.

She could still hear that voice from the trees, curling around her name like smoke.

Remember.

Sam's knuckles tightened around the steering wheel. He wanted to say something needed to, but the words caught in his throat.

Instead, he stole a glance at her.

Her profile, illuminated in fleeting flashes by the streetlights, looked carved from stone. But her eyes...

God.

She looked like someone staring over the edge of a cliff, praying the ground wouldn't give out.

When they hit the city limits, Sam finally spoke, his voice low and raw, "You should've let me pull you out of this days ago."

Lora didn't look at him, "You can't," she whispered. "You know you can't. It's not done."

His jaw flexed. "I don't care if it's done. I care about you breathing when it is."

That silenced them again. The tension thick, unspoken.

And beneath it, the sharp ache of something old, something neither of them had the strength to name tonight.

As they pulled into the precinct lot, Lora finally tore her gaze from the window.

"Sam..." Her voice cracked, quiet but steady. "What if I'm already in too deep?"

His hand twitched on the wheel, like he wanted to reach for her again, but didn't.

"Then," he said, his voice hoarse, "we find a way to drag you back."

Chapter Seven

The precinct's fluorescent lights felt too bright. Too sharp. Too clinical for what they carried in with them from the forest.

The task force room buzzed with tension voices layered over each other, phones ringing, evidence boards cluttered with photographs and maps like the frantic scribbles of a madman.

Reporters clustered outside the barricades beyond the glass, their muffled voices a relentless hum demanding answers no one had.

Lora barely noticed. She stood just inside the doorway, still, silent, her eyes fixed on the evidence board where photos of Rachel and Marcus stared back at her.

Two detectives. Two friends. Both gone.

And now a fifth waiting. Somewhere.

Sam's voice cut through the noise, sharp, commanding as he addressed the room:

"The message said to follow a path where silence screams. It's not random. Nothing about this is random."

Alvarez frowned, tapping at the map spread across the central table.

"There are a dozen deer trails through that forest that fit that description. We could spend weeks chasing dead ends."

"It's not just the trails," Lora murmured, almost to herself.

Every head in the room turned toward her, but she didn't look at them. Her gaze stayed locked on the map, eyes narrowed as if she could will the forest to give up its secrets. "It's... something else. A sound that shouldn't be there. Or isn't there at all."

Sam moved closer, studying her with that quiet, unreadable intensity.

"You think it's tied to the visions," he said, not asking.

Lora finally looked at him, her jaw tight, "I don't think, Sam. I know."

Murmurs rippled through the room doubt, fear, maybe even awe. But the air shifted, heavier, when her phone buzzed against the tabletop. A single message. Just two words. Time's running.

Lora's throat closed.

Sam leaned over, reading the message.

Every muscle in his jaw locked, the paper crumpling slightly under his grip, "Lock this number down. Now," he barked to Alvarez.

Then his gaze snapped back to her sharp, desperate, protective, "This ends now. You're off this case, Lora."

She stared at him, eyes flashing like flint. "No," she said, her voice cold steel. "You need me, Sam. You know it. I'm the only one who can read this. The only one who can see it."

Sam stepped closer, anger and fear warring in his expression, "I'm not disputing that," he said, voice rising, "but I need to keep you alive. That's my priority. You understand me?"

The room froze around them the tension electric, humming like a live wire.

But Lora didn't flinch, didn't blink. Then, quietly, like a promise, "Then stay out of my way."

The room had fallen into a tense, brittle silence.

Detectives whispered in corners, phones rang unanswered, and the hum of the precinct lights seemed louder than usual a steady, oppressive buzz that crawled into Lora's skull.

But none of it mattered.

Not when Sam's eyes locked on hers like that, "We still haven't found the first victim," she said, her voice low, shaking despite the steel beneath it. "Whoever they were... they're still out there, waiting for us to see them. Waiting for me."

Her throat tightened on that last word, but she didn't look away.

Sam didn't speak at first, instead, he stepped forward, closing the space between them. The room seemed to shrink, the noise fading until there was only the thundering of her own pulse.

Then his hands were on her shoulders, steady but trembling just slightly, grounding her and breaking her at the same time. "I know," he said quietly, the words rough and edged with something unspoken. "I know, Lora. But right now, we all need sleep. If we don't rest, we're going to miss something, and we can't afford that."

Her lips parted, ready to argue, to fight, to stay in this war until it was done.

But Sam wasn't done, "In one breath," he continued, softer now, "I'm not letting you out of my sight. Not tonight. Not tomorrow. I'm staying with you. You hear me?"

His voice cracked, almost imperceptibly. "We'll resume first thing in the morning. It might be better... in the daylight."

For the first time that night, the fight in her dimmed not gone, just quieter, buried under exhaustion and the gravity of his words.

She nodded, just once and when his arms pulled her in, she didn't resist.

For a brief moment, the noise, the chaos, the case all of it fell away, leaving just the two of them in the quiet.

They didn't speak as they left the precinct together, the night air sharp and cool, wrapping around them like a reminder that the darkness wasn't done yet.

Chapter Eight

By 06:00, the precinct was awake and humming again, tension bleeding through the walls.

The task force had gathered in the briefing room, the riddle pinned in bold red across the evidence board:

To find the fourth, follow the path where silence screams.

Empty coffee cups littered the table.

Maps of the forest were spread in every direction, marked with red circles and blue lines where the dogs had traced scents the night before.

Detective Alvarez leaned over the table, tapping a thick finger against a highlighted path on the satellite map.

"This trail here. It's the only one that cuts clean through the center of the forest but stays hidden from the access roads. It's… quiet out there. No birds. No animals. Nothing."

"Like the forest holding its breath," muttered one of the younger officers, eyes darting nervously toward Lora.

Sam ignored the mutter and focused on the room, his tone sharp but controlled.

"We move in as a unit this time. We'll cover every inch of this trail, grid the surrounding area, and sweep for signs of disturbance. No one goes off alone. Not for a second."

Across the room, Lora sat in silence, one hand loosely gripping her coffee, her gaze sharp and distant as she stared at the map.

She could almost feel it the path, the suffocating stillness, the weight of the forest pressing in.

Her chest tightened with the memory of that voice, whispering from somewhere deep in the dark.

Remember.

Sam caught her staring, his jaw tightening, "We move at 07:00," he said firmly, eyes on her. "And Lora you stay with me. Always."

She didn't argue. Not out loud, anyway but in her mind, the forest was already calling her back.

By 06:50, the task force was assembled in the motor pool, the hum of engines mingling with the crunch of gravel under boots.

The morning was grey, the kind of dim, heavy overcast that smothered the early sunlight and cast everything in muted tones. Even the flashing lights of the cruisers seemed duller, swallowed by the weight in the air.

Lora stood off to the side, arms folded, staring into the tree line that loomed beyond the access road like an endless wall. She wasn't hearing the chatter, not really. Her mind was already miles ahead, tracing the paths of the woods, mapping the echoes of the killer's presence that lingered in the shadows.

The path where silence screams...What did it mean? Why did it feel like something she should know?

Detective Alvarez adjusted his vest, side-eyeing Lora as he whispered to one of the newer guys.

"She's wired too tight," he muttered. "I don't like the look in her eyes."

The rookie swallowed hard, following Lora's line of sight into the trees. "Would you be calm after last night?"

Sam heard it, but he didn't intervene. Not this time.

His eyes stayed fixed on Lora. Always on Lora.

She was a silhouette against the early morning mist, her posture straight but her shoulders tight with tension. To anyone else, she might look like the perfect detective controlled, focused, unshakable.

But Sam knew better. She's unravelling. He hated himself for thinking it, but the truth clung like smoke.

God, Lora... I should've pulled you off this case. Should've dragged you home and locked the door. But how do I protect you from this when you keep walking straight toward it?

His hand tightened on the strap of his rifle. And why the hell can't I let you go?

"Chief Matthews," Alvarez called, snapping Sam from his thoughts. "ETA five minutes."

Sam nodded, but his eyes never left her.

"Stay sharp," he ordered, his voice cutting through the group like a blade. "We stick together. Nobody wanders. Not today."

As the convoy rolled forward, tires crunching along the dirt road, silence filled the cars a thick, heavy quiet that no one dared to break.

Lora sat in the passenger seat of the lead SUV, her gaze fixed on the tree line rushing past, her mind spiraling.

Rachel. Marcus. The riddle. The spiral. The voice...

Each thought was a jagged shard digging deeper into her resolve.

Beside her, Sam gripped the wheel tighter than he needed to, every muscle in his arms rigid.

He wanted to say something anything to break through that wall she'd built around herself.

But the words wouldn't come.

You're scaring me, Lora. And God help me, I can't lose you, too.

When they stopped, the forest greeted them with a suffocating stillness.

No birds.

No rustle of small animals in the brush.

Just silence.

Exactly the kind of silence that screams.

Sam stepped out first, scanning the perimeter as the rest of the team assembled, "Alright," he said, voice sharp, commanding. "This is where it starts. Grid teams. Check every yard of the path and keep your radios hot. We find something, we call it in."

His gaze cut to Lora.

"You stay with me. No arguments."

She met his stare, the unspoken tension crackling between them, but said nothing.

Not a word.

The forest swallowed them whole.

Every step crunched softly against damp leaves and broken twigs, the noise too loud in the unnatural quiet that pressed in around them.

No birds.

No insects.

Not even the distant hum of traffic.

Only the sound of boots on earth, heavy breathing, and the occasional static crackle of a radio checking in.

Lora stayed close to Sam, though every nerve screamed to sprint ahead, to tear through the trees and find what was waiting for them.

Patience, she reminded herself, though her chest tightened with every step.

This forest doesn't just hide him. It belongs to him.

The deeper they went, the heavier the air became, thick with damp rot and something metallic beneath it copper, sharp and unmistakable.

Blood.

Sam noticed it, too. His jaw tightened, eyes scanning the shifting shadows. He didn't squeeze her hand this time, but his presence stayed close, a steady anchor in the swirling unease.

Stay with me, Lora, he thought. Don't drift too far. Not now.

A branch snapped somewhere to their left.

The team froze.

Lora can sense everyone was jittering like nervous heartbeats.

But nothing moved. Nothing breathed.

"Keep moving," Sam whispered, though his voice sounded strange muffled, as if the forest itself was trying to swallow it.

And so, they did, deeper and deeper, until the trail narrowed into something barely more than a deer path.

Then Lora felt it.

A pull.

Not physical no sound, no sign, just a... knowing.

She stopped so suddenly that Alvarez almost collided with her.

"Matthews?" Sam's voice, sharp but low.

Her light caught on something half-buried beneath a tangle of roots, glinting in the beam like glass catching the dawn.

She crouched, brushing away dirt and leaves, fingers trembling as they uncovered a stone slab, no bigger than a shoebox lid, carved deep with strange, intertwining symbols spirals, jagged lines, something like an eye.

And at the center, in red, still wet:

"You are the key, Lora. Follow the spiral."

Her breath hitched.

"No..." she whispered.

Sam stepped closer, his shadow falling over her shoulder, his breath warm against her ear, "What the hell is this?"

Lora didn't answer. She couldn't. The symbols writhed in her mind, sharp and familiar in a way that made her stomach twist.

She traced the spiral with the edge of her glove, and for the briefest moment the forest tilted the ground vanishing beneath her feet, her head spinning as memories that weren't hers flickered behind her eyes.

Running.

Screaming.

Branches slapping against her face.

Breath tearing from her lungs.

And then blackness.

"Lora!" Sam's voice cut through the haze, his hand gripping her shoulder, yanking her back.

She blinked, breathless, trembling.

"I... I saw something," she whispered, more to herself than anyone else.

Alvarez's voice crackled through the radio. "Detective Matthews, what is it? What'd you find?"

Sam answered for her, his voice hard. "A marker. Another goddamn marker. Call for forensics. And a photographer."

As the team fanned out to secure the area, Lora stared at the slab, her chest rising and falling with shallow, uneven breaths.

You are the key.

The words weren't just carved into the stone.

They were carved into her.

The forest shifted around her, the shadows deeper now, closer, whispering along the edges of her mind.

For the first time, Lora wasn't sure if she was walking deeper into the case or deeper into the trap.

The clearing felt smaller with every second that passed.

Blue tape fluttered weakly in the damp breeze as officers began to secure the perimeter, marking the strange stone slab with numbered evidence tags. Camera flashes burst like muted lightning, bathing the twisted trees in sterile white for the briefest moments before the forest swallowed the light again.

Sam didn't move.

His hand stayed locked around Lora's, gripping so tightly it almost hurt as though if he let go, she'd vanish into the dark with the rest of the forest's secrets.

Lora stood unnaturally still.

Her eyes sharp, relentless eyes that had seen dozens of crime scenes without flinching were unfocused now, glassy, as though fixed on something none of them could see. Her lips moved faintly, but no sound came out.

She's somewhere else, Sam thought, his chest tightening. Goddammit, Lora, where are you right now?

The dull ache beneath his sternum sharpened, an anxious throb that spread like fire up into his throat. He didn't know if it was fear or anger or something else entirely.

"Chief Matthews," Alvarez said cautiously, stepping closer. "We need to pull her out of here. She's...."

"I've got her," Sam cut in sharply. His voice came out rougher than he intended, but no one challenged him.

For a heartbeat longer, he held on. His thumb brushed over her glove, the pressure meant to anchor her.

And then, without warning, Lora blinked.

The trance in her gaze didn't break not completely but her shoulders straightened, her breathing steadied, and her hand slipped from his.

"Lora..." Sam's voice lowered, a warning now.

But she didn't answer.

Instead, she turned. Slowly. Purposefully. Her boots crunched on the damp leaves, following the faint etching of spirals carved into the forest floor, a path only she seemed able to see.

"Lora."

Her name tore out of Sam like a curse as she disappeared beyond the thin veil of trees, swallowed whole by the green and the shadows.

"Goddammit, Lora!" Sam spat, snapping out of his shock.

He turned, barking orders before anyone else could move.

"Eyes up! Keep her in sight but don't spook her. Alvarez, take point and keep your safeties off." His voice cracked like a whip, sharp and hard with command, but beneath it burned something rawer: fear.

As the team fell into formation, Sam followed, his strides long and furious, his chest still tight.

She's going to get herself killed. She's going to vanish into this forest, and I....

He bit down on the thought before it could finish, muttering under his breath instead, "Goddamn it, Lora..."

The forest seemed to sense their urgency, branches clawing at their sleeves, roots rising like jagged teeth beneath their boots. Flashlight beams danced wildly between the trees, shadows slicing across their path like blades as it got darker as they walked further in.

And ahead barely visible now the fading silhouette of Lora Matthews, walking faster, deeper, as though the spiral itself had her by the throat.

The deeper they pushed, the less the forest resembled itself.

The air thickened, wet and metallic, clinging to the back of Sam's throat. Even the crunch of boots on soil seemed muted now, like the trees themselves were holding their breath.

Up ahead, Lora moved like she was in a trance, her flashlight swaying lazily in her hand, the pale beam catching on roots and damp leaves but never pausing.

"Detective Matthews," Sam hissed, the bite in his voice carrying across the darkness. "Stop. Right now."

No response.

His stomach twisted as he quickened his pace, his team following close behind. He wanted to grab her, shake her, yell at her anything to snap her out of this strange spell the forest seemed to have over her.

She's not hearing you, he thought bitterly, his jaw tight. She's somewhere else again.

Then, all at once, Lora stopped.

Not a sudden freeze but a slow, deliberate halt, like she'd stepped up to an invisible line.

Her shoulders trembled once, barely noticeable, and then her knees seemed to buckle slightly as her flashlight slipped in her grip, its beam jittering weakly across the forest floor.

Sam's breath caught in his chest.

"Lora." His voice was softer now, almost pleading. "Talk to me. What is it? What do you see?"

She didn't answer.

Her body was rigid, her breath sharp and uneven. Whatever was in front of her whatever she was staring at was something none of them could see.

"Alright," Sam said finally, his tone cracking with the weight of command. "That's it. We're calling it for tonight."

"No—"

"Yes," Sam snapped, stepping closer, his frustration spilling into his voice. "You're done for the night, Lora. We're all done. It's almost midnight, and you're... you're not steady right now. I won't risk you, not here."

Silence.

Then, slowly, Lora turned her head, her eyes hollow but defiant, fixed somewhere beyond him, beyond all of them.

She whispers barely audible, "He comes at this time."

Sam clenched his jaw, rubbing a hand across his face as he signaled to the team. "Pack it up. We move out. Now."

They began the trek back, every step feeling heavier than the last. Sam stayed close to Lora, close enough that his shoulder brushed hers as if to keep her tethered.

Halfway to the forest entrance, her phone chimed. A sharp, brittle sound that shattered the quiet like glass breaking.

Sam froze, watching as Lora absently reached into her jacket pocket.

"Give it here," he ordered quietly, his voice leaving no room for argument.

For a moment, she hesitated, then handed him the phone.

His eyes narrowed as the screen lit up.

A new message. No name. Just the number.

And below it, another riddle:

"The roots remember where the blood first fell. The spiral began with you, Lora."

Sam's hand tightened around the phone until his knuckles went white. A dull throb started in his temple, pulsing like a drumbeat.

"Jesus Christ," he muttered under his breath.

He turned, meeting her eyes, eyes that looked hollow and endless in the dim light.

"This end," he said, voice thick with something close to desperation. "Tomorrow, we end this."

Lora didn't respond. She just stared past him, back toward the darkness of the forest, as if it were calling her name again.

The forest seemed to breathe around them, its damp air clinging to their skin as they stood frozen in the dark. The message burned in Sam's hand like a live coal, its words etching themselves into the silence between them.

Lora's gaze never left the path leading back into the woods, her voice barely above a whisper when she finally spoke.

"Sam... it's witching hour."

Sam's brow furrowed. He blinked at her, confusion breaking through his simmering frustration.

"What?" His voice was tentative, as if saying the words louder would shatter the fragile thread holding her together.

Lora's head tilted slightly, her eyes still glassy, her voice cold, distant, detached.

"He comes at witching hour."

Sam instinctively glanced down at his watch. 04:12 a.m. The pale glow of its hands mocked him.

"That doesn't make sense," he muttered, almost to himself. "Dawn's breaking. It's morning."

Lora finally turned her gaze toward him slow, deliberate, a hollow stillness behind her stare that made his chest tighten.

"The forest will do that to you."

The way she said it flat, certain, like it was some eternal truth carved into the trees sent a ripple through the team.

Sam felt it, the sudden chill that slithered up his spine, coiling at the base of his neck. He swallowed hard, fighting to steady his breath.

"Jesus, Lora," he said, but his voice cracked, betraying the dread coiling in his gut.

And then she added, softly, almost reverently: "It's his favourite time."

No one moved. No one spoke.

The forest was so quiet that the hum of distant insects and the subtle groan of branches overhead became deafening. Every officer standing there felt it that collective shudder, that instinctive tightening in the chest, as though the trees themselves were leaning closer to listen.

Sam looked at her, truly looked at her the way her shoulders slumped but her eyes burned like embers, the way her lips trembled though her voice stayed eerily calm. Something in his chest ached in a way that scared him more than the forest ever could.

"Let's get out of here," he said finally, voice low and unsteady. "Now."

The walk out was silent. No one dared speak. Even the birds that usually stirred at first light stayed quiet, as though they, too, understood.

Chapter Nine

The drive back to the precinct was suffocatingly quiet.

Sam kept his eyes on the road, the steady hum of the tires against asphalt doing little to drown out the static in his mind.

She's slipping, he thought, gripping the wheel tighter, knuckles white. *Every step we take in those woods, I see her slipping further away. And I'm letting her...*

From the passenger seat, Lora stared out of the window, her reflection ghosted in the glass. The early light of morning painted her in muted gold, but her expression didn't change.

Not once.

Her thoughts were locked in a loop:

The roots remember... the spiral began with you... witching hour... his favourite time...

Her pulse thudded in her ears, each beat louder than the last.

When they reached the precinct, the team dispersed wordlessly into the dim glow of the investigation floor. Coffee cups clinked, laptops snapped open, paper shuffled the sounds of routine, but muted, dulled by something heavier lingering in the air.

Sam stopped just inside the doorway, his eyes tracking Lora as she walked straight to the evidence board. She didn't pause to take off her jacket or even sit.

She just stared.

At the message.

At the spiral photographs.

At the map of the forest with pins scattered like open wounds.

"Okay," one of the techs said, breaking the silence. "The message pinged off a tower near the east entrance. Disposable phone, untraceable. Again."

Another detective cursed under his breath.

Sam didn't move, didn't speak. He was too busy watching her the way her hand twitched slightly, the way her breathing slowed until it was almost imperceptible, the way her eyes darkened like storm clouds over still water.

Lora didn't hear the chatter around her.

She was somewhere else entirely.

The message wasn't just words. It was a hook. A reminder. A challenge. And deep down, in the quiet corners of her mind, she almost, almost swore she could hear that voice again:

Come, Lora. Remember.

Sam exhaled slowly, dragging a hand down his face.

She's not going to stop, he realized. Not until she burns herself out... or until the forest swallows her whole.

The hum of the precinct was muted. The harsh fluorescent lights overhead buzzed faintly, the steady thrum of computers and muted voices blending into a low, endless drone.

Lora stood rigid in front of the evidence board, her eyes fixed on the photographs pinned in neat, meticulous rows. The spiral carved into the slab. The Polaroids. The GPS maps of the forest, dotted with red pins marking each grim discovery.

Her lips moved, almost soundlessly at first, then soft enough for only herself to hear.

"Where's the first victim...?"

Her voice cracked on the last word, just enough to slice through the room's tense quiet.

Sam looked up from the table where the others had begun cross-referencing cell tower pings. He watched her from across the room for a long beat, the slump of her shoulders, the rigid tension in her jaw, the storm brewing just behind her eyes.

"Lora," he said softly, crossing the room until he was beside her. His voice was steady, but there was that thin edge of worry threading through it. "You, okay?"

She didn't move, didn't look away from the board.

He tried again, gentler this time, "Hey... I'll take you home in a bit," he murmured, stepping close enough that his presence cut through her trance. "I'll stay with you. Just... just for tonight."

Lora's eyes blinked, once, slow, as if dragging herself out of some deep fog. She glanced up at him a fleeting look, her gaze hollow yet sharp, like she wasn't entirely sure he was real.

Then, just as quickly, she nodded. A tiny, restrained motion.

Behind them, the task force was unravelling the riddle again, dissecting every line of the text message as if the letters themselves might hold the killer's face.

"Roots remember. Spiral began with you. Witching hour bleeds red."

"'Roots remember'..." one officer muttered, flipping through forest maps. "Could be referencing tree markers. Maybe some kind of coded location."

"Or a ritual," another countered. "This entire thing spirals, timing, silence it's classic occult symbology. We've got chatter in town about old rituals tied to the forest. The Witch's Spiral, they called it."

"And the line about witching hour."

"Could be symbolic, could be literal. The timing matches our window for both Rachel and Marcus. 2:00 to 4:00 a.m., every time."

Lora's fingers twitched against her thigh as she stared at the words on the screen, the message replaying over and over in her mind.

Roots remember.

Spiral began with you.

Witching hour bleeds red.

Her mind tried to connect the threads, but all she saw was darkness and motion flashes of Rachel running, Marcus turning toward something unseen, trees bending in strange, impossible ways.

Sam stayed close, his hand brushing her arm briefly just enough to anchor her, even as his own thoughts churned.

She's too close to the edge, he thought. If I don't pull her back now, this forest, this case, whatever this is... it'll take her. And I can't...

He forced his jaw to unclench and glanced back at the table, focusing on the discussion to ground himself.

"We should sweep the spiral site again," one detective said, tapping the pinned photo with a gloved finger. "Grid the area tighter, look for disturbed ground or markings we missed the first time."

"Agreed," said another. "If the spiral's the centre, maybe everything else radiates outward from there."

Lora finally broke her silence, her voice low, hoarse, but steady, "No. He's not radiating out... he's pulling in."

The room went quiet. Every eye turned toward her, but she didn't look at anyone her gaze fixed on the map, her finger tracing an invisible line across the pins like she could see a pattern no one else could.

Sam's eyes narrowed slightly as he stepped closer, his voice soft but careful, "Pulling in where, Lora?"

Her eyes flicked toward him for the briefest moment, something sharp and haunted in them, "To me."

The silence that followed was absolute, heavy as the forest itself.

The room felt too small.

The air too thin.

Sam's eyes stayed on her on the way her shoulders hunched slightly, like the weight of the entire forest had crawled onto her back. He remembered her like this once, years ago not in a crime scene, not in the chaos of a killer's trail, but at their kitchen table, hair a mess, still in her pajamas, hunched over case files at 3 a.m. Her stubbornness had always been her brilliance.

And her curse.

Christ, Lora. He dragged a hand over his jaw, his chest tightening with something heavier than fear.

Once, there had been laughter between them. Soft mornings. Lazy Sundays where the loudest thing in the house was the coffee brewing. She used to fall asleep on the couch, her head in his lap, while the TV hummed low in the background.

Then the job ate them alive.

The calls at all hours. The sleepless nights. The case files that followed them home like ghosts. By the time they realized what was happening, the love was still there but everything else was cracked and splintered, until they broke apart in silence.

He still loved her. God help him, he still did.

Sam cleared his throat, quiet but steady, forcing his voice to cut through the charged stillness.

"Alright," he said, stepping back from the precipice of everything unsaid. "We need to analyse everything tomorrow. Every photo, every note, every word of that message."

His gaze swept the room, sharp, commanding, "I want every missing person's file for the last two years pulled. Cross-reference with any patterns we missed. And…" His voice dipped lower, harder. "…I want to know what Meyers and Hall were working on. Every report. Every lead. Everything they touched. We reconvene here at eleven sharp."

His eyes found Lora again, softer this time, and something in his voice gentled, "No later. Understood?"

The task force nodded silently. Papers shuffled, keyboards clacked, but no one spoke.

Sam stepped closer, close enough to feel the faint tremor in her arm, "C'mon," he said quietly. "That's enough for tonight."

She didn't argue. Didn't resist when his hand found her elbow, guiding her gently out of the precinct, past the last remnants of flashing screens and murmured conversations.

Outside, the night air was cool, damp. The parking lot was empty save for the dark SUV waiting under a flickering streetlight.

Sam opened the passenger door for her. She slid in silently, her face unreadable in the dim light.

He shut the door gently before circling around, climbing into the driver's side.

The engine hummed to life. For a moment, neither of them spoke. The world outside blurred by streaks of streetlight and shadow as they slipped onto the quiet road.

Then, without a word, Sam reached over and took her hand.

Her fingers were cold.

He didn't let go.

His thumb brushed over her knuckles in small, steady circles, grounding her, grounding himself.

And though she didn't look at him, though her gaze stayed fixed on the dark ribbon of highway ahead, her grip tightened slightly the smallest, quietest sign that she was still here, still fighting.

The hum of the engine filled the silence, a low drone that wrapped around the cabin like a lullaby neither of them wanted.

Sam kept his hand on hers as they drove through the empty streets. Streetlights blinked overhead, throwing fractured patterns of gold across the dashboard, across her pale, tired face. She hadn't said a word since they left the precinct just stared out the window, lost somewhere he couldn't reach.

Then he saw it a single tear tracing down her cheek, catching the faint glow of the passing lights before disappearing into the darkness of her jawline.

His throat tightened, the ache sharp, deep. He wanted to say something anything but before he could, her voice broke through, soft and raw, almost a whisper, "I still love you."

The words hung in the air, fragile and sharp all at once.

Sam's grip on the wheel tightened, knuckles whitening, but his gaze never left her profile. "I know," he said quietly, his voice thick. "And I still love you. That's why…" His voice faltered, then steadied, heavy with unspoken fear. "…that's why I'm taking you off the case, Lora."

Her head turned slowly, her tired eyes meeting his, shimmering with defiance and something far more fragile beneath it, "No," she said softly, shaking her head, her voice barely above the hum of the tires on asphalt. "We're so close."

Sam's jaw clenched. His chest felt tight, a dull ache blooming there that refused to ease. He wanted to pull over, to take her face in his hands, to tell her that nothing no case, no forest, no killer was worth losing her again.

But the road stretched on, dark and empty, and the only sound was the quiet rhythm of their shared breath and the low growl of the engine carrying them forward.

By the time they turned onto her street, dawn was bleeding faint light across the horizon, painting the sky in shades of bruised grey and pale pink. The house looked quiet, almost too quiet, the windows dark against the creeping morning.

Sam pulled into the driveway, shifted the SUV into park, and killed the engine.

For a moment, neither of them moved.

Then Sam turned to her, his voice low, careful, "Get some rest, Lora. Please."

She didn't answer right away. She just stared ahead, her hands folded in her lap, shoulders slumped under the weight of exhaustion and something else something deeper, something that had been clawing at her since the first scream in the forest.

Finally, she nodded, a small, weary motion.

Sam reached over again, his hand resting over hers, thumb brushing gently across her skin steady, grounding.

And for a brief, fleeting second, her fingers curled around his, holding tight, as if afraid to let go.

Chapter Ten

Morning broke muted and cold, the sun climbing lazily over the horizon, its light dim and weak as though the forest itself had drained the world of its colour.

By 9:30 a.m., the precinct was alive with a quiet storm the hum of printers, the sharp clack of keyboards, phones ringing in clipped bursts, and the low, urgent murmur of voices. The investigation room looked like the mind of the killer itself, a maze of corkboards and pinned photographs. Maps of the forest stretched across two walls, red string looping like veins, and there were photos of the victims, frozen mid-life smiling, laughing, unaware of the nightmare waiting for them. And everywhere... the spirals.

Chief Sam Matthews stepped inside, coffee in one hand, files in the other, his shoulders heavy with exhaustion. Sleep had eluded him. Every time he closed his eyes, the forest replayed itself the voices, the riddle, Lora disappearing down that spiral path. And Rachel. Marcus.

And Lora. Always Lora.

She was already there, seated at the far end of the room, hair tied back carelessly, dark rings under her eyes. She didn't look up when he walked in, but she didn't have to Sam felt the pull of her presence across the room.

She'd been here all night. He could see it in the half-drunk coffee cups scattered on the table, the restless scratch of pen marks on a yellow legal pad, the obsessive scrawl of notes no one else could decipher.

The task force gathered, weighed down by fatigue and something darker grief, rage, helplessness all simmering just below the surface. Detective Harris leaned against the wall, arms crossed, sceptical gaze sharp. Forensics specialist Dana Cole set a new round of photos on the centre table: close-ups of the carved slab, the spirals burned into stone like a warning.

Sam's voice broke through the low murmur. Calm, steady, but taut.

"All right. We regroup. We break last night down piece by piece. Every riddle, every breadcrumb. We find the connection before this son of a bitch strikes again."

Lora barely heard him.

Her eyes locked on the photo pinned to the left wall the spiral etched into the stone. She felt it in her bones, humming under her skin like static.

Lora, you know what I want. Remember.

The voice was still there, deep in her mind, threading through every breath she took.

Why me? Why Rachel? Why Marcus? Why can't I see his face?

Her hands trembled slightly where they rested on the table, though her expression never cracked.

Sam noticed. God, he noticed everything. The distant stare. The tightness in her jaw. The tremor in her fingers.

Once, years ago, that intensity had been what drew him to her. But now, it scared the hell out of him because it wasn't just focus anymore. It was obsession. And it was pulling her under.

He moved closer, lowered his voice so only she could hear, "Lora," he said softly, "you, okay? I'll take you home in a bit. Stay with you."

Her eyes flicked up to his, glassy but sharp. She gave a small, almost imperceptible nod. "I'm fine," she whispered, though neither of them believed it.

Dana cleared her throat, her tone clipped and clinical. "The slab you found last night. Those symbols aren't random. The outer spiral is old maybe decades old. But the inner carving? Fresh. Within forty-eight hours. It's deliberate. Intentional."

Detective Harris scoffed under his breath. "So, what, now we're dealing with some ritualistic psycho? Great."

Dana's head snapped toward him, voice sharp. "It's not just 'psycho crap,' Harris. This is language. Someone is communicating with us."

The tension in the room thickened, officers exchanging uneasy glances.

Lora stayed silent, eyes still locked on the photographs, until her voice finally cut through the noise, quiet but steady, "Where's the first victim?"

The room froze.

Sam turned toward her, brow furrowed, "What?"

Her gaze didn't waver. "We still haven't found Victim One. Everything starts there. That's the trail we need to follow."

Sam exhaled through his nose, gripping the edge of the table until his knuckles whitened.

"Fine," he said finally, voice firm. "Today, we analyse everything. Every riddle. Every pattern. We comb through missing persons from the last year anything that fits the timeline, anything with even the slightest connection. We find out who Victim Two is. And we dig into whatever Meyers and Hall were investigating before this started. Eleven a.m. tomorrow, we regroup, and we go back into the woods. Understood?"

The quiet hum of agreement rolled through the room.

Sam turned to Lora, his expression softening as he reached for her arm, a silent plea to step away from the chaos.

"Come on," he said gently.

She didn't fight him as he guided her out, the morning air cold against their skin. They didn't speak as they climbed into the SUV, the silence thick and suffocating.

Sam reached over, his hand brushing against hers as he drove, gripping it like an anchor.

The drive to Lora's house was wrapped in silence.

Not the kind of silence that brings peace but the kind that claws, heavy and suffocating, filling every corner of the SUV.

The forest still clung to them. Its damp, earthy scent was in their hair, their clothes, their thoughts. Every shadow outside the window felt like it was following them, watching, waiting.

Sam's hand stayed on hers the entire ride. He didn't speak, didn't need to but his thumb brushed the back of her hand in small, unconscious circles, like he was trying to keep her tethered to the world and not whatever darkness was wrapping itself tighter around her mind.

Lora stared out the passenger window, her reflection ghosted in the glass. Her thoughts tangled and restless.

Rachel. Marcus. The spirals. The voice.

And that message.

You are supposed to be dead.

Her breath caught for the briefest second, and Sam noticed. He always noticed.

At a red light, he glanced over at her, really looked at her. Her face pale, her lips slightly parted, her eyes distant, far away in some place he couldn't follow. That was when he saw it a single tear slipping silently down her cheek.

"Lora..." His voice was soft, barely above a whisper, heavy with everything he couldn't say.

She didn't turn to look at him. Not at first. But then, with her gaze fixed somewhere beyond the windshield, she spoke.

"I still love you," she said, her voice quiet but unshaking, as though the words had been waiting too long to be released.

Sam's grip tightened slightly on her hand. His chest ached with a sharp, almost unbearable mix of longing and fear.

"I know," he said finally, his voice breaking just enough to betray him. "And I still love you, Lora. God, I never stopped. That's why." He paused, swallowed hard, then forced the words out. "That's why I'm taking you off the case."

Her head turned sharply toward him, eyes flashing with something raw hurt, anger, defiance.

"Sam..." Her voice trembled, but the fire in it didn't. "We are so close. You can feel it too. I can see things, things nobody else can. You need me on this."

He shook his head, jaw tight, eyes locked on the road ahead like it might offer him answers.

"I need you alive," he said, almost in a whisper. "That's all I need."

They pulled up in front of her house, the street still quiet, the early morning sun barely managing to soften the edges of the world. Sam didn't move to get out. He just sat there, engine humming, holding her hand like if he let go, she'd vanish into the spiral that had already claimed too much.

Inside the car, time felt suspended a fragile stillness that could shatter with the slightest touch.

The SUV idled quietly in the driveway, the early light creeping over the horizon, pale and uncertain. Sam's hand stayed over hers, firm but gentle, like he was holding onto a lifeline neither of them could afford to lose.

Lora didn't move, her gaze still fixed ahead, though she wasn't seeing the neat line of hedges or the cracked steps leading to her front door. She was still in the forest, still in the spirals, still hearing the voice whispering her name.

Remember, Lora. Remember.

Sam finally spoke, his voice low, steady but threaded with quiet desperation.

"Let's get you inside."

She nodded once, but it was mechanical, her body moving before her mind caught up.

The house greeted them in silence, the kind that pressed in from every corner. The familiar scent of coffee and old wood was still there, but muted, as though even the walls sensed the weight, she carried in with her.

Sam closed the door softly behind them, watching as she drifted through the hallway like a ghost, her jacket slipping from her shoulders and onto the chair by the entryway.

She didn't head for the kitchen. Didn't bother with lights.

Instead, she walked straight into the living room, straight to the evidence board she'd assembled there over the past week a chaotic map of photos, notes, red string, and jagged handwriting scrawled in ink across every blank space.

Sam followed slowly, leaning against the doorframe, arms crossed, his eyes never leaving her.

He remembered nights like this two years ago, before the job tore them apart. Nights when she'd bury herself in case files until her eyes burned, until she was shaking from exhaustion and adrenaline.

Back then, he could pull her back. Back then, she'd let him.

Now, she was slipping beyond his reach.

Lora stood in front of the board, her eyes scanning the photographs, tracing the spirals like they might suddenly open up and spill the truth.

"Why can't I see him?" she whispered, almost to herself. "Why can't I see his face?"

Her fingers brushed lightly over the photo of Rachel bright smile frozen in time and then over Marcus, his eyes forever locked on something none of them could name.

Sam stepped closer, careful, slow.

"Lora," he said softly. "You need rest. Just a few hours. You can't keep...."

"I can't stop," she cut in sharply, her voice trembling but sure. "If I stop, I'll lose it. The pattern. The... connection."

Her breathing hitched, ragged in the quiet room.

Sam wanted to argue, wanted to tell her that this case wasn't worth the pieces of herself she was bleeding out every day. But instead, he stepped closer, closing the space between them until his hand was on her shoulder, warm and grounding.

"You're going to burn out," he said, his voice barely above a whisper. "And I... I can't watch that happen again."

For a moment, just a moment, she leaned into his touch the faintest crack in her armour. Then she pulled back, shaking her head, her eyes fixed again on the board.

"Every clue leads back to me," she murmured, more to herself than him. "Every line, every spiral. It's not random, Sam. It's deliberate. He's pulling me in."

Sam's chest tightened. "And that's exactly why I don't want you out there again until we figure out what that means."

Silence stretched between them sharp, heavy, suffocating until finally, Lora's voice broke it, quiet and frayed, "We're so close."

Sam closed his eyes, exhaling through clenched teeth, fighting the urge to say what he really wanted to beg her to walk away before the forest swallowed her whole.

The evidence board blurred at the edges, the spirals twisting until they were nothing but shadows dancing across her exhausted mind.

Sam found her on the couch an hour later, still in her clothes, boots kicked halfway off, her body folded into itself like she was bracing against a storm only she could hear. Her chest rose and fell unevenly, shallow breaths catching every so often, like she was running even in sleep.

He sat in the armchair across from her, elbows on his knees, his eyes locked on her restless face.

There were no words for the ache sitting heavy in his chest. He wanted to tell her to stop, to let someone else carry the weight, but he knew Lora knew that asking her to step back from this case was like asking her to stop breathing.

I can't lose you again, he thought, though the words never made it past his lips.

The hours dragged, the house silent but for the occasional sharp gasp from Lora, the haunted murmurs slipping out of her in sleep. Names. Numbers. Sometimes just a single word.

"Remember."

Sam stayed until the first light of morning began creeping through the blinds, painting her living room in a washed-out grey. He didn't sleep. He couldn't.

The ringing of his phone jolted the stillness, sharp and demanding. Sam answered before it could wake her, his voice low but clipped. "Chief Matthews."

The voice on the other end was hurried, tight with adrenaline. "Chief we've got something. The lab came through. There's a partial match on the fibres found near Marcus's body. And... you need to see this riddle again. There's more to it. Something we missed."

Sam's stomach turned to ice, "I'll be there in twenty."

He hung up and turned to Lora. She had stirred at the sound, eyes fluttering open, glassy and heavy with fatigue, "Sam?" Her voice cracked, soft and uncertain.

He crossed the room in two steps, crouching beside her, his hand brushing her arm gently, "Go back to sleep," he said, though his tone carried the weight of a man who knew she wouldn't.

Her eyes locked on his sharp, restless, obsessive even through the exhaustion. "Something happened."

Sam hesitated. Just for a moment. Then he nodded. "The lab found something. And they want us back at the precinct."

She sat up slowly, rubbing the heel of her hand across her tired eyes, the dark circles beneath them stark in the pale light. "Then let's go."

The drive to the precinct was quiet, the kind of quiet that wasn't comfortable but wasn't suffocating either the quiet of two people teetering on the edge of something neither could name.

Sam glanced at her from the corner of his eye as he drove, noting the way she sat stiffly, her hands twisting together in her lap, her gaze fixed somewhere far beyond the windshield.

She was already back in the forest, following clues only she could see.

She's going to get herself killed, Sam thought bitterly, tightening his grip on the wheel. And I don't know how to stop her without losing her entirely.

The precinct buzzed as they walked in, phones ringing, voices overlapping, papers rustling in a frantic shuffle. Detectives moved with clipped urgency; their faces etched with tension and exhaustion.

The task force room was a chaos of evidence boards and screens glowing with lines of data.

Every eye turned when Lora and Sam entered.

"Detective Matthews," one of the techs called out, holding up a file. "You're going to want to see this."

Lora didn't hesitate, stepping forward, her exhaustion forgotten, laser-focused on whatever lay ahead.

Sam followed, his gaze never leaving her, a storm of fear and love and helplessness boiling just beneath his composed exterior.

Chapter Eleven

The task force room was humming a low, feverish energy that clung to the walls like static.

Screens blinked with maps of the forest, blown-up photos of the crime scenes, lines of coded notes. The coffee was burned and bitter, the kind that had been sitting on the warmer far too long, but no one cared.

Lora stepped inside first, her pace brisk, her expression taut. Every detective, every officer, shifted slightly as she passed, the weight of her presence quieting the room without a word.

Sam followed, a steady shadow behind her, his eyes scanning every detail, reading the tension in his people as much as the evidence on the walls.

"Report," Sam said, his tone clipped, no space for hesitation.

A young tech Harris, one of the newer faces straightened from his monitor. His voice trembled, but he kept it steady, "The lab ran secondary tests on the fibres we pulled from Marcus's jacket. It's consistent with rare nylon blends used in tactical climbing gear. Expensive, custom-made. This wasn't random."

Lora's brow furrowed. "So, we're looking at someone trained. Someone who knows the terrain."

"Yes, ma'am," Harris confirmed, flipping through a file and laying down high-resolution photos. "And... there's something else. That last riddle."

The room fell into a deeper silence, the kind that made every word sharper, heavier.

Harris brought up the image on the main screen the looping handwriting, jagged spirals curling into themselves, and beneath it, the message:

"The roots hold what you seek, but beware the hollow, for the forest remembers. Third of three. The first watches still."

Lora leaned forward, staring at the words like they were a physical wound.

The first watches still.

Her chest tightened, a sharp ache spreading outward. Victim One. The one they hadn't found. The one that haunted her in flashes of fragmented visions.

"Roots," Sam repeated quietly, stepping closer to the board. "We've already searched the core radius. What the hell does that mean?"

Lora's eyes didn't leave the screen. "It means we've been looking in the wrong places," she whispered. "It's not just about the center. It's... it's below."

Murmurs broke out around the room. Officers traded uneasy glances, theories buzzing like gnats in the stale air.

Detective Alvarez crossed his arms, skeptical. "Below what? Half that forest is a maze of sinkholes and caves. You want to dig up the whole thing?"

"It's not random," Lora said sharply, turning toward him, her voice steady but charged. "He's leading us. Every breadcrumb, every symbol they're deliberate. He wants us to find something. Or…" She hesitated, her gaze darkening. "…someone."

Sam stepped in, his presence grounding the room. "All right. Enough speculation. We focus on the evidence. If the fibers are tactical, we trace the suppliers in a hundred-mile radius. We narrow it down, we find a buyer. And we analyse every past missing-person case in the last decade anything with a tie to those woods. I want a comprehensive list by noon."

The room scattered into motion, detectives barking into phones, techs hammering at keyboards.

Lora stayed where she was, frozen in place, eyes locked on the looping script.

The roots hold what you seek… the forest remembers.

She muttered under her breath, barely audible. "Where are you?"

Sam noticed. He always noticed.

He moved to her side, close enough to feel the tension vibrating off her. "Lora," he said, softer now, pitched for her alone. "You need to take a step back. Just for a few hours. Let them work the angles."

Her head turned slowly, eyes meeting his, sharp and tired and haunted.

"If I step back," she said quietly, "I lose the thread. And we can't afford that."

His jaw clenched, frustration simmering beneath his calm. She's slipping further in, he thought, chest tightening, and I don't know how to pull her out without breaking her.

The hum of the precinct swallowed the room again.

"Then we do it together," Sam said finally, his voice steady but heavy. "No more running in alone. No more disappearing into that forest without backup. You hear me?"

There was no hesitation this time, just the faintest nod. "I hear you," she whispered.

But the look in her eyes told him the truth: the forest had its hooks in her, and it wasn't letting go.

The room moved like a living machine officers barking updates into phones, printers whirring, the sharp clatter of keyboards filling the air but for Lora and Sam, it all blurred into a distant hum.

She stood still, her gaze fixed on the spiraled message glowing on the screen, shoulders rigid, eyes ringed with exhaustion but still sharp, still dangerous.

Sam watched her from a step away, studying the way her jaw tightened, the subtle tremor in her hands she thought no one noticed.

She's burning herself alive for this case, he thought, his chest aching as if the thought itself had weight. And I'm letting her. Because part of me still believes only she can see what the rest of us can't.

"You need to eat something," he said quietly, pitching his voice low so no one else would hear.

Lora didn't move. Didn't even look at him. "I'm fine."

"No, you're not," Sam countered, just as quiet but edged with a quiet desperation. He stepped closer, close enough that only she could hear. "I know you, Lora. Better than anyone in this damn room. You're running on fumes and stubbornness, and one day soon that's going to get you killed."

Finally, her eyes shifted, locking on his and for a moment, the detective mask cracked.

"I can't stop," she whispered, voice hoarse. "I close my eyes, and all I see are their faces. Rachel. Marcus. The others we haven't even found yet. I feel it, Sam. Like I'm supposed to be out there. Like I..." She trailed off, the words caught in her throat.

Sam's hand twitched like he wanted to reach for her, but he held back, his own emotions warring beneath his steady exterior.

"You're not alone in this," he said finally, his voice barely above a whisper. "Stop acting like you are."

A beat of silence stretched between them, thick and heavy.

Across the room, Alvarez and two younger detectives pretended to be absorbed in the case board, but their quick glances kept darting toward the two of them to the quiet gravity of whatever held Lora and Sam in place, as though they were orbiting each other in a silent, dangerous pull.

Then, the intercom buzzed.

"Chief Matthews. We've got movement. Search team is ready to move back out."

Sam straightened, the moment breaking like glass. "Let's go," he said, more sharply than he intended.

Lora turned to grab her coat, the tremor in her hands gone now, replaced by a grim steadiness that told Sam she'd already shut the door on everything except the forest.

Chapter Twelve

The forest swallowed them whole again that afternoon, its silence heavier, sharper, as though the trees themselves were watching.

The search grid widened, teams fanning out in practiced patterns. The radios hissed softly with static and clipped updates.

Sam stayed close to Lora, always within reach, his eyes flicking between the narrow trails ahead and her rigid posture.

Hours bled away as they pushed deeper into the core, retracing steps and following faint disturbances in the soil, threads of evidence too subtle for anyone but Lora to notice.

Then —

"Chief, your goanna want to see this," a voice crackled over the radio.

They followed the call, the forest tightening around them until the trees broke to reveal a hollow at the base of a ridge.

It was subtle an unnatural dip in the ground, almost invisible beneath layers of fallen leaves and creeping moss. But the closer they got, the colder the air felt, as though the earth itself was holding its breath.

"Forensics flagged this," Alvarez said, crouched beside the opening, his gloved hand brushing away dirt. "Looks like a natural shaft maybe an old root cave. Could lead into something deeper."

Sam knelt beside him, his flashlight cutting through the shadowed opening, but the light didn't travel far. Just darkness. A yawning, endless dark.

Beside him, Lora didn't speak. She just stared, eyes wide, pupils dilated as though the forest was whispering secrets only, she could hear.

Sam looked up at her sharply. "Lora. Talk to me. What are you seeing?"

Her throat bobbed as she swallowed hard. "Not him," she whispered, barely audible. "Not Victim One. But... something. He's been here."

The silence that followed was suffocating. Even the birds had stopped.

Sam stood, his jaw tight. "We mark it, secure the perimeter, and get ground-penetrating radar in here by morning. No one goes in until it's cleared. Understood?"

The team nodded, scattered murmurs of acknowledgment filling the space.

Sam turned to Lora then, his voice gentler but edged with steel. "And you, you stay by me. No wandering. No running off. Not this time."

But she didn't answer.

Her eyes were still fixed on the opening, the dark below, like it was calling to her.

The team moved with quiet efficiency crime scene tape unfurling, markers set down, equipment bags unzipped but the forest seemed to hum, vibrating beneath the surface like something unseen had stirred.

Lora stayed at the edge of the hollow, her boots inches from the dark opening in the earth, her gaze fixed on the blackness that swallowed every trace of light.

Something about this place prickled along her skin, sharp and cold.

I've been here before, she thought, the certainty settling into her bones even though her mind screamed it wasn't possible. She'd never walked this deep into the forest until the investigation began, never seen this hidden scar in the earth.

And yet... it was familiar.

Like a dream she couldn't remember, just the echo of one.

Sam noticed the way her breathing hitched, the distant glassiness in her eyes. He moved closer, his voice steady but threaded with worry.

"Lora," he said, soft but firm. "Talk to me. What's going on?"

Her lips parted, a whisper escaping. "I... I think..."

The world tilted, the shadows pulling sharp and thin as the vision hit her like a cold blade flash, indistinct and fast, like trying to catch smoke with bare hands.

A woman running. Breath ragged. Branches clawing at her arms. The ground wet and slick beneath her boots. The hollow, this hollow flashing in her vision like a beacon.

And then

The number one. Carved. Deep.

Lora's knees buckled before she even registered the dizziness.

"LORA!"

Sam lunged forward just in time, catching her before she crumpled into the damp soil. Her head lolled against his shoulder, her breaths shallow and uneven, her skin clammy with cold sweat.

"Get the medics over here, now!" he barked, his voice cutting through the stillness like a gunshot.

Alvarez and two others sprinted over, radios crackling as they called for emergency kits, but Sam barely noticed. His focus was on her on the way her lashes fluttered against pale cheeks, on the tremor in her hands as if even unconscious she was bracing for impact.

"Lora," he said again, softer now, his voice cracking despite himself. "Stay with me. You hear me? Just... stay with me."

The forest pressed in tighter, thick with silence and that strange, unnatural stillness, as if the trees themselves were leaning closer, listening.

One of the officers knelt beside Sam, checking her pulse with practiced precision. "She's stable," the man said quickly, though his tone betrayed unease. "Probably just exhaustion. Dehydration, maybe. But... we should get her out of here."

Sam nodded, his jaw tight, though his hands stayed firm around her, holding her like she might vanish if he let go.

And in the hush, just before the medics arrived, Lora stirred faintly, her voice a hoarse whisper against his shoulder.

"It's... down there," she murmured, so soft he almost didn't hear it. "He's down there..."

Sam froze, his stomach dropping. "Who, Lora? Who's down there?"

Her eyes fluttered open, unfocused, haunted.

"Victim one," she breathed. "He's waiting."

The forest stood unnervingly still, the air damp, heavy, holding its breath. Even the officers spoke in lowered voices, as if afraid to disturb whatever ancient thing slumbered beneath the earth.

Sam cradled Lora against him, her weight unsettlingly light, her skin clammy against his hand. Every instinct screamed to scoop her up and run to get her as far away from this cursed place as possible. But he forced himself to stay measured, steady, because panic wouldn't help her now.

"Secure the perimeter tighter!" Sam barked, his voice cutting through the subdued chaos. "I want tape on a fifty-foot radius. No one — no one — goes near that opening until forensics and geophysics get here."

"Yes, Chief," Alvarez called back, already directing two officers to widen the cordon. Blue tape stretched between trees like veins, the hollow now encircled by a fragile barrier.

The medics arrived moments later, kits clattering as they knelt beside Sam.

"Easy," Sam muttered, his voice uncharacteristically raw, as he eased Lora into their care. He didn't want to let go, but he had to his hand lingered a fraction longer on her shoulder before pulling back.

The medic checked her vitals again, shining a light briefly into her eyes. "Pupils are reactive. She's breathing steady now. Exhaustion, dehydration and maybe shock. She needs rest, Captain."

Rest.

The word tasted bitter in Sam's mouth. Lora hadn't truly rested in weeks, not since this case had sunk its claws into her. He doubted she even remembered how.

"Chief," Alvarez called again, drawing Sam's attention. He stood a few feet from the hollow, frowning into the dark. "This thing... it's not natural. Or if it started that way, someone's worked it. These walls." he gestured with his flashlight beam, "they've been cut. Dug deeper."

Sam's gut clenched. So, it is a grave, he thought grimly, though he didn't voice it.

Instead, he turned back to the medics, his tone sharp again. "Get her ready for transport. SUV's closest. Move slow, careful. We don't risk further strain."

The retreat was deliberate, controlled.

Two officers carried gear, clearing the path. The medics worked in a practiced rhythm, securing Lora onto a stretcher as she murmured incoherently, words Sam strained to catch.

"Roots... shadows... spiral..."

Sam's jaw tightened, his chest burning as he walked close, one hand resting lightly on the side rail of the stretcher, grounding himself in her nearness.

She's in deeper than all of us, he thought. And it's tearing her apart.

The team moved out of the forest with military precision, but the sense of unease only deepened the closer they got to the tree line.

The hollow seemed to follow them, even as it disappeared behind layers of trees its dark mouth still whispering at the back of their minds.

Sam glanced over his shoulder once, the last slant of daylight bleeding into the ridge. The opening seemed wider now, hungrier, as though it had been waiting for them all along.

His hand curled into a fist. We'll be back, he thought grimly. And this time, we'll be ready.

Chapter Thirteen

Lora's eyes fluttered open to dim light, the faint smell of brewed coffee lingering in the air. For a moment, she didn't know where she was the shadows on the ceiling looked too much like the canopy of the forest, the hush too much like that suffocating silence between the trees.

Then she turned her head and saw him.

Sam sat in the chair by her bed, elbows resting on his knees, his hands clasped tightly together. He wasn't in uniform his jacket hung on the back of the chair, his tie loosened, his shirt wrinkled. He looked like he hadn't moved in hours.

His eyes met hers the second they opened.

"You're awake," he said softly, though there was a weight in his voice, the kind that came after fear had been sitting too long in the chest.

She shifted, groaning faintly as a dull ache rippled through her body. Every muscle felt like stone. "How...?"

"You collapsed," Sam said, not breaking eye contact. "The medics checked you. Said it was exhaustion, dehydration, shock. You're lucky you didn't hit your head when you went down. I..." His voice faltered for the first time, rough and strained. He cleared his throat. "I caught you."

A flicker of memory came back the darkness yawning beneath her feet, the vision clawing at her mind, then the rush of falling, weightless, before his arms had closed around her.

Her chest tightened. "You stayed."

"Of course I stayed," he replied, his tone a little too sharp, as if the very idea of not staying offended him. Then softer, almost to himself, "I couldn't leave you like that."

Silence stretched between them. The house was too still, too quiet and the quiet pressed in like the forest's silence had.

Finally, she whispered, "Sam... I saw something."

His eyes sharpened instantly, every muscle tensing. "What did you see?"

Lora swallowed, her throat dry. "The hollow. The roots. It wasn't just earth. It's been carved out... used. And I saw..." She trailed off, her gaze slipping past him, into nothing. "Number one. Victim one. He's down there."

Sam's jaw clenched. He leaned forward, his hand twitching like he wanted to reach for hers but stopping short.

"You don't know that for sure," he said firmly. "That could've been the shock talking, your mind filling gaps."

"No." Her voice was steady now, almost fierce. "I felt it. He's there. Waiting."

Sam let out a long breath, raking a hand through his hair.

Goddammit, Lora, he thought. Why is it always you who has to bleed for these answers?

Aloud, he said, "We'll check it. But not you. Not again. You're not going near that opening until forensics clear it."

Her lips parted, protest already forming, but he cut her off with a hard look. "No arguments. I mean it."

For once, she didn't push, not immediately. Instead, she studied him, the weariness in his eyes, the subtle strain in the lines around his mouth.

"You stayed," she repeated softly, like she was trying to remind herself it was real.

Sam leaned back in the chair, exhaling through his nose, and finally let his hand rest gently on the back of hers.

"Where else would I be?"

For a long moment, neither spoke. The quite stretched, but it wasn't the oppressive silence of the forest — it was softer, charged with something they'd both carried too long without saying.

Sam's hand lingered on hers, warm, steady, anchoring. She let him.

Lora's chest rose and fell, uneven, not from weakness but from the storm pressing beneath her ribs. She turned her head, eyes locking with his. In them, she saw everything she had tried to bury the man who once shared her bed, her future, her life. The man who still knew her better than anyone, even when she wanted him to stop.

"I thought I lost you in those woods," Sam said quietly, his voice rough with a truth he didn't often allow. His thumb brushed the back of her hand unconsciously, as though reminding himself she was real. "For a second... when you went down... I thought..." He broke off, jaw tightening.

"You didn't," she whispered, her lips trembling just slightly. "You caught me. You always..." Her voice faltered. "...you always do."

Sam swallowed hard, and his chest ached in that familiar way, the way it always did when she let him see the cracks. Goddamn it, Lora. I never stopped loving you.

She shifted slightly in the bed, enough to face him more fully, and the closeness made the air between them taut, fragile.

"I still love you, Sam," she murmured before she could stop herself. The words trembled out of her, like they had been waiting at the edge of her lips for years.

Sam froze. The confession wasn't a surprise not truly but hearing it now, in the dim hush of her bedroom, after the forest had nearly swallowed her whole, tore through every defence he'd built.

"I know," he said at last, his voice breaking. Then, softer, "I never stopped. That's why..." He forced a ragged exhale. "...that's why I can't watch this case take you away from me."

Her eyes glistened, but she didn't look away. She couldn't.

"We're so close," she whispered again, like a vow, like an excuse.

"And you're breaking yourself in the process," Sam countered, though his hand tightened around hers as though letting go wasn't an option.

The weight of unspoken words hung heavy between them.

The sharp buzz of Sam's phone shattered it.

He cursed under his breath, pulled it from his pocket, and glanced at the screen. The precinct.

Reluctantly, he answered. "Chief Matthews."

The voice on the other end was brisk, professional, but edged with concern. "Chief, we've secured the hollow site. Forensics is prepping ground-penetrating radar now. We should have preliminary results in a few hours. And..." a pause, softer, "how's Lora? We heard she collapsed."

Sam's eyes flicked to her, still pale but watching him intently, every bit of her willpower holding her upright. His hand was still covering hers.

"She's... resting," Sam said carefully, though his gaze never left her. "She'll be briefed when she's ready."

"Understood, Chief," the voice replied. "We'll keep you updated. Call in when you're back on-site."

Sam hung up, sliding the phone onto the nightstand.

Lora raised a brow faintly. "They asked about me?"

"Of course they did," Sam said, leaning back in the chair, still holding her hand. His voice softened, the walls slipping just a fraction. "You're the centre of this whole damn thing, whether I like it or not."

Lora exhaled slowly, the faintest smile tugging at her lips despite the exhaustion in her bones. "Then we'd better not keep the forest waiting."

Sam closed his eyes briefly, fighting both frustration and the surge of affection that came every time she spoke like that like the case was already inside her veins.

When he opened them again, his hand tightened over hers.

"We'll face it," he said quietly. "But this time, we face it together."

Chapter Fourteen

The precinct briefing room was packed tight. A quiet tension hung in the air, thicker than cigarette smoke, thicker than the sleepless haze clouding everyone's eyes. No one was speaking, not until the tech from forensics pulled the first scan onto the projector.

The hollow unfolded across the screen in ghostly white cross-sections.

"Negative for human remains," the tech said, voice clipped but uneasy. He advanced the scan. "But... there's a chamber. Roughly twenty feet down."

The air seemed to shift.

The next image showed it a large room carved into the earth. Jagged walls. A table or altar in the center. Candles lined along the edges like sentinels. And to the left... dark shapes resolved into narrow rectangles.

"Cells," the tech confirmed. His throat bobbed. "Six of them."

A ripple went through the room. Chairs creaked. Someone cursed under their breath.

Lora's nails pressed half-moon marks into her palms as she leaned forward, staring at the grainy outline of the underground chamber. Her heart clenched with both dread and certainty.

This is it. This is where he took them.

Beside her, Sam kept his face neutral, but his chest was tightening. He could feel Lora almost vibrating beside him, as though her body wanted to leap through the screen and straight into the earth itself.

"Candles, symbols on the walls," the tech went on, zooming in. "Possibly ritualistic. We'll know more when we breach, but...."

He cut himself off. The images spoke for themselves.

The silence that followed wasn't still. It was alive, crawling across skin and spines.

Sam rose first, his voice sharp, controlled. "Alright. We'll move in daylight. No exceptions. We can't risk sending people down there blind."

The team nodded, though unease flickered across every face.

Lora didn't speak. She couldn't. Her eyes remained fixed on the screen, on those black voids where cells waited. Who had been inside? Who was still inside?

Later, the SUV hummed along the quiet back roads toward her house. Dawn had stretched into daylight, but the sky still felt heavy, like it was holding something back.

Inside, the silence pressed in as tightly as it had at the precinct.

Sam drove with one hand on the wheel, the other on the armrest close enough that if she reached, he'd meet her halfway without hesitation.

"You're too quiet," he said finally, his voice low, testing.

Lora didn't look at him. Her gaze was pinned to the trees sliding past outside. "I can see it in my head. The chamber. The cells. Like I've already walked through it."

Sam's knuckles tightened on the wheel. "That's what I'm afraid of."

She turned then, her eyes sharp, fevered. "Afraid of me, or afraid of what's down there?"

"Both," he admitted, the truth pulling at him. "You're unravelling, Lora. I can see it. And I..." He exhaled hard, pain lacing his words. "...I can't lose you again."

Her throat tightened, but her voice was steady. "Then don't let go of me. Not now."

Sam glanced at her, really looked at her, and saw the fragility beneath her steel, the raw edge of obsession that frightened him but also bound him to her.

He reached across, his hand closing over hers. Firm. Grounding.

"We go down there tomorrow," he said. "Together. No more chasing shadows alone."

For the first time since the scans, Lora let herself lean into his touch. Just slightly. Just enough to know he was there.

Chapter Fifteen

T he precinct hummed with a grim purpose the next morning. Maps of the forest were spread across the long table, over-layed with the hollow scans. Officers gathered equipment: ropes, flood lamps, oxygen meters, reinforced ladders. The air was charged, as though every breath carried weight.

But for Lora, it was more than tension it was gravity.

The hollow pulled at her like a tide. Every time her eyes drifted to the scans, she felt the echo of the earth pressing down, of shadows waiting.

Why do I feel like I've been here before? Why does it feel like it's already inside me?

Sam noticed. He noticed everything. The way her jaw tightened whenever someone mentioned "cells." The way her hand trembled when she thought no one was watching. The way her gaze refused to leave the blueprints, as though the chamber itself was whispering her name.

And beneath all that, his own chest burned with fear. Fear of the case. Fear of what lay under the earth. Fear of what this obsession was doing to the woman he still loved.

Goddammit, Lora... I'd chain you to me if it meant keeping you safe.

By dusk, the team assembled at the site. Blue tape cordoned off the clearing. Generators throbbed to life, spilling pale electric light onto the forest floor. Search dogs whined, restless, as though they too sensed what was buried beneath their paws.

The opening yawned like a wound in the earth jagged, dark, waiting.

Lora stood at its edge, staring down into the void. Her breath was shallow, her palms slick with sweat despite the cool evening air. She felt the forest breathing around her, pressing in.

"This isn't just a chamber," she whispered under her breath. "It's a mouth."

Sam's voice cut sharp behind her. "Alright, rope lines are set. We'll move in formation, slow and controlled."

Officers nodded, helmets secured, lights checked.

But just as the first ladder was lowered into the hollow, Lora's voice rang out urgent, sharp.

"Stop!"

Every head turned.

She was trembling, but her eyes burned with something beyond fear. "I'll go in first."

Sam's face hardened instantly. "The hell you will."

Lora ignored him, stepping closer to the rope. "This is pulling me. You all feel it, don't you? But it's different with me. He wants me down there. If anyone should go first, it's me."

"Lora," Sam snapped, his voice rising. "I am not letting you walk into that alone. I don't care what connection you think you have."

"I'm not asking for permission," she shot back, her tone low, fierce.

For a moment, the air between them vibrated with the weight of their history partners, lovers, fractured and still tethered. Then, before he could stop her, she gripped the rope with both hands and swung a leg over the edge.

"Dammit, Lora!" Sam lunged forward, his hand grabbing the rope just beneath hers. "Then I'm right behind you."

His voice was steel, unshakable. "If you're going down, we go down together."

The rest of the team followed in grim silence, the line of descent illuminated by the cold beam of helmet lamps.

The hollow swallowed them.

Earth pressed close on either side, damp and suffocating. The smell of old soil and wax grew stronger with every rung. Shadows shifted strangely, bending light in ways that made the descent feel endless.

When their boots finally hit the floor, the chamber revealed itself.

Candles sat melted to stubs along uneven stone. The table at the centre was scarred with carvings. Symbols spiralled across the walls in jagged strokes of ash and dried blood. To the left, the cells stood like blackened mouths, iron doors rusted but still strong.

The air was cold, colder than it should have been.

Lora stood frozen, her chest heaving. Every part of her screamed familiarity. She raised a shaking hand, touching one of the symbols carved into the wall. Her breath caught.

Sam stepped close, his voice barely above a whisper. "What do you see?"

Her eyes stayed fixed on the markings. Her lips parted, and a single word escaped, ragged:

"Memory."

Chapter Sixteen

The chamber swallowed every sound. Even the scrape of boots on stone seemed dulled, as though the air itself wanted silence. Officers fanned out, securing corners, cameras flashing against the carved walls, their light stuttering over crude spirals and half-burned wax. The smell of earth, old smoke, and rusted iron pressed thick into their lungs.

Lora stood in the center, her hands curled into trembling fists. Every symbol she looked at sparked a pulse in her skull, sharp and punishing, as if each one was a nail driven deeper into memory.

I know this place... I shouldn't, but I do.

Her breath hitched, her vision swimming. Shadows warped, twisting the symbols until they seemed to writhe across the walls. She clutched at her head, staggering slightly.

"Lora—" Sam was at her side instantly, catching her elbow. His voice was low but urgent. "What's happening? Talk to me."

"It's…" She pressed her palms to her temples, her eyes wide and glassy. "It's not just a chamber… it's a story. He carved… messages into this place."

An officer's shout broke through. "Detective! Over here."

Everyone pivoted. At the far side of the altar, wedged between two stones, was a scrap of Polaroid. Dust clung to it, but when the officer eased it free, the image was clear:

Lora.

Not today. Not last week. Younger. A photo taken years ago, maybe during her academy days.

Her stomach dropped as though the floor beneath her had given way. Sam's grip tightened on her arm.

"He's playing you," Sam muttered, jaw locked. But there was fear in his eyes deep, unspoken fear.

Then, all at once, the candles flared.

Every stub flickered to life, tiny flames dancing in unison, though no one had touched them. Gasps echoed through the chamber. A chill swept over the team, the kind that sank into bone.

On the far wall, where light hadn't reached before, new words were visible. Fresh. Wet. As if painted only moments ago:

"I'm watching you."

The letters dripped.

The officers froze, weapons drawn though the chamber was empty but for them. Sam's heart hammered, his instincts screaming. He pulled Lora slightly behind him, though she resisted, her eyes locked on the message.

He's here. He's closer than we think.

Then Lora's gaze caught on something else. To the right of the cells, half-hidden in shadow, stood a narrow wooden door. Old. Splintered. A rusted chain dangled from its lock.

Drawn like a moth to flame, she stepped toward it, each footfall echoing far too loudly.

"Lora!" Sam's voice snapped like a whip. He was at her side again, his hand seizing her wrist before she could reach the handle.

Her head turned sharply toward him, eyes fever-bright, lips parting to argue.

But the look in his face raw fear, not for himself but for her froze her in place.

"Not alone," he said, his voice rough, unwavering. "Not like this."

The chamber waited, still and watching, as though holding its breath.

Chapter Seventeen

The chamber seemed to shrink around them, shadows stretching taller as if listening. The team stood taut, their beams of light jittering across the scarred walls, but all eyes fell on the splintered wooden door.

Lora's chest rose and fell too fast, every breath ragged. Sam's grip clamped firm around her wrist, grounding her and restraining her in equal measure.

"Let me go," she hissed, voice low, trembling. "I need to see what's behind it."

"No," Sam said, steel threaded through every syllable. "Not until we know what we're dealing with."

She pulled against him, just enough for her voice to sharpen, break. "You don't understand. I feel it. There's something…"

"I don't care what you feel," he snapped, louder than he meant, fear riding his tone. His eyes locked on hers, unflinching. "I care about you staying alive."

The words hung in the air, raw, cutting. The team exchanged uneasy glances, their rifles steady but their attention flicking back to the tension sparking between the two detectives.

Lora stared back at Sam, the heat in her gaze not just defiance but desperation. "If I don't go through that door, we lose him. We lose everything."

Sam's chest ached with the truth buried in her words. He wanted to shield her from all of it — the blood, the symbols, the ghosts clawing through her head. But he also knew she was right: this case was hers in a way no one could untangle.

The team shifted uncomfortably, waiting for a call.

Then it came.

The door creaked.

Every head snapped toward it. The rusted chain rattled softly as the wood shuddered on its hinges. Slow. Deliberate. The sound scraped the silence raw.

"Hold position!" Sam barked, instincts taking over as he shoved Lora gently behind him.

The door yawned open a crack, the darkness beyond thick, impenetrable. No breath, no footsteps, no sound but the groan of ancient hinges.

A ripple of dread ran through the room. One officer muttered, "Christ..." as the hairs along their necks prickled.

Lora's voice was barely audible, whisper thin. "He's inviting us in."

Sam's jaw clenched, but he didn't deny it. He raised his hand. "Weapons ready. We move on my mark."

The team closed in, rifles up, beams of light cutting into the waiting dark.

Sam's voice dropped, the gravity of command steadying the panic that threatened. "Slow. Controlled. No one breaks formation."

He glanced back at Lora, his eyes meeting hers for one brief, desperate second. Stay with me.

Then he gave the signal.

And together, the task force pushed the door wide and stepped into the darkness beyond.

Chapter Eighteen

The door groaned wider under the weight of their push, the darkness beyond yawning like a throat swallowing them whole. The air that spilled out was damp and fetid, laced with something acrid smoke, wax, and iron.

Their flashlights pierced the gloom in nervous sweeps.

The space was larger than they expected another chamber carved into the earth, but different from the first. This one was intimate, suffocating. The walls pulsed with symbols, carved deeper, etched with more precision, painted over in blackened soot and streaks of dried red. Candles littered every corner, melted into grotesque waxen stalagmites that dripped like frozen screams.

The table in the center was smaller; its surface scarred with knife marks. A rope dangled from above, frayed and darkened with stains no one wanted to name.

And against the far wall a set of iron shackles bolted directly into stone. The floor beneath them bore the scratches of desperate nails clawing for freedom.

One officer swore under his breath. Another muttered, "Jesus Christ..." as the beams of light jittered across offerings placed on the altar: bones, feathers, fragments of hair bound in twine.

Lora's breath quickened. Each object seemed to vibrate, pulling at something inside her skull. Her head throbbed. Her eyes burned. The deeper they went, the more the chamber seemed to know her.

I've been here. I shouldn't have been, but I have. Why does this place remember me?

Sam's hand ghosted near her back, steady, ready to catch her if she faltered again. His jaw was tight, his chest constricted. She's unravelling in front of me, and I can't stop it.

Then the light caught something new.

Words.

Not carved, not painted scrawled fresh across the stone wall in what looked like smeared soot or ash. The message was jagged, wild, but the letters were unmistakable:

"Oh Lora... you were the resilient one. Your spirit is strong."

The words dripped like poison, personal, intimate.

Her heart slammed against her ribs. A wave of nausea twisted her gut. She stumbled closer, her light trembling over the strokes of the message.

"He's talking to me," she whispered, her voice hollow. "Not just to me... about me."

Sam stepped forward, pulling her gently back with a hand at her arm. His voice was a low growl meant only for her. "He's baiting you. That's all this is."

But his own eyes betrayed him. The familiarity in the message chilled him, because it was true this wasn't the way their unsub taunted. This was something else.

Lora couldn't look away. The words seemed alive, as though inked into her skin rather than the wall.

The team stood frozen, every instinct screaming that the chamber itself was a trap, that the walls were closing in, that at any moment the killer would reveal himself.

But the silence held. The candles flickered.

And in that silence, Lora felt it again: not just the killer's presence, but his gaze. Watching. Breathing in rhythm with hers.

The chamber seemed to breathe.

The light of their flashlights swept across symbols and chains, but shadows clung stubbornly in the corners, thicker than they should've been. The air was damp, pressing heavy in the lungs, tinged with copper and wax.

Lora's gaze locked on the scrawled message. "Oh Lora... you were the resilient one. Your spirit is strong."

Her temples throbbed. Each letter seemed to shimmer, as though it had been burned into her skin rather than the stone.

A low hum rose in her ears not mechanical, not from the team's equipment. A tone. Almost a whisper beneath sound itself. It circled the chamber, burrowed deep into her skull.

She stiffened.

Footsteps. No... a voice. Faint. Calling my name.

Her lips parted. She swayed slightly, her eyes glassing over. "Sam..." she whispered, but it wasn't to him, it was to something unseen, something only she heard.

Sam was at her side in an instant, his hand firm on her arm. "Lora. Stay with me. What's happening?"

Her pupils dilated, her breathing shallow. "He's here. Not just the words him. I can hear him."

Sam's heart clenched, cold sweat dampening his collar. Christ, she's slipping again. But then in the corner of his own vision he swore he saw movement. A shadow that shouldn't have been there.

"Hold position," Sam barked, his voice sharp. Officers froze, rifles rising in unison.

The chamber swallowed the command, as though the walls themselves absorbed it.

Then came a sound. Subtle. A scrape against stone.

Every flashlight swivelled.

The iron shackles on the far wall rattled once. Just once. The sound reverberated in their bones.

"No wind down here," one officer muttered, voice thin with fear. "No reason they should move."

Another officer swore quietly, stepping closer to check, but froze mid-stride.

Footprints.

Fresh, damp imprints stretched across the dust on the floor. Bare feet. Leading away from the shackles... and deeper into the chamber's shadows.

The hairs on Sam's neck prickled. His grip on Lora's arm tightened.

"Eyes up," he ordered, voice low but firm. "We're not alone."

Lora's head tilted slightly, her gaze unfocused, as though listening to something no one else could hear. Her lips moved, faintly mouthing words.

Sam leaned closer, whispering urgently. "What is it? What do you hear?"

Her voice came out soft, broken, as if not entirely her own:

"He's waiting."

Chapter Nineteen

The chamber seemed to close in around them, stone pressing closer, air thinning with every passing second.

The team moved as one organism boots careful on the damp stone, rifles sweeping the corners. Every breath was audible, amplified by the suffocating silence.

Those footprints. Bare, fresh. Too fresh.

Lora's eyes trailed them like a tether, her steps mechanical, as though drawn forward by something beyond herself. The hum in her head persisted, weaving with her pulse. So close. He's just ahead. Just beyond sight. Why can't I see his face?

Sam kept his hand tight around her wrist, grounding her, though his heart was hammering. Every instinct screamed to get her out, to end this descent, but every trace of evidence dragged them further in.

The tunnel narrowed. Their beams of light barely pushed the dark back. The deeper they went, the stronger the smell wax, damp earth, faint decay.

Then.

A scuff. Ahead.

Every weapon snapped upward. Flashlights converged on the corridor's bend.

"Contact?" an officer whispered.

Sam held up a fist. Silence.

The sound came again. Lighter this time. A shuffle. Like bare feet dragging against stone.

Sam felt the heat of Lora's breath against his shoulder as she whispered, "He's toying with us."

The group pressed forward. Step by step, boots careful, hearts pounding.

A flicker.

A shadow darted across the corridor.

"Movement!" someone hissed.

The team surged, breaking the fragile pace, they'd kept. Lights cut through the tunnel, illuminating damp walls and fractured stone. A breath behind the phantom always a breath too slow.

Lora broke into a run. Sam cursed under his breath and tore after her, shouting, "Lora, wait!"

Her voice echoed back, strangled with desperation: "I see him!"

The tunnel branched. Footprints streaked through the dust. Right turn. Sharp. Downward slope. The officers thundered after her, their weapons trembling in their hands.

They weren't alone down here. Every scuff of movement just beyond reach proved it.

Then a final stretch. The tunnel sloped upward, light bleeding faintly from ahead. The sound of branches swaying in the night.

They burst through the mouth of the tunnel, spilling out into the forest.

Moonlight. Wind in the trees.

But no one there.

No shadow. No figure.

Just the hollow silence of the woods.

The dogs barked in the distance, frantic, tugging their handlers toward a direction in the trees, but then stopped whimpering. Tails tucked. Heads low.

Sam's chest burned as he caught Lora by the shoulders, spinning her to face him. She was trembling, her eyes wild, locked on the tree line as though the killer still stood there, watching.

"He was here," she gasped, voice cracking. "I swear to you, Sam, he was right here."

Sam's stomach twisted. He believed her. And yet the forest gave nothing back but silence.

The forest held its silence like a secret, the kind that gnaws at the edges of sanity. Moonlight dripped between the trees, casting fractured silver across the clearing. The team stood there, breathing hard, weapons trembling just slightly in their hands.

Lora hadn't moved. Her body rigid, her eyes locked on the dark where the tunnel mouth had spat them out. She looked like a statue carved in fear and obsession.

He was here. He was here. I could feel him, like breath on my neck. Why didn't we catch him? Why does he always slip away?

Sam's grip was still on her shoulders, firm but trembling. His chest ached not just from the sprint, but from the weight of what he'd almost lost. *She doesn't even flinch. Goddamn it, Lora. What's it going to take for you to stop before this forest eats you alive?*

The bark of dogs shattered the stillness. Two handlers broke through the tree line, flashlights shaking in their fists.

"They went crazy," one said, voice pitched high with adrenaline. "Bolted straight east like something was pulling them. Then nothing.

Just stopped cold. Whimpering, tails down. It's like ... like whatever was there vanished."

The second handler nodded, still trying to calm a trembling shepherd at his side. "Never seen anything like it. It was there. I swear. And then it wasn't."

The words fell heavy, pressing on every chest in the clearing.

A few officers exchanged glances, pale-faced, muttering under their breath.

Vanished.

Disappeared.

Like a ghost.

Sam clenched his jaw. He wouldn't let fear fracture his people. Not here, not now. "Lock it down," he barked. "Perimeter sweep. Secure the tunnel. Nothing goes in or out until we decide the next step."

But even as he gave the order, his eyes strayed back to Lora motionless, her face hollow with something more than shock. She wasn't just processing what had happened; she was feeling it. Drawing something in from the forest that no one else could touch.

Sam stepped closer, lowering his voice so only she could hear. "Lora... we'll get him. But not tonight. You hear me?"

Her lips parted, but no words came. Just the faintest shiver, the smallest nod.

And still her eyes never left the dark.

Chapter Twenty

The precinct hummed like a hive when they returned, the hour doing nothing to dim the fluorescent sting or the frantic voices bouncing from wall to wall.

Maps sprawled across tables. Evidence bags piled high. A whiteboard thick with scribbled theories and strings of connection.

The Hollow was on everyone's lips. The failed chase. The vanished presence. The dogs going mad.

Sam's voice cut through the din as he debriefed with clipped precision. "He was there. We all heard him. We saw signs of movement. But he slipped us. Again. That's not a failure it's information. It means he's confident. It means he's watching us."

Reporters shouted from outside the glass walls of the briefing room. Phones rang off the hook. Officers traded whispers like the forest had seeped into their bones.

But at the far end of the room, Lora sat alone, hunched forward, eyes glassy.

The riddle lay in front of her.

The photos.

The symbols.

Her lips moved, barely audible. "Where's the first victim? Where are you hiding them?"

Her hands trembled, knuckles white around the edge of the table. It's not random. It's a pattern. I can feel him closing in. Or maybe it's me he wants to close in on.

Sam caught sight of her across the room and excused himself from the cluster of detectives. He crossed the distance, his chest heavy.

"Lora," he said softly. No response. He crouched down beside her, his voice gentler. "You, okay? Look at me."

She lifted her eyes to him; a flicker of exhaustion mixed with fire.

"I'll take you home in a bit," Sam murmured. "Stay with me. Rest. You've done enough tonight."

Her gaze lingered on him, fragile, as if tethered by something deeper than words. Finally, she gave the smallest nod.

Behind them, the task force kept working, voices rising as theories clashed. The chalk squeak of markers against the board, the slap of photos pinned down.

Every riddle dissected. Every footprint catalogued. Every shred of the underground mapped.

But Lora? She sat in silence, staring straight through the noise, the faint echo of the forest still lodged in her bones.

The precinct ran on caffeine, adrenaline, and the brittle edge of fear. Whiteboards glared beneath the fluorescent lights, thick with names, timelines, and crude sketches of the forest and the underground hollow. Photographs were pinned in crooked lines, each one a reminder of how far behind they were.

Detective Alvarez slapped a stack of files onto the evidence table. "We've got something on Victim Two. Name's Melissa Kane. Twenty-two. Student. Went missing six months ago. Family reported her last seen heading home from the university library. Cold case file until now."

A ripple went through the room. Six months. She had been there that long beneath their feet, forgotten in the dirt and stone.

Alvarez's voice dropped. "She was found in the second chamber. Matches the Polaroid we pulled. Same carvings on her skin." He didn't need to say the rest. Everyone knew.

Another detective, Carver, scribbled furiously on the board. "Meyers and Hall's notes confirm they'd been circling this area for weeks. Cross-referencing missing women from the last year. They thought they had a lead tying them to the woods. They were working off patterns' disappearances clustered near the old mill road."

"And Lora," Alvarez added, glancing at her before continuing. "Their notes kept referencing Matthews. Said she had 'a nose for the forest,' that she sensed something off long before we did."

A murmur spread through the task force. A mixture of respect. Fear. Confusion.

Sam stood at the head of the table, jaw tight. He could feel it their doubt, their unease about Lora. They're wondering if she's cracked. Or if she's the only one keeping us ahead of him. Maybe both.

He cut in, voice steady. "Meyers and Hall were onto something. They knew the forest wasn't just a dumping ground it was part of his ritual. That's why they were there. That's why they're dead. We follow their trail. But we don't lose ourselves in the process."

For a moment, silence. The weight of the names on the board pressed on everyone's shoulders.

Lora sat slightly apart, the hum of the room buzzing around her like static. She wasn't looking at the board. Not the photos. Not even the notes from Meyers and Hall that mentioned her by name.

Her gaze was distant, fixed on a crack in the floor tile. Melissa Kane. Rachel. Marcus. How many more? How many voices are buried beneath those trees, waiting for me to hear them? And why me?

Sam broke from the table, circling toward her. He crouched again, softer this time, as if afraid she'd shatter if he pressed too hard.

"Lora," he murmured, his voice low, just for her. "Talk to me. Where are you?"

Her eyes flicked to his, and for a second, he saw it the woman she used to be. Sharp. Brilliant. Whole. Then it slipped away again, replaced by the glassy intensity that had haunted her since Rachel.

"You can't hear it," she whispered. "But I can. The forest won't let me go."

Sam's chest tightened. Goddamn it, Lora. You're slipping further every night, and I don't know how to pull you back.

He reached for her hand beneath the table, closing his fingers gently over hers. She didn't pull away. But she didn't lean into him either. Just let the contact anchor her in silence.

Behind them, Alvarez's voice rose again. "So, the question is if Kane was Victim Two, and Meyers and Hall were silenced while digging, who the hell is Victim One? And why hasn't the killer shown us yet?"

The whiteboard marker squeaked as the number 1 was circled three times.

The whole room buzzed louder. Theories spun, files were thrown open, photos rearranged, connections redrawn.

But for Lora, the din was a blur. The voices of her colleagues were drowned out by the echo in her skull—the soft, familiar hum of the forest.

And for Sam, the case warred with something deeper. He tightened his grip on her hand, whispering so low no one else could hear:

"You're still here, Lora. With me. Don't let him take that from you."

She glanced at him, eyes burning with a mix of exhaustion and something unspoken. Fragile. Fierce. A tether stretched taut between them, the only thing keeping her from unravelling completely.

The hum of the precinct thickened into a roar as strategy collided with fear. Whiteboards were filled and erased, then filled again. Notes from Meyers and Hall were pored over until the paper grew soft from handling.

Detective Alvarez tapped the riddle scrawled in thick black ink across the board.

"'To find the one who never screamed, follow the hollow's breath.' That's the new message. What the hell does it mean?"

Carver leaned in, rubbing his temple. "The 'one who never screamed' that's Victim One. He's taunting us. He wants us to know she's still out there."

"Or that she was different," Alvarez countered. "Maybe she didn't fight. Maybe she wasn't afraid. Maybe that's why she's first."

"Or maybe," another detective muttered, "she's still alive."

The room fell into stunned silence at that thought. Even the buzzing lights above seemed to hush.

Sam broke the pause. His voice was steady, commanding. "Alive or dead, she's the key. The riddle says follow the hollow's breath. That means something in that chamber we haven't seen yet. Something hidden. We go back in daylight; with every resource we've got."

Carver scowled, frustration leaking through. "And if he's waiting for us again?"

"Then we'll be ready," Sam snapped.

A nervous chuckle came from the far corner. "Ready? He's been three steps ahead every time. We're following his trail, not the other way around."

That unease spread across the table like a sickness. Lora could feel it pressing into her chest. They don't see it. They don't feel what I feel. He's not just ahead he's around us. Watching. Listening.

Her voice was barely audible, but it sliced through the noise like glass.

"He wants me."

Heads turned. Silence slammed into the room.

Sam stiffened beside her. His throat tightened. Not now, Lora. Don't give them reason to doubt you.

Alvarez cleared his throat. "What do you mean?"

She didn't answer. She couldn't. If she spoke more, they'd see the truth that the forest lived inside her now, whispering through her veins. That she wasn't sure if she could separate herself from it anymore.

Sam stood sharply, drawing the attention back to himself. "Enough for tonight. Everyone, document everything every theory, every link. First thing tomorrow, we cross-reference missing persons files for any potential Victim One. We re-examine the chamber footage. And we prepare to return."

There were mutters of dissent, exhaustion in every sigh, but the detectives began gathering their papers, stacking files, pinning photos more neatly. The frenzy dulled into a weary shuffle.

One by one, the room cleared, until the background hum was nothing more than distant chatter and the buzz of the lights.

Sam stayed rooted near Lora. She hadn't moved. She sat there with her fingers pressed into the edge of the table, eyes unfocused, lips parted like she was still listening for something.

Goddamn it, Lora. You're breaking in front of me, and I don't know how to fix it. I never stopped loving you, and now I'm watching you slip further into his world with every step we take.

Finally, he reached out, gentle but firm, his hand covering hers.

"Come on," he said softly. "It's late. Let me take you home."

Lora's gaze lifted to him, slow, heavy, as if it took all her strength to pull her eyes from the shadows in her mind. She didn't speak. She just gave the smallest nod.

Sam helped her up, his hand never leaving hers, guiding her toward the door as the precinct behind them dimmed into silence.

The tether held fragile, fraying, but unbroken.

Chapter Twenty One

S am sat in the SUV, engine idling low, the blue glow of the dashboard lights painting his face in tired shadows. The precinct lot was nearly empty now, save for a few scattered vehicles belonging to night-shift stragglers. The hum of the city felt muted, as though even it had grown wary of the forest's whispers.

Through the windshield, he could see Lora standing a few feet away from the car. She was breathing in the night air, her shoulders lifting and falling with slow, deliberate effort. A single streetlight overhead caught the faint streak of tears on her cheek, though her face was set in stone.

Sam leaned back in the seat, shutting his eyes for a moment. The weight pressed down on him harder than any case ever had.

Goddamn it, Lora. I keep saying I'll protect you, but the truth is I can't. You keep running headfirst into the dark, and I can't hold you back forever. The forest has its hooks in you, and I don't know if it's the case that's going to kill you... or yourself. I lost you once to divorce. I can't lose you again to this madness.

His chest tightened with that old, familiar pain. *And still, I love you. God help me, I never stopped.*

Lora tilted her head back, staring at the faintest hint of dawn still miles away on the horizon. The cool air scraped her lungs, but it wasn't enough to shake the crawling sensation under her skin.

It was there tonight. *He was there. So close. Breathing just behind me. Why can't they feel it? Why can't they see?*

Her fingers dug into her coat pockets, nails biting through fabric. *Melissa Kane. Rachel. Marcus. The others. The first victim. The one who never screamed. Why can't I see her face? Why won't the visions show me the truth?*

A shudder ran through her. The precinct chatter was gone now, but the forest was still with her, whispering in the silence.

And beneath it all, another truth gnawed at her: *Sam. He still looks at me the way he used to. Like I'm his anchor. But what if I'm just dragging him into the hollow too?*

She swallowed hard, forcing her body to move, her boots scraping against the pavement as she walked back toward the SUV.

Sam straightened, watching her approach. For a moment, her silhouette against the harsh streetlight looked ghostly, almost too fragile to be real. Then she opened the passenger door and slid in without a word, her profile sharp in the shadows.

Neither spoke as he pulled out of the lot. The silence wasn't comfortable it was weighted, fragile, thick with everything unspoken between them.

Sam's hand brushed against hers on the console, tentative. She didn't move away.

The small house was cloaked in stillness when they arrived, the porch light casting a faint yellow circle across the steps. Sam killed the engine but didn't move. Lora sat there, staring at the door like it belonged to someone else.

Finally, she whispered, "You're coming in, right?"

Sam nodded without hesitation. "Yeah. I'm not letting you out of my sight tonight."

Inside, the house smelled faintly of coffee gone cold and paper—case files scattered across the table, reminders of her restless obsession. Sam gently set his hand at the small of her back as she moved through the doorway, steadying her as though afraid she might shatter from the weight of the night.

Lora glanced back at him, eyes rimmed red but shining with something raw. She opened her mouth, closed it, then whispered, "I still love you."

Sam froze, every breath catching in his chest. His voice broke when he answered, "I know. And I still love you too. That's why I'm trying to keep you off this case. I can't lose you, Lora. Not again."

Her lips trembled, but she shook her head. "We're so close."

He reached for her hand again, fingers lacing with hers. For a moment, the silence between them wasn't suffocating it was fragile, intimate, like they were standing on the edge of something neither dared name.

Sam didn't let go. Not this time.

The house was dark, save for the faint glow of a lamp Sam flicked on in the living room. It cast long, golden shadows across the clutter—open case files, scribbled notes, photographs of crime scenes spread like an unfinished puzzle. Lora's obsession hung in the air, thick as incense.

Sam helped her ease out of her coat, setting it across the back of a chair. For a moment, they just stood there in the hush, too close, both of them aching with things neither dared to speak.

Lora finally broke the silence, her voice raw. "Every time I close my eyes, I see them. Rachel. Marcus. Melissa. I don't know how to turn it off, Sam."

Sam's throat tightened. He reached out, brushing a strand of hair from her face with uncharacteristic tenderness. "Maybe you don't need to turn it off. Maybe you just need someone to hold onto while you go through it."

Her eyes glistened, fragile as glass. "And if it takes me under?"

"Then I'll go under with you," he said without hesitation. "I'll pull you back."

She stared at him, searching his face for a lie and finding none. A tear slipped down her cheek, but she didn't look away.

The weight of the night pressed them both into silence again. Sam gently guided her toward the couch, and when she sat, he lowered himself beside her, their shoulders touching. He slipped an arm around her carefully, like she might resist. She didn't. She leaned in, her head settling against his chest.

His heartbeat thudded steady beneath her ear, a fragile tether against the chaos in her mind.

Sam stared into the dim room, one hand rubbing slow circles along her arm. I shouldn't be here. I should be the professional. Her boss. But goddammit, I can't let her face this alone. I won't.

Lora's breathing slowed, but not evenly each inhale was jagged, restless, as if even in near-sleep the forest whispered through her.

Morning broke pale and reluctant, leaking through the blinds. Sam hadn't slept, though he'd drifted in and out of a foggy half-doze, still holding her against him. Lora stirred, eyes snapping open as though she had never truly rested.

The shrill ring of the phone shattered the fragile cocoon of their night.

Sam cursed under his breath, reaching across the table to answer. "Chief."

The voice on the other end was clipped, urgent. "We've got updates. You need to come in. The scans of the underground chamber came back. There's more down there tunnels branching further than we thought. And... we may have a match on potential Victim One."

Sam's eyes flicked to Lora. She was already sitting up, wide awake, her gaze sharp and haunted.

The voice continued: "Her name's Elena Ward. Reported missing nine months ago. Twenty-one years old. No signs of abduction, no evidence trail she just disappeared. Until now."

Sam's grip tightened on the receiver. "We'll be there."

He hung up, exhaling slowly. Lora was already pulling her coat from the chair, her hands trembling with urgency.

"I knew it," she whispered. "She's been waiting for us all along."

Sam stepped toward her, catching her wrist before she could move past him. His voice was low, urgent, almost pleading. "Lora, don't do this to yourself. Not yet. Not like this."

Her eyes burned into his. "I don't have a choice. He wants me to follow. And I will."

The fragile tether between them stretched, pulled taut by love, by fear, by obsession. Neither spoke again as they left the house together, the weight of Elena Ward and the hollow's unfinished story driving them back into the day.

Chapter Twenty Two

The precinct felt heavier than usual that morning, as though the walls themselves carried the weight of last night's failures. Lora and Sam stepped into the briefing room together, shoulders squared but spirits frayed. The task force was already gathered tired eyes, stacks of files, laptops glowing under the pale strip lights.

Detective Harris stood at the front, flipping through a folder. "The potential match came back. Elena Ward. Twenty-one. Missing for nine months. No evidence trail, no leads. But there's more." He glanced around the room, lowering his voice. "She was deeply involved in witchcraft. Journals, forums, small covens she was linked to. She was obsessed with ritual work."

The word ritual sent a hush across the room. Everyone's eyes flicked to Lora, who sat in silence, hands clenched, staring at the photograph pinned to the board. Elena's face was pale, framed by long dark hair, her eyes sharp with defiance.

Sam shifted his weight, jaw tight. "If she was in witchcraft, we need to widen our net. I want every name, every group she was tied to. See if any local covens or occult gatherings are still operating. Quietly. No spooking anyone until we know more."

The room murmured in agreement, agents jotting notes, the quiet hum of strategy slowly building.

Lora didn't move. She sat frozen, her gaze locked on Elena's picture as if the young woman might speak to her through the glossy paper. *She looks so alive. She looks like she knew what she was walking into. Why can't I hear her? Why can't I see what happened?*

Sam's eyes flicked toward her, his chest tightening at the hollow, distant look on her face. He wanted to reach across the table, pull her out of that trance but duty demanded restraint.

"Alright," he said firmly. "The scans showed multiple tunnels branching out from the hollow. Large spaces. Possibly ritual chambers. Possibly more cells." He hesitated before finishing, "We move at noon. Forensics is already prepping. Dogs are on standby. This time, we cover every inch."

The forest waited for them like a patient predator.

By midday, the clearing above the hollow was alive with movement. Officers set up a perimeter, radios crackling, weapons checked and re-checked. Two entry points had been secured the original fissure the team discovered, and another access further east.

Sam stood at the lip of the hollow, giving orders, while Lora hovered just behind him, her presence silent yet magnetic. She looked pale, her eyes fixed downward as though she could already see the darkness stretching below.

The first team descended slowly Sam, Lora, and several officers, flanked by forensic specialists carrying equipment. Their beams of light cut jagged paths along stone walls slick with damp. The air grew colder with every step, carrying the faint metallic tang of earth and something older, stranger.

Behind them, the low growl of trained dogs echoed in the tunnels, handlers straining to keep them calm. Their ears twitched at sounds no human could hear.

Above, the second unit held their ground, radios alive, weapons ready, watching the tree line with unease.

The deeper they went, the more the walls whispered with carved symbols, some smeared, some fresh, some half-forgotten. Lora's breath quickened as her fingers brushed along one a spiral coiled inside another spiral, the same she'd seen in her visions.

Her head throbbed.

Sam caught her hand before she lingered too long. His grip was steady, grounding. "Stay with me, Lora," he whispered.

The hollow swallowed them whole.

And ahead, the tunnels waited.

The deeper they pushed into the hollow, the more oppressive the air became. Every step down the stone-cut passage felt like peeling away layers of light, surrendering to something old, damp, and breathing in the dark.

The forensics team moved carefully, documenting walls scarred with strange markings. Some looked etched decades ago, their edges softened by time; others were sharp, raw, as if freshly carved. Chalk, bone, ash smeared symbols that seemed to ripple when caught by the beam of a flashlight.

The dogs grew restless the further they went. Their ears pinned back, growls low and constant, their bodies straining against their leashes. Handlers whispered commands, but even the best-trained animals could not shake the instinctive dread clawing at them.

Sam's hand brushed the cold wall, his other gripping the flashlight, every muscle taut. He kept glancing toward Lora, who moved in silence, her face pale as though she were walking deeper into herself rather than the earth.

The air thinned. A sound water dripping, echoing mimicked a pulse.

Then Lora stopped.

Her whole body went rigid, eyes wide. She raised a trembling hand as though she were listening to something no one else could hear.

"She's here," she whispered, her voice sharp in the stillness. "I can feel her."

Every head turned. The handlers froze, forensics stopped their quiet murmur of notes. The silence rushed in, filling the void around her.

Lora gasped suddenly, clutching her chest, staggering against the wall. Her breath hitched as if the air had been stolen from her lungs. Sam lunged forward, catching her before she collapsed, his voice tight with panic.

"Lora! Breathe, stay with me!"

She struggled, lips forming words that caught in her throat. Her hand darted toward her vest pocket, fumbling for something she didn't have. She motioned desperately shaking fingers mimicking writing.

"Give her a pen! Paper now!" Sam barked.

A forensic officer scrambled, thrusting a clipboard into her shaking hands.

Lora's fingers clawed across the page, unsteady but urgent. Letters formed jagged and raw.

SHE IS ALIVE!

The words hung in the stale air like a verdict.

The tunnel seemed to constrict, the shadows crowding closer. Every officer felt it the shift, the cold spike of dread that came not from bones or bodies but from possibility.

Sam's chest clenched as he looked down at the words. Panic clawed at him, warring with the urge to keep his team grounded. His hand pressed against Lora's back, his other gripping her wrist.

"Where, Lora?!" His voice cracked under the weight of desperation. "Where is she?"

Lora's eyes fluttered, unfocused, as if she were seeing through stone and earth, into another place entirely. Her lips moved, but no sound came out only the ragged sound of her breathing.

Sam turned to the team, his voice sharp, commanding. "Fan out. Now. Find her!"

The dogs snarled, suddenly pulling hard against their leashes, noses down, claws scratching at the dirt floor. Their handlers struggled to hold them, their howls echoing down the tunnels.

The hunt had shifted.

And for the first time since entering the hollow, the forest beneath the earth felt awake.

Sam's arms locked around her trembling frame, his flashlight clattering to the ground as he pulled her close.

"Lora, stay with me," he whispered, voice frayed with panic. He could feel the erratic rise and fall of her chest against him, the frantic tremors that wracked her body. Her skin was clammy, her breath shallow, her eyes darting as though she were seeing a thousand different places at once.

Her lips parted. A broken whisper slipped free:

"Sam... she's crying... I can hear her crying."

Sam's gut twisted. He pressed his forehead briefly against hers, his hand cupping the back of her neck, trying to tether her to something solid.

She's slipping into that place again. God, she's tearing herself apart.

"Lora, listen to me," he said, soft but fierce. "You're here. With me. Not in your head. Not in his. With me."

Her nails dug lightly into his sleeve, desperate, like she was trying to ground herself through his touch. For a flicker of a moment, her wild eyes locked with his, and he saw her — not the detective unravelling in visions, not the haunted woman caught in the killer's shadow — but Lora, the woman he still loved, fragile and unyielding all at once.

Around them, chaos roared.

The dogs barked wildly, their handlers barely keeping hold. Forensics shouted updates, officers scrambled, lights sliced through the cavern. The ground felt alive beneath them with the vibrations of boots and snarls.

But to Sam, all of it blurred. His world was narrowed to her.

"Sam…" Lora whispered again, her voice softer now, tears streaking her cheeks. "Don't let me go."

He tightened his grip, jaw clenched. "Never."

A sudden howl ripped through the chamber sharp, desperate. One of the dogs had broken free, charging into the darkness. Its handler bolted after it, cursing, while the rest of the team surged to follow. The barking echoed, then split into frantic yelps deeper in the tunnel.

"Sir! They've caught a scent!" one officer yelled back, his voice bouncing against stone.

Sam cursed under his breath. He wanted to chase, wanted to lead the hunt himself. But Lora's weight in his arms anchored him, the sound of her breath ragged against his ear pulling him in two directions.

He made his choice.

"Go!" he barked to the others. "Stay with the dogs! Don't lose them!"

The tunnel erupted with movement as boots pounded deeper, flashlights bobbing into the dark. The sound of commands and barks echoed until they blended into the rumbling earth itself.

Sam stayed behind, cradling Lora against the cold stone wall. His thumb brushed against the tear at her temple. His chest ached fear, love, helplessness folding into one unbearable weight.

She was whispering still. Faint, fragmented words he could barely catch.

"Chains... red rope... the girl is waiting..."

Sam swallowed hard, his voice low and trembling. "Hold on, Lora. Just hold on. I've got you."

The tunnel beyond them thundered with the chase. But in that moment, Sam knew: the real battle wasn't just with the killer. It was with the forest, the hollow, the visions eating at Lora from the inside.

And if he lost her here, he'd never forgive himself.

Sam eased her down to sit against the cold wall, crouching low so his eyes stayed level with hers. Her breath came in shallow gasps, but her gaze wild a moment ago now seemed caught on something invisible in the air between them.

Her pupils dilated, her lips trembling.

"Lora... talk to me," Sam urged, voice raw.

She blinked, slow, almost dreamlike, then raised her hand. It hovered in the air as if tracing lines no one else could see. Her finger moved in arcs and spirals, forming shapes against the stone.

"There's something here," she whispered. "Not... not in front of us. Behind."

Sam frowned, following her trembling hand to the bare stretch of rock wall behind them. Nothing but jagged stone, damp with condensation. But her stare didn't waver she was seeing something else entirely.

Her voice grew stronger, though ragged with strain:

"Candles... a circle... symbols painted in blood. Chains."

She winced, clutching her temple as if the vision itself pressed too hard into her skull.

Sam caught her hand, squeezing tight. "Lora, there's nothing there. You're safe. You're here with me."

But she shook her head fiercely. "You don't see it, Sam. You don't feel it. There's a chamber... right here. A hollow behind the wall. That's where she is."

Sam's stomach clenched. He wanted to dismiss it, to drag her out of this cursed place, but her conviction raw and desperate cut through his doubt.

Before he could press further, the echo of frantic barking tore down the tunnels.

The dogs.

The officers' shouts reverberated through the stone: "They've got something!"

Sam snapped his gaze toward the sound, torn between the chase and the trembling woman before him.

"Stay here," he whispered, brushing a strand of hair from her damp forehead. "Don't move, Lora. I'll be right back."

But she clutched his wrist, eyes burning. "Don't let them go too far without you. He's leading them... but not where she is."

Sam's chest tightened at the warning, but there was no time to argue. He pressed her hand to his heart for a moment, then stood, flashlight in hand, and bolted after the others.

The tunnel split into two narrow arteries, the sound of boots and barking bouncing between them. Sam followed the echoes, rounding the bend just as the lead handler was nearly dragged off his feet.

The dogs strained violently, claws scraping stone, muzzles pressed to the dirt. Then suddenly they began to dig.

The earth was loose, fresher than the packed floor around it. The handlers urged them back as officers dropped to their knees, clawing away chunks of soil with gloved hands.

A shout cut through the chaos:

"Chief! We've got something!"

Sam rushed forward.

From the shallow pit, the end of a red cord emerged stained, frayed. One officer pulled gently, and a scrap of torn fabric came free, damp with sweat and soil. A woman's blouse.

Sam's heart pounded as the dogs howled again, their voices echoing up through the stone like mourning bells.

Not a body. Not yet.

But a sign. A presence.

The girl was or had been here.

The fragment of fabric fluttered in the damp air like a fragile flag of despair. Sam's gut twisted. He wanted to order the team to dig deeper, to tear through the soil until they pulled someone free, but something in his chest warned him Lora.

He spun, flashlight beam cutting through dust and shadow, and sprinted back down the tunnel. His boots echoed sharp, fast, his lungs burning with a sudden fear heavier than the air.

When he rounded the bend, relief and terror struck him at once.

Lora was still there. Still sitting against the wall. But she wasn't just breathing ragged now—she was whispering. Rapid, broken syllables, as though in conversation with something that wasn't in the chamber with her.

"Chains... dark... the smell of blood... she's crying. So tired. She doesn't know how long it's been..."

Sam dropped to his knees, gripping her shoulders. "Lora! Look at me!"

Her eyes finally snapped to his, wild and wet. "Sam... it's Elena. It's Elena Ward."

His chest seized.

The missing girl. The second victim they had traced.

"She's alive," Lora rasped. Her fingers curled in his sleeve, desperate. "I can feel her. She's in the dark... waiting. She knows her name. She keeps whispering it to herself, so she won't forget. Elena. Elena Ward."

Sam's throat dried. For the first time, her vision wasn't some vague nightmare it had a name, a focus. A pulse of truth he could feel even though every logical bone in his body wanted to doubt it.

Before he could answer, a shout carried down the tunnel:

"Chief! We found more!"

Sam squeezed her hand once, then pushed himself up. "Stay with me, Lora. Don't move."

He ran back toward the dig site, his heart a hammer in his chest.

The officers had cleared more of the loose earth, and their gloves trembled as they pulled items into the flashlight beams.

Strands of hair, matted with dirt. Fingernails, broken, some streaked red at the edges. A small chain bracelet etched with initials: E.W.

Sam's vision blurred for a second, the reality crashing into him like a wave of ice. The dogs whined and pawed at the earth, but the handlers dragged them back, unwilling to risk contaminating the site further.

The chamber seemed to shudder under the weight of the discovery.

Not bones. Not a body.

Evidence of life. Struggle. Survival.

Sam clenched his jaw and forced his voice steady. "Bag everything. Mark it. Get photos. Now. This is Elena Ward. She's been here. She's still alive."

Behind him, the hollow exhaled, its stale air curling cold around his skin.

And Sam's thoughts, despite everything, snapped back to Lora her vision, her voice, her certainty.

She's tethered to this place... to Elena. And if I lose her down here, I lose them both.

The chamber was thick with the sound of voices officers muttering, forensics debating, handlers trying to keep the dog's calm. The air tasted of soil and iron, dust stirred from the frantic digging.

Sam tried to keep control of the noise, his orders cutting sharp through the tension: "We need to decide she could be deeper. We may be right on top of her. Secure what we've got, then"

A softer voice cut through him like a knife.

"She's here..."

Sam turned.

Lora was standing now, her face pale, her eyes distant but fixed on something just beyond the edge of their flashlights. She wasn't looking at the soil or the evidence. She was looking past it. Through it.

"Don't leave until we find her," she whispered, her voice trembling.

The officers went still, all eyes shifting to her. For a moment, no one spoke. The weight of her words, the certainty in them, landed heavier than orders ever could.

Then she gasped. Her body shuddered as though an icy hand had closed around her throat. Her knees buckled, but she caught herself against the wall, her eyes widening as if she were staring into another world.

Sam was at her side instantly. "Lora, what is it? What do you see?"

Her lips trembled, then parted. Her voice came out fragile, raw, "She's curled up on the floor... knees to her chest. It's so cold. She's crying, but she's trying not to make a sound. There's water dripping. I can smell... mildew. And rope. She's so small, Sam. She's right there."

Lora's hand lifted, shaking, and pointed toward the far wall. Her finger locked on a stretch of stone that seemed no different from the rest, but her expression carried no hesitation.

Sam's breath caught. God help me, I believe her.

"Sam..." Her eyes found his, glistening. "Go get her."

For a heartbeat, the tunnel was silent only the sound of the dripping water filling the void. The officers shifted uneasily, waiting for Sam's call.

Sam swallowed, his hand brushing along the wall where Lora pointed. Cold, damp stone pressed against his glove. He turned back to his team, voice steady though his chest ached with doubt and urgency.

"Get the ground-penetrating scanner back here. Now. Focus it on this wall. If there's a chamber if she's in there we'll find it."

Forensics scrambled, hauling equipment over, the dogs barking wildly as though they sensed something alive beyond the stone.

Sam stayed beside Lora, his hand still gripping hers, his voice a low murmur meant only for her: "If you're right, we'll bring her out. If you're right, Lora... we'll save her."

And though the dread pressed heavier with every passing second, he couldn't deny the flicker in his chest hope, burning sharp and painful in the dark.

The scanner hummed to life, its high-pitched whine bouncing through the tunnel as the forensic tech pressed it flush against the damp wall. The machine's green readout flickered, jagged lines mapping density and voids behind the stone.

Everyone crowded close, breaths held, as the screen jittered and stabilized.

"There's... something," the tech muttered, his brow furrowed. "Looks like an empty cavity about six feet back. Roughly circular. But...." He hesitated, adjusting the calibration. "No clear movement. No definitive thermal signature."

Sam's heart sank. "So, you're saying you don't know if anyone's inside."

The tech's lips tightened. "Exactly, sir. Could just be an abandoned chamber. Could be nothing."

A ripple of unease swept through the officers. The weight of indecision pressed into the chamber like a second ceiling.

Then Lora stepped forward.

Her eyes were glassy, her skin pale as bone, but her voice though quiet cut sharp through the tension.

"She's in there."

Everyone turned.

Lora pressed her palm against the stone as though it were a window instead of a wall. Her body trembled, but her voice carried absolute conviction, "She's alive. Curled up on the floor. I can feel her. Hear her. Don't waste time debating she's right here."

Sam's chest clenched. His gaze swept from the uncertain scanner to the nervous faces of his team, to the woman whose hand trembled against the wall but whose eyes burned with something unshakable.

He heard his own voice before he could stop it, "Break through the wall."

The officers stared, stunned. "Chief, with respect the data doesn't confirm."

"That wasn't a suggestion," Sam snapped, fire in his voice, "Get it down. Now."

Tools came out fast portable jackhammers, crowbars, heavy mallets. The tunnel roared with the deafening clang of steel on stone. Chips of rock scattered, dust filling the air in choking clouds.

Lora staggered back, covering her mouth with her sleeve, but she didn't look away. Her eyes were locked on the wall, unblinking, as though she were waiting for it to bleed.

Minutes stretched like hours. Then...

A crack. A fissure snaked across the wall, spreading with every blow until the stone gave way with a low groan.

And behind its darkness.

A flashlight beam pierced the gap, sweeping inside. What it revealed turned the tunnel silent.

A small chamber. Cramped, damp, the floor slick with mildew. Chains bolted to the stone. And there, in the corner, a frail figure curled in on herself, knees drawn tight to her chest.

Her hair matted. Her body shivering. Her eyes flinched shut against the sudden light.

"Elena..." Lora whispered, tears streaming unchecked down her cheeks.

The girl's head lifted weakly, her lips parting in a cracked, breathless murmur. "Help me..."

Chaos erupted. Officers surged forward, voices sharp with commands as medics pushed through. The chains clattered, the girl's body flinching at every sound.

Sam's chest heaved, relief and horror colliding. He turned to Lora who was trembling, her hands clasped over her mouth, her eyes wide not with victory, but with the unbearable weight of being right.

And in that moment, Sam knew whatever tether bound her to this killer, to these victims, it was only tightening.

The precinct hummed with electric tension. Relief hung in the air, Elena Ward was alive, rescued from the shadows of the hollow but beneath it pulsed something darker. A reminder: the killer was still free, and victim number one was still missing.

Detectives and analysts filled the briefing room, voices colliding as updates came in. Forensics reported on the chamber chains, ritual symbols, offerings burned black with soot. Nothing that directly identified the killer. Just another room in his labyrinth of horrors.

Sam stood at the head of the table, jaw tight, every muscle strung taut. The team's notes on the riddle sprawled across the whiteboard, arrows linking connections, scribbles highlighting dead ends.

But the rescue had shifted the energy. This was no longer theory they had a living girl who had seen the inside of the hollow.

Lora sat in the corner, distant, her gaze locked on a photograph of Elena taken during her disappearance months ago. A vibrant young woman with dark, curious eyes, caught forever in that last image of freedom.

Her mind was restless, spiraling, reaching for threads only she could feel.

I need to talk to her, she thought, her hand tightening around the armrest of her chair. I need to hear what she saw. What he told her. Maybe then I'll understand why... why me.

Sam's voice broke through the haze. "We've bought her time. But he's still out there. And we can't underestimate him he let this happen for a reason. Elena's rescue wasn't his mistake. It was part of his plan."

The room fell silent, the weight of his words pressing down like stone.

Across the table, Lora finally looked up, her eyes locking with Sam's. Her lips parted slightly, as though she were about to speak, but the words never came. Instead, all she felt was the tightening coil inside her, pulling her toward Elena, toward the answers she hoped the girl could give her.

Toward the killer, who still held the first victim in the dark.

Chapter Twenty Three

The precinct was alive with a brittle kind of energy, the kind that follows both triumph and dread. They had saved Elena Ward, pulled her from the suffocating dark but no one could ignore the fact that her survival felt too neat, too deliberate.

Sam stood at the head of the briefing room, his voice steady though his chest ached with the gravity of his own words, "Elena is under twenty-four-hour watch," he said firmly. "Uniforms outside her hospital room, two at all times. And I want a female officer inside with her. She does not get left alone not for a second. If the killer has gone this far to keep her alive, he may try to take her back."

The room murmured in agreement, though it was the kind of agreement born of fear, not confidence. Everyone understood the risk. Everyone imagined what it would mean if the killer managed to slip past them.

Lora sat still in her chair, eyes lowered to the notes spread in front of her. Her hands rested on the edges of the paper, but her grip was so tight the pages crumpled beneath her fingers.

He wanted us to find her, she thought, her chest tight, her breath uneven. That's why she's alive. He could have killed her long ago. He didn't. Why?

Around the table, the team shifted uneasily, each officer caught in their own loop of unease.

Detective Ramos leaned forward, his brow furrowed. He left us breadcrumbs, but why? To test us? To mock us? If Elena was bait, what's the hook?

Officer Greene scribbled notes in the margin of the riddle, his pen trembling slightly. This is bigger than ritual. This is psychology. He wants control, and we're dancing to his tune.

Forensics Chief Monroe rubbed her temple, exhaustion carving deep lines into her face. Candles, chains, symbols, cells... this isn't just holding captives. This is theatre. He's staging something for us, and we still don't know the final act.

And Sam, Sam only looked at Lora.

His jaw tightened as he watched her, the woman he had once known so well unravelling before his eyes. He had loved her, still loved her, and yet he couldn't shake the gnawing fear that this case was consuming her piece by piece.

She's too close. Too tied into this. I'm losing her to the forest, to him. And I don't know how to stop it without breaking her.

Lora finally raised her gaze to the board covered in riddles and scribbles. Her voice came soft, but certain, "He kept her alive for us to find. He wanted this. But why?"

Her words cut through the noise. The team fell silent, every head turning to her, though no one dared to answer.

Sam's chest tightened. He wanted to pull her away, take her far from this madness. But at the same time, he knew she was right. Lora could see things the others couldn't.

"Tomorrow," Sam said at last, his voice gravel edged. "You'll get your time with Elena tomorrow. She needs to stabilize. And you need rest."

Lora's lips parted as if to protest, but no words came. Instead, she only nodded faintly, her gaze unfocused, already sinking deeper into the storm of questions clawing at her.

The team began to disperse, files tucked under arms, quiet voices trailing into the hallways. The hum of printers, the shuffle of papers, the faint buzz of fluorescent lights it all became a distant backdrop.

For Lora and Sam, silence pressed close, fragile and suffocating. Both too afraid to name what lingered between them: fear, love, obsession, and the killer's shadow, watching from somewhere unseen.

Tomorrow would bring answers or more torment.

The precinct wound down into its midnight hush. Files closed, chairs scraped, the last echoes of discussion faded. Sam dismissed the team with firm orders, but his eyes never left Lora. She lingered behind, still staring at the board, at Elena's photograph.

She was so close to being gone forever, Lora thought, her stomach knotted. If I hadn't... if I didn't see... she'd still be trapped in the dark. Just like the others.

Sam moved closer, lowering his voice, "Come on, Lora. Let's go."

She didn't argue, but the silence between them on the ride back was brittle, filled with unspoken words neither dared to break.

When they finally reached her house, Sam followed her inside, refusing to leave her. Neither of them acknowledged the intimacy of it, it was no longer a choice. He simply stayed, and she let him.

The night swallowed them in uneasy quiet.

Lora drifted into sleep like someone slipping beneath black water heavy, reluctant, drowning in the pull of exhaustion.

The dream came fast.

She was in the forest, the ground wet beneath her palms as she stumbled forward, breath ragged. The trees bent in unnatural ways, their shadows twisting into clawed hands. Behind her came footsteps. Slow, deliberate.

A whisper rode the night air.

Lora.

She turned, and in the dream, she saw herself not Rachel, not Elena, herself, falling. A scream cut through the dark, her scream. And then cold hands wrapped around her throat.

The killer's voice hissed against her ear, "You should be dead."

Lora jolted awake, a raw scream tearing from her throat. Her whole body trembled as though caught in a storm, sweat plastering her hair to her face.

Sam was there instantly, gripping her shoulders, pulling her into his chest. "Lora! Lora, it's me it's Sam. You're safe. You're safe."

But she was trembling too violently to hear, her breath jagged sobs against his shirt. His arms locked around her, steady, grounding, his heart hammering almost as fast as hers.

Goddamn it, he thought, fear slicing through his chest. He's breaking her. He's getting inside her head. I can't lose her. Not to him. Not again.

When her breathing finally steadied, Sam brushed damp hair from her face and searched her eyes.

"What did you see? Talk to me, Lora."

Her gaze flickered away, haunted and far. "I don't want to talk about it."

"Lora..."

"Please, Sam," she whispered, closing her eyes. "Not now."

Sam swallowed back the urge to push. He only pulled her tighter against him, silently vowing to hold her together even if it cost him everything.

Chapter Twenty Four

Morning came too soon. The call from the precinct was short and clipped Elena Ward was stabilized, and Lora's access was granted.

Sam drove them to the hospital in silence, his eyes flicking toward her every few seconds. She sat rigid in the passenger seat, staring out the window, her fingers drumming a silent rhythm against her thigh.

She's carrying too much weight, Sam thought, his chest aching as he watched her. She won't let it out. She never did. That's what broke us before. And here I am, letting it happen again, because I need her too much to pull her off this case.

At the hospital, security was tight. Uniformed officers flanked the hall, their presence as much for show as for protection. Sam's orders had been carried out to the letter.

Lora paused at the door. Through the small glass pane, she saw Elena pale, frail, sitting up in the hospital bed. A female officer sat nearby, alert. The sight twisted something sharp inside Lora's chest.

She looks broken... but alive. Alive because of me. And yet he let her live. Why? What am I not seeing?

Sam's hand touched her shoulder gently. She turned to him, her face drawn but resolute.

"Ready?" he asked softly.

Lora nodded, though her throat was dry. Her pulse thudded in her ears.

This is it, she thought. The answers are in her eyes. I have to know what she saw. I have to know why he kept her alive.

Sam stepped back, letting her move first. And as she reached for the door handle, his heart squeezed tight.

Please, Lora, he thought, his chest heavy with fear and love. Don't lose yourself in her reflection. Don't let him take you too.

The door opened, and Lora stepped inside.

The door closed softly behind Lora. For a moment, she simply stood there, the hush of the room pressing in around her. Machines hummed faintly, a slow IV drip ticked out its rhythm, and beyond it all came the fragile sound of Elena's breath.

Elena Ward sat upright in the hospital bed, her thin shoulders trembling slightly as if even the weight of her own body was too much. Her skin was pale, almost translucent in the sterile light. The female officer on watch straightened when Lora entered but didn't move, simply nodding with quiet acknowledgment.

Lora's shoes whispered against the linoleum as she moved closer. She didn't speak not yet. Her eyes searched Elena, memorizing every fragile detail, every scar of her captivity.

Then Elena looked up.

Her gaze met Lora's and froze.

For a beat too long, silence sat heavy in the room. Elena's lips parted, her eyes widening, her breath catching as though she'd just seen a ghost.

Lora's throat tightened. "Elena," she said softly, cautiously, as though the girl might shatter if her voice was too sharp.

Elena flinched, her hands tightening on the thin hospital blanket. She shook her head faintly. "No..." she whispered. "Not you."

The words cut through Lora like ice. She took a step closer, confusion flickering behind her calm exterior, "It's me. Detective Lora Matthews. I'm here to help you."

But Elena only stared harder, her body tense, her eyes filled with something between recognition and terror, "I know who you are," she whispered. "I saw you."

Lora blinked, her heart stumbling. She saw me. In what way? How?

Elena's voice was hoarse, broken from days of silence and pain. "In the dark... he told me your name. He said you'd come. He showed me." Her voice cracked, breaking apart on the weight of memory.

Lora felt the air in her lungs turn heavy. She moved closer, lowering herself into the chair beside the bed. "Elena," she murmured, steady but aching, "what did he show you?"

Elena's eyes darted to the corners of the room as though afraid he might be listening even here. She leaned forward slightly, her voice barely a breath, "Your face. Not like you are now. Broken. Hurt. Like me. He said you were his. That you'd remember."

The words rippled through Lora's chest, each syllable a blade. She swallowed hard, keeping her expression calm though her mind reeled.

He's using me. He's weaving me into this story. But why does she see me? Why does she freeze when she looks at me?

Sam's presence beyond the glass weighed on her, she could feel his eyes on her back. If she faltered, he would see it. If she broke, he would know.

So, she steadied herself, forcing her voice to remain calm. "Elena, you're safe now. We won't let him hurt you again. But I need to know what you remember. Anything. Where he kept you. What he said. Anything about him."

Elena shivered, her gaze flicking down to her trembling hands. She spoke slowly, haltingly, as though dredging words from a place she'd buried deep, "There were... sounds. Chains. Candles burning. He prayed. Not to God. To something else. And he kept saying, 'the first will lead to the last.'"

Lora's heart clenched. The riddle again. Always the riddle.

Elena's eyes found hers again, sharp with an intensity that belied her fragile state. "He's not finished. You know that don't you?"

Lora's hand, resting on the arm of the chair, tightened into a fist. She forced herself to nod, "I know."

Elena swallowed, her voice trembling as she whispered, "Then you have to be careful. Because it's not me he wants. It's you."

The words hung in the room like a curse.

Behind the glass, Sam's chest tightened as he watched. He couldn't hear every word, but he saw Lora's face the flicker in her eyes, the way her shoulders hunched as though the weight of Elena's words pressed too heavy on her.

He's closing in on her, Sam thought, his hand gripping the frame of the window until his knuckles turned white. This isn't just an investigation anymore. It's personal. And it's killing her piece by piece.

Inside, Lora leaned closer to Elena, her voice barely a whisper now, almost a promise.

"Tell me everything he told you about me."

Elena's voice shook as though every word cost her strength. She gripped the blanket in both hands, her knuckles pale.

"He talked about you all the time," she whispered. "Not me. Not Rachel. Not Marcus. You. He said... you were the only one who could hear him. That you'd been chosen long before any of us. That the forest already knows you."

Lora's breath caught in her chest. Her fingers dug into the arm of the chair, nails biting against the wood. Chosen? Long before? The words tangled with her own visions, her own dreams.

"What else did he say about me, Elena?"

Elena's eyes darted upward, finding Lora's. For a moment, fear flared there, but also something else. Recognition.

"He said you'd remember." She paused, her voice thinning, almost breaking. "That when the time came, you wouldn't fight him. That you'd walk into the dark because it's where you belong."

Lora's heart thudded in her ears. A cold weight spread through her chest, wrapping tight around her ribs.

Remember what? Why me?

"Elena..." Her voice cracked. She leaned closer, desperate now. "Did you see his face? Anything about him?"

Elena shook her head, trembling. "Always shadows. Always masks. But his voice...." She shivered violently. "Low. Whispering. Like he was everywhere. Inside the walls. Inside my head."

Her eyes filled with tears then, her voice breaking to a rasp. "And he said... when he was finished with me, you would take my place."

The air left Lora's lungs in a rush. She stared at Elena, the words stabbing straight through her resolve.

Behind the glass, Sam could see it—the way her shoulders sagged, the tremor in her hand. He couldn't hear the words, but he knew their weight. Knew what they were doing to her.

He pushed through the door, his face set in grim lines. "That's enough."

Lora turned sharply, her eyes blazing. "No! I need more!"

Sam's hand came down on her shoulder, steady, firm. He lowered his head close to hers, his voice low but commanding, "You've had enough, Lora. Look at you. You're shaking."

Only then did she realize her hands trembled in her lap, her knuckles bloodless. Her throat tightened, but still she resisted, her voice a whisper of desperation. "She knows things, Sam. I can't stop now."

Sam's hand tightened, not in anger, but in protection. "Yes, you can. I'm pulling you out." His eyes softened, just enough for her to feel the break beneath his steel. "I won't watch him destroy you too."

Lora's lips parted, but the words withered in her throat. The fight drained from her, leaving only exhaustion and that familiar hollow ache.

She glanced back at Elena. The girl had turned her face away, tears slipping silently down her cheeks, her body trembling as though her memories were still a cage.

She survived. But at what cost? And why me? Why am I in his story?

Sam guided Lora to her feet, steadying her when her knees threatened to buckle. His hand remained at her back as he led her from the room, his jaw tight, his heart heavy.

Behind them, Elena whispered into the quiet, too soft for anyone to hear, "He's waiting for you."

The door to Elena's room clicked shut behind them, cutting off the sterile hum of machines and the fragile sound of the survivor's tears. The hallway outside was quieter, but no less heavy. Officers stationed along the wall avoided looking too long at Lora, her face was pale, drained of colour, her steps uncertain as though her legs no longer trusted the ground beneath them.

Sam kept a hand hovering at her back, close but not pressing, guiding her as much as supporting her. He studied her profile: the set of her jaw, the blankness in her eyes, the tremor in her lips she tried to hide.

"You're white as a sheet," Sam murmured, his voice low so only she could hear. "You need to sit."

Lora shook her head faintly, eyes locked on the floor ahead. "I'm fine."

But her voice was thin, unconvincing.

Sam clenched his teeth, fighting back the swell of fear and anger in his chest. *She's not fine. She's unravelling, and I can't stop it. Goddamn it, why does he have to use her like this?*

They moved down the hall in silence until the waiting SUV swallowed them up. The ride back to the precinct was hollow, each of them lost in Elena's words *you'd remember... you'd walk into the dark... he's waiting for you.*

The precinct briefing room was crowded when they arrived, the team already gathered, files spread across the table, notes scrawled in frantic hands. A hush fell as Lora entered, her pale face drawing every gaze. She ignored them, sliding into her chair, eyes on the notes but mind still trapped in Elena's whisper.

Sam stepped forward, his voice sharp, commanding, trying to force the room into order.

"Ward says he spoke about Lora. He made it personal. He's been weaving her into this since the start. That means he's taunting us, or he's planning something bigger."

The team muttered, exchanging uneasy glances.

Detective Ramos rubbed his jaw. "Taunting, yes, but deliberate. If he wanted her dead, he'd have taken his chance by now. Keeping Elena alive... keeping Lora tethered... it's all part of something staged."

"Forensics confirmed the ritual site markings tie into obscure occult practices," Monroe added, flipping through her folder. "It's not just theatre it's structure. Cycles. First to last. And Lora, he's written you into that cycle."

Lora's head lifted at that, her lips parting as if to speak, then her phone buzzed.

The sound cut through the room like a gunshot.

She fumbled it from her jacket pocket, her stomach sinking when she saw the screen. Withheld number.

Her heart kicked hard against her ribs. "It's him."

The room shifted, officers half-rising, tension sparking like static.

Sam's eyes locked onto hers, steady, urgent. He signalled quickly to Officer Greene at the corner. "Trace. Now."

Greene scrambled into action, pulling cables, setting up the trace.

Sam's hand came down gently on the phone before Lora could swipe to answer. His palm was warm, firm, grounding her. He leaned close, his voice low but steady, meant only for her.

"Take a deep breath. Keep him on the line as long as you can. We'll track him."

Lora's eyes flicked up to his. For a moment, their faces were close enough she could see the worry etched into the lines at the corner of his eyes. She nodded once, shallow but certain.

Sam slowly lifted his hand from the phone. "Answer it, Lora."

She did.

"Hello?" Her voice was tight, but it didn't break.

And then the line crackled, and that familiar, chilling whisper slithered through the room:

"Lora... you're right where I want you."

The air in the briefing room was suffocating as the line came alive with that whisper, slick and deliberate, a voice that slid under the skin.

"Lora…" the killer drawled, the syllables curling like smoke. "You're supposed to be dead."

Every eye in the room snapped toward her, but Sam's gaze never wavered, he was locked on her face, watching the flicker of fear she tried to bury. His fists clenched at his sides.

The killer's voice pressed on, almost amused, "You still haven't found number one. You wander the forest like a lost child, chasing shadows, but the first piece… the first sacrifice… still waits. Do you hear her, Lora? Do you see her when you close your eyes?"

Lora swallowed hard, gripping the phone so tightly her knuckles whitened. Her voice shook but held. "Why me? Why are you doing this?"

A low chuckle spilled into the line, hollow and cruel. "Because your spirit is strong. Stronger than the rest. You were meant to break, but you didn't. And that makes you mine. Every step you take is where I place you. Every vision… every whisper in the dark… that's me, guiding you."

Sam's heart thudded in his chest as he listened, rage boiling beneath the surface. He kept his eyes on her, her trembling shoulders, her pale lips and signalled sharply to Greene. Faster. Get me a location.

On the other end, the voice slithered lower, taunting, "You will lead them all to me. And when you finally stand before number one, you'll understand. This was always your story, Lora. Not theirs."

"Trace is close," Greene hissed, fingers flying over the keys. "We almost have him."

Lora's eyes darted across the room, as if the walls themselves were closing in. Her breath hitched, and she forced herself to speak. "You're not going to win. We'll find you."

The laugh that answered her was soft, like a lullaby twisted into something vile, "Oh, my dear resilient one. You've already lost. You just haven't seen it yet."

And then click. The line went dead.

"Damn it!" Greene slammed the desk. "We almost had the ping lost it by seconds!"

The phone slipped from Lora's hand, clattering onto the table as her face dropped into her palms. The room blurred around her, swallowed by a sudden surge of visions herself, running through the forest, branches clawing at her arms, her breath sharp and ragged as something chased her just out of sight.

She gasped, choking on the phantom air of the vision, trembling as if she'd lived it.

"Lora!"

Sam was on her in an instant, pulling her up and into his arms before she could fall apart completely. He wrapped himself around her, holding tight, anchoring her against his chest. His voice was urgent but soft, whispering against her hair.

"You did good, Lora. You did good." He pressed his cheek to the top of her head, his hand rubbing her back as if to soothe the tremors coursing through her. "Come on. I'll take you home to rest. That's enough for tonight."

Around them, the team stood frozen, caught between frustration at the lost trace and awe at the toll this was taking. But Sam didn't look at them his focus was only on her, fragile in his arms, her breaths shallow but slowly evening out under his hold. He guided her gently toward the door, never letting go.

Chapter Twenty Five

T he precinct was heavy with silence after the call, the kind that thickened the air and made every sound every chair creak, every pen scratch feel too loud. The team sat scattered around the briefing table, faces shadowed with exhaustion and unease.

Greene rubbed his temples, muttering under his breath. "We were seconds away. Seconds." The words came out bitter, like he couldn't forgive himself for failing. His mind spun through the data again, hunting for the missing thread, the fraction of a second where the killer slipped through their grasp.

Harris leaned forward, hands clasped tight, voice low. "He keeps circling back to number one. He's not taunting for fun there's something there. It's either his pride... or his anchor. Either way, we can't underestimate it."

Across the table, Detective Ng stared at the whiteboard where fragments of the riddles were pinned up. Her inner voice gnawed at her: We're chasing a ghost. He's always a step ahead. But why keep her alive? Why keep any of them alive? Unless... unless she means something more to him.

The question none of them wanted to speak aloud lingered: What if number one isn't dead?

Still, the words hung, unspoken but understood.

Greene finally broke the silence. "He said it's her story. Lora's. Which means he's not just targeting victims randomly, this is personal. He's writing her into it."

The mood in the room shifted, unease sharpening into dread. They all thought it, none dared say it. Was Lora the reason for all of this?

Sam kept one hand on the wheel, the other resting lightly over Lora's. The drive was wordless, but it wasn't empty. The car hummed in the night, headlights slicing through the darkness, the silence between them a fragile cocoon.

He stole glances at her, her profile against the passing blur of streetlights, her pale skin still damp from tears, her eyes staring out the window but seeing something far away. His chest ached at the sight of her, and the words he wanted to say pressed heavy in his throat.

She's breaking, piece by piece, he thought. And I don't know how to hold her together without breaking myself.

Lora's hand shifted slightly beneath his. Her inner voice whispered in echoes: Number one. Who is she? Why can't I see her? Why does he keep her hidden? The killer's words wrapped around her mind, digging deep. But beneath the obsession, softer thoughts rose too, fragile and raw. Sam's hand is warm. Steady. I still love him. God, I still love him.

When they pulled up to her house, Sam killed the engine but didn't move. He turned to her, searching her eyes in the dim glow. "You don't have to say anything," he murmured, voice rough. "Just... let me stay tonight. Please."

For a moment she said nothing, only nodded once, as though she didn't have the strength to refuse.

Sam exhaled, relief mixing with fear, and squeezed her hand gently before stepping out. He rounded the SUV, opened her door, and offered his hand. She took it. Fragile, trembling, but she took it.

Together, they walked up to her door, fragile intimacy binding them closer than words could.

At the precinct, the air still thrummed with unease. Greene stood at the board, marker in hand, circling the phrase that had knifed through them all: "You still haven't found Number One."

He turned to the room. "If Elena was two... then Number One has to be someone taken earlier. Someone whose disappearance slipped through the cracks. We've got to cross-reference every missing woman from the past three years, especially anyone with connections to Lora—or to us."

Detective Ng frowned, pen tapping against her notepad. "Or..." She hesitated, then pushed the words out. "Or maybe Number One wasn't reported missing at all."

The thought chilled the room. A victim no one was even looking for.

Harris leaned forward, voice low but edged. "Then why keep Elena alive? Why keep anyone? He wanted her found. He's... curating this. Stage by stage."

The team exchanged uneasy glances. None of them wanted to say it out loud, but all of them thought it: the killer wasn't just playing with them, he was playing with her. With Lora.

Greene capped the marker with a sharp click. "Number One is the key. Whoever she is, she's the root. The start of this story he's writing. And until we find her, we're in the dark."

The key slid into the lock, and the door gave way with a soft click. The house was quiet, too quiet, the kind of stillness that pressed on the chest. Sam stayed close to Lora as they stepped inside, his hand never quite leaving hers.

She dropped her jacket onto the chair by habit, though her movements felt sluggish, like she was walking through water. Her eyes drifted over the dimly lit room, but her mind was still in the tunnels, still with the voices and the riddles and the unseen weight of Number One.

Sam closed the door behind them and locked it, a small but deliberate act of protection. He turned back, watching her silhouette in the living room's half-light. "You're shaking," he said softly.

Lora blinked, as if realizing it herself. Her hands trembled faintly, though she tried to still them. "I can't... turn it off," she whispered. "The forest, the visions, his voice it's still in me."

Sam stepped forward, closing the space between them. His hand lifted, hesitating for just a breath, then brushed a strand of hair from her face. "Then let me carry it with you," he murmured.

Her eyes met his, fragile and raw, and for a heartbeat the years between them seemed to fall away the divorce, the distance, the wounds left behind. What remained was the tether that had never broken, no matter how much they'd tried.

Lora's lips parted, as if to speak, but the words faltered. Instead, she leaned forward, resting her forehead against his chest. Sam's arms closed around her instantly, holding her as though she might slip away if he didn't.

Neither spoke. The silence wasn't empty this time it was full, heavy with everything they couldn't yet say.

The house lay in a hushed stillness, broken only by the faint hum of the refrigerator and the occasional tick of the old wall clock. Sam settled into the armchair across from the couch where Lora sat, but his eyes never left her. She looked as though the weight of the world pressed on her shoulders, every muscle tense, every thought tearing her inward.

"You should try to rest," he said softly.

Her head turned toward him, eyes heavy but stubborn. "If I close my eyes, Sam... I'll see it again."

He rose, came closer, crouched in front of her. His hands rested gently on her knees, grounding her. "Then I'll be here when you wake. You don't have to face it alone."

Something in her finally yielded. She let herself lean back against the couch cushions, the exhaustion of days years, really slipping through her defence's. Sam draped a blanket over her shoulders, sat beside her, and without thinking twice, let her rest against him.

Her head found his chest, the rise and fall of his breath slow and steady. She murmured, half in a dream, "Don't let go."

"I won't," Sam whispered, tightening his arm around her.

The minutes stretched. Outside, the night deepened, and inside, fragile intimacy wrapped around them both like the blanket. Lora's body finally loosened, surrendering to a restless, uneasy sleep. Her breath hitched at times, small tremors running through her as though nightmares still hunted her in the dark. Each time, Sam smoothed a hand down her arm, murmuring quiet reassurances she might never remember hearing.

In the silence, his own thoughts surfaced, sharp and unrelenting. God, Lora. How many pieces of yourself will you give before you break? He closed his eyes, forehead leaning against her hair. And why, after all this time, do I still love you like this?

He stayed awake long into the night, watching over her.

The grey wash of dawn crept through the blinds, painting faint lines of light across the room. Lora stirred first, shifting against him. Sam's body ached from staying in one position all night, but he didn't regret it for a second.

Her eyes opened, foggy with sleep. She blinked up at him, disoriented. "You stayed."

"I told you I would," he said simply.

Before she could reply, the sharp buzz of his phone shattered the fragile calm. Sam glanced at the screen Precinct. His stomach tightened.

He answered, his voice clipped. "Chief Matthews."

Lora sat up quickly, alert despite the fatigue, watching him.

On the other end, Greene's voice came through, tight and urgent. "We've got something. Possible ID on Number One. You'd better get down here."

Sam's eyes flicked to Lora's. He could already see the fire sparking back in her, exhaustion overridden by obsession.

He ended the call, exhaling slowly. "They've got a lead on Number One."

Lora swung her legs off the couch, already reaching for her jacket. "Then we go."

Sam hesitated, watching her pale, tired, still fragile but unshakably determined. He muttered under his breath, "Goddammit, Lora," then grabbed his keys.

Together, they stepped into the morning light, toward the precinct, toward Number One.

The drive to the precinct was quiet, but not in the way silence normally fell between two people. This silence was a living thing, pressed tight between them, heavy with the weight of all that was unsaid.

Sam's hands gripped the steering wheel too tightly. He glanced at Lora from the corner of his eye her profile rigid, lips pressed thin, gaze locked on the blur of the world rushing by outside the window.

He wanted to tell her to rest. To tell her he'd shield her from whatever was waiting at the precinct. To tell her that he still loved her, that he had never stopped. But the words lodged in his throat.

Instead, he muttered, "You don't have to do this alone."

Lora's head turned slightly, her voice low but steady. "I was never alone. Not really. You were always there even when you weren't."

The confession cut through him, both balm and wound. His chest tightened, and for a brief moment he reached across the console, his hand brushing hers. She didn't pull away.

By the time they pulled up outside the precinct, the fragile tether between them had been wound tighter something neither dared to name, but both felt pulling at the centre of their chests.

The task force room was already buzzing when they entered. Maps, files, photographs, and pinned notes covered every board, as though the walls themselves were closing in under the weight of the investigation.

Detective Greene stood at the front, marker in hand, dark circles under his eyes. When he saw Sam and Lora, his expression tightened. "You're just in time."

Sam guided Lora to a chair, his hand briefly resting on her shoulder before he sat beside her. He kept close, watchful.

Greene uncapped the marker with a snap. "We've cross-referenced disappearances within the last five years. Missing women. Cold cases. Unsolved vanishings." He tapped the board, where a name was scrawled in red.

Margaret Holloway – 26.

Missing: Four years.

Case Status: Unresolved.

A murmur rippled through the room.

Ng leaned forward. "She worked at the county library. No record of enemies, no troubled history, nothing that stood out. Just walked home one night and vanished."

Harris added grimly, "And the location of her last sighting, less than two miles from the forest's southern edge."

All eyes turned to the map pinned beside her name. A red dot marked her final steps, almost brushing the boundary of the cursed woods.

Lora's breath caught in her throat. Margaret Holloway. She whispered it under her breath, tasting the weight of it. Number One.

Greene's voice cut back in. "We think she was his first. The one who began this cycle. And if Lora's right..." His gaze flicked to her, a mix of fear and respect. "...then she's not just a name. She's the blueprint. Everything else builds on her."

The room shifted, officers exchanging uneasy looks. They all knew what it meant: if the killer had kept Elena alive all this time, then what about Margaret?

Sam's jaw tightened. "Any evidence that she might still be alive?"

Greene shook his head. "No proof either way. Just a ghost trail that leads straight into the forest."

Lora leaned forward, hands clasped so tightly her knuckles turned white. "She's there," she whispered, voice trembling but certain. "I can feel it."

Sam's heart twisted as he looked at her. The fire in her eyes, the cost it was taking from her, the way she seemed to live half in this world and half in the killer's. How much more can you take before you burn out completely?

The team fell silent, the gravity of Margaret Holloway Number One settling like a shadow over the room.

And in the middle of it all, Lora sat pale but unyielding, her fragile tether to Sam the only anchor keeping her from breaking.

The room hung heavy in silence, broken only by the hum of the fluorescent lights. Then, one by one, voices began to stir, as if each officer needed to unburden themselves of the dread that had settled over them.

Detective Ng leaned back in her chair, arms folded tightly across her chest. "If Margaret Holloway was his first... then everything after her is ritual. A sequence. A pattern he's perfected over years. She's not just a victim she's the foundation of all of this." Her voice faltered, but she forced the words through. "She could still be alive... or she could be a monument."

Harris slammed his pen down, the sharp clack echoing. "Four years? Nobody survives four years in captivity unless he wants them to. That's the worst part if she's alive, it's because he's kept her that way. And if she's dead, then he's holding her shadow over us like a noose." His jaw clenched. "Either way, she's, his prize."

Greene rubbed his temples, marker still in hand. "So, the question becomes why reveal Elena now? Why let us get that close? And why taunt us with Number One unless he's daring us to find her?"

The theories churned, pulling the room in every direction.

"He's orchestrating it," Ng muttered.

"He's escalating," Harris countered.

"He's testing us," Greene finished.

Across the table, one of the younger officers Daniels shifted uneasily. "Or maybe... maybe Number One's not just another victim." His voice wavered. "Maybe she's part of it now."

The words landed like a gunshot.

"Don't," Sam snapped, sharper than intended. The thought of it of Margaret Holloway transformed from captive into accomplice was a line none of them wanted to cross. He cut a quick glance at Lora. Her face had drained of all colour, her eyes fixed on the photograph of Margaret on the board.

Don't go there, Sam thought fiercely. She'll shatter if you go there.

Lora spoke at last, her voice soft but steady, carrying an authority that silenced the room. "No. She's not part of him. She's, his beginning. He built everything on her suffering. She's still there. She's waiting for us."

Her words lingered, fragile and powerful all at once.

Sam studied her profile, the tight line of her jaw, the way her hands trembled in her lap though she fought to hide it. He wanted to pull her out of the room, away from all of it, but he knew she wouldn't leave.

Greene broke the silence. "Then we don't waste time. At dawn, we go back. We sweep the forest, every inch of it. Tunnels, chambers, hallowed ground we don't stop until we find her."

The decision hit the room like a gavel.

The tension shifted into preparation files shuffled, radios checked, supply lists read aloud. The buzz of logistics filled the air, but beneath it all the unease remained: Margaret Holloway wasn't just a name on a board anymore. She was Number One.

And the killer wanted them to find her.

Sam placed a steadying hand on Lora's shoulder as the meeting wrapped, his thumb brushing lightly against her jacket sleeve. She leaned into the touch without looking at him, the tether between them taut but unbroken.

Chapter Twenty Six

The sky was only beginning to pale when the convoy assembled at the edge of the forest. The air was sharp and cold, every breath visible in the faint morning light. The dogs whined and pawed the ground, their handlers murmuring low commands. Forensics unpacked equipment, radios crackled with clipped exchanges, and officers adjusted their weapons.

Sam stood at the front, scanning the tree line that loomed dark and endless ahead of them. He turned, catching Lora's gaze. Her face was pale, her eyes shadowed from another sleepless night, but the fire inside her hadn't dimmed.

"Stay close to me," he said quietly. It wasn't an order it was a plea.

Lora only nodded, her hand brushing against his for a fleeting second before she pulled away, already turning her eyes toward the forest.

As the sun broke the horizon, painting the world in pale gold, the team stepped forward, crossing the tape and pushing into the woods once more toward Number One.

The forest seemed to inhale, waiting.

The forest greeted them like a living thing. Dawn light barely pierced its canopy, branches clawing at the sky, the air thick with a damp chill that clung to their lungs. Each footfall seemed too loud, crunching leaves echoing in the silence, as though the woods itself were listening.

The team moved in careful formation dogs pulling against leashes, handlers murmuring control; forensics with their cases strapped tight; officers scanning the treeline with restless eyes. Radios crackled now and then, but even those clipped voices sounded muted, swallowed by the forest's weight.

Sam kept Lora near him, his eyes flicking to her constantly. She walked with her shoulders tight, jaw clenched, gaze darting as though trying to peel back layers of shadow. He could see the storm inside her, the pull that had haunted her since the first scream in these woods.

Then, mid-step, she froze.

Her breath caught. Her hands trembled. Her eyes widened not seeing the forest around her, but something else entirely.

Sam turned immediately, his voice low but urgent. "Lora. What is it?"

Her lips parted. A whisper slipped out, fragile and raw. "She's alive."

The words stopped the group cold. Eyes turned toward her, uneasy silence stretching. The dogs whined, restless, as if sensing the shift.

Sam stepped closer, his hand brushing her arm. "Where is she, Lora?" His voice was steady, but his heart pounded.

Lora squeezed her eyes shut, breathing hard, straining against whatever vision clawed at her. Fragments flickered through her mind: dirt, roots, darkness, the sound of muffled crying. She reached for the image, trying to sharpen it, but it was like smoke slipping through her fingers.

Her voice cracked when she spoke. "Not in the hollow." Her breath came ragged, chest rising and falling fast. "She's somewhere else... deeper... in the forest."

The silence stretched again, heavier this time. The weight of her words settled over the group like a shroud.

Harris muttered, "Then we've been chasing shadows in the wrong place..." His voice trailed off when Sam shot him a look.

Sam steadied Lora by her shoulders, leaning close so only she could hear. "Then we'll find her, Lora. Wherever she is. But you need to hold on. Don't let it take you under."

Her eyes fluttered open, still clouded by what she'd seen. For a moment, she just looked at him lost, afraid, but unyielding. She gave the faintest nod, her voice a whisper. "Then let's keep going."

The team shifted uneasily but obeyed, pressing deeper into the forest's core. The air grew heavier, as though each step further dimmed the morning light, carrying them back into the suffocating grip of dread.

And above them, the forest seemed to lean closer, listening, waiting.

The team pressed forward, deeper into the tangle of the forest. The air thickened, damp earth and moss rising sharp in their noses. Every rustle of leaves felt amplified, every creak of branch overhead like a whispered warning.

Sam kept his place at Lora's side, his body angled toward her like a shield, though he knew no shield could keep out what was eating at her from within. He could hear her breath—measured but too quick, shallow, as if she were chasing something unseen.

No one spoke. Words felt dangerous here, as if uttering them might stir something watching from the dark. Even the dogs, usually eager and loud, moved uneasily, whining under their breath, ears twitching as if picking up frequencies no human could hear.

The forest pressed closer. Branches seemed to bend toward them, paths narrowing, the ground slick with dew and roots.

Lora stopped again. Her hand twitched at her side. "It's close," she whispered, eyes unfocused.

Sam leaned in. "What is?"

Her head tilted, listening to something no one else could hear. Her lips trembled. "Her."

The word slid like a stone into their silence, sinking deep. The team exchanged uneasy glances, their weapons shifting in nervous hands.

They pushed on, slowly, their boots sinking into softer soil, the ground dipping. The air grew colder.

Then the dogs snapped taut on their leashes, barking, snarling at the same patch of earth ahead. Their handlers struggled to rein them back, but the animals were wild-eyed, hackles raised.

Sam's heart jumped into his throat. "Easy!"

The dogs clawed at the ground, dirt flying. Something was there.

The team surged forward. Forensics dropped to their knees, shining lights, gloves already pulling soil aside with delicate urgency.

Lora staggered forward, falling to her knees, her hands digging into the dirt with a desperation that startled even the handlers. Sam dropped beside her, pulling her back gently but firmly.

"Lora stop. Let them do it."

She resisted for a moment, her fingers clawed and trembling, before finally sagging into his grip, chest heaving. Her voice cracked, nearly breaking. "This is where she was. I saw her."

The forensic light caught on something pale in the soil. A murmur rippled through the team.

Sam tightened his hold on Lora as the gloved hands worked carefully, brushing away dirt until....

A clump of dark hair surfaced, matted but unmistakably human.

The air split with silence.

Forensics leaned closer, finding more: a fingernail embedded in the dirt. Shreds of cloth. Personal effects.

One of the officers whispered, "Jesus Christ..."

Sam's grip tightened on Lora, who shook violently against him. She didn't look surprised. Not at all. Her eyes were glassy, haunted, as if she had already seen this before.

Her voice was low, hollow. "Margaret..."

The forest around them seemed to grow even darker, as if the trees themselves had leaned closer to listen.

No one moved at first. The clump of dark hair seemed to root everyone in place, as though disturbing the silence any further would awaken something deeper and older than the forest itself.

Forensics worked in measured motions, brushing dirt, bagging fragments, their gloved hands steady even as their eyes betrayed the tremor of unease. A fingernail, pale and cracked, was lifted into evidence. Torn cloth, streaked with soil. Each fragment was catalogued, yet each one carried the unbearable weight of someone's suffering.

Lora trembled in Sam's arms, her breath ragged, her head pressed lightly against his chest as if she might fall apart if he let go. Sam tightened his grip around her, his jaw clenched so hard it ached.

Hold it together. For her. Don't let her see how much it's breaking you too.

He stroked her arm, grounding her with touch. "You're here, Lora. With me. Just breathe."

Her lips barely moved. "I saw this before we came. I knew."

His chest tightened. He wanted to tell her not to blame herself, but he knew the words would be hollow against what she carried inside. He pressed his forehead briefly against her hair instead, silently begging her to hang on.

Across the site, the officers' faces flickered with conflicting emotions.

Detective Ruiz shifted on his heels, muttering under his breath, "Christ, this isn't supposed to happen. Not like this." His hands twitched at his holster though no threat had yet appeared.

Anderson's expression was harder, his eyes scanning the tree line as if expecting shadows to take form. We're being led, he thought. Every step, every clue it's not chance. It's orchestration.

Mayhew stared down at the fragments in the soil, nausea tugging at his throat. She was here, alive, buried in silence. How many times have we walked right past without knowing?

Even the dog handlers, used to grim discoveries, looked shaken. The dogs whined, still pawing weakly at the dirt, as if unwilling to stop searching.

The forest seemed to hum, every bird call stilled, every branch aching with weight.

Sam finally looked at the team, his voice low but sharp. "We push deeper. He left this here for us to find, but it's not all. There's more ahead. I can feel it."

His gaze dropped back to Lora, her eyes wide but hollow, locked somewhere between now and a vision only she could see.

Ruiz hesitated. "What if it's another trap?"

Lora stirred, her voice barely audible, cracked and raw. "It doesn't matter. She's here. She's still here. We can't stop."

The team exchanged glances, no one willing to say out loud the dread knotting in their chests.

Mayhew adjusted his flashlight. "Then we go."

Sam nodded, pulling Lora gently to her feet. She swayed, and he steadied her, his hand firm at the small of her back. Her eyes flicked deeper into the trees, glassy but resolute, as though she were tethered to something pulling them forward.

Inside, Sam's thoughts roared. She's unravelling. And I'm letting her lead us right into the wolf's den. God help me, I can't stop her. I don't want to stop her.

The team reformed, weapons raised, lights cutting thin beams into the dark. The dogs strained at their leads again, noses low, growls vibrating in their throats.

The soil behind them still whispered of pain, but the path ahead promised only more.

They pressed deeper into the forest.

The forest swallowed them whole.

Every step forward cracked against the silence like a violation. The ground was soft with moss, slick in places where roots twisted like veins just beneath the soil. Their flashlights swept in restless arcs, beams colliding against tree trunks that seemed to lean closer the deeper they went.

The air was heavy, damp, as though it had been holding its breath for centuries. Even the dogs usually eager, bounding moved with a strange caution, their hackles raised, throats vibrating with low growls that seemed to vibrate in the bones.

Lora moved in the center of the group, her steps slow, deliberate, almost trance-like. Sam never let his hand leave her, his thumb brushing across her knuckles with a subtle rhythm meant to anchor her. She hardly blinked, eyes fixed ahead, lips parted in a silence that was more disturbing than any scream.

She's breaking in front of me, Sam thought. Every step tears her apart more. But she's the only one who can see the path. And I'm letting her walk straight into hell.

Detective Ruiz kept muttering under his breath, prayers or curses no one could tell. We shouldn't be here. We're out of our depth. This isn't police work—this is something else. Something older. Darker.

Mayhew's marched stiffly, flashlight cutting sharp lines into the undergrowth. The killer's toying with us. Always a step ahead, leaving crumbs. He knows where we are right now. Watching. Waiting. He wants us to crack.

Harris's jaw worked as he scanned the tree line, fingers tightening and loosening against his weapon. We've been chasing his shadow since day one. And he keeps feeding us just enough to follow. If we don't find him soon, we'll find another body instead.

Forensics trailed close, shoulders hunched against the dread pressing down on them, every rustle of leaves pulling their gazes to the dark. Even their usual detached focus had cracked, replaced with quick, nervous glances at one another.

And then there was Lora, her inner world a storm no one else could see.

Her thoughts spiraled, fractured:

I feel her. She's close. Why can't I see more? Just pieces. Hands bound. Tears. The smell of smoke. God, why won't it come clear? Why show me fragments and not the truth?

Her breath caught, shallow. She whispered to herself, though Sam heard. "She's alive. She's afraid. But... he's near."

Sam's chest tightened. He squeezed her hand harder. "Don't lose yourself, Lora. Stay with me. Just stay with me."

No answer. Only her trembling, her eyes glassy as if seeing something just beyond the reach of the beam.

Then, a sound.

Not loud, but enough. A faint scrape of something against bark, ahead in the blackness. The dogs bristled instantly, barking sharp, frantic, straining at their leads so hard the handlers nearly lost grip.

The team froze. Every gun lifted, beams of light converging.

Ruiz hissed, "Movement. There was movement."

Mayhew's pulse roared in his ears. It's him. Finally, him. Right there.

Lora jerked suddenly, gasping. She pointed into the dark. "There! There's something!" Her voice cracked with desperation.

The team surged forward. Heartbeats thudded against silence. Branches snapped underfoot. The dogs tore ahead, their barks ricocheting between the trees.

And there, against the roots of a gnarled oak, they found it, another breadcrumb.

A crude wooden effigy, bound in twine and streaked with what looked like blood. Symbols carved deep into its torso, spiraling patterns echoing those they had seen underground. At its base, a strip of fabric stained, torn too real to dismiss as prop.

The forest seemed to close in tighter.

Lora's knees buckled. Sam caught her under the arms, pulling her against him as her body shook.

He's taunting us. He left this here knowing she would feel it. Knowing it would break her more.

Sam's fury burned hot beneath his fear. I swear to God, Lora, I'll end this before he takes you too.

Around them, the team's faces reflected raw dread and exhaustion. No one spoke. There was nothing to say.

The breadcrumb lay between them and the dark, promising nothing but deeper descent.

The effigy sat at the roots of the oak like an offering. Twine cutting into wood. Symbols gouged deep, raw, almost fresh. Blood or something meant to be blood streaked the grain, dark and tacky under the flashlights.

The strip of fabric stirred faintly in the night breeze, fluttering like a flag of surrender. Or a lure.

No one moved at first. The only sounds were the frantic panting of the dogs and the wind threading through the high branches.

Detective Ruiz broke the silence, voice low, unsteady. "This… this is ritual. Straight ritual. We're chasing a ghost that knows the forest better than we do."

"Forensics," Sam barked, forcing steadiness into his tone, "bag everything. I want photos, soil samples, fibers, all of it." He swallowed hard, eyes never leaving the effigy. "And be careful. This wasn't left by accident."

NG muttered through clenched teeth, "He's toying with us. Every step we take, he's leading us somewhere he wants us to go."

Mayhew exhaled sharply, scanning the tree line. "Yeah. Straight into the ground."

Sam kept one hand clamped on Lora's arm, grounding her. Her skin was clammy, her body taut like a wire stretched too far. She wouldn't look away from the effigy.

Her thoughts spiraled, pressing against her temples like needles: He wants me to see this. For me. Always for me. Why? What am I to him? Why do I feel like I know this?

Her voice finally broke the silence. Barely above a whisper. "She's alive. He's keeping her… like he kept Elena. But this…" She motioned weakly toward the effigy, her hand trembling. "…this is a promise. A warning."

Sam turned her toward him sharply, his own fear leaking through his sternness. "Lora. You need to stop doing this to yourself. He wants inside your head."

She stared back at him, pale and unflinching. "He's already there."

The words hung between them like a knife.

One of the handlers tugged back the dogs, who whined and strained toward the effigy, teeth bared. Even animals sensed what the humans were struggling to admit: the forest itself felt wrong.

The debate spread through the team.

"We push deeper. If there's more, we need to see it." Harris's voice was hard, clipped, trying to hide the tremor in his hands.

"No," Ruiz countered, shaking his head. "This isn't police work anymore. This is him pulling us apart, step by step. If we go deeper, he'll bleed us dry."

"We can't leave this trail cold," Mayhew argued, though the strain in his face betrayed his doubt. "Every clue ties closer to the victims. We might be one step from finding number one."

"And one step from joining them," Ruiz snapped back.

Sam's chest ached as he listened. The weight of every choice pressed against him: Chief, leader, ex-husband, man still in love with the woman trembling under his arm.

His inner voice roared: If I push, I risk losing them all. If I retreat, I risk letting the killer win. Goddamn it, what's the right call?

He looked at Lora. Her eyes locked on his, glazed but resolute. "She's not here, Sam. Not tonight. He just wants us to feel it. Wants us to break."

Sam's decision came like a blade. "We're pulling out."

The team hesitated. Relief and frustration battled across their faces.

"That's an order," Sam snapped, forcing steel into his tone.

Forensics bagged the effigy, gloves shaking slightly. The strip of fabric was sealed in another pouch. The blue light strobed faintly against the trees as officers marked the site with tape and GPS coordinates.

The retreat was controlled, careful but every step back through the trees felt heavier. No one spoke. Only the crunch of boots, the low growls of the dogs, and the silence of the forest pressing close.

Back at the precinct, emotions erupted.

The effigy lay under harsh fluorescent lights in the evidence room, stripped of the forest's dread but no less grotesque. The carved spirals, the blood, the fabric they looked almost clinical now. But the chill they carried clung to everyone.

Ruiz slammed his hands on the table. "We're being strung along like fools. He's making a game of this, and we're playing right into it."

Mayhew snapped back, "So what's the alternative? Sit on our asses while he keeps killing?"

Voices overlapped, tempers frayed. Forensics presented early findings yes, human blood, type still being tested, fabric consistent with women's clothing but too torn for an immediate match.

Through it all, Sam stayed standing, his eyes darting from the evidence to Lora.

She sat motionless, pale as paper, staring at the effigy through the glass as if she were somewhere else entirely. Her inner thoughts wound tighter: He's close. Closer than they know. And he wants me to keep following. Every breadcrumb is a string pulling me deeper into his design. But why me? Why always me?

Sam's chest burned. He wanted to shout, to shake her, to tell her to stop sacrificing herself for this case. But instead, he whispered inside his own head: I can't lose you again. Not to this forest. Not to him. God help me, I'll follow you into hell if I have to.

The team's voices grew louder. Grief, rage, theories spilling across the room. But between Sam and Lora, a fragile silence stretched, unbroken an unspoken tether fraying with every clue they found.

The night boiled around them, unresolved.

Chapter Twenty Seven

The shouting, the clatter of files against tables, the scrape of chairs none of it touched the small pocket of silence where Sam and Lora sat.

She was still staring through the glass at the effigy, unmoving, like her soul was tethered to the crude figure sealed inside the evidence bag. Her fingers twitched against the edge of the table, restless, needing to hold onto something but refusing to reach for anyone.

Sam sat across from her, elbows on his knees, eyes never leaving her face. The room swirled with fury and fear, but for him, there was only her.

She's slipping further away with every clue we find. Every vision drags her closer to him, and further from me. Goddamn it, Lora, I need you here. With me. Not in his forest, not in his riddles.

Her lips parted faintly, words too soft for the chaos around them. "He wants me, Sam. Every breadcrumb, every symbol it's all for me. Not the team. Not the department. Just me."

Sam leaned forward, lowering his voice so only she could hear. "Then he's going to have to go through me first. I'm not letting him take you."

Her eyes flicked to his, and for the first time that night, they softened. Haunted, yes but also touched with the fragile thread of something she had buried for years.

He still loves me. Even after everything. Divorce. The walls I built. And here he is, holding me together when I'm barely whole.

Her hand trembled as she reached for the edge of his sleeve, brushing it like testing if he was real. Sam covered her hand with his own, fingers closing around hers, grounding them both.

The moment held, fragile and unspoken, until the noise of the room surged again and pulled them back into the reality they couldn't escape.

The team's debate spiraled deeper into exhaustion.

Ruiz was pacing, voice hoarse from hours of argument. "We've been led in circles. He doesn't want to be caught. He wants us to unravel until we're as broken as his victims."

Harris fired back, slamming a palm on the table. "He does want to be caught but on his terms. He's choreographing this. Every symbol, every effigy, every breadcrumb, it's a dance, and we're following the steps."

Meyers rubbed at his temple; his words sharp with fatigue. "Or maybe we've been wrong from the start. Maybe there's no victim number one. Maybe that's the trick. Keep us chasing shadows while the real prize is somewhere else entirely."

Forensics shuffled through photos, their voices clipped, technical. "The blood matches female, though no confirmed ID yet. Spiral carvings are consistent with symbols from the hollow. The fabric...

looks torn from clothing. We'll need to cross-reference with missing persons."

Every word layered more weight on the air. The precinct hummed with desperation like a machine running too hot, gears grinding, ready to break.

Inside each mind, the storm churned:

Ruiz's inner voice: We're outmatched. He's ahead of us in every move. And we're fools to keep walking into his traps.

Harris's: If we stop now, he wins. If we keep pushing, maybe we bleed for it—but at least we bleed forward.

Mayhew's: There has to be a logic to this madness. A reason for number one. Goddamn it, what are we missing?

Sam's: They're all spinning, grasping at threads. But the one thread that matters is sitting across from me, hollow-eyed and breaking. If she goes, we all go.

Lora's: They don't see it. None of them. He isn't talking to the team. He isn't talking to the police. He's talking to me. And I can't stop listening.

The clock dragged past midnight. The debate dulled to murmurs, exhaustion pulling at every face. Files lay scattered, coffee cups half-empty, the effigy still sealed and staring from the evidence table like a silent witness.

Sam finally stood, voice firm. "Enough. We're circling the drain. Everyone get four hours of rest. Back here at dawn. No exceptions."

Grumbles of protest died quickly. Weariness won. Officers shuffled out, heads low, shoulders bent.

Only Lora lingered, her eyes still on the evidence.

Sam touched her arm gently. "Come on. You can't stare it into giving up answers."

Her gaze broke from the glass, flicking to him. Fragile. Haunted. But she rose, letting him guide her out, their silence heavier than any argument.

Chapter Twenty Eight

The SUV cut through the night in silence.

No radio. No hum of conversation. Just the low growl of the engine and the rhythm of tires on wet asphalt. Outside, the forest gave way to empty highways, streetlights casting fractured shadows across the windshield like fleeting ghosts.

Sam's hands gripped the wheel tighter than he realized, knuckles white, veins raised. His eyes flicked between the road and the reflection of Lora in the passenger window. She hadn't spoken since they left the precinct. She barely moved head, tilted against the glass, eyes unfocused, lips parted as if words wanted to come but wouldn't.

She's not here. Not really. The case has her by the throat. And every mile we drive, I'm losing her piece by piece. Goddamn it, Lora, why can't I protect you from this?

He flexed his fingers on the wheel.

Because you don't want protection. You want the truth. Even if it kills you.

Lora's thoughts spiraled like smoke.

He's out there, smiling in the dark, knowing I'm chasing. He leaves me crumbs because he knows I'll follow. Sam thinks he's keeping me safe, but how can I explain? I'm not afraid of dying not anymore. I'm afraid of failing. Of not finding her. Of not stopping him.

She glanced sideways at Sam. His jaw was tight, shoulders rigid, but his eyes the same eyes that had once looked at her across a dinner table, across their wedding vows, across the quiet unravelling of their marriage still burned with the same fierce devotion.

He still loves me. I can see it. Feel it. And I...God help me, I still love him. But I can't give him peace. I can only drag him further into the dark with me.

The weight of unspoken words thickened the air.

Finally, Sam broke the silence, his voice low. "You scare the hell out of me, you know that?"

She didn't answer at first. Her eyes stayed on the dark blur of trees rushing past. Then, softly, "I scare myself."

He reached across the console, tentative, his hand brushing against hers. For a moment, she didn't move. Then her fingers curled around his, weak but certain.

The fragile tether held. For now.

Early Dawn approached quickly, it was four in the morning dawn was making another appearance. Sam had planned that the team all meet at five A.M at the precinct and get started on unravelling the case again.

Sam got up early after a restless night, Lora stirred, Sam looked across at her, grabbed his clothes and dressed as he left the room to go downstairs to make coffee. Lora got up from the bed to shower as Sam re-entered the bedroom and handed Lora her coffee with a weary smile.

The precinct felt hollow, drained by exhaustion. Coffee steamed in paper cups, but no one touched it. Files were spread open like wounds across the table. The effigy's photos stared back at them from the corkboard; the spirals carved into its body burning like brands into the team's-tired eyes.

Detective Ruiz slouched in his chair, eyes red, muttering, "It's like we're feeding on ourselves. Every night in that forest, we come back emptier."

Hall rubbed his hands across his face. "We're running out of time. If number one is still alive and that's a big if we're not moving fast enough."

Meyers tapped a pen against the table, staring at the symbols. "It's not random. He's leaving us a path. A map maybe. But it's written in a language we don't understand."

Forensics set down another stack of preliminary reports. "Blood on the effigy confirms female, O negative. No match yet in the system. The fabric... possibly from a dress, red or dark maroon, but degraded."

The words were clinical, detached. But the faces listening was anything but.

Lora sat at the edge of the table, silent, eyes dark-rimmed and distant. She hadn't slept. Couldn't. Her fear curled tighter with every minute.

He's pulling me deeper. It's like I'm tied to him. What if I can't cut the string? What if the only way this end is with me?

Her hand twitched against her thigh. Her chest felt tight, her breath shallow. She looked at the photos of the effigy, then at Elena Ward's case file, then at the blank space still marked Victim One: UNKNOWN.

Her voice cracked the silence. "She's still alive. I can feel it. Just like Elena. He hasn't killed her yet."

The room shifted. The others stared. Some skeptical. Some afraid to admit they believed her.

Sam leaned forward, eyes locked on her, voice low but firm. "Then we find her. But Lora." His jaw tightened. "You don't do it alone. Not anymore. You hear me?"

She nodded faintly, though inside her head the storm raged on.

He'll never understand. I'm already alone in this. I've been alone since the first scream.

The team sat in silence for a beat too long, exhaustion pressing down like a second skin. Each one trapped in their own fears, their own fragile theories.

The clock ticked forward. Dawn began to bleed pale light through the precinct windows.

The case wasn't slowing. And neither was the killer.

Chapter Twenty Nine

T he morning air was sharp and clean, carrying the faint bite of damp earth and city exhaust. Sam guided Lora out of the precinct's heavy doors, his hand at the small of her back. The inside of the building had felt suffocating walls pressing in, voices circling the same theories until they blurred together. Out here, under the pale grey wash of dawn, there was at least space to breathe.

Lora wrapped her arms around herself, her jacket pulled tight though the chill wasn't what made her shiver. Her eyes roamed unfocused, distant. The fragile tether between them vibrated with every unspoken thought, every tremor in her chest.

After a long silence, her voice broke through, so quiet Sam almost missed it.

"Something's wrong, Sam."

He turned, his brow furrowing. "What do you mean?"

Lora's gaze flicked up to him, tears already shimmering in her eyes. "I'm not sure. It all... it all seems like déjà vu. Like I've been here before." Her hand pressed against her chest, trembling. "My mind keeps reverting back like I'm inside someone else's body. Running. Always running. And the fear… it's crushing me. Like I can feel what they felt."

Her words cracked, her breath catching as though each memory scraped her lungs raw. She clutched her chest harder, as if the ache were clawing from the inside.

Sam didn't hesitate. He closed the gap, wrapping his arms around her. His warmth pressed into her cold, his hand sliding protectively across her back as he pulled her against him. He could feel her shaking.

"Hey, hey… Lora." His voice softened, barely above a whisper, meant only for her. He rested his chin gently against her hair. "It's going to be okay. I've got you. We're going to catch them. I promise."

She pressed her forehead against his chest, her breath unsteadies, caught between sob and silence. For a moment, the world stilled the hum of traffic, the looming weight of the case, even the shadows of the forest that waited. It was just the two of them, clinging to the thin line that tethered them together.

Sam closed his eyes, holding her tighter, wishing he could pour his strength into her, wishing his promise was enough.

But promises didn't stop killers.

Sam and Lora headed back Inside the precinct; the briefing room buzzed with restrained urgency when they re-entered. Maps of the forest stretched across the table, pins marking each discovery effigy, tunnel entrances, the chamber. The air smelled of stale coffee and damp paper.

Mayhew pointed to a sector on the east side of the map. "The scans didn't cover this ridge. It's possible there's another access point here. If Lora's vision is right if number one isn't in the hollow we may find a new trail in this area."

Harris leaned in, frowning. "We'll need dogs again. And extra ground units. If he's still moving her, we have to assume he's close."

Ruiz exhaled sharply. "Close and watching. He knew we were in the tunnels. He wanted us to see that effigy."

The team's tension rippled across the room. Every word pressed heavier on the already fraying edges of their exhaustion.

Lora sat beside Sam, silent, eyes fixed on the map. She didn't need to speak for him to know what she was feeling the pull, the dread, the weight of déjà vu still heavy in her chest.

Sam placed a hand on the table near hers, close enough she could feel the heat of his skin. His voice steadied, cutting through the swirl of unease. "We prepare for dawn. We go in careful, methodical. We take every piece of equipment, every unit we can spare. No one goes off alone."

His eyes slid to Lora. Especially not you.

She met his gaze for only a second before looking away. But the fragile tether between them tightened all the same.

The forest awaited.

The house was quiet, the kind of silence that pressed against the walls like a tide. Lora sat curled into the corner of the couch, her body still taut, her eyes wide though exhaustion clung to her face. Sam sat across from her at first, watching the subtle tremors in her fingers as she held her cup of tea. He wanted to tell her to sleep, to beg her to rest, but he knew like always her mind wouldn't let her.

When she finally shifted closer, sitting beside him, Sam felt his chest tighten. She didn't speak, but the way she leaned into him, her head gently resting on his shoulder, said everything. He slid his arm around her, pulling her close.

The intimacy between them was fragile, delicate, born of wounds and the firestorm of the case pressing against them. They didn't speak of love, but it lingered between every glance, every breath. Sam pressed a light kiss into her hair, whispering softly, "We'll get through this, Lora."

Her reply was quiet, trembling. "If I close my eyes, I see her. I see him. I feel like... like I'm already gone."

Sam tightened his hold, refusing to let her slip into that darkness. "You're here. With me. And I'm not letting you go."

That night, sleep came only in restless fragments for her, while Sam stayed awake longer, listening to the uneven rhythm of her breathing, keeping watch like her silent guard. The tether between them was thin, but it held.

Chapter Thirty

Dawn broke in shades of pale gold and grey mist clinging to the forest's edge. The team gathered where the SUVs were parked, their breath visible in the chill morning air. The atmosphere was taut, laced with fear and determination.

Detectives Mayhew, Ng, Greene, and Harris stood slightly apart, watching Lora as she shifted uncomfortably near Sam.

Mayhew's inner voice churned: She looks like she's unravelling... but she's, our compass. Without her, we're blind.

Ng crossed his arms, his sharp eyes narrowing. Chief doesn't want her exposed. But every time she's led us, we've found something. We can't ignore that.

Greene rubbed his jaw, unease carving into his face. This isn't procedure. Following visions? We're already out of line, but the forest doesn't care about procedure. It's her or nothing.

Harris finally broke the silence, stepping forward. "Chief... we need to unleash Lora. We follow her with the dogs. She's the key."

Sam bristled, his jaw tight. "No way! Absolutely not! I'm not letting her!"

"Hang on, Chief," Harris interrupted, his voice steadier than he felt. "We'll be right behind her. But you know as well as I do, this case didn't start with us. It started with Meyers, Hall, and Lora. They were onto something in these woods and now Meyers and Hall are dead." His words cut heavy through the cold morning air. "As I said... Lora is the key."

Sam's heart clenched. He glanced at Lora, pale and withdrawn, yet with that same sharp focus buried beneath her fragile exterior. He wanted to keep her safe. He wanted to lock her away from this nightmare. But Harris wasn't wrong.

His voice broke softer, quieter. "She doesn't remember..."

The detectives looked at each other. Then Ng spoke firmly, "We know. Trust us, Chief."

Sam hesitated. His fists clenched, his pulse hammering. Then slowly, reluctantly, he nodded. "Fine. But no one leaves her side."

The team pressed into the forest, boots crunching against the damp earth, the dogs straining at their leads. The spot they had left only a day ago looked darker somehow, the mist still curling low around the undergrowth.

Lora froze. Her eyes glazed, her lips parting as though she were listening to something far away. Her body trembled. She trailed off mid-step, whispering words no one fully caught.

"Vision," Sam muttered, his heart stuttering as he raised a hand to halt the others.

Everyone snapped to red alert, eyes scanning the trees, ears straining for movement.

Then, without warning, Lora bolted forward, the dogs reacting instantly. The handlers followed, and the team surged after her. She cut through the underbrush with a kind of clarity that frightened them all.

They broke through into a clearing. Lora dropped to her knees, her hand pointing to a patch of disturbed earth. Her breath came in quick, shallow bursts, her eyes locked on the ground as if she could see through it.

Sam's voice cut sharp, commanding. "Clear that spot! Now!"

The team moved, shovels and hands tearing into the damp soil. Sweat mixed with dirt as the ground gave way.

Lora stayed kneeling, her eyes wide and unblinking, fixed. Watching. Almost as if she already knew.

Minutes stretched taut as the digging deepened. Then came the sound a dull scrape against something not earth.

They uncovered a large, mud-caked cardboard slab, wedged flat beneath the soil. With effort, they pulled it free.

And then... silence.

Their shock and horror hung thick in the air.

But none of them spoke.

Not yet.

Chapter Thirty One

T he clearing had fallen into a suffocating silence, the air thick with the smell of damp soil and decay. The team stood in a half-circle around the gaping wound they had carved into the earth, their faces pale, every breath caught somewhere between disbelief and terror.

Something about the cardboard slab its placement, the way it had been buried felt wrong, deliberate. A taunt. A trap.

Detective Greene muttered under his breath, "What the hell is this...?" His voice cracked, barely audible.

Sam came rushing forward, his boots slamming against the soft ground. His heart hammered as dread surged like fire through his veins. "Move! Let me see!"

But the detectives reacted fast. Harris and Mayhew grabbed his arms, their grips iron strong as they dragged him back from the edge. "No, Chief!" Harris barked, his voice raw with fear.

Sam struggled against them, his chest heaving, muscles burning as he tried to break free. "Goddammit, let me go! Let me see!"

Mayhew's voice was desperate, almost pleading. "We can't let you."

Sam thrashed again, finally twisting enough to turn his head. He looked at Lora, but she wasn't there.

His heart lurched. The space where she had been kneeling moments ago was empty.

"Lora?" His voice was hollow, cracked. His eyes darted frantically across the clearing, searching, panic clawing up his throat. "Lora!"

Confusion spiraled into terror. He shoved harder against the detectives holding him back, adrenaline tearing through his body. With a guttural roar, Sam ripped himself free and staggered forward, his boots slipping in the churned earth.

He dropped to his knees at the edge of the hole. And there, there she was.

Lora.

Her body lay half-buried, cradled in the cruel earth like a grotesque mockery of rest. Her skin pale, lifeless, her hair tangled with dirt.

"No..." The word barely escaped his throat, strangled and broken. His hands reached out, trembling, pulling her from the shallow grave with desperate care. He cradled her against his chest, rocking back and forth as grief tore through him like blades. "Lora! Lora, no, come back to me, please!" His voice cracked into sobs, his body shaking violently as he held her tighter, as if sheer will could bring her back.

Behind him, the detectives froze, the horror in front of them burning into their minds. Mayhew fumbled for the radio, his hands trembling. "We.... we need paramedics. Now. The site's compromised, we've got a victim...Detective Lora..." His voice broke. "She's not... she's not responding."

The crackle of static came back with a delay before the grim reply: "ETA... one hour. Repeat, one hour."

The words felt like a death sentence.

Sam didn't hear them. He pressed his forehead against Lora's hair, tears soaking into the strands, his entire body racked with grief. Rage and despair collided inside him, bursting out in shouts that tore at the air.

"LORA! Goddammit, Lora! Don't leave me! Don't you dare leave me!"

The forest swallowed his voice, the sound reverberating through the trees like an unholy echo.

The detectives stood back, helpless, their own eyes burning as they watched their Chief unravel in the dirt, clutching the lifeless body of the woman he loved, his grief raw and unbearable.

And somewhere, hidden in the shadows of the trees, the forest seemed to watch.

Time stretched cruelly in that clearing. Every second dragged like an eternity, every breath from the detectives standing back sharp and shallow. Sam clung to Lora's body, rocking her against his chest, his grief pouring into the soil beneath him.

"Hold on, sweetheart... come back to me," he whispered brokenly, his tears cutting mud-streaked lines down his face. "I can't lose you. Not you."

The forest remained still, suffocating, as though the trees themselves held their breath.

The minutes bled into what felt like hours before the sharp wail of sirens pierced the distance. Lights flickered faintly through the branches, growing closer. The team stirred, snapping into frantic motion, clearing a path through the woods.

But Sam didn't move. He refused to loosen his grip on Lora, refused to surrender her to the world that had already taken so much from them. His hands clung tighter as footsteps thundered into the clearing.

The paramedics arrived in a rush equipment bag slamming to the ground, voices sharp with urgency.

"Chief, Chief, we need to get in."

"No." Sam's voice was raw, jagged. He tightened his arms around her, his entire body trembling. "You check her here. You check her while I hold her."

One paramedic exchanged a glance with the other before kneeling beside him, his gloved hands moving quickly but carefully. He pressed fingers to her neck, to her wrist, his face unreadable as seconds ticked by.

Sam held his breath, tears streaking his face. "Please... please..."

Then, sudden and sharp, "We have a pulse!" The paramedic's voice cut through the night, triumphant but tense. "It's weak, but it's there. She's alive!"

The forest seemed to exhale all at once.

Sam's entire body sagged with relief, sobs tearing free, though his grip on her never loosened. He pressed his forehead to hers, voice breaking.

"Thank God... thank God," he whispered, kissing her hair through his tears. "Lora, hang in there, baby... you're safe now. I've got you. I won't let go."

The paramedics worked swiftly, sliding oxygen into place, preparing fluids, one of them murmuring updates as they stabilized her. Yet Sam still held her close, unwilling to surrender her warmth, even as they tried to ease her onto the stretcher.

"Chief," one paramedic urged softly, "we need to move her now."

Sam hesitated, his eyes locked on her face, still pale, still fragile, but alive. Finally, with hands shaking, he eased her down onto the stretcher, his fingers lingering against hers.

As they strapped her in and lifted her, Sam walked alongside, never letting go of her hand. His voice stayed with her, a constant thread of love and desperate reassurance.

"You're safe, Lora. You hear me? You're safe now. I'm right here. I'm not letting go."

And though her eyes remained closed, Sam swore he felt the faintest twitch of her fingers in his hand.

The forest closed in around them like a silent witness, its shadows heavy, its air thick with the echo of grief and fragile hope. Sam walked beside the stretcher as the paramedics rushed Lora out, his hand never leaving hers, his voice a soft murmur of desperate promises.

The detectives trailed behind, their faces pale and grim, their silence heavier than words. Relief and horror mingled in the air, thick and choking.

The blue lights of the ambulance cut through the trees, flashing against the bark like warnings. Sam climbed in after them, still clutching her hand as the doors slammed shut.

And for the first time all night, he dared to breathe.

Chapter Thirty Two

The hospital smelled of antiseptic and urgency. The moment they wheeled Lora through the doors, Sam was forced to slow his pace, though his eyes never left her pale form as nurses and doctors swarmed.

Dry blood matted her hair at the temple, a crimson stain against her skin. Ugly bruises darkened her arms and cheek, spreading across her like shadows that refused to fade. The X-rays revealed several broken ribs fractures from blunt force, the kind that told a story of violence, of struggle.

Sam stood just outside the room, his fists clenched at his sides, his body aching to be closer, to protect her. His chest was tight with fear, every beat of his heart echoing in his ears.

She fought for her life. The thought wouldn't leave him, each repetition heavier, darker. She fought, and God knows what he did to her, what she endured before we got there.

It terrified him. Not just the idea of losing her, but the image of her alone, trapped, hurt. The strongest woman he'd ever known brought low, broken.

And yet, she had held on.

Sam pressed his hand against the glass of the observation window, his throat raw. His mind replayed the feel of her lifeless body in his arms, the weight of her head against his chest, the way his heart had shattered in that moment.

I can't lose her. Not again. Not like this.

Every instinct screamed at him to storm into the room, to sit beside her, to never let her out of his sight. But he knew he had to let them work. So, he stood guard, his body still trembling from the fear that had consumed him in the forest, his love for her burning brighter and sharper than ever before.

And when he finally saw her chest rise and fall, steady under the oxygen mask, his knees nearly buckled with relief.

She's alive. She's still fighting. And I swear to God, I'll fight for her until this is over.

The night in the hospital stretched long and heavy, a silence broken only by the occasional shuffle of nurses' shoes and the steady, fragile beeping of Lora's heart monitor. Sam sat at her bedside, his body hunched forward in the uncomfortable chair, but he didn't care. He wasn't leaving her.

Her face was pale beneath the fluorescent lights, framed by bruises and cuts, her chest rising and falling shallowly beneath the thin hospital blanket. The sight gutted him.

Sam leaned forward, his elbows braced on his knees, his fingers trembling as he brushed lightly against hers. For a moment, he just stared at her hand so small, so delicate in his, yet still calloused from years of carrying a badge, still strong in ways most people couldn't imagine.

She came back for us, he thought, his chest aching with a mixture of grief and awe. All those visions... every step, every breadcrumb. It wasn't just the killer leading us. It was her. Her spirit... pulling us to her, to the victims. She never gave up. Not once.

His thumb stroked her knuckles gently, and at that touch, the heart monitor suddenly sped up, its beeps quickening, filling the room with urgent rhythm. Sam froze, then leaned closer, his breath catching.

"Lora?" His voice cracked. He swallowed hard. "You know I'm here, don't you?"

The monitor continued its staccato rhythm, and he felt a tremor pass through her fingers faint but real.

Sam's throat tightened, his eyes burning with tears that spilled freely now. He bowed his head until his forehead rested against her hand. "God... Lora..." His voice trembled as words poured out of him, words he'd been holding back for years.

"I love you. I never stopped. Not once. Even when everything fell apart between us. You—your spirit—came and got us. You brought us to you, to the truth, to the others. You're stronger than anyone I've ever known. Stronger than me."

His tears soaked her skin as his grip tightened, though gently, afraid of hurting her fragile body. The monitor kept beating faster, steady and alive, as though answering him.

Sam lifted his head, his eyes locking on her still face, and whispered through his tears, "Stay with me, baby. Please. You've fought this long, fight a little longer. I need you. I'll always need you."

And with that vow heavy in the room, Sam settled back into the chair, her hand still in his, his body weary but unrelenting in his vigil.

The world outside could rage and collapse, but here, in this room, he would not move.

The hours bled together in the hospital room, time marked only by the steady beeping of Lora's heart monitor and the mechanical sigh of the machines keeping track of her vitals. Sam hadn't moved. His body ached, his eyes burned, but he didn't care.

He sat forward, her hand still cradled in his, his thumb brushing across her skin as though trying to memorize its shape. His mind wouldn't stop running looping through every moment that had led them here.

How did I not see it?

He thought of her pale complexion, the dark smudges under her eyes, the way she'd refused sleep so many nights, brushing it off with excuses he'd accepted too easily. He thought of how she would stare too long into the dark, how her breathing sometimes caught when she woke in the night.

Her sleep patterns... her exhaustion... she didn't remember the case at the time, but she was part of it all along. Every sign was right in front of me. I was blind.

Sam clenched his jaw, his chest twisting with guilt. He had replayed it in his head a hundred times already tonight, each time the same conclusion burned deeper into him. I should have known. I should have seen the truth before it nearly killed her.

He bowed his head, pressing her hand to his lips, whispering against her skin: "I should have protected you. I should have seen it. God forgive me, Lora, I won't let you slip again."

The heart monitor beeped steadily in answer, her pulse fragile but alive. That rhythm became his anchor, keeping him from drowning in the tide of grief and guilt.

Sam sat through the night in silence, his thoughts circling, his eyes never leaving her face. Every twitch of her fingers, every flicker of her eyelids sent a jolt of hope through him. He stayed until the first weak light of dawn began to seep through the blinds.

Chapter Thirty Three

The door opened softly, breaking the fragile cocoon of the room. Detectives Harris, Mayhew, Ng, and Greene stepped inside, their faces lined with exhaustion, eyes shadowed with dread.

Sam straightened but kept his hand on Lora's. "How long?" His voice was low, raw from the night. "How long was she in there?"

Detective Harris was the one who answered, his tone heavy. "Five days. That's what the doctors estimate based on her condition and what they found."

Sam closed his eyes, the words slicing through him. His voice broke as he spoke again: "So that night...the night we were called to the scene was when she was taken. Along with Meyers and Hall?"

The silence stretched until Detective Mayhew nodded. "Yes. The others, most of them had been there longer. A few weeks, give or take more."

Sam's grip on Lora's hand tightened as his gaze dropped back to her pale face. His chest burned with grief and fury. "The killer has been busy," he muttered, his voice bitter with rage. His thumb brushed over her knuckles, softer now. "Lora, Meyers, Hall... they were so close. They knew who it was. That's why they were silenced."

The room held still, the team exchanging weary glances but saying nothing more. The weight of the truth pressed down on them all. Sam kept his vigil, unwilling to leave her, unwilling to let go.

And through it all, the monitor kept its fragile song, proof she was still here. Proof there was still something left to fight for.

The hospital night stretched on like a punishment.

Sam hadn't moved in hours, his body stiff in the unforgiving chair, his hand wrapped around Lora's pale fingers as if letting go would let her slip back into the earth. The faint beeps of the heart monitor tethered him to hope, each sound a fragile reassurance that she was still here, still fighting.

He leaned in close, his voice a whisper only for her: "You came back for us. All those visions, the sleepless nights... they weren't just signs. They were you leading us. You led us to Elena, to the others. You pulled us through the dark."

His chest ached as he brushed his thumb over her knuckles. "How blind was I? You were screaming in ways no one could hear, and I didn't see it. I should have known. God, Lora... forgive me for not knowing."

A tear slipped onto her hand. The monitor responded with a sudden quickening, just for a moment, and Sam's breath caught. He lifted his head sharply, searching her still face.

"You feel me, don't you?" His lips trembled as he kissed her hand. "You know I'm here. I love you, Lora. And I'm not letting you go."

The door opened quietly. Detectives Mayhew, Harris, Ng, and Greene re-entered, their faces shadowed by exhaustion. They lingered near the wall at first, watching Sam in silence, as if afraid to intrude on something sacred. Then Harris cleared his throat.

"Sam... we've been reviewing the files, the timelines, the evidence. We think..." He hesitated, glancing at the others. "We think Lora might have been number one."

Sam froze. His head snapped up, fury flickering in his exhausted eyes. His grip on her hand tightened.

"No," he said, sharp and final.

Mayhew stepped forward. "Listen. Look at the evidence. She was buried alive. She had visions of running, of being chased. She fits the pattern. Maybe the killer kept her alive for...."

"Stop." Sam's voice cracked like a whip, raw with grief and rage. "That's what he wants. He wants us to believe she was his first. To reduce her to a victim, a pawn. But she's not. She's the reason we found Elena. She's the reason anyone's still alive."

The room fell into a heavy, charged silence.

In the corner, the detectives leaned toward each other, lowering their voices so Sam wouldn't hear.

Ng whispered, "What if he's right? What if the killer is twisting the truth to break her and him?"

Greene shook his head. "Or what if Sam's blinded by his feelings? She's been showing signs for weeks. Pale, sleepless, visions. Maybe she doesn't even realize what she went through."

Harris crossed his arms. "Doesn't matter. If she was his number one, it changes everything we thought we knew about his pattern. Why keep her alive? Why let her lead us here?"

Mayhew rubbed his temples. "Maybe that's the game. To keep her alive long enough to bring us deeper. To unravel her. To unravel Sam."

Their voices faded into a low hum, a background current of doubt and theory.

But Sam didn't hear them.

His world had narrowed to the still figure in the hospital bed, the fragile weight of her hand in his. He brushed her bruised cheek with his thumb, his voice breaking into the silence:

"You're not a number, Lora. You're not his. You're mine. You're the light that's been cutting through his darkness. And I swear I'll keep you here with me."

The heart monitor continued its slow, steady beat thin, fragile, but alive. An anchor in the storm.

And Sam clung to it. To her.

Even as the detectives whispered in the background, arguing over riddles and theories, Sam's inner vow cut through it all:

You came back once. You'll come back again.

The night hummed with machines and whispers. Sam's world shrank to the fragile pulse beneath his fingers, the bruised face on the pillow. The others might have whispered about numbers, patterns, and games, but to him, there was only this: Lora was still breathing, and as long as she was, he would not move, not bend, not let her go.

Behind him, the detectives murmured: what if she was number one? Their words slithered into the silence, but Sam didn't turn. He pressed his forehead against Lora's hand, shutting out everything but the rhythm of her heartbeat.

The monitor beeped. Steady. Fragile. Alive.

The unbearable tension Sam's fierce, unyielding vigil, and the team's whispered doubts floating like smoke in the sterile hospital air.

Chapter Thirty Four

By morning, the room smelled faintly of coffee and disinfectant. The detectives had gathered in the small consultation alcove outside Lora's hospital room. They spoke in low, clipped voices, the kind meant for war rooms and battlefields, not sterile corridors.

Detective Harris leaned forward, elbows on his knees. "We can't ignore it anymore. The killer's been playing with us, yes but everything points back to her. If Lora was his first intended victim, then what does that mean?"

Ng shook her head. "No, not intended. He kept her alive. That changes everything. Maybe she was supposed to be number one, but he decided differently. Maybe she's the thread binding his entire ritual."

Greene muttered, "That's even worse. It means this whole thing has been circling around her from the start."

Mayhew rubbed the back of his neck. "Think about it Meyers, Hall ... all of them detectives. All of them connected to this forest investigation. He's been cutting us down, one by one, forcing Lora into the center of it. This isn't random it's targeted. It's deliberate."

The group fell silent, the weight of the words sinking in.

Sam finally stepped into the hallway. He looked like he hadn't slept in days, eyes red-rimmed, jaw tight, his shirt creased from the chair he'd refused to leave. But his voice was steady when he spoke:

"You're wrong."

The detectives turned toward him, startled.

Sam's gaze swept across them, cold, unflinching. "She wasn't his number one. She was his obsession. He kept her alive not because she's a victim, but because she's the one who can stop him. That's why he taunts her, why he leads her with riddles. He needs her in this game. He wants her to play."

Harris frowned. "Then what's his endgame?"

Sam clenched his fists. He glanced back at the hospital door, where Lora lay inside, fighting her way back to him. His chest ached as he spoke.

"To break her. To break all of us. To prove that even the strongest spirit can be bent, twisted, destroyed. He doesn't just want bodies he wants despair."

The detectives exchanged uneasy glances. For once, no one argued.

And Sam haunted, exhausted, but unshakable returned to the chair at Lora's side, holding her hand like an anchor.

The killer had written his warnings, taunted them with riddles, scattered the forest with symbols and bones. But Sam knew now, with a clarity that burned:

This was never about numbers. It was about Lora.

The hospital room was quiet except for the beeping of monitors, a sterile rhythm that Sam clung to as though it was her heartbeat itself. Lora's hand lay limp in his, pale fingers dwarfed by his own, and he traced circles along her knuckles as if the motion alone could keep her anchored here.

He hadn't slept. He hadn't left. He wouldn't.

Through the thin wall, he could hear the low cadence of the detectives gathered in the alcove, voices rising and falling like waves. They thought they were being discreet, but Sam caught fragments, enough to know the shape of their debate.

"She fits the profile..." Mayhew's voice, steady, careful.

"Ritualistic pattern, not random..." Harris, firm.

"Obsession. He's binding her into it..." Ng, clinical, precise.

"...manipulative. Everything is control..." Greene, heavy with unease.

Sam shut his eyes, leaning forward, resting his forehead against the back of Lora's hand. Their words pressed against him like a tide he couldn't hold back. Profile. Ritual. Obsession. All words that carved her down into pieces, fragments, theories.

Not a woman. Not his partner. Not the woman he still loved. Just another line in a case file.

His jaw tightened. He whispered into her skin, "They don't know you, Lora. They don't see what I see. You're not just part of his game you're stronger than him. Stronger than me. Stronger than all of us."

The monitor beeped steadily in reply, fragile but certain.

Outside, the voices sharpened.

"We've seen this before," Harris argued. "Killers who elevate one victim, turn them into something sacred in their sick worldview. He's ritualistic. He stages the bodies, carves the messages. He's using her."

Mayhew added, "No, he's fixated on her. That's different. Ritual is about process. This is about obsession. He doesn't just kill, he stalks, manipulates, draws them in. Everything circles back to Detective Matthews."

Ng's voice dropped lower. "Then she's both: the ritual and the obsession. He needs her to complete whatever game he's playing."

Greene muttered, "And she's alive, which means he hasn't finished."

Silence fell, heavy and sharp.

Sam lifted his head, staring at Lora's still face. Her cheek was bruised, her lip split, her dark hair fanned across the pillow. But to him she was still the fire that burned through the forest, still the woman who had fought her way back from a shallow grave.

His chest ached with a mix of rage and tenderness. He wanted to storm out there, shout them all down, tell them to stop dissecting her like she was just a puzzle piece. But his voice cracked into the still air instead, only for her:

"You hear that, Lora? They think they've figured him out. Ritual. Obsession. Manipulation. They don't know him. Not like you do. Not like I do. You've been one step ahead of him from the start even when you didn't know it. That's why you came back. You're not his victim, you're his undoing."

He bent and pressed his lips against her hand, holding it as though it were the only thing left keeping him alive.

The detectives debated on. Theories sharpened, voices clashed. But Sam's vigil never wavered. His world had narrowed to the fragile tether between him and Lora, a line the killer could not sever.

Not now. Not ever.

Sam's lips lingered against her knuckles, his eyes shut tight as if he could will her strength back into her body. Outside, their voices blurred into theories and labels, ritual, obsession, manipulation but to him, none of it mattered. What mattered was the fragile weight of her hand in his.

"She's not his victim," he whispered, voice breaking against the silence. "She's, his end."

The monitor beeped on, steady and frail. Sam bowed his head. He would not leave. He would not let go.

The detectives debated. The hospital lights buzzed. And the night stretched long, leaving them all suspended in a quiet that felt one breath away from shattering.

Chapter Thirty Five

The dawn was thin, grey, and heavy when the precinct team pulled themselves back together in the hospital's small conference room. Their eyes were rimmed with exhaustion, their nerves frayed, but no one dared speak of rest. They had none left to spare.

Detective Mayhew stood, files spread out before him. "We need boots back in the forest at first light. Whatever he's staging out there, it's not finished. The effigies, the disturbed ground they're messages. He's leaving us a trail."

Ng leaned forward, fingers tapping against the table. "And we need a tighter net around the victims he failed to kill. Elena Ward first. Twenty-four-hour guard, two female officers inside rotation, surveillance on every entrance. If he's obsessed with Lora, Elena might still be leverage. We can't risk it."

Greene's voice was low, heavy. "And Lora. We double security here, outside her room. No visitors without clearance. If he's bold enough to dig graves under our noses, he's bold enough to come for her in a hospital."

Detective Harris shook his head. "Not just bold obsessed. He won't stop. He's circling her, and us with her. That means he'll escalate. We have to be ready."

A grim silence settled over the table. No one wanted to voice what they all knew: the killer's game wasn't done, and every move he made was drawing them closer to something none of them yet understood.

Through the cracked conference door, Sam could hear pieces of their plans as he sat motionless at Lora's bedside. He hadn't moved all night, his hands still wrapped around hers, his eyes fixed on the faint rise and fall of her chest.

Search the forest.

Guard Elena.

Double security.

Words that barely reached him. His world had narrowed to the fragile thread of her pulse beneath his fingertips.

She was here. She was alive. That was his anchor.

But beneath the relief sat a quiet terror he couldn't shake: if the killer had buried her once, he would try again.

Sam leaned forward, resting his forehead against her hand, and whispered, "They're coming for him, Lora. But I'm not leaving you. Not now. Not ever."

The monitor beeped in steady reply, fragile but defiant.

The small hospital makeshift conference room smelled faintly of burnt coffee and antiseptic, the air heavy with exhaustion. Files and photographs littered the table. The detectives leaned forward, hollow-eyed, the weight of their choices pressing into their shoulders.

Detective Mayhew rubbed at his temple, staring at the spread of maps on the table. We should have seen this sooner. Every breadcrumb he left wasn't just for Lora it was for us too. He's taunting us, daring us. And now we're chasing shadows. How much time do we even have?

His jaw clenched. He wouldn't let another life slip through because they were one step behind. Not again.

Ng crossed her arms tight against her chest, her voice low and sharp. "We triple security around Elena. He let her live for a reason, and that reason terrifies me. She's leverage, bait… maybe worse." She didn't say the rest aloud that maybe Elena was never meant to survive at all, that perhaps keeping her alive was just another sick performance. In her gut, a quiet dread whispered: He's not finished. He's watching us scramble.

Greene leaned back, staring at the ceiling for a moment before speaking. His hands trembled slightly, hidden under the table. I've walked crime scenes, I've carried bodies, but this is different. This one feel like he's in the room with us every step of the way. He exhaled heavily. "If we don't stop him soon, we're going to lose more than we already have. And if he comes here…" His eyes flicked toward the door where Sam kept vigil. God help us if he comes here.

Detective Harris sat forward, elbows on the table, his tone steady but eyes rimmed with grief. "This case started before we got pulled into it. Meyers, Hall, and Lora were already circling something. Now Meyers and Hall are gone. We can't let her join them." His throat tightened. They were my friends. My brothers in this job. I owe them justice, and I owe her the chance to breathe free. He pressed his palms together, voice steady even as his chest ached. "That's the line. We guard her, and we hunt him. No compromises."

The detectives all fell silent, their individual fears coiling into the heavy stillness. For all their experience, for all their training, each of them knew the truth: they weren't chasing a man they were chasing a ghost who knew the forest, their fears, and now their team better than they did themselves.

Through the open crack of the conference room door, Sam heard every word, though his eyes never left Lora. Her hand lay in his, fragile, bruised, threaded with IV lines, and still the warmest thing he had ever held.

Triple security. More guards. Search the forest. Do this. Do that.

The words barely touched him. His mind was caught in a loop he couldn't break: the image of her body pulled from the earth, lifeless in his arms. The blood, the dirt, the silence.

He brushed his thumb across her knuckles, whispering so low the monitor nearly swallowed his voice and repeated his words feeling guilty with her. "You came back to us, Lora. You led us, even when you weren't here. How the hell did I not see it? How could I let it get this far?"

His chest burned with guilt. She was pale. She never slept. She was unravelling before my eyes, and I told myself it was stress, trauma, anything but this. She was number one, buried and fighting to reach us, and I couldn't even see it. Blind. I was blind.

The monitor beeped steady, faint but insistent, and Sam's tears slid down his cheek. He bent low, forehead brushing the back of her hand. "I love you," he whispered, the words breaking like glass in his throat. "And I'm not leaving you again. Not for anything."

Behind him, the detectives' voices rose and fell in sharp debate, their fears stitched into tactical plans guards posted, searches launched, every contingency drawn from desperation. Each of them knew time was against them, each carried the silent weight of two detectives already lost.

But Sam heard none of it. His world had narrowed to the fragile rise and fall of her chest, the trembling warmth of her hand, and the haunting truth echoing in his mind: She came back for us... and she's still not safe.

The room, the arguments, the entire case all of it blurred into a low hum. The only reality left was her.

And in that fragile vigil, the tension hung unbroken, suspended like the breath before a storm.

Chapter Thirty Six

The night had bled into dawn, and the detective's whispered debates hardened into sharper edges. The conference room walls seemed to hold their fear like smoke thick, suffocating, inescapable.

Detective Mayhew's voice was the first to cut through the low murmur. "We're dealing with someone ritualistic. Obsessive. Everything he does is deliberate every candle, every effigy, every breadcrumb. He's not killing at random; he's crafting." His eyes darkened. "And Lora is central to it."

Ng added, her tone clipped but heavy with unease, "He kept Elena alive because she meant something to him. Leverage, maybe a message. But this fixation on Lora..." Her throat tightened. "It isn't about her as an investigator it's about her as prey. He wants her."

Greene's fists clenched on the table. Wants her. Or needs her. God help us if it's the latter. His voice shook despite himself. "That's why Meyers and Hall died. They were orbiting too close to whatever truth ties Lora to him. He made sure they didn't live to uncover it."

Detective Harris leaned forward, voice gravel deep. "So, we tighten the net. Elena gets round-the-clock security, nobody in or out without clearance. We push harder on the forest grid, every dog, every set of boots on the ground. But let's not lie to ourselves the killer isn't hiding from us. He's circling us. Waiting."

A heavy silence fell, the kind that made every creak of the walls seem louder.

Through the open door, Sam finally moved.

He rose from the chair by Lora's bedside, every muscle stiff from hours of stillness. His hand lingered on hers just a heartbeat longer before he let go. His eyes red, exhausted, burning with something deeper than sleep could ever cure lifted to the glow of the conference room.

Step by step, he crossed the threshold. He didn't sit. He didn't lean. He stood in the doorway like a man carved from stone. The detectives fell quiet instantly.

For a long moment, silence hung. Sam's gaze swept over them, these men and women he trusted with his badge, his life, but not with her.

Then his voice came low, steady, and cold, "Action it. Make Elena safe."

No one moved, no one dared to breathe.

"As for Lora and me..." His jaw tightened, the fury in his chest barely contained. "...let's hope that son of a bitch comes for her. Because I'll be waiting."

The words struck like a hammer. Every detective in the room knew Sam well enough to hear the truth behind them. There would be no mercy. No hesitation.

Ng swallowed hard, glancing at the others. If he comes for her, Sam won't just stop him. He'll end him.

Greene felt his stomach tighten. And God help anyone who tries to get in his way.

Harris leaned back in his chair, his expression grim. I've seen Sam in the field. Seen what happens when his fury is unchained. He won't stop. Not until that monster is dead.

The team exchanged uneasy glances, but none of them spoke against him. They all knew the truth, Sam's rage was surfacing, dark and unyielding, a fire stoked by grief and love.

In the doorway, his fists curled at his sides, his breath slow but unsteady. His eyes burned with the single promise that lived inside him now: he would protect Lora at all costs. And when the killer finally showed his face, Sam would be the last thing he ever saw.

The silence that followed was suffocating, a pact unspoken but understood.

War had been declared.

The first grey light of dawn pressed through the blinds, thin and cold. In the hospital room, Sam sat once more at Lora's side, her pale hand cupped between both of his. The rhythmic beep of the monitor was steady now, her breath shallow but even.

Sam's eyes lingered on her bruises, the cracked skin near her temple, the faint tremble of her chest with each inhale. He leaned closer, whispering so low the words barely stirred the air.

"You're still here. That's all that matters. They won't touch you again. I swear it."

For a fleeting second, her fingers twitched against his. Sam's breath caught. He didn't know if it was reflex or recognition, but it was enough to keep him anchored. Enough to keep him from unravelling.

In the conference room down the hall, the detectives had resumed their hushed debate. But none of them could forget the way Sam's voice had sounded in the doorway cold, final, dangerous.

Detective Ng scribbled notes with a stiff hand, her mind racing. If Sam goes too far... if he acts on pure rage... do, we lose him to the same darkness we're chasing?

Mayhew leaned back in his chair, staring at the ceiling. He's, their Chief. He's supposed to guide us, steady us. But right now? He looks like a man standing on a knife's edge.

Greene tapped his pen against the table, jaw tight. I'd follow him anywhere. We all would. But this...this isn't leadership. This is vengeance. And vengeance can blind even the sharpest hunter.

Detective Harris's gaze hardened on the door that led to Lora's room. He spoke low, almost to himself. "Sam's rage... it'll either be the fire that burns this bastard down... or it'll consume him."

No one disagreed.

Back in Lora's room, Sam rested his forehead lightly against her hand. He could feel the warmth of her skin against his lips, fragile and faint, but real.

"I'm not letting you slip away, Lora. Not now. Not ever." His voice cracked, the fury beneath it burning through his grief. "He thinks he broke us, but he has no idea. When he comes, I'll be ready."

The words were a vow, whispered into her stillness. A promise to her, to himself, to the darkness waiting in the forest.

Dawn crept higher, filling the sterile room with pale light. And in that fragile, suspended quiet, Sam's rage coiled tighter fuel for the hunt that was far from over.

The hospital room was wrapped in the hush of early morning, a silence so deep it seemed to press against Sam's chest. Dawn's light crept across the floor in muted bands, pooling against the edges of Lora's bed.

Sam hadn't moved for hours. His hand remained locked around hers, the fragile anchor keeping him tethered when everything else threatened to pull him under.

Her skin felt warmer now, but her face still pale and bruised still haunted him. He traced the line of her cheekbone with his eyes, remembering laughter, the softness of her smile, the fire in her gaze when she was unshakable. And then, just as vivid, the sight of her limp in his arms in the forest. That memory would never leave him.

A lump rose in his throat. I should have seen it sooner. I should have protected you better. Never again.

Her heart monitor pulsed steady and calm. The sound was the only thing keeping him from collapsing. He let his thumb brush gently over her knuckles, a trembling gesture of devotion and guilt.

Sam leaned closer, his lips hovering against her temple. "I love you," he whispered, a truth he'd carried for too long in silence. His eyes burned, his chest heavy. "And I swear to God, Lora… he'll never touch you again."

Outside the room, the faint murmur of the task force filtered through the walls. Plans were being drawn, strategies debated. But Sam remained where he was, locked in vigil. To him, this was the only war that mattered, the fight to keep her breathing.

And in that suspended dawn quiet, Sam vowed again: there would be no mercy.

Chapter Thirty Seven

The sun had fully risen when Sam finally stepped into the conference room. He hadn't showered, hadn't eaten. His shirt was wrinkled, his face drawn, his eyes burning with exhaustion and something darker.

The detectives fell silent the moment they saw him.

He stood in the doorway, broad shoulders rigid, the weight of his presence commanding the room. For a long moment, he said nothing. The air thickened.

Then, in a voice low but edged with steel, Sam broke the silence.

"Action it. Double the detail on Elena. Twenty-four-hour surveillance, inside and out. No blind spots. No gaps." His gaze swept over each of them like a blade. "As for Lora and me..." His jaw tightened, and for a heartbeat, the mask slipped, revealing the fury underneath. "...let's hope that son of a bitch comes for her. Because I'll be waiting."

No one spoke. They all knew Sam well enough to hear what he wasn't saying that when the killer came, Sam wouldn't be calling for backup. He would finish it himself.

"There will be no mercy." The words cut the silence clean in half.

The detectives exchanged uneasy glances. They respected him. They trusted him. But they also feared him in this state.

Detective Harris shifted in his seat, his mind heavy. God help whoever crosses Sam now. But God help us too, if his rage blinds him.

Detective Ng scribbled notes with trembling fingers. We're walking into a storm, and he's the lightning.

Mayhew exhaled through his nose, his eyes narrowing. The killer thinks he's in control. He has no idea what's coming for him.

And in the center of it all, Sam stood tall, unyielding, his vow burning in his chest like fire. Lora was alive. Barely. And for that alone, Sam would hunt the man responsible into the ground.

No matter the cost.

The hospital hummed with its endless monotony, monitors, distant footsteps, the quiet shuffle of nurses outside. Inside Lora's room, time held its breath.

Sam hadn't spoken in hours. He just sat there, eyes fixed on her pale face, the steady rise and fall of her chest. His mind looped through everything her visions, her collapse, the grave in the forest. She came back for us. She led us here. And I almost lost her.

In the makeshift conference room down the hall, the detectives' voices drifted like murmurs of ghosts.

"She was number one all along..."

"No, the killer wants us to think that."

"If Sam's wrong."

"He won't hear it."

The debate flickered in hushed tones, but they never let it reach his ears. They knew better.

Sam leaned closer, pressing his forehead gently to Lora's hand, whispering words only she could hear. "I've got you. No matter what."

The detectives' doubts bled into silence. Fear, determination, and uncertainty clung to them like fog.

And so, the night closed suspended in tension: Sam's vigil unbroken, the team's whispered theories unresolved. Two currents pulling against each other yet tied to the same fragile tether Lora.

The dawn was coming, and with it, the next move.

Chapter Thirty Eight

When dawn finally cracked through the blinds, it carried no warmth. Just a pale light spilling across the floor, touching the edges of Sam's hunched figure.

He rose stiffly from the chair, every muscle tight with exhaustion and rage, and walked down the hall. The detectives were waiting in the makeshift conference room, their notes spread across the table, their faces drawn.

Sam stood in the doorway for a long moment, silent, his presence heavy enough to still the room. Then, at last, his voice broke the air.

"Action it. Make Elena safe. As for Lora and me…" He paused, the words sharp as glass. "…let's hope that son of a bitch comes for her. And I'll be waiting."

The detectives exchanged wary glances. They all knew Sam too well. Knew the promise in his voice. The vow.

"There will be no mercy."

Silence gripped the room. No one dared challenge him.

Detective Mayhew's stomach knotted. He means it. He's not talking about arrest, he's talking about an execution. I've seen him controlled, methodical... but this? This is the raw side. If the killer comes, Sam won't stop until there's blood.

Detective Ng swallowed hard, eyes shifting to the folders in front of her. He's the Chief. If his rage burns too hot, we're all at risk. But... maybe that's what we need. Someone unflinching. Someone willing to go further than the rest of us can stomach. God help us if it breaks him.

Detective Harris leaned back in his chair, arms crossed. I've fought beside Sam before. He's a man of principle. But love changes men. Love can turn them ruthless. And with Lora at the centre of this... I'm not sure whether his rage is our shield or the fuse to the powder keg we're standing on.

Detective Greene scribbled absently on a notepad, not writing anything. He's right about one thing: the killer will come. It's only a matter of when. And when he does, Sam will be there, waiting like a storm. Maybe that's what tips the scales. Maybe Sam's fury is the one thing the bastard doesn't expect.

The room seemed to tighten with the weight of their unspoken thoughts. None of them dared speak against Sam not because of fear of him, but because deep down, they knew he wasn't wrong. The killer had already pushed them past procedure, past reason. This was war now.

And in war, mercy was a luxury none of them could afford.

Sam's hand gripped the doorframe as he fixed each of them with a steady, burning gaze. His voice, low but ironclad, sealed the moment:

"We catch him. Or we bury him. Either way it ends."

The team said nothing, but their silence was not dissent. It was wary acceptance, each of them steeling themselves in the shadow of Sam's vow.

Sam turned back down the hall, back to the room where Lora lay. His tether. His reason. His breaking point.

And behind him, the detectives sat in the heavy silence, each of them knowing the truth. If the killer came for Lora, it wouldn't be a trial. It would be retribution.

The words still echoed in the detectives' ears as Sam turned and walked away from the room. His vow hung heavy in the air like smoke after a gunshot.

The corridor was dim and quiet, sterile white light spilling in shallow pools across the floor. Sam's boots carried him back, each step heavier than the last, until he pushed open the door to Lora's room.

Inside, everything slowed.

The machines hummed softly, steady, her breaths shallow but present. The beeping of the monitor was the only sound anchoring him. He sat down in the chair beside her again, lowering himself with a long, tired exhale, the rage in his chest still burning hot—but it faltered here.

With her.

Sam leaned forward, elbows on his knees, staring at her face. Bruised but still achingly familiar. The storm in him softened, just a fraction, as he reached out and carefully brushed a strand of hair from her forehead.

"You don't know what you do to me," he whispered, voice cracking under the weight of everything. "One second I'm ready to tear the world apart... and the next... you bring me back."

Her hand lay still against the blanket, pale, fragile. He took it gently, curling his calloused fingers around hers. The monitor ticked a little faster at his touch.

Sam's throat tightened. She feels me here. Even if she's not awake... she knows.

"I made them a promise, Lora," he murmured, eyes burning. "I swore to them and to myself that if he comes for you, I'll end it. No hesitation. No mercy. But God help me... I don't know if that's to protect you or because I can't live in a world where he breathes while you suffer."

He bowed his head, resting it against the back of her hand, the contrast inside him tearing him open: fury and tenderness, vengeance and love, all tangled in the same fragile tether.

For a long time, he stayed there, silent except for the broken sound of his breathing.

The storm was still inside him, wild and hungry. But beside her, in this fragile stillness, Sam let himself feel something else too something gentler, almost unbearable.

Hope.

Hope that she'd wake. Hope that when she did, she'd still see him not as a man consumed by rage, but as the man who loved her more than anything.

And as dawn stretched thin across the blinds, Sam whispered one last vow, quieter than the rage-filled promise he'd left with the team:

"I'm here. I'm not leaving. Not now, not ever."

He sat there, keeping his vigil, the thunderstorm in his chest held back by the fragile calm of her presence.

The calm after thunder.

Chapter Thirty Nine

Dawn broke pale and thin over the precinct, the kind of light that felt too fragile for the weight it had to hold. The detectives gathered one by one, some with red-rimmed eyes, others with coffee clutched in shaking hands. Exhaustion pressed on all of them, but beneath it was something sharper, harder: resolve.

Detective Mayhew leaned over the spread of maps and photographs. "The forest's hollow stretches further east. We've only scratched the surface." His voice was steady, but in his chest a coil of unease wound tighter with every word. *We're chasing something we don't understand. And Sam's rage... God, what happens when that finally breaks loose?*

Ng's jaw was tight as he traced a finger across the routes. "The riddle pointed to cycles, to something unfinished. If Lora's visions are pulling us, then maybe she's still the compass we follow." He hesitated, lowering his voice. "But how much of her is left to carry that burden?"

Greene rubbed his temples. He'd seen too many cases where obsession hollowed detectives out. *She's burning from the inside. And Sam,* he'll let himself burn right beside her if it means keeping her breathing. He looked around the table. "We need to be smart. Not reckless. The killer's taunting us using her, using him. Don't let him win twice."

Harris's voice cut through the silence like steel. "Then we do this by the book. Sweep teams in pairs. Secure every inch of the hollow. Dogs up front, forensics behind. If the bastard is still down there, we flush him out." He clenched his fist. I've buried enough colleagues. I won't bury her too.

For a long moment, no one spoke. The weight of what lay ahead pressed heavy on every shoulder.

And yet beneath the maps, the riddles, the endless theories each detective thought of Sam. His vow. The rage simmering behind his eyes. They needed him, but they also feared what that rage might unleash when the killer finally stood in front of him.

The clock ticked toward deployment.

Back at the hospital, Sam sat at Lora's bedside, still holding her hand. He hadn't slept. He wouldn't.

The hunt was resuming without him. But the storm inside him whispered: Soon. Very soon, it will be me and him. And when that moment comes, there will be no mercy.

The team readied themselves to enter the forest at dawn, hardened determination pushing against exhaustion, fear, and doubt. They carried Sam's vow with them into the trees like a shadow none of them could shake.

The detectives moved out at dawn, their boots crunching on gravel as the SUVs rolled toward the forest's edge. Engines rumbled low, radios crackled, dogs barked sharp in the morning chill. The hunt had begun again, the weight of Sam's vow shadowing every step, though he was not with them.

Sam remained at the hospital. His place was here, rooted at her side. He hadn't left the chair in hours his back stiff, his eyes hollow, but his grip on her hand unbroken.

The steady beep of the monitor filled the room. It had become his lifeline, proof she was still here. Proof that the storm inside him had reason to hold back.

Then soft. Barely there.

Her fingers twitched against his.

Sam's head shot up, heart hammering. He blinked once, twice, terrified it was a trick of exhaustion. But no, her hand moved again. Slowly, weakly, it lifted, trembling as it brushed against his head.

"Lora…" His voice cracked. He leaned closer, eyes burning, as her fingers slid through his hair in a fragile stroke.

With her other hand she tugged at the oxygen mask, weak but determined. Sam panicked, "No, no, you need that, "but before he could stop her, she slipped it free and drew in a shaky breath on her own.

Her eyes fluttered open, pale but alive, and found his.

Sam's chest broke open. He surged forward, kissing her face, her temple, her bruised cheek, her lips anywhere his tears fell. "I love you, baby," he whispered against her skin, voice wrecked with relief. "God, I thought I was going to lose you."

The monitor picked up speed as her breaths trembled through the room.

The door burst open nurses rushing in, eyes wide, gasps filling the air. "She's awake!" one called out, shock and relief colliding in their voices as they rushed to her side.

Sam didn't let go of her hand. Not for a second.

His forehead pressed to hers, tears spilling freely as he whispered again and again, "I love you. I love you. You came back to me."

And for the first time since the forest, the storm inside him gave way not to silence, not to rage. but to fragile, haunting relief.

The nurses moved quickly, checking vitals, murmuring orders, adjusting IV drips. But to Sam it was all background noise distant, muffled because the only thing that mattered was her hand still clutching his, her eyes fluttering but fixed on him.

"Stay with me," he whispered. "Don't you dare leave me again."

Her lips parted, dry, soundless at first. He leaned closer, catching the faintest thread of her breath. "...Sam."

It broke him. He kissed her hand, her forehead, his tears soaking into her hair. "I'm here, sweetheart. I'm not going anywhere. You're safe now."

Safe. But even as he said the word, he didn't believe it.

The rage simmered, coiled tight beneath his relief. Every bruise on her face, every bandage across her ribs, every line of dried blood whispered what she had endured. What he hadn't stopped. What someone out there had done to her.

Sam tightened his grip. He would never let that happen again.

The nurses exchanged hushed words behind him, voices tinged with awe. "It's a miracle she's awake... she shouldn't be this strong after five days..."

Sam tuned them out. He only heard the faint sound of her breath, the steady rhythm of the monitor. Each sound stitched him back together, just enough to keep him from unravelling.

He brushed her hair back gently, studying the pale complexion he'd missed beneath the bruises. He remembered every sign he'd ignored, her exhaustion, her fragile sleep, the way her visions pulled her away. All the clues, and he hadn't seen them.

"I should've known," he whispered, his voice thick with guilt. "I should've seen it."

Her eyes opened again, faint but steady. She shifted her fingers, barely enough to squeeze his hand. And though she had no strength to speak, her gaze told him: You did find me.

Sam bent forward, resting his forehead against hers. His shoulders trembled, his breath catching. "You're right. You came back for us to find you. You brought us to the victims... to you. God, Lora, you fought harder than anyone I've ever known."

The nurses dimmed the lights, leaving only the soft glow of monitors and the faint hush of machines. The world outside the hunt, the killer, the danger faded.

It was just the two of them.

Sam sat back down, never releasing her hand. The chair creaked beneath his weight as he settled in for another vigil. His thumb traced circles over her skin, grounding himself in the fragile reality of her presence.

Somewhere in the city, his detectives pushed forward, chasing shadows through the dawn. But Sam didn't care. His battlefield was here, beside her, where silence and devotion met.

He stayed that way until exhaustion finally pressed his head against the edge of her bed, her hand still entwined with his, as the night stretched on.

Chapter Forty

The hospital was quiet at dawn, corridors hushed, the scent of antiseptic sharp in the air.

Sam stirred awake to the faintest touch against his hair. His eyes snapped open, meeting hers open now, clearer, though her face remained pale and fragile.

She pulled the oxygen mask aside, just enough to speak. Her voice was ragged, barely above a whisper. "Sam..."

He leaned close, instantly alert. "I'm here."

Her lips trembled, eyes glistening. "He's coming."

Sam froze.

"The killer," she whispered, her voice breaking on the words. "He's coming here... for me."

Sam's breath caught like ice in his chest. For a moment, the world seemed to narrow into just her words thin, fragile, yet heavy as stone.

"He's coming here... for me."

Her voice trembled, her eyes wide, glistening with a mix of fear and certainty. This wasn't just delirium. It wasn't confusion. Sam knew that look. He'd seen it before, every time a vision had torn through her.

He leaned in, one hand cupping her cheek as if to anchor her to the present. "Lora, listen to me." His voice was low, steady, but a storm raged beneath it. "If he comes... he won't get near you. I swear it."

Her lips parted, but no words followed. Just a faint shudder, her fingers tightening weakly around his hand, as if to say don't let go.

Sam pressed his forehead against hers, eyes closing. His voice cracked as he whispered, "I thought I lost you once. Never again. I don't care who he is, what he thinks he can do—if he steps into this room, I'll end him. You hear me? I'll end him."

The monitors beeped softly, filling the silence that followed his vow. The rage inside him burned hotter than it ever had no longer just anger, but a lethal promise etched into bone.

He pulled back, reached for the small handset by the bed, and pressed the call button. Within moments, nurses rushed in. Their eyes widened at the sight of Lora awake, mask lowered, her hand gripping Sam's.

"She needs monitoring," one nurse said quickly, moving toward the IV.

Sam lifted his other hand, stopping them with a look that carried the weight of command. "She stays safe. No one comes in here unless I clear it." His voice was steel, quiet but undeniable.

The nurse hesitated, nodded, and slipped out to alert the floor.

Sam's other hand moved to his phone. His thumb hovered for only a second before dialling through to the detectives. His voice when they answered was sharp, stripped of hesitation:

"She's awake. She says he's coming here. Lock this hospital down. I want every entrance sealed, every floor covered, plainclothes and uniforms both. Nobody in, nobody out without clearance. Move now."

On the other end, silence then hurried voices, the shuffle of chairs, boots against the precinct floor.

Detective Harris's voice came steady but urgent: "Understood, Chief. We're on our way. ETA fifteen minutes."

Sam ended the call and slipped the phone back into his pocket, his hand returning immediately to Lora's.

She watched him, pale and trembling, but her eyes softened as his thumb brushed her knuckles. He leaned close again, speaking just for her. "Let them come. Let him come. He thinks you're alone. He thinks he can finish what he started." His jaw clenched, eyes dark. "He doesn't know I'm here. He doesn't know what I'll do."

Lora's lashes fluttered as exhaustion pulled at her, but she whispered back, breath hitching against the mask: "...Sam..."

He kissed her hand gently, whispering like a prayer, "Rest. I've got you."

The room stilled again machines humming, dawn light pushing weakly through the blinds, yet the air felt heavy, braced for something unseen.

At that same hour, across the city, the precinct was a storm of motion. Detectives Mayhew, Ng, Greene, and Harris abandoned their case files, their coffee, their exhaustion. They grabbed jackets, weapons, radios, all of them knowing the same truth at once: if the killer was coming for Lora, everything was about to converge.

Each carried the weight differently.

Ng felt her chest tighten, the dread of déjà vu Meyers, Hall, almost Lora already. Could they stop history repeating?

Greene clenched his jaw, telling himself not to think, just move, just act.

Harris felt the weight of his words from before, that Lora was the key. Now the key was in danger.

Mayhew thought only of time: fifteen minutes, maybe less. Every red light, every second was another chance for the killer to slip closer.

Engines roared to life. Sirens stayed silent stealth mattered.

They weren't just going to the hospital. They were running into the jaws of the trap.

Engines roared. Tires bit into wet asphalt as the convoy of unmarked cars and cruisers tore through the streets.

No sirens, no lights. Just grim faces behind the windshields, hands clenching wheels, radios alive with clipped orders.

Every detective felt it pressing in the knowledge that the clock had started ticking the second Sam's call ended.

Ng's stomach was in knots; she kept replaying Lora's words in her head. He's coming here. What if they were too late?

Greene fought to keep his mind blank. Better to focus on the hunt than imagine what might already be happening inside those hospital walls.

Harris ground his teeth, his chest burning with guilt. He'd been the one to say Lora was the key. If she was hurt again if she was taken it would be on him.

Mayhew watched the minutes on his dashboard clock. Fifteen to get there. Fifteen too long.

The city blurred by in streaks of sodium light and shadow. All of them knew it: they weren't just rushing to protect Lora. They were rushing into the killer's hands.

The trap was set.

Back in the hospital, silence pressed down like a second skin.

Machines ticked in soft, rhythmic beeps. Weak light filtered through the blinds, striping the bed in pale grey.

Sam sat close, his body angled protectively toward Lora. He hadn't moved since the call. His hand still wrapped around hers, his thumb brushing over her knuckles in small, steady circles, as if that alone could keep her tethered.

Her eyes fluttered, her chest rising and falling shallowly, but her lips curved faintly beneath the mask. She knew he was there.

Sam leaned closer, his voice rough but steady. "They're coming for us, Lora. But they won't touch you. Not while I'm breathing."

Her lashes flickered. Her hand, trembling, pressed weakly back against his.

Sam bowed his head over her hand, eyes burning. "I love you. And if he wants you, he'll have to go through me."

The monitor beeped, steady.

The hospital halls beyond were quiet. Too quiet.

The hunt was already on its way and Sam was waiting.

Chapter Forty One

The hospital room was quiet too quiet. Machines hummed in soft, steady rhythms, a mechanical lullaby that should have felt safe. But Sam sat rigid in the chair by Lora's bed, hand still wrapped around hers, and something inside him whispered that safety was an illusion.

He lifted his head at the faintest sound. A scrape. Not loud, not obvious just a whisper of rubber soles against polished tile. His eyes flicked to the door, to the thin shadow pooled beneath it.

Lora stirred in her half-sleep, lips parting around a broken murmur. Sam leaned close, trying to catch the words. Her voice was raw, fragile, but carried a thread of warning: "He's... here."

Sam's heart clenched hard against his ribs. He tightened his grip on her hand, fighting to keep his voice steady. "I'm right here, Lora. No one's getting near you. Not while I breathe."

But even as he said it, the scrape came again closer this time. Then silence. A silence that weighed too much.

Sam rose slowly, every muscle taut, and shifted himself between the bed and the door. His hand hovered near his weapon. Lora's eyes opened weakly, just enough to watch him, her lips trembling as if she wanted to speak more but the oxygen mask pulled her words back.

"Rest," he whispered. "Don't be afraid. I've got you."

The silence stretched. His pulse roared in his ears. Then...

The scene cut outward like a snapped wire.

Red and blue strobes washed across the hospital lot as the detectives arrived, their vehicles skidding into place. Doors slammed open. Detective Mayhew barked orders as officers sprinted toward every entrance, sealing them off. Detective Harris led the second wave into the lobby, weapon drawn, eyes sharp and darting.

Every hallway lit up with radio chatter and the pounding of boots. They knew the killer's pattern sudden, slippery, a ghost in plain sight. The hospital wasn't just a building anymore. It was a hunting ground.

Inside, Sam didn't move. He stood watch at the door, jaw clenched, every nerve tuned to the quiet beyond. The detectives were coming he could hear the echo of their advance down the corridors. But whether they were early enough, or already too late, he couldn't yet know.

Sam didn't move. He stood at the door, jaw clenched, one hand hovering over his weapon.

Every nerve screamed with the quiet beyond that thin strip of shadow under the frame.

The detectives' footsteps were coming closer now he could hear the echo of their boots and clipped orders in the corridor.

But what waited on the other side of this door what dared to come for her was already here.

The air was a taut wire, about to snap.

Chapter Forty Two

T he handle twitched. That was all Sam needed.

The door cracked open, and he launched. In a single blur of movement, Sam ripped the figure inside and slammed him against the wall so hard the plaster split. The intruder grunted, tried to twist free, but Sam was already on him, fists driving forward with a violence no training manual could sanction.

Blow after blow. Bone cracking. The sharp spray of blood painting sterile white walls.

"You think you can touch her?!" Sam roared, voice jagged, not even human. "You think you can take her from me again?!"

The killer if he even deserved the word man choked and coughed, arms flailing weakly as Sam dragged him down and beat him across the floor.

Behind him, the team had reached the doorway. They froze, not in shock, but in grim silence.

Detective Mayhew gave the slightest shake of his head. Radios were switched off.

Detective Harris thumbed his body cam until the little red light went dark.

The uniformed officers followed without a word, cameras cut, every lens gone blind.

No one was going to stop him.

Sam had bled for this team, commanded them, saved them. And now they stood guard not for the law, but for him. For Lora.

Every punch was a promise. Every broken rib, a prayer. Every howl from Sam's throat was grief made flesh.

The killer's body convulsed under him, but Sam didn't stop. Couldn't stop. His rage was tidal, bottomless, a storm year in the making.

In the corner, Lora stirred weakly in her bed. Her lips parted, eyes glassy, and she whispered his name.

"Sam..."

For the first time, his fists slowed. His chest heaved, blood dripping from his knuckles as he looked up, eyes wild, face drenched in sweat and tears.

The room reeked of iron, violence, and something far older than justice.

And still the detectives held their silence.

Because they all knew this wasn't just Sam protecting her. This was Sam unleashing everything he'd carried, every failure, every death, every moment he almost lost her.

And none of them dared pull him back.

The silence broke at last. Boots moved across the floor, the detectives stepping in, slow and cautious, not to stop Sam but to circle the wreckage he had made.

The man on the ground was barely breathing, face ruined, body limp. Yet even in his broken state, he managed a sound.

A laugh. Thin, gurgling, blood-soaked but a laugh. Sam froze, his fist still cocked above him.

The killer wheezed words through shattered teeth. "She'll never be yours, Sam... she'll be mine. Even if I have to take her piece by piece..."

The rage snapped back into Sam like a whip. He grabbed the bastard by the throat, hauling him up until their faces were inches apart. His breath was fire, his eyes wild with something primal.

"She will never be yours," Sam growled, every word vibrating with lethal promise.

The killer smiled through blood. Mocking. Daring.

Sam drew back one last time, his knuckles already raw, and slammed his fist into the man's face with a bone-jarring crack.

The body went limp instantly. Out cold.

Sam let him drop, sneering down at the unconscious husk sprawled across the sterile floor. His chest heaved, blood dripping from his fist. For a long, terrible moment, the only sound was the rhythmic beep of Lora's monitor and the heavy breathing of every detective in the room.

Detective Harris finally moved, crouching by the body, checking the ruined face for breath. He glanced up. "Alive. Barely."

Detective Mayhew wiped a hand across his mouth, unsettled. "What the hell do we do now?"

No one answered immediately. They all looked at Sam. The man who had just shown them the truth of what he was willing to do. The man they feared and followed in equal measure.

Behind them, Lora stirred again in the bed, her whisper carrying like a ghost across the room.

"Sam..."

Her voice broke something in him. The animal rage drained, leaving only the trembling shell of a man, his fists dripping, his chest heaving. He staggered back from the body, turning toward her as if the rest of the room didn't exist.

And the detectives, hardened though they were, felt the weight of it the fragile tether between Sam and Lora, and the blood-soaked cost it had already claimed.

The killer lay beaten. But the war was far from over.

Chapter Forty Three

The hospital's sterile corridors echoed with a chaos that felt muffled, like voices drifting through water. Gurneys rattled, radios crackled, and uniforms swarmed but inside the room itself, the silence was still absolute.

The killer's body was bound, shackled at wrist and ankle, guards dragging him out with grim, nervous faces. Even unconscious, he radiated something foul, something that seemed to crawl under the skin of anyone too close.

Detective Harris muttered under his breath, almost to himself: "Monster."

Mayhew didn't disagree. His jaw was locked tight, eyes tracking every inch of the killer's battered frame as if afraid he might rise from the stretcher like a revenant.

Forensics moved in next, sealing evidence bags with quick, precise hands. Bloodied sheets, Sam's torn knuckles swabbed for record, the cracked linoleum underfoot scraped clean. It was all procedure, but no one in the room could pretend this was just another case.

Sam stood apart, his chest still rising and falling like a man coming down from the edge of war. His knuckles were wrapped now, trembling beneath gauze, but he hadn't taken his eyes off the door since they wheeled the killer away.

The detectives avoided his gaze. They all knew what he had done in that room was beyond the line. But they also knew none of them would ever put it on paper. Radios had been switched off. Cameras cut. What happened here would remain in the dark.

Because every one of them had felt it when the killer laughed, when he taunted Lora's name it wasn't law that answered. It was blood. And Sam Matthews had bled for all of them.

Across the room, Lora shifted weakly in her bed, her eyes half-open. Her voice was barely audible, but it anchored Sam like a chain. "Sam..."

He moved instantly, crouching at her side, his large hand cradling her fragile fingers. His voice broke as he answered her, a softness no one else ever heard. "I'm here. I'm not leaving. Ever."

Behind them, the team filed out into the hallway, their whispers low but heavy with dread.

Harris: We've got him secured. But he wanted this. Why?

Ng: Because it's not over. It never is with people like him.

Greene: Sam won't let this go. He'll kill him outright before we ever get answers.

Mayhew: Wouldn't you? After what he did to her?

The corridor swallowed their words.

Sam stayed where he was, forehead against the back of Lora's bruised hand, whispering something no one else could hear. The world could rage outside these walls, but in here, there was only this fragile tether.

The killer was in custody. Preparations for interrogation were already underway. But everyone every single one of them knew that this wasn't the end.

It was the beginning of something worse.

Lora stirred again, her eyes fluttering open in the dim wash of fluorescent light. Her voice was raw, weak, but her words cut through the silence like glass.

"Keep him alive, Sam..."

Sam froze, his breath catching in his chest. Her hand trembled against his, frail but insistent.

He leaned closer, tears sliding down his bruised cheeks as he pressed a tender kiss to her forehead.

"Anything for you," he whispered, his voice breaking.

But even as he spoke the vow, something inside him twisted. He knew those words weren't just mercy, they were warning. There was more buried inside Lora's visions, more about this killer, more about the victims. She carried it, even if she didn't know how to name it yet.

Sam's jaw clenched. The rage was still there, thrumming under his skin, but now it was tangled with fear. Fear of what she knew, fear of what he didn't, and fear of what was still to come.

He stayed like that, forehead pressed against her temple, until her breathing steadied again. The world outside the hospital door could wait.

Chapter Forty Four

The killer's transfer was carried out under heavy guard. Shackles clinked with every step as uniforms hauled him down the sterile hallway, flanked by detectives whose hands never strayed far from their weapons.

No one spoke. No one wanted to.

When they wheeled him into holding, the air shifted. The usual ritual of booking and processing felt wrong too clinical for someone like this. Too clean.

The attending medic gave him only the bare minimum: a quick swab, a few cursory stitches across his split brow, and a perfunctory check of his ribs. There was no kindness in their hands, no real care. Just procedure. He wasn't a man to them; he was evidence barely kept breathing.

Detective Ng stood in the corner, her stomach tight with unease. We should want him alive, she told herself. We need answers. But God help me, I wanted Sam to finish it right there on the floor.

Harris paced like a caged dog, his mind racing. We've got him. We've actually got him. But what if he wanted this? What if we're walking into his design?

Greene leaned against the wall, arms folded, his eyes like flint. Let Sam interrogate him. He'll break him faster than any of us. But... maybe that's exactly what the bastard wants.

Mayhew's gaze never left the stretcher as it rolled past the glass. Two detectives dead. How many victims gone. And now he's here, breathing. If this isn't justice, what the hell is it?

Inside the holding cell, the killer stirred under the dim light. His face was swollen, his lip split, one eye puffed shut. Still, a crooked, bloodstained smile tugged at his mouth.

He coughed once, spat red onto the floor, and rasped a laugh that rattled like dry bones.

The detectives watching felt it in their bones: this was far from over.

And somewhere upstairs, Sam still sat with Lora, her whisper echoing in his chest, Keep him alive, Sam.

Alive, for now.

But every man and woman in that precinct knew what it would take to keep him that way.

The killer's transfer was carried out under heavy guard. Shackles clinked with every step as uniforms hauled him down the sterile hallway, flanked by detectives whose hands never strayed far from their weapons.

No one spoke. No one wanted to.

When they wheeled him into holding, the air shifted. The usual ritual of booking and processing felt wrong too clinical for someone like this. Too clean.

Chapter Forty Five

The room was hushed except for the steady beeping of the heart monitor. Sam hadn't moved all night; he sat slouched in the chair, his hand still wrapped gently around Lora's. His thumb brushed across her knuckles in slow, absent motions, as if to remind her and himself that she was still here.

A tremor stirred in her eyelids. Her lips parted, a faint whisper slipping out before she could even wake.

"...running..."

Sam leaned forward instantly. "Lora? Baby, I'm here. You're safe."

Her breathing hitched. She gripped his shirt with surprising strength, her voice no louder than a rasp. "They're... they're running. In the woods. Cold. I can feel it."

Her words fractured, her body trembling with effort.

Sam tightened his arms around her. His pulse hammered, half in fear for her, half in anger at what she was being forced to carry. She's still seeing them. Still feeling it. My God, what did he do to her?

"Shh. Easy," he soothed, pressing his cheek to her temple. "You don't have to force it. Whatever comes, I've got you."

But Lora shook her head weakly, her voice cracking. "No... you need to listen. He's not done. Not with me. Not with any of them."

Sam closed his eyes, every word carving deeper into him. He kissed her damp hair, his whisper hoarse.

"I swear, I won't let him touch you again. Not now, not ever."

Her breathing softened, her body sinking back against the bed, but the fragments lingered in the air between them running, cold, woods.

Sam stayed by her side until nurses slipped in to check her vitals. Only then did he force himself to leave, though every step away from her bed felt like treason.

Back at the precinct, the mood was heavier than stone. The killer sat shackled at a steel table, bruised and bloodied, yet smug.

Detective Harris loomed against the wall, arms folded, jaw clenched. Mayhew shuffled the case files, her hands trembling just enough to betray her exhaustion. Greene's eyes were fixed sharp on the killer's every move, cataloguing the smallest twitch. Ng leaned on the doorframe, watching silently, her gut coiled tight with unease.

The killer lifted his head slowly, swollen eye cracking open. A grin broken tooth smeared red spread across his face.

"Where's my audience?" His voice was a rasping mockery. "Where's the one who sees me? Where's Lora?"

Every detective stiffened.

Harris slammed a fist down on the table, leaning in close. "You don't say her name."

But the killer only chuckled, a low, rattling sound. "Oh... but she says mine. All the time. In her sleep. In her pretty little visions. She feels me, doesn't she? The woods, the running, the fear... I made her mine before you ever found me."

Mayhew's knuckles whitened as he gripped his pen. Greene's stomach turned. Ng looked away, trying to steady her breath.

Behind the glass, Sam stood silently, his face unreadable. He wasn't supposed to be there, but no one dared ask him to leave. His eyes burned through the barrier, through the killer, through every word.

Because in his chest, all he could hear was Lora's whisper from the hospital bed: He's not done.

Sam knew she was right.

Chapter Forty Six

The hospital room was dim, the first fingers of dawn pressing faint light through the blinds. Sam hadn't moved all night, still anchored at her bedside. Lora stirred, her breath quick, her eyes fluttering as if chasing something only she could see.

"Sam..." her voice cracked, fragile but sharp with urgency.

He was already leaning over her, his hand brushing sweat-damp hair from her forehead. "I'm here, baby. I'm right here."

Her fingers tightened around his wrist, trembling, as though she was holding on for both their lives. Her gaze drifted beyond him, to some unseen point only her visions could show.

"They're still out there," she whispered. "Running. Cold. I can hear them crying. Sam, they're waiting for you."

Sam's stomach clenched. He reached into his jacket, pulled out his phone, and hit the speaker. "Team, you are hearing this?" His voice was low, steady but inside, it felt like standing on the edge of a cliff.

Across the speaker, the detectives went silent. Every breath in the room was heavy.

Lora gasped, her body jolting as if struck by something unseen. Her hand clawed for Sam's shirt, pulling him closer. "You interrogate him," she rasped. "Finish it. Find the bodies. Find them, Sam. I'm with you."

Her words shook him to his core. His throat burned, and it was all he could do to nod, lowering his forehead to hers, whispering back: "Then we do this together. Always."

Inside, his mind roared. She's guiding me again. She trusts me to finish what we started. God help me if I fail her now. I won't. I can't.

Sam kissed her forehead softly, letting the moment brand itself into him. Then, straightening, he left the room with a final glance back carrying her words like armour.

The door slammed behind him, the sound reverberating through the sterile walls of the precinct's interrogation room.

The killer looked up, bruised and swollen, lips curling into a smile that still somehow carried mockery. "Well, well. The great Chief finally comes down from the tower. Where's your ghost girl?"

Sam pulled out the chair, sat down slowly, and placed both hands flat on the table. His eyes locked on the killer with a stillness that made every detective watching hold their breath.

"She's alive," Sam said evenly. "And because of her, so are you. For now."

The killer chuckled, his split lip leaking fresh blood. "Alive... for now. But you know she was mine first, don't you? I let her breathe so she could find me again. So, she could lead you right here."

Sam leaned closer, his voice a growl low enough to rattle bone. "Then you already know how this ends. You tell me where the bodies are, or I make sure you never speak her name again."

The killer's eyes glittered with something sharp hunger, obsession, maybe even delight. He leaned forward until their faces were inches apart. "You're close, Chief. But you're looking in the wrong place. The ground isn't the only thing that hides them."

The room stilled. Harris's jaw tightened. Mayhew scribbled furiously. Greene's pulse kicked into his throat. Ng's eyes narrowed, parsing every syllable.

Sam didn't move. He let the silence hang like a blade, his heart hammering with one truth pounding louder than the rest:

Lora was right. He's not done. And I won't stop until he is.

The killer tilted his head, lips twitching into a grotesque grin despite the swelling. "You keep digging in the dirt like desperate little dogs. But the ground..." He paused, savouring the silence, eyes darting between Sam and the detectives behind the glass. "...the ground only swallows what's left. The others, Chief, the ones you can't, see? They're hidden in plain sight."

Sam's jaw tightened. His pulse thundered, but his face stayed stone. "Plain sight where?"

The killer laughed, the sound scraping like rusted metal. "Ah, that's the riddle, isn't it? Where would you put something so precious if you wanted everyone to walk past and never know?"

Harris cursed under his breath from behind the glass. Mayhew leaned forward, whispering to Greene, "He's taunting, but it's something. There's a layer here we're missing."

Sam leaned in, voice low, deadly steady. "I don't play riddles. Give me something real."

The killer's swollen smile widened, exposing bloodied teeth. He whispered like a conspirator, eyes gleaming. "Look up, Chief. Look higher than you've ever searched. Graves aren't always dug down."

Sam's knuckles flexed against the table, rage straining to break free. But he forced stillness, knowing every word mattered. Look up... higher...

The killer leaned back, closing his eyes as if sated. "Number one... oh, she's closer than you think. She watches you even now."

For a heartbeat, the room seemed to close in. The words hung like smoke, wrapping around each detective's throat.

Ng muttered, "Jesus. He's saying she's above ground! Elevated! What the hell does that even mean?"

Mayhew's pen scraped furiously. "Closer... watches... It's deliberate."

Greene swallowed hard, eyes locked on Sam. "Chief, he's playing with you."

Sam didn't blink. Didn't look away. His voice came out like broken glass. "If you so much as breathe her name again, I'll end you. Right here. Right now."

The killer smiled wider, his swollen face grotesque. "Then I win, Chief."

The silence that followed was suffocating, broken only by the faint buzz of the overhead light. Sam finally stood, his chair scraping back, towering over the restrained figure.

"Enjoy this cell while you can," Sam growled, low enough to rattle. "Because when I find them and I will there'll be nothing left of you but a name in a file."

He turned on his heel, every muscle burning with the weight of the breadcrumb. Look up. Closer. Watches.

Behind the glass, the detectives shifted uneasily, each one parsing the killer's words through their own fears.

But Sam already knew whatever this meant, Lora would see more. She always did.

The interrogation room was empty now, the killer dragged away in cuffs and restraints, his mocking words still bleeding into the air.

Behind the glass, the detectives lingered, each face etched with unease.

Detective Harris broke the silence first, shaking his head. "Look up. What the hell does that mean? What's higher than the graves we've been digging?"

Ng leaned against the wall, arms folded tight, chewing the thought. "Elevated ground. Old mines. Maybe the forest's ridge. It could be literal."

Mayhew shook his head, his eyes narrowed. "No. No, he's cleverer than that. Symbolic, maybe. Look up like towers, attics, rafters. Somewhere you don't look because you're always focused on the ground."

Greene rubbed at his face, exhausted but restless. "Or he's lying. Throwing us off, making us waste time chasing shadows. He knows Sam's close to breaking."

Silence stretched, heavy and brittle. Each of them felt it the weight of the breadcrumb, the possibility that number one was right above their heads, hidden in plain sight all along.

But none of them dared to say what they feared most: that the killer's obsession with Lora meant the answer might circle back to her.

Through the one-way glass, the empty chair where Sam had sat still seemed alive with rage.

Chapter Forty Seven

Sam didn't linger for the debate. His boots pounded the hospital corridor until he was back in Lora's room.

She stirred as he entered, her pale face turning, eyes soft but haunted. Her hand lifted weakly, reaching for him.

He crossed the space in two strides and lowered himself beside her, taking her fingers into his palm. His voice cracked, raw. "He said something. A breadcrumb. 'Look up. Closer than we think. She watches.'"

Lora's breath hitched. Her gaze unfocused, as if already being pulled into something beyond the room.

Sam's chest tightened. He wanted to stop her, shield her from it, but he couldn't her visions had carried them this far.

Her lips moved, a whisper at first. "Above... not buried. Elevated. Watching. Sam..." Her eyes fluttered shut, her voice trembling. "I can see... rafters, beams... wood... it's dark. She's there, curled like she was waiting."

Sam's heart slammed against his ribs. He leaned closer, holding her hand tighter, grounding her. "Where, Lora? Tell me. Where is she?"

Tears welled at the corners of her eyes. She gasped as if she could barely breathe the words.

"Somewhere high. A place no one looks. He kept her where she could see everything... but no one could see her."

Sam brushed her hair back gently, his throat burning. "We'll find her. I swear, baby, we'll find her."

Her fingers clenched weakly at his. "You have to, Sam. Before he moves her again."

The room went still the fragile tether between them the only anchor against the storm outside.

Sam's words seemed to hang in the sterile air of the hospital room, echoing in the space between them. Lora's hand trembled faintly in his, her breath uneven.

Her eyes drifted shut again not from weakness this time, but because she was elsewhere.

Sam leaned in closer, afraid to break the moment. "Lora... what do you see?"

Her lips parted, her voice barely more than a breath. "Wood... beams... above my head. It smells like dust, like old rope. I hear... faint dripping... not water, something thicker..."

Her fingers tightened suddenly around his. Sam swallowed hard, forcing his voice steady.

"Stay with me. What else?"

Her body shivered as though she was lying in that place, not in the hospital bed. "It's narrow, but I can see out... slats of light through cracks. It's high. Above ground. She's curled there, knees to her chest, eyes red from crying. She's waiting. Watching. But no one looks up. No one thinks to look."

Sam felt his stomach twist. The way she said waiting made his skin crawl.

Lora's voice cracked, her breathing jagged. "She whispers... not to me, but... to herself. She says, they'll never find me here."

Her eyes flew open suddenly, glassy, unfocused. "Sam... she's still alive. But if we don't hurry..."

Sam squeezed her hand tight, anchoring her back. "No. Don't do that. Don't finish that thought. We will hurry. We will find her."

For a moment, silence pressed against the walls of the room, heavy, suffocating. The only sound was the steady, thin beep of her monitor.

Lora's gaze locked on his, fragile but unyielding. "He hid her in plain sight. High. Where the forest looks down on itself. You have to tell them. Before he moves her again."

Sam kissed her forehead gently, his throat raw with emotion. "I'll tell them. But right now, rest. I've got you. I'm not leaving."

The tether between them hummed fragile, frayed, but unbroken. Outside the room, the storm of the hunt pressed closer.

Sam hadn't realized he was still gripping her hand until his knuckles ached. Slowly, he eased his hold, brushing his thumb across her palm like he was reminding himself she was real, flesh and bone not another ghost the forest had stolen.

Lora's eyes fluttered, her voice thin but certain. "You'll find her, Sam. You always do."

Sam's throat tightened. He wanted to believe that, wanted to lean into her faith the way she leaned into him but the images in her head weren't just clues. They were weights dragging her closer to something he couldn't reach.

"I swear to you," he whispered, bending close so only she could hear, "whoever he's keeping, wherever... we'll bring her home. And him...." his jaw locked, voice rough with steel, "he won't touch you again. Not while I'm breathing."

Lora let her head rest against his chest, the faintest trace of a smile flickering. "I know. That's why he hates you."

Sam closed his eyes, holding her there, letting the fragile silence between them stretch. The tether, thin as gossamer, still held.

But beyond the walls of this room, the hunt was already moving.

Chapter Forty Eight

At dawn, the precinct was alive with urgency. The room hummed with overlapping voices, the whiteboard scarred with scribbled maps of the forest.

Detective Mayhew slapped a hand against the latest aerial scans. "She said look up. That means elevated. Watchtowers, lofted cabins, old fire lookouts. We start with every elevated structure within the forest perimeter."

Detective Harris leaned over the table, jaw tight. "There are at least four abandoned ranger posts that fit. Maybe more if we count hunting platforms."

Ng's eyes flicked across the data, her voice low. "If she's alive, we can't waste time. He's taunting us. Keeping her in sight of the ground search, knowing we won't look higher."

Greene exhaled sharply. "We should've thought of it sooner."

For a beat, silence settled a quiet admission of guilt. Then Mayhew broke it. "No. None of us could have. Only she could."

And though Sam wasn't there, his presence hung over the room, his vow carved into their minds.

Harris clenched his fist. "So, we follow her words. Every tower, every loft, every platform. Dogs up. Drones up. We don't stop until we find her."

The team nodded, determination hardening in their eyes. The forest awaited and above it, the truth hidden in plain sight.

The precinct briefing room was heavy with the smell of burnt coffee and sleepless bodies. Papers rustled, pens tapped, and the whiteboard looked like a battlefield arrows, maps, notes sprawled across it in a frenzy of desperate order.

Detective Mayhew stood at the front, voice clipped. "We've been thinking wrong. He's above us. Elevated structures ranger posts, lofted cabins, hunting blinds. If Lora says look up, then we adjust the search grid. Everything we missed on the ground, we cover from the air."

Detective Ng's eyes were dark, lined with exhaustion but sharp. "We don't know how much time we've got. He taunted us with those effigies that means he's watching. He wants to see if we'll find her."

Harris leaned forward, both palms pressed flat against the table. "Four abandoned ranger stations, all within six miles of where we pulled Lora. Plus, half a dozen hunting platforms that aren't marked anymore. The killer could've restored any one of them."

Greene's voice broke the tense quiet. "So, we split it. Teams of two. Drones deployed. Dogs cross-tracking scents. Every high point in that forest is checked. No hesitation."

A silence followed, heavy and unanimous. They all felt it this was closing in. No more blind circling.

Mayhew's jaw tightened. "If she's alive, she won't last much longer. This is it. Either we bring her out today... or we lose her."

No one argued. No one breathed too loud. They all knew it was true.

The forest met them with its usual silence, but under the pale bleed of dawn it felt different watchful, expectant.

Boots pressed into damp soil, dogs straining at their leads, radios crackling low. Every detective tilted their gaze upward as they moved: to the thick canopy, to the faint outlines of structures swallowed by branches, to every crooked shadow that might hide something built above the earth.

Harris felt the weight of it in his chest Lora's visions, Sam's rage, the promise that nothing about this case was ordinary. Ng's hand brushed her holstered weapon every few steps, a reflex she barely registered. Greene caught himself studying the treeline, almost whispering under his breath: She's up there. She has to be.

And Mayhew, leading point, forced himself to believe Lora's words. Look up. If they ignored that, they'd be blind all over again.

The dawn hunt had begun, every nerve stretched taut and above them, hidden in the shadows, the truth waited.

Chapter Forty Nine

The forest was a cathedral of muted greens and browns, pierced only by the pale dawn light and the occasional flutter of startled birds. Every step the team took pressed them deeper into the shadowed heart of the woods, the earthy scent of damp leaves and soil mingling with the metallic tang of anticipation.

Detective Mayhew moved ahead, eyes scanning the treetops. "Keep your eyes up. Every platform, every ledge... he could've put her anywhere above the ground."

Dogs strained against their leashes, noses quivering, tails stiff. Harris leaned down, whispering instructions, "Follow the scent. Don't let it escape. Stay focused."

Ng's gaze flicked constantly upward, every shadow twisting into possibilities. "I swear I saw movement in that old fire tower. Could've been nothing... or it could've been her."

Greene cursed under his breath, taking slow, deliberate steps around a fallen log. "Nothing about this is nothing. Every detail counts."

The forest closed in around them, every snap of a twig or rustle of leaves sending a spike of adrenaline through the team. Their minds replayed Lora's words, the visions she had shared: look up, high, where no one thinks to look.

Mayhew signaled the team to pause at a clearing. Above, a rickety structure rose, half-hidden in the canopy. The beams looked old, but signs of recent use faint scratches, footprints, a piece of fabric caught on a nail made the hair on the back of their necks stand on end.

Harris tightened his grip on the dog leash. "She's here. I can feel it. Something's off. Too quiet... almost like it's waiting for us."

Ng's voice was tight. "We've got to move carefully. One wrong step and he'll know. One wrong step and she could be gone again."

Mayhew exhaled, trying to steady his nerves. "Alright. Split teams. Harris, Greene, Ng with me. Dogs in the lead. Eyes up. Every step matters. We get her out today we will get her out."

The forest seemed to press closer around them, shadows twisting, branches creaking like whispered warnings. Each detective felt it: the unseen presence of the killer somewhere above, watching, knowing, waiting.

And every heartbeat carried the weight of Lora's vision.

Mayhew signaled the team to circle the base of the rickety fire tower, boots crunching on damp leaves, eyes darting upward. Every creak of the timber sounded amplified in the still forest, each shadow a threat.

Harris's dog stopped suddenly, tail stiff, ears pricked. The canine began whining and pawing at the ground, signaling a scent. Greene leaned down, whispering, "She's close... she's here."

Ng's flashlight swept the beams of the tower, catching on a frayed piece of cloth fluttering faintly in the morning breeze. "There! look!" Her voice was tight, urgent.

Mayhew's stomach clenched. "Get a rope up there. Carefully. We go slow. Eyes everywhere."

As they ascended, every creaking plank and snapped twig rattled nerves. Then, at the top, they found it: a small platform hidden in the thick canopy. A thin mattress, blankets, and signs of recent human presence. The smell of sweat and fear lingered.

Harris scanned the edges, a gloved hand brushing against a water bottle and some personal effects. "She's alive. I can feel it. We're right here."

Mayhew whispered, voice caught between relief and dread, "Stay sharp. He's left traces, but no one's up here with her. Not yet."

The platform was exactly as Lora had seen elevated, almost hidden, a place where the killer could monitor without being seen. The first breadcrumb was found, confirming her vision.

Every detective froze for a beat, absorbing the truth. Above the forest floor, hidden in plain sight, the captive waited just as Lora had foreseen.

Harris glanced down at the team, voice low, tense. "Move carefully. She could be frightened. Any sudden noise..." He trailed off, the unspoken terror hanging between them.

The forest remained eerily silent below, the canopy above shifting as the wind whispered through the leaves. And every heartbeat carried the weight of the hunt, the tension of what might come next, and the unbroken thread of Lora's visions guiding them forward.

Every movement was measured. Mayhew crouched at the base of the fire tower, radioing instructions, while Harris and Ng slowly secured the ropes and harnesses. The dogs whined softly, sensing the tension, tails stiff, ears twitching at every rustle in the canopy.

Harris ascended first, gloved hands gripping the rough wood, muscles taut. At the platform, he froze for a heartbeat the thin blanket shifted, and a small hand appeared, trembling. "It's okay," he whispered, voice low. "We're here to help. You're safe now."

The girl blinked up at him, eyes wide and frightened, but alive. Mayhew motioned from below. "Go slow, Harris. We don't want her falling or him knowing we're here."

Ng steadied the ropes while Greene kept watch on the surrounding trees. Every snapping branch, every flicker of shadow sent a jolt through their nerves. It was as if the forest itself held its breath, waiting.

Harris gently lifted the girl, wrapping the blanket around her. "It's going to be okay," he repeated, soft but firm. Her weight was slight, her body shivering, but she clung to him, fragile yet alive.

Mayhew's voice crackled over the radio. "Lower her slowly. Keep the line taut. Eyes everywhere. Move."

The descent was agonizingly slow, each footstep of Harris on the precarious beams measured. Below, Greene scanned the treeline, heart hammering. "Something's watching," he muttered, voice barely audible.

Ng's hands were steady on the ropes, but her mind raced. If he's here, he'll know we found her. He'll come for us... or worse, for her again.

Finally, the girl's feet touched the forest floor. Harris knelt, easing her down, whispering reassurances. "You're safe. You're safe now."

Mayhew let out a long breath, eyes scanning the treetops once more. "Check the perimeter. Now. Nothing gets past us this time."

The team gathered close, surrounding the girl protectively. Every sense was alert every shadow, every rustle a potential threat. But for the first time in weeks, hope pulsed through the forest, fragile but undeniable.

And though the immediate danger was still unknown, the first breadcrumb of Lora's vision had led them true.

Sam's hands were still trembling as he held Lora's, the hospital-like calm of their tether stretching across the tension-filled forest. He hadn't left her side since the morning briefing on the telephone, and now, knowing and seeing the girl brought down safely, relief and fear collided inside him.

Lora's eyes, wide and unblinking, followed the movements of the team through the victim's eyes. Her breaths were shallow, chest rising and falling with the weight of adrenaline and lingering visions. "She's... she's safe," Lora whispered, her voice fragile, almost a tremor.

Sam tightened his grip around her hand. "Yes. Thanks to you, baby. You saw it. You led them here."

A tear slipped down Lora's cheek, one she didn't bother wiping away. "It wasn't me," she murmured. "It was... I don't know. I just... I saw." Her other hand reached up, brushing Sam's hair back gently, the faintest touch of connection in a forest that still felt like a battlefield.

Sam's voice broke slightly, caught between relief and lingering fear. "I don't care how it happened. You guided them. You saved her. And I... I don't know what I'd do if anything had happened to you."

Lora leaned into him, one arm wrapping around his waist, the other resting on his chest. Her head rested lightly against him. "I'm here," she whispered, almost to herself, "and I'm... still here with you."

Sam lowered his forehead to hers, eyes glistening. "I'll never leave your side again. Not now. Not ever."

Around them, the forest hummed with quiet tension the dogs sniffed the ground, the detectives secured the perimeter, and every shadow seemed to press against the team, but in this small pocket of space, Sam and Lora existed together from the scene, suspended in fragile intimacy, a tether holding them steady while the hunt continued around them.

Chapter Fifty

The clearing had been turned into a makeshift command post. Radios hissed, dogs circled on taut leashes, and uniforms shuffled equipment into tighter grids as the rescued girl was taken toward the waiting medics. Relief rippled outward but no one allowed themselves to exhale fully. Not yet.

Detective Harris crouched over a marked map laid across the hood of a squad SUV, tracing lines with a gloved finger. "We got her out, but this doesn't close the circle. Whoever left her alive left her here for us to find." His jaw tightened. "Which means he's still ahead of us. Watching."

Detective Ng added, voice low but clipped, "The site inside the hollow wasn't random. Rituals like this aren't abandoned. There will be another chamber, maybe more. And he's taunting us with them."

Mayhew glanced toward the trees, eyes scanning shadows as if expecting them to move. He's still here. I can feel it. His thoughts twisted bitterly: two detectives already dead, a dozen close calls, and now a girl pulled half-alive from the earth. How much longer could they chase smoke before it turned on them?

Greene tapped a pen against the notebook in her hand, restless. "If Lora felt her, if she knew where to lead us that means she's still connected. We can't ignore that anymore. Sam might hate it, but she's the key."

A hush lingered around the SUV. No one spoke the thought out loud, but every detective there was turning the same fear over in their minds: the killer hadn't finished. He'd left his game open-ended, and Lora's fragile link to it was both their compass and their most dangerous vulnerability.

At the edge of the perimeter, Sam stood apart with Lora still folded against him. He hadn't moved since she had whispered, I'm still here. His hand rested protectively over hers, eyes never straying far from her face. He heard the voices behind him strategy, maps, caution but none of it mattered in that moment.

All that mattered was the fragile, living warmth in his arms.

Sam's inner voice clawed at him with equal parts rage and relief: She's the reason we're this close. And he knows it. He's after her. If he comes for her again, I won't hold back. I'll end it myself.

Lora stirred faintly, her eyes catching Sam's. She didn't need to speak; he saw the unspoken truth in her gaze. She knew the killer's pull hadn't ended. She knew they weren't finished.

Behind them, Harris straightened from the SUV and spoke grimly to the team: "We regroup. We go again. And this time, we don't stop until we've closed every last tunnel."

Sam only tightened his arm around Lora. He didn't care about tunnels or maps or protocols. All he cared about was keeping her breathing, keeping her tethered here with him.

The forest wind whispered across the clearing like a warning, and the detectives fell back into motion, each carrying their private dread as the hunt prepared to resume.

The forest refused to sleep.

Floodlights bathed the clearing in harsh white, casting long, fractured shadows that quivered with every gust of wind. The air buzzed with the static of radios, the low rumble of generators, the constant shuffle of boots as detectives rotated shifts. Dogs growled now and then, ears pinned to unseen movements in the dark.

Sam stayed rooted watching everything on the screen, with one hand stroking Lora's hand, the other clutching the comm receiver that streamed every channel. At his insistence, the cell feeds were piped through too vitals, witness logs, even the faint hum of the secure room where the unconscious killer lay asleep under guard. Sam wanted it all. Every wire, every whisper, every shadow within his reach.

Lora began to sit up, Sam helped her and wrapped in a blanket around her, that one of the Detectives wives gave for Lora, pale but focused. Her eyes half-closed, head bowed slightly, she seemed caught between here and somewhere else. The team had grown used to the silence that preceded her visions, a silence heavier than any scream.

Then, without warning, her lips moved.

Her voice was raw, uneven. "He... did not kill alone."

The words cut through the clearing like gunfire.

Detectives froze mid-motion. Harris, standing closest to the perimeter, swung his head toward her sharply. Ng muttered a curse under his breath. Greene tightened her grip on the radio mic.

Sam turned to look at her, his eyes locked to hers, his hand gripping hers tight. "Lora. Say that again."

Her gaze trembled, unfocused. She shook her head weakly, but the words fell out anyway, trembling like breath on glass. "He wasn't alone... not always. More than one. I remember... watching."

Sam's heart hammered. His jaw clenched, and when he stood, his voice carried like steel across the comm.

"Listen up," he barked to the detectives, his voice slicing through the static. "We are not dealing with one man. That son of a bitch we've got on ice had help. Maybe still has help. Everyone stays sharp. No assumptions. You hear something, you see something you call it. Understood?"

"Understood," Harris echoed, though his stomach twisted. More than one. Christ, how deep does this go?

Sam turned back, his chest tight as he looked at Lora again. She looked so fragile, trembling beneath the blanket, yet the truth she carried was heavier than any weapon. He smoothed his thumb over the back of her hand, hiding the quake in his own voice. "You're safe with me. No matter how many of them there are."

But even as he said it, a darker vow coiled in his chest. If there are more... I'll kill every last one before they touch her again.

Around them, the team resumed motion, but the air had shifted. The night stretched taut, as if the trees themselves were listening. No one rested. No one dared. They stayed braced for dawn, knowing the hunt had just grown larger, stranger, deadlier.

Chapter Fifty One

The next day bled into the next night. By the time the task force gathered back at the precinct briefing room, exhaustion hung off them like smoke. Maps covered the walls. Case files spread across the long table in chaotic stacks. Coffee cups littered every surface.

The discovery of multiple killers was no longer speculation it was a weight pressing into every theory, every plan.

Sam sat at the head of the table, posture rigid, his eyes sharp though shadows carved deep beneath them. Lora wasn't there; she remained under hospital observation, and Sam felt every inch of distance like a blade. Still, he carried her words into the room as though she were seated right beside him.

Detective Harris spoke first, his voice hard but frayed at the edges. "If he wasn't acting alone, then the man in custody is either a pawn or a partner. Either way, we're blind. We don't know how many more are out there."

Ng crossed her arms. "The rituals, the tunnels, the effigies it all points to structure. This isn't one lunatic carving symbols in the dark. This is organized. They've been at it for years."

Greene tapped his pen against the table, eyes flicking between the notes and Sam's silent figure. He's holding himself together for her, but how long before his rage breaks us too?

Mayhew leaned forward, voice low. "Then we have to start thinking bigger. Broader net, tighter surveillance on the hollow, on Elena, on Lora. If she's right, she's already marked."

The room fell into silence, each detective drowning in their own doubts and fears. Sam finally broke it, his voice low but steady:

"Lora's right. He didn't kill alone. And if they're still out there, they'll come for her. Which means we don't chase them. We make them come to us."

The team absorbed his words with a mix of dread and reluctant acceptance. They knew what it meant: to make bait of the one person Sam loved most.

The air was heavy, suspended in the terrible choice before them.

The precinct briefing room was a nest of exhaustion and dread. Coffee cups crowded the table, untouched. Maps layered the walls, thick with scribbled notes and pins marking too many sites. The air hummed with fatigue, but no one dared leave. The weight of what Lora had said he didn't kill alone hung over them like a noose.

Sam wasn't in the room, but his presence was felt. His voice came steady through the comm speaker at the centre of the table, connected to the hospital where he remained at Lora's side. A live feed streamed back to the hospital too, so that Lora, pale but alert in her bed, could watch the detectives argue.

Harris leaned forward, his hands pressed flat against the table. "We're not chasing one man anymore. God knows how many are out there. For all we know, the one we've got in custody is the weakest link bait to distract us. What if the real leader is still at large?"

Greene rubbed his temple, eyes burning with lack of sleep. We've buried two detectives already. We pulled one woman barely alive from the ground. How many more bodies are hidden out there? "If this is structured if it's a group then we're not looking at random killings. This is ritual. Organized. Coordinated."

Ng's jaw tightened, her gaze darting to the live camera feed of Lora in the hospital bed. "And if that's true, then she's more than just another target. She's part of it somehow. Every breadcrumb has been tied to her. Either she's their obsession... or their endgame."

On the hospital side, Sam bristled. His hand tightened around Lora's, his voice sharp over the comm: "She's not their endgame. She's the key. They've been circling her from the start because she can see what we can't."

Mayhew spoke then, voice quieter, though the weight of it silenced the room. "And that makes her the only one who can draw them out."

The words landed like a verdict. The silence that followed was suffocating.

Harris shifted uncomfortably, his throat dry. We're supposed to protect her, not dangle her in front of wolves. But he didn't say it. He knew Sam already heard the thought behind every silence.

Greene's fingers drummed nervously on his pen. If we use her, and she breaks under the pressure, what then? What happens to her? What happens to Sam?

Ng let out a rough sigh. "Look, we've been reactive this whole-time chasing shadows, cleaning up bodies. If Lora's visions are the only thing leading us forward, then maybe... maybe the bastards want her close. Fine. Let's turn it against them. Use the tether they built against them."

Sam's voice cut through, gravel low with fury and resolve: "You're talking about using her as bait."

A long silence. No one denied it.

Lora shifted in the hospital bed. Her pale fingers tightened over Sam's, her voice faint but steady as it came through the comm. "He's right, Sam. They'll come for me. I can feel it. It's always been about me. If I'm the tether, then let me be it. Draw them out. Finish this."

Sam turned toward her, his chest aching at the fragility in her voice and the steel behind it. His rage burned, but so did his fear. How can I ask her to carry this weight when she's already given everything?

Back in the briefing room, the detectives exchanged wary glances. They didn't need to speak to know the decision was already sliding into place. Their fear, their doubts, their determination all folded into one unspoken truth: the only way forward was through Lora.

The debate was ending. A plan was taking shape.

It meant putting everything, everything on her shoulders.

The silence after Lora's words weighed heavy, filling the precinct briefing room like smoke. No one moved, no one spoke until Harris cleared his throat.

"She's offering herself up. And as much as it tears me apart to even say it... she's right. The tether only works if it's real. If she's in play." His eyes flicked to the live feed of her pale face in the hospital bed, and guilt coiled through him like barbed wire. We swore to protect her. Now we're letting her volunteer to bleed for us again.

Greene leaned forward, voice clipped but trembling at the edges. "Then it has to be controlled. We're not dropping her into the woods and hoping for the best. We use every tool we've got. Eyes on her twenty-four-seven. Dogs, drones, radios. And Sam."

Mayhew nodded, slow and certain. "Sam doesn't leave her side. Not in the hospital. Not in the field. If she's the bait, then he's the trap waiting to spring shut."

Across the comm, Sam's hand tightened around Lora's. His jaw worked, a muscle twitching in his temple. "You're damn right. If she's in this, I'm in it with her. She doesn't breathe without me next to her."

Ng raised a hand. "Then we make the hospital the anchor. Everything routes back to her room. Live feeds, comms, tracking. If she says a word, if she sees something, we move. The team reacts in real-time. She's not bait, she's command."

All eyes shifted back to the monitor where Lora lay. Her breathing was shallow, her frame bruised and battered, but her voice cut through steady and unshakable: "Sam. Go with them. I'll still be here. I'll see what I see. I'll hear everything. You'll hear me. If they come for me, I'll feel it. But you need to be with the team. You need to end this."

Sam's chest ached. Her hand felt too small in his, too fragile, yet she was the one steadying him. His voice broke as he answered, "Baby, I can't...."

"You can," she whispered, her gaze locking onto his. "You have to."

The detectives exchanged glances. Fear whispered through each of them, but determination settled like steel. Harris thought of the makeshift grave where they'd found her. Greene of Meyers and Hall, buried by the same hands. Ng of the bodies still waiting to be uncovered. Mayhew thought of the other monsters they still hadn't caught, somewhere out there, watching.

They didn't want this. None of them did. But the path forward was drawing itself, step by bloody step.

Mayhew finally spoke, voice low but resolute: "Then that's the plan. Lora holds the tether. Sam hunts with us. We draw them out, and when they come, we finish it."

Sam bowed his head, torn between love and fury, between protector and hunter. His rage was a storm, but her hand in his was an anchor. If this is what it takes to end it, then so be it. But God help anyone who comes near her again.

The first sketch of the plan lay on the table. Fragile. Dangerous. Final.

And no one doubted what it would cost.

Sam stayed silent as the detectives' voices faded. The room, the screens, the hum of comms it all fell away until there was only feeling Lora's hand in his, her fragile fingers curled into his palm like a plea, like a promise.

Her eyes found his, weak but unyielding. You have to, Sam.

He rose slowly from his chair, the weight of every detective's gaze following him as the camera which was motion censored followed him around the hospital room. For a long beat, he said nothing, the storm in him visible only in the tightness of his jaw, the hollow fury in his eyes. Then, with a voice scraped raw by grief and love, he gave his vow.

"Action it. Lora leads the tether. We all follow her visions. And I'll be with you when it ends." He looked at each of them in turn, letting the words sink like stone. "But hear me now if they come for her, if they touch her again..." His voice cracked into steel. "There will be no mercy this time."

The detectives didn't answer. They didn't need to. They knew Sam too well knew what lived in him when rage was stoked, knew what he was capable of when the woman he loved was threatened.

The fragile, dangerous outline of the plan hung in the air, a vow and a curse bound together.

And no one dared breathe as the night pressed in around them.

Chapter Fifty Two

Dawn seeped through the hospital blinds in thin grey ribbons, painting Lora's face in a light that looked too fragile to touch. Sam hadn't moved from her bedside. Her hand lay inside his, her pulse faint but steady, and for the first time in days, he allowed himself to breathe.

She stirred, her lips parting, eyes glassy but aware. "Sam…"

He leaned close, his thumb brushing over her knuckles. "I'm here, baby. I'm not going anywhere."

"You have to," she whispered, her voice a rasp carried on breath and will. "Go with them. I'll see what you see. I'll be with you."

Sam's chest tightened. Every part of him wanted to refuse, to chain himself to this chair, to guard her with his own life. But her eyes the clarity in them, the stubborn will he knew too well held him still.

Uniforms filed quietly into the room, followed by two detectives he trusted. They posted themselves at the door, weapons at their hips, eyes scanning like sentries at a fortress. Sam's gaze lingered on each of them, silent command passing without a word. Protect her. With your lives.

He bent, kissed Lora's forehead. "I'll come back," he promised, voice breaking. "And I'll finish it."

Her lips curved into the smallest ghost of a smile. "Find them, Sam."

When he finally left, the hospital's corridors felt hollow, like echoes of all he was leaving behind. At the precinct, the exhaustion of the night still clung to the air, but Sam moved through it with steel in his veins. He went straight to his office and pulled the fresh set he always kept folded in the bottom drawer a ritual of a man who knew the job could call him at any hour. Headed to the shower room and stripped off the blood-creased clothes,

The shower was quick, but felt good, the water burning against his skin as if it could scour away the dread. It didn't. But it sharpened him, pulled him back to the man the team needed.

The SUV hummed down the road, tires slicing through the wet dawn silence. Beside him, the small monitor flickered with Lora's image. She lay in her hospital bed, oxygen mask still close at hand, eyes fixed on him with a tether that cut across miles.

"You, watching me?" he asked softly.

Her lips moved, and the comm crackled: "Always."

Sam's grip tightened on the wheel. She was still with him. That was all that mattered.

The forest loomed when they arrived black-green and endless, its silence already holding its secrets close. The air smelled of damp earth and pine, and the cold bit through even their layered jackets.

Detectives Mayhew, Harris, Ng, and Greene were already at the perimeter, maps stretched out on the hood of an SUV, dogs straining at leashes as if the earth itself had stirred them restless.

Sam killed the engine, stepped out, and felt the shift in the air as the team turned toward him. Their chief. Their anchor. Their storm.

And with Lora's face still glowing on the monitor inside the SUV, he walked toward them, ready to lead them into the dark.

Chapter Fifty Three

The forest breathed a low, steady silence as the team spread across the clearing. A damp fog clung close to the ground, curling around boots and equipment cases. Every sound the click of a radio, the low growl of a dog, the scrape of a shovel against gravel felt amplified against the hush of the trees.

Maps were pinned to the hood of the SUV, laminated pages marked with red circles, lines cutting across like veins. A portable monitor fed from the command vehicle flickered with Lora's hospital room, her faint silhouette a reminder of what tethered them all here.

Detective Mayhew traced a finger across one map, his jaw tight. We missed something last time. Someone was here, above us, watching. We walked straight under their shadow.

Detective Ng adjusted her vest, tightening the straps until the edges bit into her shoulders. We're walking into a maze again. But Sam's here now. Sam doesn't bend. If he's leading, maybe we come out alive.

Detective Greene leaned against the SUV, hands buried deep in his jacket pockets, eyes on the treeline. This forest doesn't want us here.

Every instinct says turn back. But there's no turning back. Not while Lora's visions keep calling us forward.

Detective Harris crouched, his hand firm on the leash of a restless shepherd. The dog's hackles bristled, nose quivering as if catching a scent carried on the fog. The dogs know. Something's ahead. Something alive. God help us if we're not ready for it.

Sam stood apart for a moment, his gaze moving over each of them, then lifting toward the forest's dark sprawl. His rage simmered just beneath his calm, but his mind was precise, sharp. This ends. No more graves. No more bodies hidden in the soil.

Behind him, the comm crackled. Lora's voice, soft but steady: "I can see you all. Stay sharp. He's not alone."

The words dropped like stones into the silence. The detectives exchanged quick looks fear, determination, doubt. Then all eyes turned back to Sam.

He gave a single nod. "We move."

Suddenly the fog appeared out of nowhere, but it was thin as they crossed into the trees. Dogs surged ahead, noses to the ground, pulling handlers forward with urgent snaps of the leash. Radios hissed with clipped check-ins, the kind of controlled chatter that masked unease.

The forest swallowed them whole, the canopy above blotting out the early light. Every branch looked like a claw, every hollow a mouth. The air thickened, heavy with damp rot and something sharper anticipation, dread.

They pushed deeper, boots pressing into soft earth, breath clouding in the cold. And with every step, it felt less like they were hunting, and more like they were being led.

The air seemed to grow heavier the deeper they went. Branches knit themselves into a canopy so thick the daylight barely pierced through.

Radios whispered in static, the dogs pulling, straining, but not barking not yet. It was worse than barking. It was expectation.

Every step sounded too loud. The crunch of boots on damp soil, the rattle of gear, the breath caught in chests. Sam's gaze swept left, right, ahead, the muscles in his jaw locked tight. It feels like walking inside a throat, he thought, like the whole forest is about to swallow us whole.

Detective Mayhew's hand never left his weapon. We've been here before, all of us. Different case, same damn fear. Meyers and Hall walked these woods, and they didn't come out alive.

Detective Ng counted her breaths, steady, deliberate. Don't think of the trees. Don't think of the holes. Just think of Lora — watching from the hospital, tethered to us. If she can face this from her bed, I can face it on my feet.

Greene brushed against a low branch, its wet leaves slick like flesh. This place isn't silent. It's listening.

Then, the comm flared with a burst of static Lora's voice breaking through. Weak, ragged, but cutting through the quiet like a blade, "Stop."

Everyone froze.

Sam's hand shot up, halting the line. He pressed his earpiece tighter. "Lora? What is it?"

Her breath came in quick bursts, the faint sound of the heart monitor in the background. "He's... watching you. Right now."

A cold ripple tore through the team. Harris tightened his grip on the shepherd, who whined and pulled hard to the right.

"Where?" Sam demanded.

Silence. Then a gasp, sharp and strangled. "Above."

All heads tilted upward.

A crack. A shift in the branches. The forest exhaled then erupted.

The dogs barked violently, straining against their leads, teeth bared at the canopy. Weapons snapped upward, barrels following the phantom movement overhead.

"Contact!" Mayhew hissed.

"Hold your fire!" Sam roared, his voice cutting through the chaos. His pulse hammered as he tried to command two worlds at once his team with rifles trembling toward the treeline, and Lora's fragile voice gasping in his ear.

"I see him," she whispered.

Sam's chest tightened. "Where, Lora? Tell me."

But the branches above only swayed empty, or not, the forest held its breath once more.

Chapter Fifty Four

It happened in a rush branches snapped high above sharp, splintering, too heavy to be wind. Bark rained down on helmets and shoulders. The dogs went wild, howling, clawing at the earth to break free.

"Movement!" Greene shouted, already raising his weapon higher into the shifting canopy.

Shadows darted. Leaves shook. The whole team spun in unison, rifles sweeping the treetops like searchlights.

"Hold position!" Sam barked, though his voice was hoarse, his chest hammering. He strained against the urge to fire blind into the green gloom.

Through the comm, Lora's cry tore across the line. "He's running!"

Every nerve in Sam's body lit up. His eyes raked the branches the blur of something, someone, leaping from trunk to trunk. Too fast. Too deliberate.

"Eyes on!" Harris shouted. "North side!"

Then, just as suddenly as it began, it stopped.

The forest fell still. Leaves swayed gently, as though rocked by some ghostly hand. But there was no sound of footsteps, no crack of escape. Only silence.

The team froze. The dogs whined, ears pinned back, pacing in frantic circles but no longer pulling.

"He's gone," Ng whispered.

"No," Sam muttered, sweat dripping into his eyes. His voice was low, raw. "He's here. He wants us to chase."

The forest pressed in, suffocating, as if waiting for them to make the next move that unbearable stillness, the dread coiled tighter than ever.

The silence shattered.

The dogs lunged as one, snarling, tearing free from their handlers with sheer animal force. Harris cursed, stumbling after them as the line buckled.

"Go! Go!" Mayhew roared, the forest erupting as boots hammered into soil, rifles raised, branches whipping at faces.

Sam ran with them, breath scorching his lungs, his earpiece buzzing with Lora's voice urgent, fractured, "He's pulling you deeper! Don't Sam, he's pulling you."

Her warning bled into static.

Above, something moved. A streak of dark, a body vaulting from one limb to another. The detectives fired upward, bark exploding, woodchips raining down. No cry of pain. Just that taunting, inhuman speed.

"Left! He's left!" Greene shouted, veering off. Harris followed, the dogs straining to match the predator's path.

Sam's chest burned. His instincts screamed at him to push harder, to tear through the underbrush, to end this now.

But then the woods opened into a clearing, the air unnervingly still. The trail ended cold.

The dogs circled, confused, hackles raised, but their wild certainty faltered.

"Where the hell!" Harris gasped, spinning in a full circle.

Branches swayed. The shadows shifted. But the quarry was gone.

Or waiting.

Sam raised a clenched fist, freezing the team mid-motion. His breath came in ragged bursts, his eyes cutting through the trees with the cold fury of a man who knew he was being played.

"He's baiting us," Sam said flatly. His voice was steady now, deadly. "He wants us in his ground. Every step forward is his."

The detectives stood frozen in the clearing, their weapons still up, their eyes on Sam. The forest seemed to breathe around them, holding its secrets close.

Through the comm, Lora's voice returned faint, fragile. "Sam... don't let him lead you. He's waiting."

The team didn't move. Couldn't.

They were caught between hunter and prey knowing they were both, the decision of whether to push deeper hung heavy in the silence.

"Hold!" Sam's voice cut through the static, sharp as a blade. His raised fist froze the squad in place. The dogs snarled, straining at their leashes, but no one moved.

The forest breathed heavy. Every branch looked like a weapon, every shadow a waiting hand.

"No one steps forward," Sam growled. "This clearing isn't ours — it's his. He wants us in."

Harris nodded grimly, sweat glistening at his temple. Greene's jaw clenched tight, rifle locked on the treeline. Even Mayhew, stubborn to his core, didn't argue.

But the silence pressed harder, unbearable. Seconds stretched into hours. The quarry had vanished or was circling above, unseen.

Then it snapped, Detective Roland muttered, "To hell with this," and broke rank, pushing past the line. He shoved into the brush, rifle up, breath ragged.

"Roland!" Sam barked, but it was too late.

Branches cracked like gunshots. Leaves scattered. Roland vanished into the dark undergrowth.

The dogs howled, pulling violently toward his path. The comm in Sam's ear crackled with Lora's voice sharp, panicked.

"Sam! He's not alone don't let him go."

Sam lunged forward two steps, fury igniting in his chest. The rest of the detectives looked to him, torn between following Roland and obeying Sam's command.

The forest seemed to close in tighter, a snare tightening its noose.

"Hold!" Sam's voice cracked through the comms, hard and commanding. His raised fist froze the squad mid-step.

The forest seemed to still with them. The dogs strained at their leads, teeth bared, low growls reverberating in their throats.

"No one steps forward," Sam said. "This ground isn't ours, it's his. He's waiting for us."

The detectives exchanged quick, wary glances. Mayhew swallowed hard, his knuckles white on his weapon. Greene shifted his weight, tension humming off him like a wire about to snap. Harris muttered something under his breath, unreadable, but he didn't break rank.

Then it happened. Detective Roland exhaled a sharp, bitter curse. "Screw this waiting," he hissed, and before anyone could stop him, he shoved past Harris and plunged into the undergrowth.

"Roland!" Sam roared, surging forward, but the forest had already swallowed him whole.

Branches cracked violently, the sound too loud, too fast. A startled cry cut through the dark, jagged and short-lived then silence. Dead, suffocating silence.

"Roland?" Mayhew's voice wavered into the comm, but there was no answer.

The dogs barked furiously, tugging toward the sound, whining as though they could scent the blood and fear rolling invisible through the clearing.

Lora's voice sliced through the comms, trembling, urgent, "Sam! Don't follow—don't—you'll all fall with him."

Sam's chest tightened, rage burning, fear burning hotter. His fists clenched at his sides as the detectives turned toward him, eyes wide, waiting for the call.

He could feel it the snare closing, the forest holding its breath.

One choice. Go after Roland and risk losing the whole team or hold the line and leave a man behind.

The silence pressed in, unbearable, Sam's jaw tightened. His decision sat on the edge of his tongue.

"Hold position!" Sam barked, the command sharp enough to cut the air. His voice carried the weight of iron, brooking no argument.

The detectives froze, their boots rooted in the damp soil, weapons raised but trembling. The dogs lunged at their restraints, snapping at the unseen, desperate to chase what they scented in the shadows.

"Chief Roland's out there." Harris started, but Sam's glare cut him down before the words could finish.

"No one moves," Sam said again, lower this time, deadly, as if the forest itself needed to hear it.

The order was clear. Final. Unbreakable, and yet, inside, Sam's chest cracked open with torment. He could hear Roland's strangled cry replaying in his skull, could picture the detective dragged into the trees, broken and alone. Every fibre in him screamed to run after him, to tear the woods apart with his bare hands until Roland was found.

But he couldn't. Not this time.

Because he'd heard Lora's voice through the comms, trembling, warning. Don't follow—you'll all fall with him. Her words clung to him like chains, binding him to the ground. He trusted her visions more than he trusted his own instincts, more than the rage pumping through his blood.

Sam ground his teeth, fists flexing at his sides. He felt the detectives' eyes burning into him, demanding action, demanding rescue. He could feel their doubt like knives in his back—was he abandoning Roland? Was he dooming him?

The torment ate at him, clawing deep. He wanted to be the man who could save everyone. But the leader in him knew the truth: chasing Roland now would be chasing death.

Sam's throat worked, but his voice was steady when he forced the words out, "We hold. That's an order."

The silence that followed was worse than any scream.

The forest seemed to tighten around them after Sam's command, every creak of a branch, every rustle of leaves sharpening into accusation.

Harris's jaw clenched. He muttered low, not daring to raise his voice against his chief but unable to swallow the bitterness, "Roland's out there alone. We can't just...."

"Shut it," Mayhew snapped, though his own eyes flickered with unease, "You heard him. We hold."

Ng shifted her stance, hands trembling around her weapon. She didn't speak, but her silence was heavy, loaded with all the things she wanted to say.

Greene, the youngest, shook his head in disbelief. He whispered to himself, too quiet for Sam to hear but loud enough for the others, "This isn't what we do. We don't leave our own."

The team's doubt rippled like a current, pushing against Sam's iron resolve. He felt it pressing in, testing for cracks. The air grew heavier, the woods listening, waiting.

Still, Sam didn't move.

The forest held them like a clenched fist. No one spoke. Every twig seemed to snap louder, every breath too sharp. Sam's jaw locked, the weight of command crushing him as his thoughts circled one truth: if I move wrong, they all die. If I do nothing, Roland dies alone.

The detectives shifted uneasily.

Harris whispered to Ng, "We can't just sit here., "He's one of ours."

Ng shook her head, fear etched into every line of her face. Greene's fingers hovered near his trigger, torn between discipline and the raw urge to move.

Sam felt it all, their doubt, their anger pressing against him like a storm. Inside, he was unravelling. God, Roland. Hold on. Don't let them take you too.

It came. A scream ripped through the trees, raw, cut short by the deafening crack of a gunshot. The forest swallowed the sound, leaving nothing but the echo in their bones.

The dogs erupted, snarling and straining at their leads. The team froze, every muscle coiled, weapons up. Sam's eyes darted into the darkness where Roland had gone, and for one heartbeat he saw nothing only the endless shadows staring back.

The silence after was worse than the noise. A silence that said: he's gone.

Sam's chest burned. He wanted to run, to tear through the trees until his fists found whoever had done this. But he held himself barely, the others were watching, because if he broke now, they all would.

Still, his voice cracked when he barked, "Hold your ground!" even as his hands trembled around his weapon.

In that moment, with the echoes of Roland's scream still hanging in the night air, every detective knew they were standing on the edge of something they might not walk away from.

Inside, his torment was a storm. He could hear Roland's cry echoing, imagined the worst that broken body they'd find later, another name added to the dead. Rage and grief twisted inside him, each breath a war.

But above all of it, Lora's warning held him steady. Her trembling voice through the comms. Don't follow—you'll all fall with him.

Sam's hands curled into fists. He forced himself to stand still, shoulders squared, back rigid against the doubt of his detectives, against his own breaking heart.

The silence stretched. The dogs strained harder, whining now, their instincts screaming chase. The forest creaked and shifted, as if mocking their stillness.

Then somewhere in the distance, a sharp crack. A branch breaking. The sound of something or someone moving.

The detectives' heads snapped toward the noise, fear flaring in their eyes.

Sam didn't flinch. He lifted his hand slowly, signalling them to hold, every muscle in his body screaming to run, but his command remained iron.

The moment teetered, unbearable, the line between restraint and chaos razor thin, then silence again.

Suspension. A knife's edge, waiting to break.

The dogs pulled harder, nearly dragging their handlers into the trees. Their barks echoed like a chorus of alarm, leading straight into the black maw where Roland had vanished.

Harris's face was pale, eyes wide with disbelief. "We can't just leave him." His voice was hoarse, breaking under the weight of grief and fury.

Ng's whisper was almost a prayer. "It's a trap. It's what they want."

Sam stood rigid, weapon in hand, every muscle screaming to run after Roland, to bring him back. But the other truth pressed heavier: if he went, if they all charged forward, they might all join Roland in whatever hell had swallowed him.

Inside, Sam's rage was volcanic. They took Meyers. They took Hall. They almost took Lora. And now Roland. I swear to God, I will burn this forest to the ground if that's what it takes to end this.

He clenched his teeth so hard his jaw ached. "Nobody moves until I say," he growled, the words more vow than command.

The detectives exchanged glances, fear in their eyes but also a flicker of something else. They trusted him. Even in his fury. Even when Roland's scream still rang in their ears.

The forest waited, holding its secrets just beyond reach.

Sam knew this was only the beginning.

The forest pressed down on them like a living thing, listening, waiting. The silence after Roland's scream was a silence that cut into bone.

The dogs strained and snapped at their leashes, their barks echoing like desperate warnings. The handlers held tight, every tug reminding them they were fighting instincts sharper than their own.

Detective Harris's face was hard, but his eyes betrayed him. He kept replaying Roland's voice in his head, that scream that ended too soon. I should've gone with him. I should've had his back.

Ng stood frozen, whispering words under her breath that no one could catch. Her hands trembled around her weapon. She wasn't praying for Roland anymore—she was praying they wouldn't be next.

Greene's jaw clenched so tight the muscle pulsed. His mind spun with rage. They're hunting us, making us bleed one by one. If Sam won't let me move, I'll move myself. Better to die fighting than wait to be picked off.

Harris cut a look at Sam. "Chief, we can't just…" His voice cracked. He didn't finish.

Sam didn't look at him. His eyes stayed locked on the shadows where Roland had vanished, his body coiled tight, trembling from the effort of holding still. Inside, he was splintering. Goddamn it, Roland. I should've stopped you. Should've tied you down if I had to.

But Lora's voice echoed in his memory, fragile and steady at once: He's coming. I'm with you.

Sam's throat burned. His rage surged, threatening to tear him apart. He wanted blood. He wanted to put his hands on the thing that had taken Roland. But if he let go now, he knew what would happen. The trap would close. The forest would win.

Finally, he forced the words out, low and sharp, every syllable dragging against his teeth.

"Hold your ground."

The detectives stiffened. Some wanted to argue. Some wanted to break. But the command carried weight it was more than an order. It was Sam's vow.

Ng glanced at Harris, then back to the darkness. "This isn't over," she whispered.

It wasn't. The forest still waited. The killers still watched. And Roland's scream still hung in the branches like a curse.

The team stood there, caught between fear and fury, knowing the next step could cost them all.

The forest stayed frozen around them, every branch a blade, every shadow a mouth. Sam's command—Hold your ground—hung in the air like a steel chain binding them together.

But then the dogs went rigid. Their barks cut off mid-snarl, replaced by low growls, deep and trembling. They were staring upward.

Slowly, every detective followed their gaze.

Leaves shifted high above, though no wind moved through the forest. A single branch creaked underweight. Then another.

Ng's breath caught. "Up there..."

Greene raised his weapon, eyes narrowing, but the canopy was too thick. Whatever was above them was moving with practiced silence, staying just beyond sight. Watching. Choosing.

A single pinecone fell, landing between them with a soft, deliberate thud.

Sam's eyes burned as he stared into the trees. His chest heaved with the effort of holding back his rage. Inside, a vow coiled tighter than ever: You're not leaving this forest alive. Not one of you.

The silence returned but now it wasn't empty. It was crowded, oppressive, thick with unseen eyes.

The killers were up there. Waiting.

The team knew it.

Chapter Fifty Five

The forest was still. Too still.

Sam stood at the center of the formation, every muscle wound tight, his eyes scanning the canopy as if sheer will could peel back the shadows. Around him, the detectives held position, weapons raised, but their breaths were ragged, uneven. Even the dogs had gone silent, their hackles bristling, bodies trembling at the invisible pressure that seemed to hang above.

"Don't move," Sam ordered, his voice low, edged like a blade. "They want us to break."

But doubt was creeping through the ranks like smoke. Harris shifted his grip on his rifle. Roland's absence pressed on all of them he'd vanished into that same silence, swallowed whole by the trees.

This is wrong, Sam thought. We're being drawn in. Step by step, they're shaping the board, waiting for us to make the wrong move.

A whisper broke the fragile quiet. Mayhew. "They're herding us." His tone was hushed, almost reverent, as if admitting the thought gave it power.

Nobody answered. Nobody had to. The truth of it was in the tension pressing down on every one of them, the sense of eyes above, watching, waiting.

Sam glanced at the monitor clipped to his vest Lora's face flickered on the tiny screen, pale but steady, her gaze locked on him even from miles away. He drew strength from that tether, but the rage in his chest pulsed hotter with every passing heartbeat.

They think she's bait. They think they can circle us, pick us off. Not while I'm breathing.

A faint sound cut through the air a scrape of bark, a rustle of leaves high above. Every rifle snapped upward in unison. The dogs snarled, breaking their silence, straining against their handlers.

Something shifted in the branches. Too quick, too deliberate. Not an animal. Not the wind.

"They're up there," Harris hissed, eyes wide, finger tight on the trigger.

The forest held its breath again. Sam's jaw clenched, his heart pounding in his throat. He knew what came next. This was the killer's way stretch the silence, stretch the fear, until the moment snapped like bone.

And then, with a sound like a branch breaking underweight, the forest moved.

The forest moved.

Branches snapped above, the sound sharp as gunfire in the stillness. Weapons lifted, dogs barked, and the team braced for the strike.

Then Lora's voice burst through the comms, raw and urgent, pulling every head around.

"He's there!" she cried, her breath ragged through the speaker, "The head of the cult is there!"

Sam froze, confusion cutting through his rage like ice. The head? His mind rebelled he'd nearly killed the bastard himself back at the hospital. That man was supposed to be the leader. The one pulling strings. The one who wanted Lora.

But Lora's voice sharpened, shattering that fragile certainty. "No—you don't understand. You've been played. He's dangerous and he's a cop."

The detectives went still, exchanging looks that carried both disbelief and dawning horror. A cop.

Sam's blood ran hot. His grip tightened on his rifle until his knuckles burned.

"His name…" Lora's voice cracked with strain, but she forced it out, cutting through the noise of the forest as if speaking into their bones. "Detective Simon Swayers."

Every head turned. Faces pale, eyes wide. They knew him.

Sam's mind reeled back through the investigation room Swayers leaning against the wall, his eyes too sharp, too curious, asking questions he had no business asking. Watching. Listening. Testing their silence.

Goddamn it, Sam realized, his stomach turning. He's been in the room the whole time. Watching us close the net. Laughing behind his badge.

The comms hissed with silence, every detective reeling. Then Lora again, her voice breaking but fierce. "Be careful. He's dangerous. More dangerous than the others. He's not like them, he owns them."

Before anyone could speak, the strike came.

The trees above erupted. A figure dropped through the canopy with terrifying speed, a blur of dark fabric and steel glinting in the fractured dawn. Gunfire cracked, dogs lunged, and the forest exploded into chaos.

Sam raised his weapon, fury and betrayal burning through his veins.

"Swayers!" he roared, the name tearing out of him as the hunt twisted into something far darker than any of them had prepared for.

The forest detonated in violence.

Swayers landed like a predator among them, low and fast, his blade flashing as he drove one of the dogs back with a savage slash. The animal yelped, handler screaming, but Swayers was already moving, weaving through muzzle flashes with a speed that seemed impossible.

"Hold formation!" Sam bellowed, his voice ripped raw with fury, but the team scattered under the sudden, surgical assault. Gunfire lit the trees, deafening in the close air, bullets tearing bark where Swayers had been a heartbeat before.

Sam lunged forward, eyes locked on him. How many times had this bastard stood in front of me, all polite nods and steady eyes? How many times had I let him close?

"Simon!" Sam's roar cut through the chaos. "You son of a bitch!"

Swayers turned, just for a flicker, and Sam saw it, the calm, amused gleam in his eyes. Not the frantic desperation of a cultist. Not the madness of a zealot. Cold calculation.

"You never were as sharp as you thought, Chief," Swayers taunted, his voice carrying with unnatural clarity over the gunfire. "She figured it out before you did." His chin lifted, eyes narrowing as if he could see Lora through the comms. "Always the girl."

Sam surged, finger tightening on the trigger, but Swayers melted back into the trees.

"Eyes up!" Detective Harris shouted, but his words were drowned by another volley of movement overhead. Shapes flickered above them—others, smaller, following Swayers' lead. Shadows of the cult, scrambling along the branches, raining down broken silence and dread.

"Shit, there's more of them!" Greene shouted, swinging his rifle skyward.

The dogs barked, handlers straining, and the team spun, formation unravelling as fear clawed into their guts.

Sam stood rooted for a breath, his rage sharpening into a deadly edge. His comm hissed, and Lora's voice broke through, thin but fierce.

"Sam—listen to me—don't chase him blind. That's what he wants. He knows these woods. He's setting the trap."

Her voice tethered him, cutting through the storm. Sam's chest heaved, finger still on the trigger, every cell in his body screaming to run Swayers down and tear him apart.

Instead, he forced himself to breathe, to lock down the rage before it consumed them all.

He spat the words into the comm, voice like iron. "No one moves. Hold your ground. We do this my way."

The team froze, glancing at each other in the shadows of the trees, fear in their eyes—but also trust.

For one ragged moment, the forest held its breath, every sound stretched thin, as if the whole world was waiting for who would strike next.

Chapter Fifty Six

The silence shattered.

A scream tore through the tree line high, raw, and human. Detective Greene staggered back, hand clamped to his shoulder as blood seeped hot between his fingers. The shadows above had struck, fast and precise, a blade dropped from the branches like a viper.

"Contact!" Harris bellowed, dragging Greene behind cover, muzzle flashing fire into the canopy. The dogs lunged, handlers screaming, but the branches above erupted with movement, bodies slipping in and out of sight. Too fast. Too many.

Sam's gun was already up, rage flooding his veins. First blood. Ours. Always ours. His jaw clenched so hard it hurt. He sighted, fired, bark splintering inches from a shadow. A hiss of pain told him he'd clipped something, but it wasn't enough.

"Eyes sharp!" Sam shouted, forcing command into the terror. "They want panic they want you scattered. Stay tight!"

Another cry ripped out Ng this time, knocked flat by a figure that dropped out of the branches. Sam spun, firing, but the attacker rolled, rising with a blade gleaming red. Ng scrambled back, teeth clenched in agony, rifle lost in the dirt.

"Son of a bitch!" Sam lunged forward, emptying two rounds into the figure's chest. The body jerked, collapsed into the underbrush. For a heartbeat, stillness. Then more movement, like insects pouring from the trees.

Sam's comm hissed, Lora's voice breaking through, tight and urgent, "Sam—he's here. Swayers. Don't let him vanish this is what he does. He bleeds you piece by piece until you break."

Sam's grip tightened around his weapon, his fury almost blinding. Not tonight. Not with her watching. Not while she still breathes.

He snarled into the comm, voice raw steel, "Then we bleed him first."

The team braced, rifles raised, the dogs snarling against their leashes as the forest itself seemed to tilt toward blood.

And above them, a laugh carried cold, familiar, echoing down through the branches.

The forest was alive with violence.

Branches snapped underfoot as the team scattered and reformed in a brittle, desperate pattern. Dogs lunged, teeth bared, barking ferociously as the attackers rained down from above, some swinging from ropes, some dropping silently from the canopy.

Sam moved like a predator, firing, ducking, striking with brutal precision. Every moment stretched thin; every breath counted. Detective Mayhew took a slash across his arm but fired back without flinching. Harris blocked a thrown knife, rolling into cover while Greene wrestled with a shadow, fist meeting metal and flesh with a sickening thud.

"Hold your positions! Don't let them outflank us!" Sam roared, voice hoarse, the edge of rage cutting sharper than any blade.

Above, a figure twisted, spinning a rifle, firing into the ground near Sam's feet. He dove to the side, feeling the air hiss where the bullet passed. Every second was measured chaos; every heartbeat a gamble.

Then, like a cold wave, Lora's voice whispered in his ear not over comms, but inside his mind.

Sweat slicked across Lora's brow, hand gripping Sam's sleeve as if he were the tether holding her to reality. Her vision fractured, scenes exploding in her mind: Sam dodging, rolling, firing; the dogs lunging; her team taking hits—each blow ripping through her chest like she were the one being struck.

"Sam—don't—watch out!" Her voice came out a whisper, dry and broken, though her lips didn't move. The monitors beeped steadily, but inside her skull, the world of the forest and the hospital blurred.

Sam's eyes met hers, and though she was weak and pale, she felt the fight too. He squeezed her hand tightly, murmuring, "I see it, baby. I'm right here. Stay with me."

Each strike Sam landed, each grunt of pain from the team, reverberated inside Lora's vision. It was a tether of terror and connection; every movement, every cry, every bullet traced the line between life and death for them both.

The cultists surged, and the team pushed back harder, trading blows, the fight jagged and unrelenting. And Lora, despite weakness, watched it all unfold, every strike, every close call, every moment of their survival threaded through her mind like a living nightmare.

The chaos intensified.

Sam's boots pounded through wet leaves, gun in one hand, the other signalling his team. Branches cracked above as the cultists tried to scatter, but Sam had anticipated their paths. Greene and Harris flanked him, firing and moving in sync. The dogs yipped and lunged, pinning two attackers against trees.

Then came Swayers, the true head dropping silently from the canopy, eyes wild, a knife glinting in his hand. Sam's breath hitched for half a second as recognition sparked fury. He's here. He's real. And he's mine.

Lora's voice, thin and urgent, cut into his mind through the visions, "Sam... left... right... he's going for the slope... corner him!"

Sam pivoted instantly, directing his team. Mayhew and Ng intercepted Swayers' strike as Sam fired, grazing the man's shoulder. The cult leader spun, feral, lashing out with a chain. Sam deflected, felt the metal scrape his forearm, and gritted his teeth.

Every move Lora saw, every blow she felt through the visions, sharpened Sam's focus. Her whispering guidance kept him alive and allowed him to anticipate Swayers' attacks with uncanny precision.

A cultist lunged at Harris, knife slashing across his chest. Sam dove, intercepting the strike with his forearm, pain shooting up his arm, and he slammed the attacker into the forest floor. Greene fired, taking another down. The team moved like a well-oiled unit under chaos, but Swayers was unpredictable, darting through shadows, mocking, striking where they least expected.

Then, a scream from Lora cut through the comms she hadn't spoken, but her tone echoed inside Sam's mind. Her hand clenched the monitor cable in the hospital room, eyes wide.

"Sam... he's going to vanish... now!"

Sam's pulse surged, adrenaline and fear locking his senses. He barked orders, pushing the team to tighten formation while keeping Swayers in view. The leader tried to escape, but the dogs, guided by subtle commands and instinct, boxed him in.

The forest seemed to hold its breath. Every movement, every growl, every snap of a twig amplified the tension. Sam's eyes darted between

Swayers, the team, and the shadows trusting Lora's visions entirely, knowing she could see what they couldn't.

Then, Swayers slipped misstep on the mossy slope. Sam pounced, grappling him to the ground. Rage and control fused; Sam's fury was a living thing, yet Lora's presence, fragile and tethered, kept him from crossing the line. Every strike he delivered was calculated, precise, lethal—but not fatal... yet.

Above it all, Lora's vision sharpened to one final thread: Swayers' hand twitched toward a hidden knife. Sam anticipated, slammed his knee down, twisting Swayers' arm, disarming him. The cult leader's eyes widened in shock for the first time, Sam had the upper hand.

For one fleeting heartbeat, the forest seemed suspended in a silent, suffocating pause. Sam's chest heaved, rain and sweat streaking dirt and blood across his face, yet every strike, every movement was sharpened by Lora's presence in his mind. Through the visions, he could see the enemy's intentions before they struck. He could feel her trembling pulse echoing inside him, tethering him to her even though she was miles away, safe—or trying to be—in the hospital room.

"Sam... left... corner... now!" her voice threaded through his thoughts. He didn't hesitate. He ducked, twisted, disarming one cultist before a dog lunged, biting another. Every command he barked, every movement he made, was informed by her fragile, ghostly guidance.

The chaos raged around them, but for Sam, time slowed. Lora's presence was a lifeline steadying, sharp, intimate. He saw the flash of Swayers' eyes, the glint of a knife, the calculated danger. And he struck—swift, precise, controlled fury knowing she knew, that she was with him in this brutal dance.

Then the tide shifted. With Sam's iron grip and the team moving as a single unit, Swayers faltered. Dogs nipped at ankles, Detective

Greene blocked a strike, Harris landed a blow. Swayers stumbled and went down. Sam pinned him, rage and relief colliding. His hands were firm, controlled, but his chest heaved as if he could absorb the forest itself.

A final glance upward reminded him of Lora, her eyes wide in vision, hands clutching the comm, tethering them together. She was the unseen guide, the pulse that had led him here. And in that tethered instant, Sam's mind swore she was safe, and he would never let go.

The remaining cultists were rounded up, restrained, their murmurs of panic swallowed by the forest. Dogs circled, snarling, their work done. The team exhaled collectively, adrenaline slowly giving way to comprehension. Swayers' capture was complete.

Sam lingered for a breath longer, kneeling over Swayers, eyes scanning the shadows. His fingers twitched, half in readiness, half in disbelief at the magnitude of the hunt. Then he reached for the comm, calling back to the hospital.

"Lora... it's done. We've got him," he whispered, voice breaking slightly.

Across miles, in a quiet hospital room, Lora exhaled, trembling, but with a soft, fragile smile. "I know... I saw it," she murmured, her hand brushing her forehead, still catching her breath. Their tether, across space and danger, held them together unbroken.

The team regrouped, checking restraints, evidence, and injuries. Sam's gaze returned briefly to the forest, then to his phone, then to the hospital monitor. He could feel Lora's pulse even now, steadying his own.

The aftermath stretched silence punctuated by low murmurs, the forest exhaling its dark secrets, the team digesting the weight of what had just occurred. But Sam's focus remained fixed, tethered, unwavering. Lora had led them here. And together, they had survived.

The forest, once alive with the chaos of battle, now hummed with an uneasy stillness. Leaves whispered under a soft wind, the scent of damp earth mingled with sweat and blood. Sam remained kneeling by Swayers, hands still firm on the restrained killer, eyes scanning the shadows for any hint of movement. Every sense was on edge, yet one thread held him steady: Lora.

Back at the hospital, her hand rested lightly on the monitor's soft glow, heartbeat steady, but her mind still pulsing with the residue of visions. Through the comm, Sam could hear the murmurs of his team, the low, tense voices of Mayhew, Harris, Greene, and Ng as they processed the capture, double-checking restraints and recounting injuries.

"She wasn't kidding," Mayhew muttered, eyes scanning the bound cultists. "This guy… he's meticulous. Every move calculated."

Harris exhaled, frustration threading her voice. "And he had back-up. Could've been more out there. We're lucky—Sam and Lora's call kept us alive."

Ng shook his head, voice low. "I still can't believe she guided him. Saw it all. If we hadn't had her—" He trailed off, swallowing, eyes flicking to the shadowed treeline.

Greene's lips pressed together, jaw tight. "We did our part. But Sam… he went in hot. That was dangerous. Too close."

Sam didn't speak. He felt Lora's presence, her pulse threading through the comm, and it anchored him more than any words could. Leaning back, he allowed himself a moment, brushing a strand of hair from his forehead, eyes softening as he imagined her in the hospital room, fragile, steadying herself after the ordeal.

He finally exhaled. "Everyone check your evidence logs, all re-straints, injuries, and positions. Debrief fully when we're back at the precinct," he ordered, voice calm but carrying the undercurrent of iron resolve. The team moved efficiently, their fear, doubt, and adrenaline threading into a careful orchestration.

Sam's focus shifted again to Lora. Through the comm, a faint voice reached him: "Did you get him?" Her words were soft, trembling, but full of certainty.

"I did," Sam whispered, as though she could hear the truth in every beat of his heart. "We've got him. You're safe."

Her fingers brushed her lips in a soft, almost imperceptible gesture, a silent acknowledgment of the tether they shared. Sam's chest tightened. He wanted to rush to her side, hold her, reassure her in person, but the team still needed him here to secure the scene.

He stood slowly, giving one last glance to the captured Swayers, and then spoke into the comm: "Lora... I'm coming to you. You stay there, breathe. You're okay now."

And with that, the forest's dark tension began to ease, leaving behind the echoes of struggle, the weight of what had been uncovered, and the fragile, unbroken tether between Sam and Lora steady, pulsing, alive.

Even as the team processed the capture, cleaned up evidence, and secured the remaining cultists, Sam's thoughts never left her. Each step he took toward the hospital, each breath, was a careful balance between relief and the gnawing knowledge that the hunt might not yet be over but for now, Lora was safe, for Sam, was enough.

The fluorescent lights of the hospital corridor cast a pale glow across the room as Sam entered, boots quiet against the tile. Every movement was careful, deliberate he didn't want to startle her, didn't want to shatter the fragile tether that had kept him tethered to reality through the chaos of the forest.

Lora lay propped slightly, blankets pulled around her, hair dishevelled, eyes wide and vivid despite exhaustion. Her gaze lifted to him the moment he stepped closer, and a faint smile flickered across her lips, tentative and fragile.

"You made it back," she whispered, voice hoarse, but the relief in her eyes was unmistakable.

"I promised," Sam replied softly, his hand reaching out to brush a loose strand of hair from her face. His thumb traced her cheek, lingering near the corner of her mouth, careful not to move too quickly. "And I always keep my promises."

She reached up weakly, stroking his head, her fingers gentle. "I... I kept watching," she murmured, voice trembling. "Even when I thought I couldn't... even when it hurt, I saw... everything."

Sam swallowed, emotions tight in his chest. "I know, baby. You came back for us. You came back for the victims. I saw it in every step, every vision you gave us. You're incredible."

Her eyes flicked to the monitor, the small feed showing the forest now cleared, the team wrapping up evidence, Swayers secured. A shiver ran down her spine. "He... there's more. We didn't get them all. He isn't done."

Sam's hand tightened gently on hers. "Then we'll finish this. But right now... you rest. You need your strength. I'll be right here. Always."

She leaned closer, one arm weakly wrapping around his waist, the other resting on his chest, heartbeat to heartbeat. "I know," she whispered, a tear tracing down her pale cheek. "I know you'll keep me safe."

The hospital was quiet around them, a fragile bubble against the storm they had survived. Outside, detectives were still debriefing, evidence being processed, and questions about the rest of the victims swirling but, in this room, time slowed. Sam held her, soft murmurs exchanged, breaths mingling. For now, nothing else mattered but the tether that had been tested in fire and chaos and yet, somehow, remained unbroken.

As the night stretched on, Sam remained vigilant. Every twitch of her eyelid, every shallow breath, every faint murmur drew his attention. He whispered reassurances, ran his fingers over her hand, and let the exhaustion settle into a quiet rhythm. He thought of every narrow escape, every vision Lora had given them, every threat that had been narrowly avoided. And through it all, he repeated silently: She came back. She's here. I will not let go.

Morning light filtered weakly through the blinds as Sam remained at Lora's side, gently brushing a strand of hair from her temple. She stirred slightly, still pale but alert enough to follow the small monitor in front of her. The team was already back at the precinct, gathered around maps, evidence boards, and laptops, dissecting every scrap Swayers had revealed during his initial questioning.

Detective Mayhew leaned over a tablet, pointing at a series of symbols found in the underground ritual sites. "We've catalogued everything Swayers admitted to, cross-referenced with known missing persons. The network is bigger than we thought... he didn't act alone."

Detective Ng added, eyes scanning the floor plans of the forest and tunnels, "There are patterns to the locations. Each site was meant to teach or punish ritualistic, symbolic. And these victims weren't random. Swayers wanted them to leave a trail for someone... someone like Lora."

Sam's gaze flicked between the screen and Lora, who had her small hand resting lightly against the monitor, following every movement. He could feel her tension, the remnants of her visions from the night before still echoing through her. She whispered, almost inaudibly, "He was always watching... studying us. I saw him... there's someone else, Sam. Another."

Sam's chest tightened, and he squeezed her hand. "Then we find them. But we do it smart. You stay with me, okay?"

Her eyes met his, faint fear lingering beneath the steel in her gaze. "I'll help. I need to."

He swallowed, nodding. "I know. And we will. But right now, your safety comes first. You can guide us, but I'm not letting you go anywhere dangerous."

The detectives continued their analysis, debating who might still be at large, how far Swayers' influence extended, and which missing victims' cases needed immediate reopening. Each comment drew Sam's attention, his mind bouncing between the threat they still faced and the fragile figure beside him. Every new detail the team uncovered seemed to heighten the tension in the room.

Lora, listening, murmured fragments of her visions, small pieces: a hidden room under the forest floor, a smell of incense, chains. Sam repeated each word softly, committing it to memory, guiding the team through her perspective without ever letting her leave the bed.

Detective Harris glanced up, voice low and cautious, "Chief, if Swayers has a network, we need to consider the possibility that the others are watching, even here. We can't underestimate the risk."

Sam's jaw tightened. "I know. That's why Lora stays here. She's our tether, yes, but she's also the target if we slip. I won't risk her again."

The room fell quiet for a moment, tension heavy in the air. Lora shifted slightly, finally speaking clearly, "I saw a path... underground. There's more. I can lead you, Sam—but you have to trust me."

He brushed a kiss across her forehead, feeling her pulse steady beneath his hand. "I trust you more than anyone, baby. You show me the way, and we finish this together."

The detectives took a breath, absorbing every detail, eyes exchanging glances filled with fear, respect, and determination. Sam remained a constant presence at Lora's side, his hand never leaving hers, silently reinforcing the fragile tether that had carried them through every nightmare so far.

It was quiet, tense, and deliberate every heartbeat measured, every breath synchronized before the plan began to crystallize. Lora would guide, the team would move, and Sam would hold the line between vision and reality, safety and chaos.

Chapter Fifty Seven

The precinct briefing room felt heavier than the forest had. Maps covered the walls, marked with pins, circles, and hastily scrawled notes. The air hummed with fatigue and dread, but also a sharp, rising urgency.

Sam stood at the head of the room, his eyes fixed on the live feed of Lora's hospital bed on the corner monitor. She was propped up now, oxygen mask gone, her colour returning slowly. The bruises along her cheek and ribs were still visible, but her gaze was steady stronger than he'd seen since she'd first woken. Every detective noticed it too.

She was healing. And with each day, her visions were sharpening.

On the comm link, her voice was faint but firm. "There are more... I saw them again. They're waiting, trapped, maybe still alive. You'll find them if you go back to the forest. But not where you were last time. It's deeper... beneath."

The room stilled. No one dared to interrupt.

Sam's jaw worked as he looked from her image on the screen to his team. "You heard her. We're not just chasing shadows anymore we're searching for survivors. Every second we waste is another they don't have."

Detective Harris spoke, cautious but steady, "Chief... what about Swayer? He's still holding back. We could press him."

Sam cut him off, voice low and absolute. "No. Not yet. The bastard wants to talk, he wants to gloat. But until we've got every victim we can find out of those woods, I'm not giving him the satisfaction. We use Lora. Her visions are the truest lead we've got."

He cast a glance back at the monitor. Lora, weak but defiant, lifted her chin as though to reinforce his words.

Detective Ng shifted uneasily, murmuring half to herself, "We're letting her carry this weight. She's tethered to him, to them it's killing her."

Sam's fists clenched at his sides. He could feel her pulse even from here, through the tether they shared, and the thought of her suffering tore at him. But he also knew if he denied her, if he tried to shield her completely, she would fight him.

"I'm not letting her carry it alone," he said at last, his voice rough. "She leads, I oversee. Every move we make goes through me. Nobody takes a step in those woods without me knowing. Clear?"

The detectives nodded, though unease lingered in their expressions. They trusted Sam, but they also knew what his vow meant he would bleed for her, kill for her, and maybe, if it came to it, die for her.

On the screen, Lora's hand moved slowly, as if reaching for him across the distance. "Sam... we'll find them. Together."

His chest ached at the strength in her voice. "Damn right we will."

The logistics came next. Dogs were being redeployed, floodlights readied for night search, ground-penetrating radar and drone support requisitioned. Every detail mattered, because Sam demanded it. He oversaw it all with the precision of a soldier and the ferocity of a man possessed.

Yet even as the room filled with talk of strategy, Sam's eyes returned again and again to the screen. To her. To the fragile tether that bound their fight to something bigger than vengeance.

And he swore silently, as the preparations rolled on: they would find every victim. They would rip out every root of this cult. And Swayer would not draw another breath of triumph before he had given up everything.

Not until it was finished.

The room emptied slowly as the detectives dispersed to prepare for the operation. The air buzzed with clipped voices, the scrape of chairs, and the low growl of police dogs being walked out. Sam stayed behind, rooted where he stood, his gaze fixed on the hospital monitor.

Lora sat upright in her bed now, hair damp from a nurse's gentle wash, her eyes pale but clear. She looked stronger than she had in days, though he could see the tremor in her hand when she moved it to adjust the blanket.

"Sam," she whispered through the comm.

He leaned in instinctively, like she was in the same room. "I'm here."

Her lips curved into the faintest smile. "Don't lose yourself out there. You're my anchor, remember?"

His throat tightened. He pressed his palms flat against the table as though steadying the whole world. "And you're mine."

For a long moment, the only sound was the faint hum of the monitor and her slow, measured breaths. He wanted nothing more than to walk out of the precinct, get in his car, and drive straight back to her. But he couldn't—not yet.

"Rest," he told her softly. "I'll handle the forest. You guide us. I'll bring them home."

Lora's lashes fluttered closed, though her lips moved just enough for him to catch the shape of her words. I believe you.

Sam swallowed the ache in his chest, then finally turned away from the monitor. The hunt was waiting. This time, it would end.

Dawn came grey and muted, the forest swallowing the light before it touched the ground. The team moved in a tight column, dogs straining at their leashes, boots crunching over dead leaves that seemed too loud in the oppressive silence.

Every ear wore an earpiece, every eye flicked between the trees and the canopy above. And every so often, Sam's low voice cut through the comms, steady as a lifeline.

"Keep formation. Eyes up. Nobody breaks rank."

But another voice guided them too, softer, thinner, carried from a hospital bed miles away Lora's, "Left of the clearing... slow down, the ground changes here. You're close."

Her words rippled through the column, every detective adjusting at once. The dogs' ears pricked, noses pulling toward unseen trails.

Detective Harris muttered under his breath, more prayer than report, she's tethered right into this forest. Like she never left it.

Sam heard him but said nothing. His grip tightened on the radio instead, his entire body thrumming with the fragile, unbreakable thread that connected him back to Lora. She was with them. Every step, every breath.

The forest deepened around them, so did the sense that they were not alone.

The forest seemed to breathe around them slow, heavy, watchful. Every step forward carried a weight of silence that pressed against the detectives' chests.

The dogs moved with nervous energy, ears flicking, noses darting to the air as though they smelled something the humans couldn't. Detective Ng kept glancing upward, every shifting branch reminding him of the ambush days ago. Detective Greene muttered under his breath, trying to steady the rhythm of his own heart.

Sam stayed at point, his radio pressed close, his gaze never straying far from the monitor strapped to his vest where Lora's pale face flickered in real time.

"Keep steady," Sam murmured. "She's with us."

She was.

From her hospital bed, Lora's voice broke the silence in the detectives' ears. Faint, fragile, but certain, "Further ahead... the trees narrow... you'll see a split. Take the left. Something's waiting."

The team shifted as one. Harris shot a glance at Mayhew, unease etched in every line of his face. She's leading us blind, his thoughts churned, but she hasn't been wrong once.

Greene gripped his weapon tighter, jaw clenched. If she's right again, then what the hell are we about to walk into?

Branches clawed at their sleeves as the forest tightened around them. The air grew damp, the smell of soil and rot thickening.

Suddenly, the dogs stiffened. Their hackles rose, low growls vibrating in their throats.

"Hold," Sam ordered, raising a fist.

The detectives froze in formation, breaths caught, hearts pounding in sync.

Then Lora's voice cracked softly into the comm, trembling but clear, "Stop. You're close. Look down."

Every eye followed Sam's lead as he crouched, brushing aside wet leaves and branches. His stomach turned cold.

There, half-buried in the earth, was a rope frayed, dirt-stained, knotted into a cruel binding. Beside it, something darker: the faint outline of bones, picked clean by time and weather.

Ng whispered, his voice shaking, "Jesus... another one."

Mayhew's throat tightened, bile rising. How many graves has this forest swallowed?

Sam rose slowly, his jaw set, his eyes burning. His voice was low but carried to every ear.

"This wasn't just Swayers. There were more. Maybe there still are."

On the monitor, Lora's eyes welled with tears. She whispered, more to herself than to them, "I told you... he didn't kill alone."

The forest pressed closer, darker, as the team stood suspended at the edge of discovery.

Chapter Fifty Eight

The forest held its breath. No one moved. The rope sat in the dirt like a wound torn open, the bones pale against the dark soil. The dogs whined, pulling against their leads, unsettled by what lingered in the air.

Sam finally broke the silence. His voice was steady, but beneath it simmered a fury that none of them missed, "Secure the perimeter. No one moves in or out without my word."

Ng and Harris immediately fanned wider, weapons up, scanning the tree line. Greene dropped to a knee near the remains, careful not to disturb the site, his eyes narrowing as he took in the knots on the rope.

"Looks fresh," he muttered, glancing up. "Not years old. Months. Maybe less."

Sam's jaw tightened. *How many did they bury out here while we were chasing shadows?*

He keyed his radio, his voice cutting through the comms to Lora, "We've got bindings. Bones. You were right again."

On the hospital feed, Lora's face paled further, her eyes fluttering as if visions clawed at the edges of her mind. She whispered, "They used that place. More than once."

Sam clenched his fist around the radio, "We'll find every one of them. All of them."

Then, to the team, "Mark this site. Get forensics here immediately. And keep the dogs moving. This forest is hiding more than bones."

The detectives exchanged looks, the weight of his words sinking in. Each of them knew the truth: they weren't just searching for graves. They were chasing ghosts of victims, of killers, of mistakes buried in the soil.

The forest, thick and watchful, seemed to close in tighter around them as they prepared to push deeper.

For a long moment, no one spoke. The forest pressed in, the air damp and heavy with rot, the kind of silence that felt alive.

Ng swallowed hard, his voice low, "Every time I think I've seen the worst of it..." He trailed off, unable to finish.

Greene's hand hovered above the rope without touching it. His thoughts flickered to Elena Ward, to the survivors, to the faces of victims who hadn't made it. How many of them ended here, their last breath tied into these knots?

Detective Harris crossed himself under his breath, a gesture so small the others barely noticed. But his eyes were burning, jaw clenched. He wasn't a man who prayed often, but the sight stirred something raw in him.

Mayhew muttered, "We've been chasing ghosts. Meanwhile, they were doing this." His fists tightened at his sides, knuckles whitening.

The dogs were restless, tugging, whining, as though sensing the stain in the ground. Their handlers whispered sharp commands, but even the animals seemed unsettled, straining noses to the air as if something still lingered.

Sam stood a step apart, his shoulders squared, his rage simmering in silence. Inside, though, the storm churned. Lora saw this. She's felt it all along. And I didn't stop it in time.

His radio crackled faintly, Lora's voice threading through, fragile but steady, "Sam... don't stop. This isn't the only place."

Every detective froze at the sound of her conviction. They shared glances fear, doubt, and grim understanding etched across their faces. If she was right, this forest wasn't just a hunting ground. It was a graveyard.

Sam lifted his chin, eyes sweeping the tree line. His decision cut through the suffocating stillness, "Mark this. We push deeper. Stay sharp. Whatever they left for us here this is just the beginning."

The detectives nodded, their fear coiled tight with determination. Boots shifted, rifles adjusted, and the line reformed. The dogs strained forward, pulling them toward the unseen depths of the forest.

The team pressed on swallowed once more by the endless, watching trees.

The forest closed tighter the deeper they moved, the canopy blotting out what little grey daylight bled through. Every footstep seemed too loud, every breath carried like a flare in the silence.

The line advanced slowly, boots sinking into soft earth, dogs pulling harder now snouts low, whines sharp, urgent.

Then Greene's hand shot up, "Wait."

The team froze, weapons half-raised, breath caught in their throats.

Ahead, not ten feet from the path, a shape jutted out of the soil a crude wooden post lashed together with the same rough rope they'd just uncovered. Symbols had been carved into the wood, shallow but deliberate, spiralling down its length.

Ng whispered, "Christ... it's another marker."

Harris's chest tightened. He thought of the killer's arrogance, the way the forest itself seemed littered with warnings no one had seen until now. How long have they been building this? How many of these are still out there?

The dogs barked and strained against their leashes, their fury bouncing off the trees, echoing back at the detectives like a war drum.

Sam stepped closer, his voice a low growl, "They wanted us to find this. A trail. And we're going to follow it every last step."

The others nodded, though their faces were pale, every instinct screaming this was a trap. Still, they moved forward, weapons drawn, following the breadcrumb deeper into the forest's throat.

The hospital room was hushed, the only sound the steady rhythm of the monitor at Lora's bedside. She lay still, her breathing shallow, until a sudden jolt tightened her chest. Her eyes flew open, unfocused at first, then sharpened on something beyond the ceiling tiles.

Her fingers twitched against the blanket. She felt it the marker.

"Sam," she whispered, her voice hoarse but steady enough.

Sam was already there, leaning forward, alert. He touched her hand. "What is it, Lora?"

Her eyes glistened with the strain of what she was seeing. "Symbols... carved in wood. Not random. They're... instructions. A warning. No, a path." She gasped, trying to catch her breath. "They're standing in front of it now. Tell them tell them not to touch it until they understand it."

Sam immediately hit the comms, his voice sharp. "Team, hold. She's seeing it."

In the forest, the detectives froze mid-step. The marker loomed before them, crude and heavy with symbols scorched into its surface. The dogs whined uneasily, tugging against their leads.

Detective Ng squinted at the carvings, running a gloved hand just above the lines. "It's not just decoration. This is ritual. A map maybe."

From the comms, Lora's voice carried through, fragile but unyielding. "The circle... that's the heart of the forest. The lines branching out they're trails. But the broken one..." She trailed off, her voice trembling. "That's where they buried them. That's where you'll find what's missing."

Detective Mayhew swallowed hard, the weight of her words sinking in. "She's seeing this while lying in a hospital bed. Jesus Christ."

Detective Greene muttered under his breath, "This isn't a clue left for us. It's a message to her. Always her."

Sam's grip on the comm tightened. His voice was low, controlled, but the rage underneath rippled through. "Then we follow her lead. No mistakes. This forest is speaking, and she's the only one who hears it clearly."

The team gathered around the marker, their flashlights cutting across the carved symbols. Each stroke seemed to pulse under the beam, alive with menace. The silence stretched, suffocating, until Detective Harris finally said what they were all thinking:

"Whatever's buried out here it's waiting for us."

Through the comm, Lora whispered the final word, as if carried on the wind, "Runes."

The forest closed in, thick with dread.

The hospital monitors hummed softly beneath the tension. Lora's eyelids fluttered as if each vision pulled her further from the room, her breath uneven. Sam sat forward, headset in hand, watching her fight the pull.

Her fingers tightened around his, "They're standing at the marker," she whispered, her voice thin but urgent, "It's not just carved it's... written in grief. Every cut means a name. The forest remembers them."

Sam's jaw tightened, "Then we'll remember them too," he said softly, and pressed the comm. "Team, she's seeing something deeper. Hold your ground."

In the forest, breath steamed in the cold air as the team circled the marker. The night sounds had gone silent no insects, no wind, even the dogs uneasy.

Detective Greene muttered, "We can't just stand here. We need to move. There could be remains."

Mayhew cut him off sharply, "And walk right into another trap? You saw what these freaks left last time."

Ng's voice was low, tense, "She's the only one who's been right, every single time. We wait for her word."

A growl of frustration from Harris. "We're chasing ghosts through a graveyard! The killers are in custody. How the hell could this be happening?"

The comm crackled. Sam's voice came through, firm but strained. "Enough. Lora's still seeing it. She said the marker's a map every line leads to a victim. We don't move until she tells us which one is still speaking."

The team fell into uneasy silence. The flashlights glared against the wood, the symbols dancing in their beams. Each detective felt it the suffocating awareness that someone, or something, was watching.

Then Lora's voice came faint and broken over comms, as if the vision was tearing at her.

"Sam... the ground there... soaked in memory. Not the blood of one. Many. They called it the harvest."

Her breath hitched, monitors beeping faster. Sam's free hand clenched the radio until his knuckles went white. "Lora, hold on. Don't push it. You're safe. I'm right here."

But she shook her head weakly, eyes still half-seeing something beyond the room. "You need to listen to the forest... the wind will tell you where to dig."

Sam swallowed hard, the weight of helplessness pressing on his chest. He could see her on his wrist monitor pale, trembling, but unyielding and he knew she was paying for every revelation.

In the forest, the detectives looked to him for orders, their faces drawn tight. He spoke at last, voice edged with steel, "We wait for daylight. We follow the broken line first. And we don't dig blind. Lora's sight got us this far we move when she can guide again."

No one argued. The air itself seemed to thicken, every shadow alive with meaning. The marker loomed behind them, a jagged monument to the dead and the lost.

Back in the hospital, Lora slumped back against her pillows, spent. Sam watched the monitors settle and whispered, "You're stronger than any of us."

Her lips curved faintly, barely audible, "Find them, Sam. Before he does."

Her voice drifted into sleep, and the room fell silent again.

Chapter Fifty Nine

The hospital room was dim but soft with early light. The machines whispered, steady now, the air scented faintly with antiseptic and rain.

Lora stirred, her eyelids fluttering open. For a moment she didn't know if she was awake or still within the vision's pull. The line between this world and that other place the one filled with roots, bone, and whispering trees had become paper thin.

She turned her head, saw the monitor on her bedside table. Sam's live feed flickered faintly on the small screen: the team huddled in the forest, still and waiting.

Her pulse quickened. She could feel it again the same hum she'd felt before every revelation. The tether. Sam. The forest breathing with her.

"Sam..." she whispered, voice rough.

He heard her through the comms at once. "I'm here, Lora."

Her eyes closed briefly, as if listening to something far away. "It's changing," she said softly. "The dark is thinning. The forest doesn't want to keep them anymore."

There was a pause, static carrying the weight of her words back across the miles. Sam's voice came back, low, reverent. "Then we move at first light."

Dawn crawled over the horizon, thin gold bleeding through the trees. Mist drifted low along the forest floor. The air smelled of damp moss and secrets finally loosening their grip.

Sam raised a hand to signal the team forward. Boots sank quietly into the softened earth, dogs tense but silent, ears flicking toward the shifting sounds ahead.

The deeper they went, the less oppressive it felt. The forest that once seemed endless and suffocating now breathed open, shafts of pale sunlight breaking through the canopy. Branches no longer tangled above them like claws; instead, they reached skyward, open, almost yielding.

Detective Ng murmured, "It's like the place is... letting us through."

Sam didn't answer. His eyes were fixed ahead, following the faint rope trail half-buried beneath roots and leaves. It wound in the same broken pattern carved into the marker.

Through his earpiece, Lora's voice came again clearer this time, stronger, "You're close, Sam. I can feel the ground shift when you step. Follow the line until it dips toward the hollow. That's where they rest."

He nodded once, though she couldn't see it, the tether between them alive and steady.

The detectives fanned out as the trees began to thin, sunlight striking the ground in fractured gold. Every sound, the drip of dew, the whisper of boots in the loam, felt amplified.

When they reached the clearing, the air itself seemed to still.

The rope disappeared into the earth ahead of them, trailing beneath a mound half-swallowed by vines and roots.

Sam stepped forward slowly, "This is it."

Behind him, Mayhew swallowed hard, "You think we'll find them here?"

Sam didn't answer. He could hear Lora's breathing in his ear, calm but fragile.

The forest had become almost beautiful, lighter, gentler but every beam of dawn light seemed to land on the mound like a revelation waiting to break.

No one moved.

The clearing held them in a kind of spell, birds gone silent, the low mist curling like breath from the earth. The rope trailed into the mound as if pointing to the forest's last confession.

Detective Mayhew's fingers flexed around the handle of his spade. Every time we find one of these places, he thought, it takes something from us. He could feel that same old pull — the weight of what they were about to uncover pressing against his chest.

Ng scanned the tree line, her heart a measured drum. Light in the forest, light in the case, she tried to tell herself, but the brightness only made her more uneasy.

Greene crouched near the mound, tracing the damp soil with his glove. Too soft, he thought. Too new. The realization sent a chill up his spine.

Behind them, Harris stood guard, eyes flicking between his team and the open forest beyond. Something about this feels wrong, he thought. Too quiet. Like it's waiting for us to see.

Sam stood at the front, motionless, staring at the mound. The rope ended at his boots, half buried, frayed. His breath came shallow. The forest light touched his face, gilding the exhaustion in his eyes.

He could hear the faint hum of the hospital machines through his comms Lora's steady pulse, her breath. It was almost like hearing her heartbeat through the trees.

She said the forest doesn't want to keep them anymore, he thought. So why does it still feel like it's watching us?

Lora's voice brushed his ear, faint, trembling, "Sam... don't move yet."

He froze. The rest of the team followed his stillness instinctively.

"There's something beneath," she whispered. "Something heavy... old... not just them. There's something... buried with them."

Static swallowed the end of her sentence.

Sam closed his eyes, jaw tight, every nerve wound taut as wire. What did they bury with them? Evidence? A name? Or something worse?

The silence stretched, until it felt like the whole forest was holding its breath with them.

Then the mist shifted, curling toward the mound as if pulled by an unseen hand.

Lora gasped in his ear, "Now."

Sam opened his eyes, "Let's dig."

The first shovelful of dirt hit the ground with a dull, wet sound. Then another. And another.

The forest seemed to flinch at each one.

Sam knelt near the edge, helping them move the soil by hand once the layers turned soft. The scent of decay rose in waves old leaves, earth, and something metallic beneath.

Through the comms, Lora's breathing quickened, "I can see it," she said, voice tight. "A circle of rope, red cloth... bones tangled together. They were bound."

Sam's shovel hit something solid. The vibration travelled up his arm like an electric shock. He exchanged a look with Mayhew. They both crouched, brushing away the loose soil.

The outline of a small shape emerged a child's shoe.

Harris swore softly under his breath, stepping back, hand clenching the air as if to ward off the weight of it. How many more? he thought. How many did we miss?

Ng turned her face away, forcing her breathing to stay steady. Don't let it break you now.

Greene whispered, "There's more. Look."

Another piece of fabric surfaced then bone, pale against the dark earth.

Lora's voice came faint but certain, "They wanted them hidden together. He said the forest would guard them."

Sam stopped digging, every muscle trembling. His vision blurred with sudden wetness. They were kids. Innocent. Buried like secrets.

He closed his eyes, forcing his breath through his teeth. "Lora," he said quietly, "how many?"

The line crackled. Her whisper came back like a gust through leaves, "Six. Maybe more. But... one of them is new."

Sam's eyes opened, sharp, hard. "New?"

"Yes," she breathed. "Not from before. From after."

The words landed like thunder.

Sam rose slowly, his voice turning cold steel, "Bag everything. No one leaves this site. We've got a fresh kill."

The detectives froze, the forest spinning around them, dawn's light now too bright, too clean against the grave they'd just unearthed.

And through the comms, Lora's voice faded to a whisper again, drained but certain, "He's still out there, Sam... one more... one watching."

The trees rustled or maybe they didn't.

Sam's gaze lifted toward the shifting canopy above, his hand hovering near his weapon. The tether between them hummed, alive and taut. The forest had released its secrets but not all of them.

For a long moment, no one spoke, only the forest breathed.

The grave lay open before them, bones, rope, fragments of cloth like petals scattered over damp soil. The early light had turned sharp, gilding the raw edges of what they'd unearthed.

Detective Mayhew sank to one knee, head bowed. We were too late, he thought. Always too late.

Ng stood rigid beside him, staring at the fragments with an expression that flickered between fury and sorrow. Harris moved away from the mound and braced both hands on his knees, breathing through the nausea that rose in his throat.

Greene murmured, "Jesus... this wasn't supposed to happen again."

Sam didn't answer. His gaze was fixed on the monitor clipped to his vest on Lora's pale, sweat-slicked face as she guided them through the vision. Her breathing was shallow now, her lips barely moving.

Then the feed trembled. Her head sank back into the pillow. The monitors spiked.

"Lora?" Sam's voice cracked through the comms, raw with panic. "Lora!"

The forest blurred around him as the team turned sharply toward the sound of his voice. On the other end of the connection, nurses rushed into Lora's room the camera jolting as one leaned close, gently tapping her cheek.

"Lora, can you hear me? Come on, sweetheart, open your eyes."

A heartbeat later, her lashes fluttered. Her voice small, dry drifted through the comm, "I'm here."

Sam's knees gave slightly, a trembling sigh escaping him. Relief flooded his chest so suddenly it hurt.

On the monitor, the nurse looked up toward the camera, speaking firmly, "She's exhausted, Chief. You both need to let her rest."

Lora turned her head faintly, the oxygen mask shifting as she whispered, "I'm fine."

The nurse gave her a look that said she didn't believe a word of it. "You need to rest, Lora."

Sam rubbed a hand over his face, helpless. "Yeah," he murmured. "Yeah, she's right."

He turned to his team, voice low but steady, "We stay here. We gather everything. I want full sweeps of this area. Every inch. Every clue."

The detectives nodded, quiet, subdued by the weight of the discovery.

Sam stood a moment longer, half turned toward the forest, half toward the glowing screen where Lora's image rested. She was watching him weak, eyes heavy, but still there. She gave a slow nod.

Something in that look made his breath hitch not just exhaustion, but warning.

Her lips moved, no sound coming through the mic, Sam felt it, a pull deep in his gut, something unspoken. In that instant, realization began to bloom like frost inside him.

Chapter Sixty

S am froze. The world seemed to narrow around that small, fading screen around the shape of Lora's mouth and the faint tremor of her eyes.

It wasn't random exhaustion. She was trying to tell him something.

He replayed the last few seconds in his mind the way she'd said "new," the shift in her tone just before she'd collapsed.

The tether between them hummed with residual static, alive even through the distance.

Then it hit him. The killers in custody… weren't all of them.

Sam's heart stuttered once, then began to hammer.

He turned sharply toward the others, "She wasn't warning us about the grave." His voice dropped, hard as gravel. "She was warning us about someone else."

The detectives stared back, confused, waiting.

Sam's hand clenched around his comm. "There's another one. Still free."

The words fell like a shockwave through the clearing.

Ng whispered, "How can, you be sure?"

Sam's eyes lifted toward the pale sky bleeding through the canopy, "Because she felt it. And because I can too."

The forest had gone utterly still again, as if it had heard somewhere in that silence, something unseen shifted faint, deliberate, and close.

The silence that followed Sam's words was almost physical. It pressed against their ribs, thick with disbelief and the echo of dread that no one wanted to give voice to.

Detective Mayhew was the first to move. He crouched beside the unearthed grave, staring down at the disturbed earth. We've been chasing ghosts, he thought bitterly. And all the while, one of them was still breathing the same air we are.

Ng swallowed hard, her throat dry. "Sam... if there's another one...."

"There is," Sam cut in. His tone left no room for question.

Harris muttered something under his breath a half-formed curse, half prayer. Greene shifted his weight, scanning the tree line with the muzzle of his rifle raised slightly, as if expecting the forest itself to answer.

They were all thinking the same thing: We thought it was over.

Sam stared at the monitor on his chest the small, flickering image of Lora lying in her hospital bed. Her eyes were closed now, her breathing slow but steady. The faint light around her made her look almost spectral, caught between this world and whatever place her visions came from.

He spoke quietly into the comm, his voice rough. "Lora... if you can hear me, we're still here. We found them. You did it."

There was a long pause a fragile heartbeat of static. Then her voice, barely above a whisper:

"No, Sam... not all of them. There's one more."

Her tone changed thin, trembling, but full of knowing.

Ng flinched at the sound. Even through the distance, something about Lora's voice carried weight. It filled the clearing like a ghost's breath.

Sam's stomach turned cold. "Lora," he said softly, "tell me. Who?"

The others watched him the leader who'd once seemed unbreakable now caught between fear and determination, tethered to a woman half a world away by a wire and a heartbeat.

Lora's breathing crackled through the comms. "He's close," she said finally. "He's been watching. You've seen him too."

Harris looked up sharply. Seen him?

Sam's pulse thudded in his ears. "Lora, look at me," he whispered, though she couldn't. "Who is it?"

Her voice dropped even lower, trembling. "The one who stayed silent when they questioned the others. The one who waited. Detective Roland Mayhew."

The words landed like a gunshot.

The team froze. Mayhew's head snapped up eyes wide, confusion flickering across his features, "What the hell is she talking about?"

Ng took a half-step back, her hand brushing her holster. Greene's jaw tightened. Harris looked between them all, torn between disbelief and instinct.

Sam didn't move. His eyes locked on Mayhew, studying every twitch of his expression the flicker of guilt, or fear, or perhaps outrage.

Inside his chest, something twisted. Please, God, don't let it be true.

Lora's voice came again, weaker now. "He was there, Sam. The night it all began. I saw him. He didn't run from the cult... he ran with them."

For a moment, no one breathed. The forest had gone still again that same unbearable stillness before everything breaks.

Sam lowered his weapon slightly, his tone soft but iron beneath it. "Roland," he said, "you'd better tell me that's not true."

Mayhew shook his head, voice shaking. "You can't believe this. She's—she's delirious, Sam. You saw her condition. The visions mess with her."

But Sam didn't answer right away. He could feel Lora's presence still pulsing faintly through the comm fragile, but sure.

He drew a breath, low and steady, "We'll end this tonight," he said into the comm, eyes never leaving Mayhew.

Lora's weak laugh came through the static the faintest, weary sound. "I know," she whispered. "And I believe you."

A long silence hung between them Sam staring at the monitor, Lora watching him through tired eyes from her hospital bed. That fragile tether, stretched across miles, was all that kept the world from falling apart.

She smiled faintly a crooked, exhausted smile that told him she knew this was the end.

Sam's throat tightened. He nodded once, the weight of it pressing into his chest.

Tonight, he thought. This ends tonight.

The team around him began to move in slow, cautious motion Harris signalling the others to flank, Ng's hand still trembling near her weapon, Greene scanning the trees again.

Mayhew stood perfectly still, eyes darting between them, the early light catching the sweat on his temples.

Sam turned back to his men, voice low, final, "Lock it down. No one moves. No one breathes until I say."

The forest seemed to darken around them, as though the dawn itself was holding its breath.

And miles away, in a hospital room bathed in cold light, Lora closed her eyes whispering a single word that only Sam could hear, "Finish it."

Chapter Sixty One

The clearing had gone soundless, the kind of silence that feels like the air itself has turned solid. No birds. No wind. Only the soft hiss of the open comm linking them to Lora's steady, distant breathing.

No one wanted to be the first to speak. No one wanted to be the one to make it real.

Sam's pulse hammered beneath his vest. Roland? No… it can't be Roland.

He forced himself to look at him really look past the familiar lines of a partner he'd trusted on night watches, shared bad coffee and worse jokes with. Now, those same eyes looked too alert, too calculating.

Ng shifted her stance, trying to keep her voice even. "Boss… what if she's mistaken?"

Her tone said she didn't believe that, not really.

Sam didn't answer. He couldn't. The thought of it of Roland Mayhew, standing there among them, knowing every pattern of the case because he'd helped make it pressed against his ribs like a knife from the inside.

Greene's knuckles were white around his rifle. Harris's mouth twitched, trying to form words that wouldn't come. The forest, once their crime scene, now felt like an open wound they were standing inside.

Lora's voice crackled faintly in Sam's ear again: "Sam... he's lying. He always lied."

Then silence. Just the soft, exhausted rhythm of her breathing.

Sam took one step toward Mayhew, "Roland." His voice came out low, controlled. The same tone he used when coaxing confessions out of broken men. "You want to tell me why her vision matches too many details we never released?"

Mayhew's jaw clenched. "Because she knows things, Sam. You've seen it. She dreams up half the damn case before we even touch it. That's not evidence its hallucination."

Sam stared at him remembering the first weeks of the investigation, the way Mayhew always arrived first on scene, the way he'd touched every file, every photo. The way he'd flinched when they uncovered the second grave.

You didn't flinch because it was new, Sam thought. You flinched because you remembered it.

"Look me in the eye," Sam said. "And tell me you weren't there."

Roland's gaze faltered. Only for a second but it was enough.

Ng whispered, "Oh my God..."

Greene stepped closer, weapon half-raised, but Sam held up a hand.

Inside, Sam felt everything at once rage, grief, the sick, cold betrayal that numbed his fingertips. How long were we eating at the same table while you hid this? How many times did you help me look for yourself?

He felt Lora in his ear again, faint but clear: "He's afraid, Sam. Not of you of what's still out there."

Sam's stomach twisted, "What do you mean, still out there?"

But the comm went silent again.

Roland laughed. Low, bitter, "You still don't get it," he said. "You think I was leading them? No, Sam. I was following orders. Just like you."

The words sliced through the air. Greene swore. Harris took a step forward, fury breaking through the fear.

"Orders from who?" Sam demanded.

Roland's eyes lifted toward the canopy, where the light was filtering through the thinning trees. "You'll find out soon enough. We all do."

His hand twitched toward his jacket pocket. Sam's weapon was up before thought could catch up the safety clicking off, every muscle coiled.

"Don't," Sam said, voice breaking.

Roland froze. The clearing held its breath again.

Through the monitor, Lora whispered Sam's name not as a warning, but as a plea.

Sam didn't lower his gun. He couldn't. The man in front of him wasn't his partner anymore. He was the last piece of a nightmare that refused to die.

"Roland," Sam said quietly. "You tell me everything. Now. Who's still out there?"

Roland's smile cracked a weary, broken thing. "Someone you already know."

Then his hand moved. The forest exploded.

Time shattered. For one heartbeat the forest was a photograph dew trembling on leaves, breath hanging in the air, every face turned toward the movement of Roland's hand.

Then sound rushed in. The crack of a weapon. The bark of a tree tearing apart. The dogs howling. A blur of motion Roland dropping, Sam lunging forward, hands burning with adrenaline, "Roland, don't—!"

But it was already happening.

Sam hit the ground beside him, pinning the arm that still twitched toward the inside pocket. A cold glint of metal slipped out not a gun, but a small recorder smeared with dirt and blood.

Ng was shouting something a command, maybe, or a prayer. Greene had his rifle trained, shaking, waiting for an order that wasn't coming. Harris's voice cracked over the comm: "We've got shots fired! We've got—"

Sam barked back, "Stand down!" though his own pulse was a cannon inside his skull.

Roland gasped once, eyes wide, a mixture of shock and bitter satisfaction. The breath rattled through him like the last wind of a storm.

"You still... don't see it," he choked, blood catching at the edge of his mouth. "They're still... watching."

His gaze flicked upward, past Sam's shoulder, into the thinning canopy as though the forest itself leaned closer to listen.

Sam followed the look, saw nothing but the shimmer of morning light breaking through the branches. But every instinct screamed that something unseen had just shifted.

The comm crackled. Lora's voice faint, terrified, "Sam... above you."

Sam's stomach dropped. He swung his weapon up toward the trees just as the leaves exploded outward something moving fast, too fast, a blur of black motion across the treeline.

The team scattered, weapons raised. Greene shouted, "Contact! Movement, north ridge!"

Roland's last breath turned into a laugh, a wet, broken sound that curdled in Sam's ears.

Sam turned back, hands shaking, voice raw. "What did you do?"

Roland smiled with blood on his teeth. "Opened the door."

The words hung there and then the forest erupted again, a volley of sound that swallowed every thought.

Sam dove, dragging Greene down as branches splintered above them. The comm filled with shouts Lora screaming his name, the dogs barking, someone calling for backup.

And in that instant, just before the world drowned in chaos, Sam looked up and saw a shadow move across the canopy, huge and deliberate, slipping deeper into the trees.

Not Roland. Not any of them. Someone else.

The air vibrated with the weight of it. Sam's heart clenched around the single, searing thought that Lora had been right all along — the real leader was still out here.

The roar of the forest swallowed his next breath. Then silence.

Everything froze. The world hung on the sound of Sam's ragged breathing and the faint, broken static of Lora's voice whispering through the comm.

"Sam..." she said, weak but steady. "It's not over."

Then nothing.

Chapter Sixty Two

The forest was breathing again. Slowly, like a creature waking from a nightmare.

Smoke from the gunfire curled upward, thin and grey, vanishing into the canopy. The scent of burnt soil and blood clung to the damp air. Sam rose from where he'd fallen, his knees grinding against the mud. The echoes of the shots still rang in his skull. His ears were full of ghosts.

"Everyone sound off," Sam rasped, voice hoarse.

Ng, Greene, Harris each voice came through the comm, trembling but alive.

"Roland's down," Greene added quietly. "He's gone."

Sam didn't answer. He already knew. His eyes flicked toward the still form half-covered in leaves. A smear of blood stretched toward the roots of an old oak, seeping into the earth like the forest was drinking it.

Then Lora's voice cut through the static, "Sam... he's still here."

Her tone was faint but unwavering, a thread of sound that wrapped around him like a heartbeat.

Sam swallowed hard, looked up into the dark branches. The morning light had shifted again too fast. Shadows leaned where there shouldn't be any. Every instinct screamed that they weren't alone.

"Direction?" he asked, his voice low.

"North," Lora whispered. "Past the ridge... he's moving fast. He's watching you."

The team exchanged glances fear flickering behind their eyes. None of them wanted to believe it, but after all they'd seen, belief no longer mattered. Only survival did.

"Form up," Sam ordered, snapping back into command. "Harris, take the east flank. Ng, dogs with you. Greene, you're on me."

They moved without hesitation, weapons raised, boots crushing the wet earth. Every branch overhead seemed alive, every gust of wind heavy with breath.

As they advanced, Lora's voice kept guiding them through the comm short, clipped phrases between shallow breaths, "There's a trail... it's faint... he's trying to pull you off course."

Her breathing hitched. "Sam, he's—" Static swallowed her for a moment, "—he's close."

Sam clenched his jaw, "Stay with me, Lora. You hear me?"

Through the small monitor strapped to his wrist, her image flickered pale, sweat shining on her temple, eyes wide open but seeing something far beyond the hospital room. He could almost feel the tremor in her hand as she pressed it to the sheets, reaching for him through the distance.

"I'm here," she whispered. "Just... don't go where the ground breaks."

Sam's gaze swept the terrain ahead uneven roots, damp patches of disturbed earth. The forest was shifting, rearranging itself under their feet.

Greene muttered under his breath, "Feels like it's breathing."

Harris shivered. "I hate this place.

"Ng stayed silent, the dogs whining low as if they felt the same dread.

Then movement. A rustle just ahead. A branch snapped.

"Contact!" Greene hissed.

Weapons came up. The dogs lunged forward, barking violently into the undergrowth. But there was no figure, no shape only the echo of footsteps fading deeper into the woods.

Sam's voice was a snarl, "We move."

They pushed forward at a run, branches slashing at their faces, the forest thinning as dawn spilled through like fire. Each heartbeat echoed through the comm Sam's, Lora's, the dogs.

All in rhythm, one tethered pulse.

Then Lora gasped sharp, broken, "Sam stop!"

The entire team froze.

"What do you see?" Sam demanded, scanning the ground.

Her voice was barely audible now, the faint tremor of someone balancing on the edge of two worlds, "He's not running... he's leading you... there's something buried... beneath the water."

Sam turned his head slowly. Ahead, just beyond the rise, the forest opened into a clearing — a shallow creek cutting through, its surface still as glass. Mist hung low over it, curling like breath.

The others caught up behind him, panting, their eyes wide. The silence of the clearing pressed against them like a weight.

Sam lifted his comm, "Lora, we've got it. You were right. We've got him cornered."

There was no answer for a moment only the faint hum of hospital machines in the background. Then, weakly, "No, Sam… you've got his altar."

A chill sliced down Sam's spine. The air felt colder now. The light dimmer. He looked again at the water saw something glint beneath the surface, half-buried in the mud. Symbols. Bones.

He stepped forward, pulse thundering, and the dogs began to whine again.

Behind him, the team spread out cautiously, circling the creek's edge.

Sam didn't breathe. The forest felt alive again. Like it was waiting for something.

Lora's voice returned faint, breaking, "Be careful… he's closer than you think."

Just as the words reached him, a ripple moved across the water.

Chapter Sixty Three

The ripple widened. Circles spread across the shallow creek, touching the banks where moss clung to stone. Sam froze at the edge of the water, his breath a cloud in the cold morning air.

The forest had gone completely still. Even the dogs stopped barking, their bodies tense, noses low, whimpering softly.

A faint metallic tang reached Sam's nose, blood, but old. Too old to be from any fresh kill.

He crouched, staring down into the murk. Beneath the film of silt and rotted leaves lay a patchwork of shapes, not random, not natural. There were lines carved into the creek bed, etched deep, intersecting symbols that pulsed faintly in the fractured dawn light.

Greene's voice came from behind, hushed, reverent, "What the hell is this place?"

Sam didn't answer. His eyes followed the markings, tracing them like veins in the earth. Some part of him knew the pattern before he could name it something Lora had drawn once in a dream, her hand trembling across the hospital notepad, sketching circles and intersecting lines while her pulse spiked.

Lora's voice came through the comm, faint and shaky, "It's where they... finished them. The final rites."

Sam's heart stuttered. "Lora, what do you mean 'finished'?"

Her answer came through broken breaths, "They brought them here after... after the hunt. They... offered them to him."

The silence that followed was unbearable. Greene swore under his breath. Harris turned away, bile rising in his throat. Ng's knuckles were white around her weapon, her face unreadable except for the trembling at her jaw.

Sam felt it differently not as shock, but as an old, dull ache tearing open again. Every buried rage, every sleepless night waiting for justice to make sense. This wasn't a crime scene anymore. It was an open wound.

"Everyone spread out," Sam ordered quietly. "No one touches anything."

They moved like ghosts through the clearing, careful and deliberate. The air grew heavier the farther they went, as though the forest itself disapproved.

Ng stopped near the far bank. "Chief..." Her voice cracked. "You'll want to see this."

Sam crossed the creek in two strides, water soaking his boots. When he reached her, he saw it a half-buried mound, the soil recently disturbed. A thin corner of fabric jutted out, faded blue beneath the mud.

Sam's stomach dropped, "Start clearing it. Gentle."

Harris knelt beside Ng, using a trowel to peel back the dirt. Greene joined them, his breath shallow. The smell hit them first decay, sharp and sweet, mixed with the rot of the forest floor. Then the shape emerged: a human hand, pale and stiff, the skin stretched tight over bone.

Lora gasped through the comms, her voice a cracked whisper, "Sam... that's her."

Sam froze. "Who?"

"The first one," Lora said. "The one we never found."

Greene's hands shook as he cleared more soil. "Jesus Christ..."

A wrist. Then an arm. A woman's body, twisted, her face half-hidden by the mud, eyes long gone.

Harris whispered a prayer under his breath. Ng stared at the body, jaw trembling, a mix of fury and grief written across her face.

Sam stepped back, chest tight, eyes burning. The forest tilted around him. He'd spent years chasing ghosts, but standing here seeing the truth unearthed, smelling it, it didn't feel like victory. It felt like failure.

Then Lora's voice broke the silence again, weaker than before, "There's more."

Sam turned toward the sound of her voice through the comms, his heart pounding, "How many, Lora?"

A pause, "...Seven."

Ng's eyes widened. "Seven?"

Lora's breathing quickened. "They... they buried them in a circle. Seven points... to bind the ritual."

Sam's hand tightened on his radio until his knuckles blanched. "We're finding all of them. Everyone. You hear me, Lora? We're ending this here."

Through the faint hospital feed, he saw her nod fragile, pale, tears slipping down her temples, "I know, Sam," she whispered. "You already are."

The team worked in silence. One by one, the outlines began to appear shallow graves beneath the roots, small markers of ritual, rope bindings, fragments of jewellery, scraps of fabric. Each body told a story of pain and sacrifice, of control and cruelty.

Ng muttered under her breath, "Swayers didn't plan this alone."

Greene nodded grimly. "He didn't have to. The cult had roots."

Sam's voice was a low growl. "And we'll dig up every one of them."

He stood at the center of the clearing, looking around at the unearthed circle. The dawn had risen fully now, thin light filtering through the trees, illuminating the pale shapes in the soil. For the first time, the forest didn't seem endless it seemed exposed.

Sam's thoughts drifted to Lora, her face on the monitor, the way her lips trembled when she spoke the truth. She had seen all this long before he had, lived it in her mind, suffered through visions that tore her apart. And he'd been too slow to stop it.

He whispered into his mic, just for her, "It's over, Lora."

Her voice came faint, tender, "Not yet, Sam... the last one still walks."

The words chilled him. He looked to the tree line the forest still, but not silent. Somewhere in the distance, a crow cawed, low and mournful.

Harris whispered, "What did she mean, 'the last one'?"

Sam didn't answer. His pulse was thudding in his throat. The cold certainty pressed against him like a hand.

Because even as the dawn light touched the graves, he could feel it, someone was still watching.

Chapter Sixty Four

The static on Sam's comm hissed once, then cleared. He thought it was Lora again but the voice that came through wasn't hers.

"You should've stayed away from the woods, Chief."

The words slithered through the channel, low, controlled, familiar. Every detective froze. The sound was coming from their own network, not the outside frequencies.

Greene looked up sharply. "That's... internal, sir. That's our signal."

Sam's gut clenched. "Trace it."

Harris already had his tablet out, scanning the waveforms. The colour drained from his face. "It's bouncing from the precinct. From inside the damn building."

The forest seemed to tilt again, the wind whispering through the treetops like a warning. Sam's mind snapped to the people left behind, Elena, the techs, the uniforms guarding Lora's room.

He clicked the mic. "Lora—talk to me. Lora!"

No response. Only the hum of interference, faint and rhythmic, like breathing through static.

Ng's voice shook. "Sir... if he's in the precinct."

Sam was already moving. "Pull the team out. Now. Full evac to the vehicles. Greene, get the dogs back. Harris, stay on the line until you lose signal."

They moved fast, hearts pounding, the clearing behind them already feeling cursed again. Sam didn't look back. He couldn't—not with Lora's last words echoing in his skull. The last one still walks.

By the time they reached the SUVs, Harris had the trace triangulated, "It's coming from the upper east wing. Security corridor outside the evidence lockup."

Ng frowned. "That's restricted. Only the detectives have that access."

The truth hit like cold water. Sam whispered, "He's one of us."

The silence that followed was suffocating.

Inside the hospital, Lora stirred. Her eyes snapped open, the monitor beside her blipped faster. The nurse at her side leaned in, startled, "Detective? Are you—"

Lora's voice was a rasp, almost not her own, "He's there... not in the woods. He's behind you."

The nurse turned just as the hallway lights flickered. A shadow moved past the glass uniformed, calm, purposeful.

Lora tried to rise, her body screaming in protest. She grabbed the comm mic beside the bed and pressed transmit.

"Sam—it's someone in the precinct... in uniform..."

Her voice broke in a crackle of static. Then silence again.

Sam's convoy tore through the trees, mud spattering the windshields. His thoughts were a blur of Lora's voice, the graves, the pattern etched into the creek bed—seven points. Seven victims. But there had always been eight names on the missing list.

The last one still walks.

He gripped the steering wheel hard enough to hurt. In the rear seat, Greene murmured, "Sir, if it's someone inside... who would have the clearance? The codes?"

Harris looked up from his screen, his voice hollow. "Chief... there's one detective who never turned in his badge after the raids. He was on medical leave when the arrests went down."

Sam's breath caught. "Who?"

Harris swallowed. "Detective Rowan Vance."

The name hung in the air like a ghost.

Ng whispered, "Vance was on evidence duty last month—he had keys to the entire lockup."

Sam's pulse thundered in his ears, "Vance was at the hospital rotation last night."

Greene met his eyes. "Then Lora's not safe."

They hit the precinct lot twenty minutes later. The building loomed quiet, its windows dark behind the grey dawn. Too quiet. Sam signaled the approach, weapons drawn, every sense stretched to breaking.

Inside, the security lights flickered. The lobby smelled faintly of bleach and gun oil. Somewhere deeper, a door clicked open and shut again.

Sam's radio crackled with Lora's voice—faint, terrified, "He's in here, Sam. I can see him..."

He froze mid-step, eyes on the stairwell leading toward the holding cells. The last one wasn't running anymore. He was waiting.

The drive back from the forest felt endless. The air in the SUV was thick no one spoke, no one dared.

Every radio check came up the same: static. Only Lora's faint breathing through the hospital comm gave any sign of life on the other end.

Sam kept one hand on the steering wheel, the other tight around the comm unit, knuckles white. His heart hadn't stopped hammering since she said it — He's in uniform.

He knew what that meant. He had trained with every cop in that precinct. He'd eaten with them, laughed with them, trusted them. One of them had spent years pretending to be on his side.

Vance. It had to be him. It explained everything, the vanishing evidence, the double signals, the way the cult always seemed a step ahead.

He swallowed hard and turned to Greene in the passenger seat, "Greene you go to Lora. Now. Don't stop for anyone. She's priority one."

Greene nodded without hesitation. "Yes, Chief."

Sam handed him the backup comm and a spare weapon, "Keep eyes on her at all times. I don't care who tells you otherwise, if anyone tries to stop you, they're not one of us."

Greene's jaw tightened. "Understood."

He slipped out at the hospital turnoff, lights off, vanishing into the fading dawn.

Sam watched him go, feeling the tether between them all tighten Lora in her hospital bed, Greene rushing toward her, and himself barreling toward the heart of something he'd feared all along.

The precinct loomed ahead hollow, grey, and silent.

No patrol cars outside.

No lights in the windows.

No sign of life.

Sam's pulse kicked into overdrive. He parked half a block away, motioning for Harris and Ng to stay low as they approached on foot. The air smelled wrong metallic, sharp, as if the building itself had been holding its breath too long.

Ng whispered, "Sir, there's no guards posted. Nothing."

"Keep your safeties off," Sam murmured. "He's in there."

As they drew closer, faint echoes filtered from inside. Not screaming — talking.

A man's voice, shaking with conviction, echoing through the corridors.

"...This city was blind. We had to open its eyes. They wouldn't understand... but you do. You always did."

Sam froze — he knew that voice.

Captain Jansen.

Then another voice overlapped his — darker, calmer, cruelly patient.

"Don't lie to me, Captain. You all saw what they did. You all walked past it. You buried them, case after case. I'm just finishing what you were too scared to start."

Vance. There was no mistaking it now.

Sam's stomach turned to stone. He gestured Harris toward the side door, whispering, "Get a perimeter. Quiet."

Then to Ng, "You're with me. We go slow."

They slipped inside.

The fluorescent lights flickered weakly down the main corridor. Blood streaked one wall — smeared, not splattered, like someone had been dragged.

A body? A warning?

Sam didn't want to think about it.

His boots made almost no sound, but his heart thundered so loud he was sure Vance could hear it.

Stay sharp, stay breathing, stay calm. Every fiber of him screamed to run, to tear through the halls until he reached Lora, but discipline was the only thing keeping him from shattering.

He caught faint voices ahead three, maybe four. Vance had company.

Hostages.

Then a muffled shout, "Vance! This isn't the way."

A gunshot cut it off.

Ng stiffened. Sam's blood iced over. They were out of time.

Chapter Sixty Five

The precinct reeked of smoke and fear. Sam moved through the holding corridor like a ghost, weapon drawn, pulse pounding in his ears. The overhead lights buzzed and flickered, dying one by one.

He could hear Vance's voice now, clearer, steadier, as if he were preaching.

"…They thought I was weak. They thought I didn't see. But I saw everything. The hollow wasn't a curse it was a gift. A cleansing."

He stood in the middle of the holding area, one gun in his hand, the other trained loosely on the room of bound uniforms and detectives. His face was streaked with sweat and grime. His smile was almost tender.

When Sam stepped into view, Vance turned, eyes bright, "Chief Matthews. I was wondering when you'd get here."

Sam kept his weapon steady. "It's over, Vance. Drop it."

Vance laughed soft, almost pitying, "You still think this is about you chasing a killer, don't you? You think I joined them." He tilted his head. "I led them."

Ng swore under her breath.

Vance took a step forward, blood from a cut at his temple glinting under the lights.

"I saw the rot, Chief. The corruption. The evidence that vanished, the reports that never saw daylight. We were supposed to protect this city but it's sick. The cult just gave me the strength to cut it open."

Sam's trigger finger twitched. He could see his Captain on the floor, wrists bound, still breathing but bleeding. Hostages lined against the wall, eyes wide, waiting.

Vance's grin widened. "And she, Lora she understands. That's why she sees. She's the mirror, the conduit. You think she survived by chance? She's part of it."

"Shut your mouth," Sam snapped.

"She called me," Vance said quietly. "In the dark. Her soul reaching for mine. She showed me what we were meant to do."

Sam lunged forward but froze as the faintest crackle came through his earpiece.

"Sam… I'm here… Greene's with me… Don't let him speak."

Lora's voice thin but alive.

Sam's chest tightened. "You're safe?"

"For now. But he's not done. He's got followers still inside."

Almost on cue, Vance's smile turned slow, deliberate. He raised his free hand and pressed a button on a small remote at his belt. A low rumble answered from somewhere deeper in the building, cells unlocking, bolts disengaging.

Ng's eyes went wide, "Oh, no…"

The sound of movement echoed through the hallway multiple footsteps, rising and spreading like a storm.

Vance stepped back toward the corridor, his laughter echoing, "Welcome home, Chief. Time to finish what you started."

Meanwhile, in the hospital, Greene burst through Lora's door. She was sitting upright, trembling but alert, eyes glowing faintly under the low light.

He dropped the comm link to the bedside screen, "Sam's inside. He's got eyes on Vance."

Lora's breath caught, "It's started. They're waking the others. The ones he kept below. You have to tell him   don't let him chase them alone."

Greene hit transmit. "Chief, she's awake. She's seeing something."

Static. Then Sam's strained voice: "I hear you. Stay with her. Whatever happens, don't move."

Sam stood in the threshold of the holding corridor, heart thundering, as the doors along the lower cells began to swing open one by one. Figures emerged disoriented, feral-eyed, half-mad. Vance watched it all with a calm, religious serenity.

Sam aimed, shouting, "Don't do this, Vance!"

Vance turned slowly, eyes wild now, "Oh, Sam. It was never me you were meant to save."

With that, he dropped the remote and whispered something Sam couldn't quite hear a prayer, or a curse as his followers surged forward into the dark.

Chapter Sixty Six

The corridors of the precinct had erupted into war.

Gunfire cracked through the flickering lights, shadows leaping across walls as Sam and Ng fought to hold the line. The cult's remnants, Vance's hidden followers poured from the cells like phantoms crawling out of the dark. Screams echoed. Smoke burned their throats.

"Fall back to the evidence room!" Sam barked, his voice hoarse.

Ng nodded, reloading as she covered the retreat.

Sam's comm crackled with static, then Greene's voice, breathless, urgent, "Chief — we've got movement at the hospital. Four of them, all armed, heading straight for Lora's floor."

Sam froze. "How the hell?"

"Already here, Chief! They're inside!"

The connection filled with chaos gunfire, glass breaking, shouts in the background.

Greene grunted, voice strained, "Two down, three, no, four, all neutralized!"

A metallic clang, then silence.

Sam's hand tightened around his weapon, "Greene, talk to me!"

"All four down... but Chief, Lora... she's...." His voice faltered, disbelieving. "She's up. She... she's moving."

"What do you mean moving? She's supposed to be on bed rest!"

"She just got up, Chief. Like she wasn't even hurt. She picked up her clothes, walked to the bathroom.......she's changing. I tried to stop her, she looked right through me. She's... it's like she's somewhere else."

"Greene, keep her there. Do not let her leave that room!"

"I can't! I've tried! Chief... she's in a trance...... she's walking like she knows exactly where to go!"

Sam slammed a fist against the wall, teeth clenched in fury, "God-dammit, Lora!"

Ng glanced over from the corridor. "Chief?"

"She's coming here," Sam said, voice breaking. "She's walking straight into this nightmare."

From across the room, Vance's laughter echoed soft, knowing, al-most joyful. He stood amid the chaos like a prophet in the storm, smoke swirling around him.

"So, she's coming," he said quietly, almost reverently, "She's an-swering the call."

Sam raised his gun, aiming dead center on Vance's chest, "Yeah," he snarled, "she's coming to finish you."

Vance smiled, the kind of smile that made Sam's blood run cold, "Then let her. She's always belonged here, with us. You just never had the courage to see it."

Sam took a step closer, every muscle coiled. "You so much as look at her again, and I'll—"

"Kill me?" Vance cut in smoothly. "And what then, Chief? You think it ends with me? It never ends. Not until she stops fighting what she is."

"Don't you dare talk about her!"

"Why not?" Vance's voice softened to a whisper. "She's the bridge between worlds, she sees what we can't. She was chosen long before you ever pulled her out of that grave."

Sam's vision narrowed, rage and dread burning in his chest. He could feel her presence even now faint in the back of his skull, the tether humming through every nerve.

Lora.

He saw her as if she stood beside him, walking barefoot through the hospital hallway, her gown fluttering, eyes unfocused but glowing faintly gold. Greene followed, desperate, pleading.

"Lora, please don't do this. He said stay here! You're hurt!"

She turned to him, voice distant and hollow, "I have to end it, Greene. If I don't...he'll never stop."

Her bare feet left faint, bloody prints on the tile as she walked.

Back in the precinct, the sound of boots echoed down the stairwell — the rest of Sam's team closing in, weapons ready, faces drawn with exhaustion and fear.

Ng caught Sam's eye, "Orders?"

Sam looked toward the holding corridor, where Vance stood calmly amid the wreckage, gun still in hand, "Hold your positions," Sam said, voice low. "We end this when she gets here."

Vance chuckled softly, as if savoring the moment, "She'll come. She always comes. The light needs its shadow."

Sam's grip tightened around the trigger, his voice barely more than a growl, "Not this time. This time, she's the one holding the light."

Chapter Sixty Seven

The night inside the precinct felt unmoored from time. Smoke hung low, the emergency lights pulsing red against walls streaked with dust. Every sound, the drip of a burst pipe, the creak of cooling metal, seemed to carry a heartbeat of its own.

Greene had just reached the main corridor when the outer doors slid open with a sigh. He turned, half expecting another wave of Vance's people. Instead, a thin figure stepped through the haze, barefoot, hair damp from hospital rain, eyes lit from within.

"Lora," he whispered.

She didn't answer. Her movements were slow, deliberate, as if guided by something just beyond sight. She walked past him to Sam's office, the light above the door flickering as she entered.

Greene followed, hesitating in the threshold. He watched her cross to the locked cabinet and rest her hand against the steel. The lock clicked open without the key. She reached inside and drew out Sam's field shotgun, not raising it, not yet. Her face remained calm, otherworldly, her skin pale against the black metal.

When she turned, she caught Greene's wide stare and lifted a finger to her lips, "Don't say a word," she breathed barely sound at all.

Greene swallowed hard. "Christ," he murmured, not sure if it was prayer or disbelief.

She loaded the weapon with slow, steady precision, every movement measured. Then she looked up not at Greene, but through him, her gaze fixed on something only she could see.

Down in the holding corridor, Sam stood opposite Vance, every muscle burning with the need to end this. Behind Vance, the surviving followers waited in the half-light, eyes fever-bright.

Then, a sound the echo of footsteps. Soft. Certain. Coming closer.

Vance's smile faltered. Sam felt the shift before he saw her.

Lora emerged from the smoke at the end of the corridor, shotgun lowered at her side, her expression calm and terrible in its clarity. For an instant, the red strobe caught her face and Sam saw both woman and spirit the mortal and whatever force had chosen her.

"Lora," Sam said, his voice cracking with relief and fear.

She didn't answer; her eyes were on Vance.

"So," Vance murmured, trying to sound amused though his voice trembled, "you came after all."

Lora stepped forward, the echo of her bare feet sharp against the tile, "You thought you could control me," she said quietly. "You thought I was yours to lead."

Her tone was almost pitying, "You never realized, Vance, I was the one leading you."

The followers shifted uneasily. Sam's team glanced at one another, the truth dawning in fragments, that every step of this night, every trap that had closed, had done so by her hand.

Vance's confidence cracked. "What are you?"

"You're finished," she said. "All of you."

The lights flared white, a wind tearing through the corridor though no doors were open. The glass in the observation windows shuddered, and every gun barrel in the room tilted downward, as if pressed by invisible weight.

Sam shielded his eyes, heart hammering. He saw her then not the wounded woman from the hospital, but the survivor who had carried them this far, the one who had walked through death and come back burning with purpose.

"Lora, stop," he managed, stepping toward her. "You don't have to."

She turned her head slightly toward him, and for the first time her eyes softened, "It's already done."

The wind died as quickly as it had come. Vance and his remaining followers dropped to their knees, their weapons sliding from limp hands. The air felt drained, hollow, as though the storm itself had exhaled.

For a long moment, no one spoke. Sam's team stood frozen, stunned, shaken, and in awe of what they had just witnessed.

Lora let the shotgun rest on the floor, her strength finally leaving her. Sam caught her as she stumbled, his arms closing around her before she could fall.

"I've got you," he whispered.

She managed the faintest smile. "Told you... it would end tonight."

Sam looked over her shoulder at the silent corridor, the unconscious followers, the man who had thought himself untouchable. The nightmare was over or at least, this part of it.

But inside him, the tether still hummed the quiet certainty that light and darkness were not yet done with them.

Chapter Sixty Eight

T he silence that followed was unreal, too clean, too sudden, the kind that pressed against the skin like static.

Smoke curled through the holding corridor, soft grey ribbons twisting in the emergency light.

The sharp scent of burnt wiring and spent rounds lingered, mingling with the copper tang of blood and disinfectant. Everything was still, save for the faint drip of water from a cracked ceiling pipe and the shallow, uneven sound of breathing.

Sam stayed crouched, Lora's weight cradled in his arms. Her head rested against his shoulder, her pulse fluttering fast beneath the skin of her throat. He could feel her trembling not from fear, but from exhaustion, from the sheer force of what she had unleashed.

He whispered her name once, then again, quieter. Her eyelids flickered but didn't open.

She was alive, he could feel that much but whatever had driven her here had burned through the last of her strength.

Behind him, the rest of the team moved in slow disbelief. Harris lowered his weapon, his hands shaking as he exhaled. Ng leaned against the wall, eyes darting between the unconscious followers and the broken figure of Vance on the floor, even Greene, usually all composure, had gone pale. He wiped his mouth with the back of his hand, his voice breaking when he spoke.

"Is she—?"

Sam didn't answer. He just pressed his forehead against hers, breathing with her, forcing his own heart to match the rhythm of hers.

He'd thought he'd lost her once. He wasn't going to let that happen again.

When the medics arrived, the corridor filled with harsh light and clipped voices.

But none of it seemed real. Sam stood back only long enough to let them place Lora on a stretcher, oxygen mask returned to her face, a line threaded into her arm before he followed, silent and grim, his eyes fixed on her the entire way.

Vance was carried out separately under guard, his head lolling, a faint smear of blood down his temple. He wasn't dead, though a small, ugly part of Sam wished he were. He had wanted this man to face justice but not the courtroom kind. He had wanted him to feel it. The weight of every name, every grave. And yet, seeing Lora lying there so pale she seemed almost transparent, he understood that vengeance would never undo what had been taken.

Ng touched his shoulder lightly as they passed through the ruined hallway, "Sam," she said softly. "We need to secure the scene. We'll handle this."

He nodded without looking at her, "Do it."

Outside, the night air hit like a shock. Blue strobes lit the wet asphalt, the hum of generators underscoring the chaos. Detectives moved like ghosts, bagging evidence, sealing off doors, recording statements that none of them had the strength to believe.

Sam stood near the ambulance where Lora lay, the doors open, a medic checking her vitals.

She looked fragile against the white sheets, her hair damp, her lips cracked but peaceful now, as if some part of her had finally found quiet. He reached out, brushing his thumb along her cheek. Her skin was cool. He remembered the warmth of her laughter once the way it had sounded before the forest, before the blood and the graves and the endless whispering nights.

He closed his eyes. You brought us here, didn't you? All this time, you were showing us how to end it.

The medic spoke, breaking his thought. "She's stable. Weak, but stable. We'll take her back to the hospital."

He nodded again, voice low. "I'll follow."

Back inside, the team stood amid the wreckage, staring at what was left.

Harris broke the silence first, "She took them down," he said quietly. "All of them. How the hell did she?"

Ng cut him off, her voice rough. "Does it matter how? She did what we couldn't."

Greene leaned against the wall, rubbing his temples. "She shouldn't have had to," he muttered. "She's still recovering. She shouldn't have even been here."

Ng turned toward him, eyes glassy. "Would any of us have stopped her?"

No one answered they all knew the truth: none of them could have. Lora had walked through the darkness alone before and she'd done it again, only this time, she hadn't come back untouched.

Sam's voice echoed from the hallway, "Secure the prisoners. Get Vance into an isolated cell. No contact, no press, no one near him without my say-so."

His tone was cold, stripped of emotion, the professional mask barely holding over the storm beneath. The others watched him disappear toward the ambulance, shoulders rigid, every step the measured pace of someone holding himself together by force of will.

Inside the vehicle, Sam climbed in beside Lora and took her hand. Her fingers twitched faintly, her breathing shallow but steady. For the first time in days, there was no screaming in his head, no scent of decay clinging to his clothes only the faint antiseptic sting of the ambulance and the slow beeping of the monitor beside her.

He watched the road blur past through the window, city lights reflecting in her pale skin. She'd saved them all. She'd walked into fire to drag him out of it and still, even now, she looked peaceful, like the eye of the storm that refused to close.

His throat tightened. He whispered, "You did it, baby. It's over now."

But even as he said it, some quiet part of him the part that had learned to listen to the spaces between her breaths knew it wasn't truly over. The forest might be done giving up its dead, but something else lingered, just out of reach.

He would stay right here, tethered to her heartbeat, until it showed itself.

Chapter Sixty Nine

The world came back in fragments. Soft beeping. The sterile hum of fluorescent lights.

The faint scent of antiseptic and metal, hospital air, scrubbed too clean, too empty.

Lora's eyelids fluttered. For a moment, everything felt distant, like she was watching through glass. Shapes blurred at the edges of her vision, white coats moving in and out of the room, monitors blinking their soft, unrelenting rhythm.

Then she saw him.

Sam sat slumped in the chair beside her bed, his head bowed, his elbows resting on his knees. His clothes were still creased from the night before, faint smudges of dried blood along his sleeves. His hair was a mess, his eyes hollowed with exhaustion but the moment her breathing changed, he was awake.

"Hey..." he whispered, his voice cracked from lack of sleep. He reached for her hand before he even knew he was moving. His fingers were rough, warm grounding.

Lora's lips trembled into the faintest smile. "Sam…" Her voice was barely a breath, weak and raw. He leaned closer, afraid to miss a single word.

"Thank you," she whispered, the corners of her eyes wet.

He blinked hard, swallowing the lump that rose in his throat. "Don't thank me. You saved us all."

She tried to shake her head, but the effort cost her. "We… saved them." A pause. Her gaze softened on him, tracing the exhaustion that sat heavy in his shoulders. "It's over now, isn't it?"

Sam hesitated, his thumb brushing over her knuckles. He wanted to tell her yes. That it was finished. That the monsters in the dark were all gone. But the silence between them said otherwise.

Outside the hospital room, the team was gathered in the corridor, huddled around a series of screens and folders spread across a rolling desk. Ng's eyes were red-rimmed; she hadn't slept. Greene had a bandage across his cheek from the fight. Harris stood apart, leaning against the wall, arms folded tight across his chest.

The whiteboard in front of them was filled with names, photographs, scribbled connections lines crossing through Vance's face, looping toward others still unknown.

Detective Ng spoke first, her voice low, "Vance was the visible head the one we could find, but look at this."

She tapped a photo clipped to the corner. A woman's face. Smiling. Ordinary, "He wasn't acting alone. Not just in the field he had handlers, financiers, people feeding him information from inside departments."

Harris frowned. "Inside departments? You mean…"

Ng nodded grimly. "Law enforcement. At least three precincts touched this case in the last year. Some of the data leaks we blamed on bad storage. Those were deliberate. They've been covering movement for months."

A heavy silence fell. The hum of the hospital's fluorescent light filled it.

Greene exhaled slowly. "So, what are you saying? That this goes higher?"

Ng's eyes flicked to the window to where Sam sat beside Lora's bed, visible through the glass. "I'm saying this isn't over. Vance was one head of something bigger."

Harris cursed softly, rubbing his jaw. "And Sam?"

"He won't rest until he finds the rest," Greene said quietly. "But right now... he just needs her to wake up."

Inside, Lora stirred again, watching him. The morning light filtering through the blinds caught the edge of her face, softening the bruises that mottled her skin. She could feel the soreness in her ribs, the dull ache behind her eyes but deeper still, there was something else: the faint echo of the forest. The smell of pine, the feel of cold air. It lived under her skin like memory, faint but insistent.

"Sam..." she said after a moment. "Did they find everyone?"

He hesitated, looking down. "We found enough. The burial sites, the markers, the altar it's all over the news. They're linking it to Vance and the others. But Ng thinks there's still more out there. Connections we haven't seen."

She nodded faintly, as if she'd expected that, "I can feel it," she murmured, her voice distant. "It's quieter now, but... not silent."

He looked at her then really looked and saw the shadow in her eyes. The same one he'd seen the first night in the tunnels, the one that told him she had seen too much, carried too much.

"You don't have to do this anymore," he said gently. "You've done enough."

Her lips curved into a small, sad smile. "You know that's not true."

Sam exhaled, pressing his palm to her cheek, his thumb tracing the fading bruise there, "Yeah," he said softly. "I know."

By afternoon, the team had pieced together more fragments of the cult's network. Names cross-referenced. Transfers flagged. Old cases reopened.

It wasn't just local the pattern stretched across states, linked through the same symbols and rituals they'd found buried in the forest.

Harris leaned forward, jaw tight. "We shut down their main cell, but there's still activity out there. Small groups, maybe waiting for orders."

Ng rubbed her temples. "Orders from who? Their leader's locked up. Their field men are dead."

Greene glanced at the monitors. "Then maybe that's why they'll lash out. The power vacuum could make them desperate."

Sam stepped into the doorway, silent until then. The room turned toward him instinctively.

He looked drawn, pale under the hospital lighting, but his eyes, those sharp, storm-grey eyes were clear again.

"They'll come for her," he said simply. "Not tonight, maybe not tomorrow. But they'll want her because she ended what they worshipped."

A grim silence followed. Then Ng nodded once, resolute. "Then we'll be ready."

Back in the room, Lora dozed again, her pulse steady now. Sam sat by her side, watching the slow rise and fall of her chest. The monitors beeped softly, rhythmic, almost soothing.

For the first time in months, he allowed himself to breathe. To really breathe.

He thought of the faces of the dead. The colleagues. The victims. The darkness of the forest and the smell of rain. He thought of Lora the woman who had come back from the grave to finish what she'd started and felt something he hadn't felt in a long time.

Not victory. Not closure. But hope.

He leaned closer, whispering against her hair, "Rest now. I've got you. And whatever's left out there we'll finish it. Together."

Her lips moved faintly, a whisper barely audible. "Together."

For that one, fragile moment, it felt like dawn again the kind that might finally hold.

Chapter Seventy

M orning came grey and restless. The storm that had threatened the night before finally broke in a slow, sullen drizzle, rain tapping against the hospital windows like quiet fingers.

Sam stood there for a long time, watching the blurred shapes of the city outside. His reflection ghosted over the glass sleepless eyes, stubble, a weight that hadn't yet lifted.

Behind him, Lora stirred. She was stronger now colour returning to her cheeks, her body no longer shaking when she moved. The doctors had said she was recovering faster than they expected. But Sam could see what they couldn't: the strain that still lived behind her eyes, the way her hands trembled just slightly when she reached for the water glass.

"Couldn't sleep?" she asked softly, voice still rough but steadier.

He half-smiled, "Didn't try."

Lora studied him for a moment. "You still think it's not over."

He turned toward her, and the way he didn't answer was answer enough. He crossed the room, sat beside her bed again. "We found evidence yesterday. Transfers, falsified files, badge numbers that don't belong to anyone still serving. Someone in the precinct's been feeding them information."

Her eyes darkened, "Someone close."

He nodded. "Has to be."

Lora looked down at her hands, her fingers tracing the IV line absently, "They won't stop, Sam," she said quietly. "Not while any of them are still out there. The cult was never about one leader it was about faith twisted into control. There'll always be another who thinks they can pick up the torch."

Her voice trembled slightly, but there was steel underneath it, "But I'll fight. You know that don't you? I'll fight until the last one is gone."

Sam reached out, covering her hand with his, "Not alone."

For a heartbeat, they just sat there, the rain whispering against the window, the faint hum of monitors the only sound between them.

Across town, the precinct was waking in fits and starts.

Coffee machines hissed. Phones rang. The stale air smelled of bleach and burnt toast.

Detective Ng was the first to notice it, small things, almost nothing at first. A missing evidence tag in the property room. A file drawer unlocked when it should've been sealed.

And later, a surveillance log entry that had been tampered with the timestamp rewritten, the footage replaced by static for exactly six minutes.

She stood over the monitor, jaw tight. Greene appeared at her side. "You're seeing it too, huh?"

Ng nodded. "Yeah. Somebody's been inside the system again."

"Vance is dead."

"I know." She exhaled through her nose, leaning in. "But his followers aren't. And whoever's in here... they know the system. They know what to erase."

Greene frowned. "Could it be Mayhew's old team?"

"No," Ng said quietly. "This feels fresher. Smarter."

They both looked up when Sam walked in. He looked more himself now — showered, cleaner, but still carrying the storm in his shoulders.

Ng turned the screen toward him. "Look familiar?"

Sam's eyes scanned the timestamp. He froze. "That's last night. That's the hour we secured the evidence from the holding cells."

Greene added, "Whoever did this had clearance. High clearance."

Sam's jaw clenched. "Check the logs. Every keycard entry from that time window. Every motion sensor."

Ng's fingers flew over the keyboard. A list flickered onto the screen rows of names, timestamps, and access levels. Halfway down the list, one name pulsed back at them, faint and wrong.

Detective T. Lang.

Greene frowned. "Lang? He's been on leave since the second raid."

Ng's face paled. "Then someone's using his ID."

Sam stepped back, cold realization settling like ice in his gut, "They're inside," he said quietly, "Still inside."

Back at the hospital, Lora sat up slowly, her back against the pillows. The window had fogged from the rain. She could see her reflection in the glass pale, haunted, but alive.

Then something flickered at the edge of her perception that faint electric hum she'd come to recognize as the onset of another vision. It wasn't like before, not overwhelming, not violent. This was quiet. Subtle. A whisper threading its way through her mind.

She saw flashes a figure in a hallway, gloved hands opening a locker, sliding something into an evidence box. Then the smell of pine, faint and wrong. A voice, low, calm: You can't stop what you can't see.

Lora's breath hitched. The room tilted. She gripped the sheets, eyes wide.

The nurse appeared in the doorway just as Lora gasped, "Sam— tell Sam they're still here."

The nurse blinked. "Ms. Matthews, what—?"

"They're still inside!"

Back at the precinct, Sam's phone buzzed sharply. Ng glanced at him as he answered. The nurse's frantic voice spilled through the line, disjointed, frightened.

"Detective— she's awake— she said to tell you— they're still inside—"

Sam's stomach turned cold. His eyes met Ng's, "Lock the precinct down. Now."

Ng didn't hesitate, "On it."

Greene was already moving, shouting orders down the hall. Sirens blared inside the building, the metal shutters beginning to fall over the main entrances.

Sam's pulse pounded. The room suddenly felt smaller, tighter. He turned back to the screen the tampered feed, the erased footage, the impossible timestamp.

For a second, the monitor glitched again. Static flared. Then, for the briefest flicker, a face appeared pale, almost smiling before the screen went black.

Lora's words echoed in his mind like thunder: They're still inside.

This time, Sam knew she wasn't just talking about the precinct.

She meant the rot itself. The thing that had been festering behind every badge, every sealed file, every quiet disappearance.

The cult wasn't dead. It had simply changed its skin.

Sam turned toward the team, his voice low, steady, and colder than the rain, "Everyone arm up. We're not done yet."

Chapter Seventy One

The sirens still echoed through the precinct a shrill, mechanical scream that bounced off the steel shutters and glass walls, twisting the air into panic.

Detectives scattered through the dim corridors, weapons raised, eyes sharp with suspicion and exhaustion. The hum of emergency lights painted everything in pulsing red and white.

Sam stood at the center of it all in the bullpen his voice cutting through the noise.

"Every floor locked. No one in or out until I say. Check every ID, every locker, every goddamn shadow. We end this tonight."

He turned toward Ng and Greene, "Comms open. Keep Lora on channel one. If she sees anything — anything — you call it out."

Greene nodded, already keying his mic. Through the static, Lora's voice drifted in faint, trembling, but steady, "Sam? I can see the hall... the west corridor. Someone's moving there. Alone."

Sam froze. "Who?"

There was a pause a breath like wind across wire, "I can't see his face... but there's blood on his hands. He's heading toward the holding cells."

Ng's eyes met Sam's. "That's where we found Vance."

Sam's jaw tightened. "Move."

They pushed down the corridor, boots thudding against the linoleum, the overhead lights flickering as if the building itself held its breath. The silence pressed in every sound amplified: the click of safeties, the scrape of boots, the metallic drip of water from a burst pipe.

At the far end, a door stood slightly ajar.

Sam motioned for the others to flank. Greene on the right, Ng on the left. He stepped forward, weapon ready, heart pounding like thunder in his chest.

Inside, the holding cells flickered with the strobe of red emergency lights bars casting warped shadows across the walls and there, standing just beyond the last cell, was Detective Lang.

He turned slowly at the sound of their approach uniform torn, eyes glassy, a faint smile curling at the corners of his mouth.

"Sam," Lang said, voice disturbingly calm. "You shouldn't have come."

Ng hissed, "Lang, drop it. Now."

Lang shook his head slowly. "You don't understand. He's not gone. Vance was never the leader. He was just the voice."

Sam's pulse thundered. "Then who the hell is?"

Lang looked past him as if seeing something only he could. "He's already here."

The lights went out.

For three heartbeats, there was nothing but blackness and then the sound of a shot.

Sparks lit the room. Greene shouted, diving behind a pillar. Ng screamed Lang's name.

Sam moved on instinct, rolling forward, weapon raised. Another shot cracked the air, grazing the wall beside him. He caught a glimpse, Lang, staggering, his own gun shaking.

"Don't make me do this!" Sam yelled.

Lang laughed high, broken, "It's not me, Sam! It's—"

Another flash. Another report.

Then silence.

Lang collapsed backward, the gun clattering from his hand. His eyes rolled up toward the ceiling as if seeing salvation that would never come.

Sam stood frozen, weapon still aimed, breath heaving. Ng crept forward, checking the pulse and shook her head slowly.

Sam's stomach twisted. He dropped to his knees beside Lang, staring down at the man who had once been a brother-in-arms. The smell of gunpowder and blood hung thick in the air.

Lora's voice broke through the comm, raw and strained, "Sam?"

He swallowed hard. "It's over, Lora."

But even as he said it, he wasn't sure he believed it.

Ng exhaled shakily, wiping her brow. "What if he was right? What if there's someone else?"

Sam holstered his weapon slowly, his voice hoarse. "Then we'll find them. And we'll end it."

He looked at Lang one last time, eyes dull beneath the flashing red.

The precinct was silent again, the storm outside fading into the whisper of rain against glass. Sam closed his eyes and whispered, "It ends now."

And somewhere, on the other end of the comm line, Lora finally let herself exhale the sound soft, almost a sob of release.

Chapter Seventy Two

Spring crept back into the city quietly, the way healing often does one gentle sunrise at a time.

The precinct was repaired, the walls repainted, the ghosts still lingering but quieter now.

The cult's files had been sealed, their remaining followers in custody, the rot finally dug out root by root.

Lora's hospital room was bathed in sunlight. Her hair had grown back where the IVs and bruises once were. She stood near the window now, the gown traded for soft clothes, her hand resting over the faint scar on her arm.

Sam knocked lightly on the doorframe, leaning in, "You look like trouble," he said with a tired smile.

She turned, her grin small but real. "You'd miss it if I wasn't."

He laughed, stepping closer. The lines on his face had softened, though the weight of everything they'd survived still lived in his eyes, "You're not wrong."

Lora studied him the faint twitch at the corner of his mouth, the way his shoulders eased for the first time in months, "You got the reports?"

He nodded. "All of them. Cults gone. Network dismantled. What's left… we'll keep watching."

She stepped closer, searching his face. "And you?"

He hesitated, then smiled faintly. "Still here."

Lora tilted her head. "Barely."

He laughed then reached into his pocket. For a second, she thought it was another case file. But then she saw the small velvet box.

Her breath caught, "Sam—"

He opened it quietly. Inside, the ring gleamed against the soft fabric the same one she'd lost in the chaos months ago, cleaned and whole again.

"I asked you once," he said softly. "Before all this. Before the blood, the visions, the madness. I never stopped meaning it."

Her eyes filled with tears.

He took her hand steady, warm. "Lora Matthews," he said, his voice low, steady. "You came back from hell with me. You saved us all. So, I'm asking again will you marry me?"

She couldn't speak for a moment, only nodded as tears slipped free. Sam smiled, slid the ring onto her finger, and kissed her softly, reverently, as if sealing a promise not just to her, but to the life they'd fought so hard to reclaim.

Later that evening, the team gathered at Greene's favourite dive bar a dim, familiar place that finally felt like home again.

Ng sat nursing a drink, staring at the row of empty stools the ghosts of those they'd lost still beside them.

Greene raised his glass. "To the ones who made it out. And the ones who made it matter."

Sam nodded, clinking glasses. "And to Lora," he said quietly, "for showing us light when all we had was dark."

Lora smiled, leaning against him. "We all found it together."

For a moment, no one spoke. The rain outside had stopped. The night was still.

Ng whispered, "Think we'll ever be free of it?"

Sam looked around at the laughter, at the warmth, at the small, steady glow that filled the bar, "Maybe not," he said. "But tonight... we get to breathe."

Later, walking back through the quiet streets, Lora slipped her arm through his. The city lights reflected off puddles, the world clean and alive again.

She looked up at him, smiling softly. "Feels strange, doesn't it? No sirens. No shadows."

Sam squeezed her hand. "Feels right."

They stopped beneath the streetlamp the light pale gold across their faces.

Lora looked up at the sky clear for the first time in weeks. Her voice was a whisper. "It's over."

Sam brushed a strand of hair from her face, "Yeah," he said. "We made it through."

And as dawn broke over the city quiet, unbroken, and bright Sam kissed her once more, their tether no longer bound by fear or visions, but by love and survival.

For the first time in a long time, they were finally free.......

For now.......

Epilogue

Three weeks later, the city had thawed into early spring, the streets washed clean by rain. Morning light poured through the trees lining the park outside Sam and Lora's small townhouse a house too quiet for two people who'd once lived by police radios and nightmares.

The days were different now, Sam still rose before dawn, the habit of vigilance too deep to break. He brewed coffee, checked the windows, listened to the hum of life returning the neighbour's dog, the bus braking at the corner, the slow rhythm of safety.

Inside, Lora moved through the kitchen barefoot, a soft robe brushing against her knees. Her hair was loose, her movements slower but stronger now. The bruises had faded, the scars softened into silver traces of what they'd survived.

She smiled when she saw him watching her, "Still keeping guard?" she teased, her voice rough from sleep.

He smiled faintly. "Old habits die hard."

She walked over, pressing a kiss to his jaw. "You can let your guard down, Sam. It's over."

He nodded but didn't answer. The silence between them was comfortable, threaded with everything they didn't need to say.

Outside, the mail truck rattled away. Sam went to the door, sorting through bills and flyers and then froze.

Among them was a plain white envelope. No return address. Just his name, typed neatly: **Detective Samuel K. Hale.**

Lora noticed the change in his expression. "What is it?"

He tore it open slowly. Inside was a single photograph.

It showed the clearing in the forest the altar long since dismantled but in the far background, blurred and small, a figure stood among the trees. Watching.

No date. No caption. Just the faint imprint of a fingerprint on the edge of the glossy paper.

Lora came to his side, her breath catching when she saw it, "Sam..."

He looked up, scanning her face, then the quiet street outside.

"It could be nothing," he said softly. "Could be old."

But even as he said it, the fine hairs on the back of his neck rose. Lora slipped her hand into his. Her voice was steady, though her pulse wasn't, "If it's not... we'll face it together."

He met her gaze the same fierce calm that had carried them through every hell, "Always," he said.

They stood there for a long moment, side by side in the doorway, the morning light stretching across their faces the world still and peaceful again, but just at the edges, something unseen shifting in the shadows.

Somewhere, a phone began to ring. Neither of them moved.

The sound echoed once... twice...and then faded into the hum of the waking city

As the light caught the corner of the photograph, Sam turned it just enough to see the faint handwritten scrawl on the back, **"See you soon, L."**